# REFLECTIONS OF A MISFIT

*To my beloved family of misfits, who make and keep life so very interesting and fun! Trust God always! Love you forever!*

*Mom, Gramma,*
*PTL Persin*

# REFLECTIONS OF A MISFIT

## P.T.L. Perrin

Copyright © 2014 by P.T.L. Perrin.

Library of Congress Control Number:     2014920018
ISBN:
    Hardcover    978-1-5035-1560-4
    Softcover    978-1-5035-1561-1
    eBook    978-1-5035-1562-8

All rights reserved. No part of this book may be reproduced or transmitted in any form or by any means, electronic or mechanical, including photocopying, recording, or by any information storage and retrieval system, without permission in writing from the copyright owner.

Any people depicted in stock imagery provided by Thinkstock are models, and such images are being used for illustrative purposes only.
Certain stock imagery © Thinkstock.

Unless otherwise indicated, all Scripture is taken from THE MESSAGE, Copyright © 1993, 1994, 1995, 1996, 2000, 2220, 2002. Used by permission of NavPress Publishing Group.

Cover design by Ewald Sutter

Coverpicture: © Niserin | - Beautiful Ocean And Sunset, Dolphin Jumping Photo

Some names have been changed to protect the individual's privacy.

Although Gramma and Grampa may seem misspelled, they are the proper names our grandchildren call us.

This book was printed in the United States of America.

Rev. date: 11/14/2014

**To order additional copies of this book, contact:**
Xlibris
1-888-795-4274
www.Xlibris.com
Orders@Xlibris.com
698492

# CONTENTS

Foreward ..................................................................9
Preface ...................................................................11
Introduction ...........................................................13

The Unconscious Search ........................................ 15
What Are The Rules? .............................................. 21
What Comes Next? ................................................. 31
Sour Lemons Or Lemonade? ................................. 51
It's All About Relationship ..................................... 61
A Gathering Of Misfits ........................................... 67
What Is That Gibberish? ......................................... 75
What Is Normal For A Misfit? ................................ 83
A Matter Of Life Or Death ..................................... 93
Breathe Gratitude .................................................... 99
Who Are We, Really? ............................................ 105
A Misfit And The Holidays .................................. 115
Is Jesus The Messiah? ........................................... 135
A Walk Through Seasons .................................... 147
A Family Of Misfits .............................................. 163
A Misfit Hits The Road ........................................ 171
A Misfit's Journey Through Fear ........................ 189
Surviving Storms .................................................. 213
A Misfit's Month In Proverbs .............................. 225
That Misfit David ................................................. 251
The Longest Psalm ............................................... 269
A Misfit On The Roman Road ............................ 289

# DEDICATION

*The Oxford Dictionary* defines a misfit as a person whose behavior or attitude sets them apart from others in an uncomfortably conspicuous way. *The Collins Dictionary* says a misfit is a person not suited in behavior or attitude to a particular social environment. I'm happy to say that I am, according to God, set apart and unsuited to the prevailing social environment.

In 1 Samuel 22:1-2, David assembled a band of misfits. They became mighty warriors, and his closest friends when he later took the throne of Israel.

In Luke 14:12-14, Jesus told the host of the dinner he attended that he should invite the misfits to his next dinner. Even if they can't return the favor, Jesus said, "the favor will be returned – oh, how it will be returned! – at the resurrection of God's people."

In 1 Corinthians 4:10, Paul says "We're the Messiah's misfits."

I love the old King James Version of 1 Peter 2:9: "But ye are a chosen generation, a royal priesthood, an holy nation, a peculiar people that ye should show forth the praises of him who hath called you out of darkness into his marvelous light…" I love being peculiar!

I dedicate this book to my patient and loving husband Bill, and our own band of misfits -- the parents of our grandchildren, to whom is given the awesome responsibility of teaching their children about God. To them I say, teach them that he loves them with an extravagant love. He has a plan and a purpose for each of them. They are infinitely valuable because he knew them before they were born, and he sent his own Son, Jesus Christ, to make a way for them to find God, be forgiven of all their sins, and to get to Heaven someday where so many who love them will be waiting.

I dedicate it to my siblings and my parents, fellow misfits on the journey God gave us. I wouldn't be who I am, and there would be no book without their significant influence and help.

Mostly, I dedicate every word I write to the Holy One of Israel, the Creator of the universe, my Lord and Savior Jesus Christ, who reminds me of the craziness of my life and how his love has protected me, sustained me, fed me and grown me. He's amazing! His generous love has given us misfits a place in the Son.

God is real, God loves you, God has a plan for you. It's a blessing to be considered one of Messiah's misfits!

# FOREWARD

As second in line of five siblings, I have looked up to my big sister, Patty Perrin, all my life. Growing up in a military family the way we did, moving from place to place and country to country, the feeling of never really "fitting in" was pervasive. Dealing with that feeling – especially during the adolescent years – forced me to confront the questions; "Where do I fit into the overall scheme of things? What is my life all about?"

God, in His mercy gave me and the rest of the family the answer through His son Jesus, our precious Savior. Whatever we might "miss" in our humanity, He makes to "fit" into His perfect plan for our lives.

Through these snippets of real life experiences - at times humorous, at times serious, always real - Patty not only invites the reader into the inner circle of her life, she also teaches deep and practical Spiritual truths. Truths that will help you overcome in your daily walk as one of God's "Misfits" as well! Enjoy!

Dan Tracy<br>
Director of Derek Prince Ministries Germany

(Dan and his wife Cindy have been missionaries to Germany since 1976 and have raised their six children there. The family serves the Lord in music, ministry of the Word and other areas of service to the Body of Christ.)

With a sincere Christian faith Patty Perrin tackles subjects that many shy away from. Opponents try to sway her away from her Christian stance and beliefs, without success. Many a healthy discourse is started because of her. The truth on important subjects is often hidden from the regular public, but Patty brings it to light.

> Rev. Paul Norman, Senior Pastor
> First Baptist of Saura Valley, NC

It has been my privilege to be Patty's Pastor since 1998. At the very first, as I read her musings I encouraged her to publish them.

One of the things that I think is so great about this book is that it is a 'gratitude project.' Patty is writing to express her gratitude and devotion to the Lord for all His love and faithfulness to her over the years. Serving the Lord has been a wonderful journey for her. She clearly states she is not a Bible scholar or an apologist but merely someone who loves Jesus. These inspirational encounters come from heart and memory as well as devotional time with the Lord.

I saw her reflections as uplifting, well written and enjoyable. I have always enjoyed reading what people write as an expression of their thinking. It gives insight into human nature and, in this case, the person's thoughtfulness while showing how the Lord works through and for someone who trusts in Him.

While you read this you have the opportunity to see the working of the Holy Spirit in a life that is on a life-long journey serving our Lord and Savior.

> Scrivner Damon
> Pastor, New Life Community Church

# PREFACE

*Reflections of a Misfit* began as a gratitude project on FaceBook. I intended to post something I was grateful for at least once every day leading up to Thanksgiving. I found I couldn't stop. It soon morphed into daily reflections as the Lord reminded me of times in my life that related to the Scriptures I read that day. My Pastor, my friends, and some of my family soon began to encourage me to put them into book form. This book is the result of their prompting and the Lord's nudge to get it done.

I gratefully acknowledge everyone who has had a hand in this project. Dan Tracy, Paul Norman and Scrivner Damon, thank you for your kind words and the time you spent writing a foreward. Sharon Willson, your proofreading and editing skills are priceless! Ewald Sutter and Mike Sardina, thank you for the time and love you put into designing the cover – both for the one I chose and for the other. You guys rock!

I am grateful for all of you who prayed for me as I wrote and re-wrote, and fussed and fumed during the birth process of this book. Thank you!

I am immeasurably grateful for my patient, longsuffering husband who never complained about being neglected as I focused on getting this project done. Thank you, Bill, for all the meals you've scrounged, all the dishes you've washed, and all the ways you've ministered to me. You truly exemplify the love of Christ to me. You're amazing.

More than anything, I hope this book reflects the deep gratitude I have for my Lord and Savior Jesus Christ, without Whom life would be empty. I'm humbled and happy to be counted among His misfits.

# INTRODUCTION

I am a misfit. If you're human, if you're from Earth, or if you're an alien from another planet or dimension – if you aren't perfect, then you may be a misfit, too.

The Bible is full of misfits, from Abraham to Moses, from David and his band of misfits, to Daniel and the prophets. The ultimate misfit is our Lord and Savior Jesus Christ. The religious leadership of the day considered him a dangerous radical because he didn't follow, or preach, their religious dogma. They literally hounded him to death, but only because he allowed it.

As a new Christian, I wanted to learn everything I could about how to be a Christian. What is acceptable? What isn't? What do I have to give up? What happens when I mess up? What are the rules?

Some churches have well-defined procedures to follow. Scriptures can be confusing, but we can find instructions to follow there, too. Some folks are wired to obey rules, and they do it very well. There was a time when I envied them, because I am not wired that way. Did that make me a bad person -- a bad Christian? If we're to be like Jesus, isn't there a mold we should fit into?

Stretch, fold, squirm, or squeeze -- as much as I tried, I still couldn't fit the Jesus Mold. Only God knows how often I apologized and repented, and imposed penance on myself for being incorrigible. Wisdom comes with age – sorry young'uns, you really don't know it all – and as time continued to plod forward, I began to see that when God gave us Jesus, he broke the mold.

If there's no mold to fit into, then how do we know how to BE?

Jesus is our standard. We don't have to be the standard, but how wonderful that we have such a One to follow. Each of us has gifts. Each is a unique individual with a role to play in the Christ-life. We live, we love, we learn, we grow, and sometimes we're called into battle. Jesus is our Commander in Chief. He's our role model. He's also our Healer and the Lover of our souls. We can't go wrong if we follow the Jesus Standard.

Is there room in Christianity for misfits? You'd better believe it!

# THE UNCONSCIOUS SEARCH

"Open the eyes of my heart Lord
Open the eyes of my heart"

~ Paul Baloche
Integrity's Hosanna! Music

## *I Needed a Friend*

I was pretty much a loner growing up. I could count the number of my friends on one hand. We were a military family and lived in Europe where I met and married my first husband.

The two of us moved to the States and lived in a Cuban barrio, where Spanish is the main language. My husband was the only person I could speak with in English -- and we didn't communicate well at all. Even before I knew the Lord, I prayed for a friend; just one, please.

The Apostle Paul addressed his friends in 2 Thessalonians 1:1-12. "You need to know, friends, that thanking God over and over for you is not only a pleasure; it's a must. We have to do it. Your faith is growing phenomenally; your love for each other is developing wonderfully. Why, it's only right that we give thanks. We're so proud of you; you're so steady and determined in your faith despite all the hard times that have come down on you."

Paul went on to describe the coming day when Jesus "appears out of heaven in a blaze of fire with his strong angels."

"Because we know this extraordinary day is just ahead, we pray for you all the time – pray that our God will make you fit for what he's called you to be; pray that he'll fill your good ideas and acts of faith with his own energy so that it all amounts to something. If your life honors the name of Jesus, he will honor you. Grace is behind and through all of this, our God giving himself freely, the Master, Jesus Christ, giving himself freely."

I didn't know that the friend I was praying for was listening and answering. I found the Lord there, in the loneliness. He was my first friend, and he has since led me to many, many others. Whatever you believe, or don't believe, know this: I thank God for you and I ask him to strengthen you, to bless you, to fill you with joy and to reveal the truth to you as you go about living your life.

----------

## *Persistence Pays*

My brother Mark and sister Sharon were persistent in their campaign to make a believer out of me. They sent tracts and books and even the Bible in the form of a graphic novel, thinking it was one way I'd actually read it. Mostly, they prayed for me.

I resisted for a long time because I was afraid I'd have to change my lifestyle to fit my image of what a "Christian" was supposed to be. I was sure I'd never be good enough, and, quite frankly, I didn't want to be! I figured Christians were bound by a bunch of rules I refused to follow.

To my surprise, I found that I was in good company! The Apostle Paul wasn't about to let a bunch of rules define his life, either, and he made it plain in Galatians 2:17-21.

Paul said, "Have some of you noticed that we are not yet perfect?" That's no surprise.

"If I was 'trying to be good,' I would be rebuilding the same old barn that I tore down. I would be acting as a charlatan."

Wow. Did Paul say that if he had acted like a believer is supposed to act, according to popular opinion, he would have been a hypocrite?

"I tried keeping rules and working my head off to please God and it didn't work. So I quit being a 'law man' so that I could be God's man. Christ's life showed me how, and enabled me to do it. I identified myself completely with him."

Jesus bucked the establishment. He was considered a radical by the prevailing religious leaders. They didn't like him because he didn't act the way they thought he should, and he wouldn't shut up. So they crucified him.

Paul continued, "Indeed, I have been crucified with Christ. My ego is no longer central. It is no longer important that I appear righteous before you or have your good opinion, and I am no longer driven to impress God." Let's be honest. What can any of us do to impress God?

What Paul said next gave me the green light to surrender to Christ and be happy about it. "Is it not clear to you that to go back to that old rule-keeping, peer-pleasing religion would be an abandonment of everything personal and free in my relationship with God? I refuse to do that, to repudiate God's grace. If a living relationship with God could come by rule-keeping, then Christ died unnecessarily."

When God moves in, darkness moves out. No rule book can do that.

----------

## *Temper, Temper*

My longsuffering sister was fed up with my bad temper. She'd been trying to get me to open up to the Gospel she kept sharing with me, but I was stubborn. Then one day, she threw her hands up and shouted a challenge to me, "Why don't you just ask God to make himself real to you? Would you listen then?" Yes, Christians can lose it, too.

I shouted back, "Okay! I will!" And I did.

In 1 Kings 18, Elijah was fed up with Israel. He was one prophet against 450 priests of Baal, the "god" that Ahab led Israel to worship. So, he challenged them, like Sharon challenged me.

They built an altar, laid it with firewood and slaughtered an ox as a sacrifice. Then they prayed to Baal to set fire to their offering. They prayed aloud, shouted, jumped, stomped on the altar, and even cut themselves in a brutal ritual. They used every religious trick and strategy they knew, all morning and into the afternoon, calling on Baal to do this one little thing. Finally, Elijah put a stop to it and declared it his turn.

He took twelve stones, one for each tribe of Israel, and built an altar. He laid the firewood and ox on it and then poured twelve buckets of water over the top, filling the trench around the altar. He prayed once, saying, "O God, God of Abraham, Isaac and Israel, make it known right now that you are God in Israel, that I am your servant and that I'm doing what I'm doing under your orders. Answer me, God; O answer me and reveal to this people that you are God, the true God, and that you are giving these people another chance at repentance."

I imagine that Sharon cried out to God the day she challenged me. I'm sure her prayer sounded much like Elijah's. "Show this stubborn girl that you are the one true God!"

Back to Elijah: "Immediately, the fire of God fell and burned up the offering, the wood, the stones, the dirt, and even the water in the trench."

God showed them! Israel turned back to God, and killed the Baal prophets. What did Elijah do after all this drama? He went off by himself and sulked. How human.

So, did God prove himself to me? Yes he did -- supernaturally, and undeniably, but with far less drama. It was enough to show me that he is real, that he cares enough about us to answer my sister's prayer, and that he is a loving and forgiving God. He had a lot to forgive!

----------

## God Proved Himself

My first encounter with the Lord was a supernatural experience for which I had no earthly explanation. I had challenged God to show me he's real. Full of skepticism and vinegar, I had the nerve to shout my challenge to the heavens. He saw the tiny spark of hope in me that I didn't know was there, and he made himself real in a way he knew I'd get – because he knows me.

Gideon was very familiar with Baal, a god who supposedly created the universe and then left it to run itself. His father had built an altar to the false god. Baal worshipers didn't expect miracles to happen. Their god was disinterested in the affairs of mankind.

In Judges 6, the one true God called on Gideon to defeat more than 32,000 Midianite warriors who were ready to invade his land. That would require a miracle, and Gideon was skeptical that God could do such a thing. He considered himself the least of all the Israelites, and he was insecure and afraid, so he put God to the test.

Gideon asked God to prove himself by laying out a fleece and asking him to send dew to the fleece and nowhere else. The next morning, he wrung a bucketful of water out of the fleece, and everywhere else was dry.

Okay; maybe the sun dried the surrounding dirt before it dried the fleece, so Gideon asked that this time, the dew would appear everywhere except on the fleece.

God didn't strike him down. He didn't get impatient and he didn't go find someone with more faith. He did as Gideon asked. Why? It was because God knew him.

Gideon defeated the entire Midianite army with just 300 men. God knew the Midianites, too, and he worked on their minds so that their defeat was inevitable. God knows us – individually and as a race of human beings. Even the strongest of us is weak in some way, and God shows his strength through our weakness.

Because he knows me and loves me anyway, God showed up in a way I couldn't refute. Who wouldn't want to serve a God like that?

# WHAT ARE THE RULES?

"Take the shackles off my feet so I can dance
I just wanna praise You

"You broke the chains, now I can lift my hands
I'm gonna praise You"

~ Mary Mary
Song: *Shackles (Praise You)*
From the album *Go Get It*

Words and music by Ricky M.L. Walters,
Alvin G. West, Erica M. Atkins,
Trecina E. Atkins, Don Milla

## *Walking on Eggshells*

As a new Christian, I worried about a lot of things. Would I be able to follow the rules, even though I didn't know what they were? Did I, or would I, do something so bad, so stupid, so unforgiveable that God wouldn't let me into Heaven? I walked on eggshells every day, afraid to make the wrong move, say the wrong thing, or give someone the wrong impression. I was hungry for God, but didn't know what he expected of me.

I jumped at the first chance for a one-on-one Bible study. It was with someone who, I later learned, had been taught a lot of falsehoods and was passing them on to me. I hope she's found the truth by now.

In Matthew 7:13-24, Jesus warned us to be careful about what and who we believe. He said, "Don't look for shortcuts to God. The market is flooded with surefire, easy-going formulas for a successful life that can be practiced in your spare time. Don't fall for that stuff... The way to life – to God! – is vigorous and requires total attention." It seems that self-help programs have been around for millennia!

He went on, "Be wary of false preachers who smile a lot, dripping with practiced sincerity...Don't be impressed with charisma; look for character. Who preachers are is the main thing, not what they say." I thank the Lord every day for our honorable, genuine pastor and his equally wonderful wife. Pastor Scrivner and Dolores Damon live out their faith.

And then he shared this clincher, "Knowing the correct password – saying 'Master, Master,' for instance – isn't going to get you anywhere with me. What is required is serious obedience – doing what my Father wills."

If he'd left it there, I would have had good reason to worry and walk on eggshells! My being obedient is like ice water catching fire – highly unlikely.

He went on to say, "These words I speak are not incidental additions to your life .... They are words to build a life on." These verses follow what Jesus said about the golden rule. If we live a life of love, which is what Jesus did, then the rest will follow.

We don't have to do it all ourselves, and we don't have to walk on eggshells. God has our backs. He's the One who is growing us up. Trust him!

----------

## *Enthusiastic Beginnings*

I've always been an enthusiastic beginner. I'll start a project full-on, enjoying every minute of it — for a while. I can't tell you how many unfinished projects have cluttered my closets over the years. So when I became a Christian, it was with total enthusiasm, and with a twinge of worry about how long it might last.

I had taken a course in college called The Bible In Literature. It was pretty dry, and I didn't see how anyone could get into reading the Bible on a regular basis.

When I reluctantly opened my brand new Bible as a brand new Christian, I was amazed at how it spoke to my heart! Every word suddenly made sense! It was as if God himself was speaking directly to me. One story, in particular, stood out.

In Luke 8:4-15, Jesus said, "A farmer went out to sow his seed. As he was scattering the seed, some fell along the path; it was trampled on, and the birds ate it up. Some fell on rocky ground, and when it came up, the plants withered because they had no moisture. Other seed fell among thorns, which grew up with it and choked the plants. Still other seed fell on good soil. It came up and yielded a crop, a hundred times more than was sown." (NIV)

He had to explain the parable to his disciples. "The seed is the word of God. Those along the path are the ones who hear, and then the devil comes and takes away the word from their hearts, so that they may not believe and be saved. Those on the rocky ground are the ones who receive the word with joy when they hear it, but they have no root. They believe for a while, but in the time of testing they fall away. The seed that fell among thorns stands for those who hear, but as they go on their way they are choked by life's worries, riches and pleasures, and they do not mature. But the seed on good soil stands for those with a noble and good heart, who hear the word, retain it, and by persevering produce a crop."

As soon as I read it, I saw myself along the path, on rocky ground, and among the thorns. I was afraid that this would be another thing I'd be excited about at first, and then fall away from. I prayed, "God, make me fertile ground. Change me so that I'll persevere."

I'm still an enthusiastic beginner, and not much of a finisher, but where God is concerned, I am sold out. Just to set the record straight, I still pray that prayer. I haven't arrived at the finish line yet.

----------

## What Happened to the Red Letters?

The first time I picked up a Bible that didn't have the words of Jesus in red letters, I wondered, "How will I know when it's Jesus talking?" I was so new.

The Bible I'm reading now, The Message, doesn't have the words of Jesus in red letters, either, but there's never any doubt that he's the one talking.

Jesus said, "Are you tired? Worn out? Burned out on religion? Come to me. Get away with me and you'll recover your life. I'll show you how to take a real rest. Walk with me and work with me – watch how I do it. Learn the unforced rhythms of grace. I won't lay anything heavy or ill-fitting on you. Keep company with me and you'll learn to live freely and lightly." (Matthew 11:28-30)

I love learning the "unforced rhythms of grace" and I'm happy to leave the heavy stuff up to him. He can handle it, and in return, I get rest and joy and light and freedom and love. Who wouldn't want to live that way?

----------

## Uncomplicated

We have grandkids who have memorized so much scripture that they've won competitions or placed very highly. We're proud of them for their accomplishments, but also because they're growing in grace and character and will make a difference in the world. I can say the same for all of our grandkids.

Memorization is not my strong suit. I have trouble remembering our children's names at times, so I admire those who undertake what our grandchildren have done. They're hiding God's Word in their hearts, and someday, they'll have a deep well to draw from when they need a reminder.

One reason I read the Bible through, over and over again is because I hope something will stick. So much information can seem overwhelming, but in Matthew 7:1-12, Jesus said that it's not that complicated.

"Don't pick on people, jump on their failures, criticize their faults – unless, of course, you want the same treatment. That critical spirit has a way of boomeranging."

"Don't be flip with the sacred...Don't reduce holy mysteries to slogans."

"Don't bargain with God. Be direct. Ask for what you need."

"Here's a simple rule-of-thumb guide for behavior: Ask yourself what you want people to do for you, then grab the initiative and do it for them. Add up God's Law and the Prophets and this is what you get." We know this one as the Golden Rule.

In the NIV it goes like this, "So in everything, do to others what you would have them do to you, for this sums up the Law and the Prophets."

There's much more in this chapter, and all of it straight from the mouth of Jesus. There's much value in memorizing scripture, but the real value is in learning how to live the way God wants you to. Jesus reminds us that it's not that complicated.

----------

## *You Had To Be There!*

I can almost hear the Latin rhythms and unique sound of Santana in my mind. Nothing compares to the immediacy and intimacy of the music and the play of drums at one of their concerts. You had to be there!

Now imagine being in a crowd of people. You're listening to someone whose voice reaches into your heart. You watch him heal the sick – perhaps even you. You're fascinated by his words, which are radically different from what the religious leaders are teaching. You gasp as demons show themselves in their victims, and he casts them out right before your eyes.

Obviously, not everyone was at the concert, and none of us was alive when Jesus physically walked among us. Yet, we have the recorded music, and we have his recorded words. Here are a few nuggets from that day, from Luke 6:17-49:

"Your task is to be true, not popular." If only our kids would get that!

"Ask yourself what you want people to do for you; then grab the initiative and do it for them."

"I tell you, love your enemies. Help and give without expecting a return. You'll never – I promise – regret it. Live out this God-created identity the way our Father lives toward us, generously and graciously, even when we're at our worst. Our Father is kind; you be kind."

"Don't pick on people, jump on their failures, criticize their faults – unless, of course, you want the same treatment."

"Give away your life; you'll find life given back, but not merely given back – given back with bonus and blessing…Generosity begets generosity."

"It's who you are, not what you say and do, that counts. Your true being brims over into true words and deeds."

How I wish I could have been there – not for the entertainment, but for the heart-changing, mind-bending message of kindness, generosity and love. It still satisfies a hunger in us that nothing else can touch. Oh, wait -- the day is coming when we might all be there, listening to Jesus, basking in his presence. That's a gathering I don't want to miss!

----------

## Preoccupation with Details

I called to get a prescription filled. The pharmacist was very nice and told me it would cost $196 for a 90 day supply. I nearly choked! The last time I had it filled, it was only $46 for 90 days! What happened?

As I searched for a better price online, my old computer started acting up. I figured God wanted me to pay attention to him, so I went to read the Word.

His timing amazes me. I read Luke 12:22-32, where Jesus told his disciples not to fuss and fret about things like food and clothing. God takes care of the birds and flowers, and aren't we more important to God than those? So how does this relate to pharmacy prices?

In verses 29-32, Jesus spoke directly to me: "What I'm trying to do here is to get you to relax, not be so preoccupied with getting so you can respond to God's giving." Really, Lord? How did he know I was agitated? How did he lead me to this verse, on this day, when my mind was occupied with this problem? Isn't he amazing?

He continued: "People who don't know God and the way he works fuss over these things, but you know both God and how he works. Steep yourself in God-reality, God-initiative, God-provisions. You'll find all your everyday human concerns will be met. Don't be afraid of missing out. You're my dearest friends! The Father wants to give you the very kingdom itself."

Wow. I rebooted the computer, called the insurance company, offered to pray with the sweet customer service lady who couldn't give me any answers, went online and found a CVS Health Savings Pass that would save me a bundle on the prescription.

In fact, it's cheaper than it was when I was paying less under the insurance plan – and it's the same pharmacy! I highly recommend it!

I even more highly recommend spending time with the Lord whenever the cares of this world tend to agitate you – as they do me. He has all the answers, and he cares!

----------

## *Five Things Your Pharisee Won't Tell You*

"Ten Things Your Doctor Won't Tell You." "20 Things Your Flight Attendant Won't Tell You." Sound familiar? I read the *Reader's Digest* from cover to cover every month. The articles are informative, concise, and good reading. I admire the editors who can cut the word count down without losing the integrity of the story. It takes a lot of skill to do that.

Luke was the only writer of the four Gospels who had not been one of the companions of Jesus. He told a story based upon eyewitness accounts the disciples related to him, and events he knew about but hadn't experienced himself. His style reflected his medical background in the concise way he wrote, and in the events that most caught his attention. He gave us much more detail about the births of John the Baptist and Jesus than the other Gospel writers.

In Matthew 9:23-27, he told us "Five Things Your Priest Won't Tell You." He was writing in the day of the Sanhedrin and those priests were not fans of Jesus.

He reported that Jesus said:

{1} "Anyone who intends to come with me has to let me lead. You're not in the driver's seat – I am."
{2} "Don't run from suffering; embrace it. Follow me and I'll show you how."
{3} "Self-help is no help at all. Self-sacrifice is the way, my way, to finding yourself, your true self. What good would it do to get everything you want and lose you, the real you?"
{4} "If any of you is embarrassed with me and the way I'm leading you, know that the Son of Man will be far more embarrassed with you when he arrives in all his splendor in company with the Father and the holy angels."
{5} "This isn't, you realize, pie in the sky by and by. Some who have taken their stand right here are going to see it happen, see with their own eyes the kingdom of God." (The Message)

I don't know about you, but it seems less complicated to follow the instructions of Jesus than those many detailed laws enforced by the priests of that day; and we're going to see the kingdom of God with our own eyes!

----------

## The Cycle is Broken

In college, I passed a Modern Literature class with an A without having to take the final exam. My professor and I met, by chance, at a coffee shop. Our conversation soon turned to the latest book we were reading, and I described to her my theory that all literature – in fact all of life – is a series of intersecting globes.

There are no straight lines in nature (with the possible exception of crystals), and everything, from seasons to life-cycles, is cyclical. Themes, writing styles, the works themselves, overlapped in areas and were unique in others.

John Donne wrote, "No man is an island." I contended that no literary work could be self-contained without intersecting with others. I had trouble verbalizing what was a pretty vague idea, but she bought it, and I aced the class.

Now I know that Scripture tells us the same thing. "What has been will be again, what has been done will be done again; there is nothing new under the sun." (Ecclesiastes 1:9 NIV)

History repeats itself. We never learn from it. We forget too easily. And yet, there is one thing that was done once and will never be repeated.

Under the Jewish Law, sacrifices were to be made on a regular basis for the atonement of sin. In the New Testament, we're introduced to the Lamb of God who became the final sacrifice for the sin of all mankind.

When he said his last words on the cross, "It is finished," (John 19:30 NIV) he broke the endless cycle of never-enough and opened the door of Heaven for everyone who appropriates his sacrifice for all time.

Jesus Christ did the one new thing that had never been done before and will never have to be done again. Love broke the cycle.

# WHAT COMES NEXT?

"In this world of wonder, where color chases color,
There's so much yet to see and so much more to learn.
A lifetime isn't long enough to solve the mysteries
You have placed here long ago, just so we might see."

~ Amber and Ewald Sutter
Song: *Harvest Dance*
From the album *Collecting the Past*

Lyrics and music by
Amber and Ewald Sutter

## *Yoga Meditations*

I took a yoga class a few years ago, and asked the instructor what the words meant in a soothing tape he played while we were meditating at the end. He said it was a musical recitation of some of the names of the gods. I still think the purpose of the music was to drown out the snoring of one of the exhausted devotees.

I told him that I meditate on the names of the One True God and that those other gods are false and meaningless. I didn't make a friend that day.

God told the Israelites in Exodus 15:26, "I am God your healer." In Hebrew, Adonai Roph'ekha is the Lord who heals you. God heals. He heals us physically, mentally, emotionally and spiritually. He's been healing me since he first saved me.

I needed a lot of healing, and still do…every day. I'm so glad he doesn't expect us to be perfect in this life.

Adonai Tov ve'Salach is Hebrew for "the Lord is good and forgiving." As messed up as I was, healing and forgiveness had to go hand-in-hand. I thank my God that he does both

----------

## *It's a Bird! It's a Plane! It's Chuck Norris?*

Our grandsons love Chuck Norris jokes. "Chuck Norris is so strong that instead of push-ups, he pushes the earth down." "Chuck Norris counted to infinity – twice." "Chuck Norris can do a wheelie on a unicycle." You get the drift. Chuck Norris is the modern-day Superman.

In ancient Israel, those jokes might have referred to King Solomon. He was the wealthiest, wisest and most handsome man in ancient history. His armies were the strongest. He had multiple wives and concubines, everything money could buy, and he kept himself busy trading horses, building cities, and learning everything he could about everything. What a guy! And yet, Solomon was bored and depressed.

Having learned everything there was to know, he came to the conclusion that life is just smoke. Guess what? I know something he didn't know.

In Ecclesiastes 3:19-22, King Solomon had this to say, "Humans and animals come to the same end – humans die, animals die. We all breathe the same air. So there's really no advantage in being human. None. Everything's smoke. We all end up in the same place – we all came from dust, we all end up as dust. Nobody knows for sure that the human spirit rises to Heaven. Who knows if there's anything else to life?"

I do. During his last Passover supper with his disciples, Jesus hinted at what was about to happen – namely his death. In John 14: 1-3, Jesus told his disciples, "Don't let this throw you. You trust God, don't you? Trust me. There is plenty of room for you in my Father's home. If that weren't so, would I have told you that I'm on my way to get a room ready for you? And if I'm on my way to get your room ready, I'll come back and get you so you can live where I live." Solomon wasn't sure about Heaven, but Jesus said we can be sure of it.

What does it take to be more super than Solomon? Place your trust in God, accept that Jesus is your Savior, and know that your spirit will rise to Heaven when it leaves this earth. I can't wait to fly!

----------

## *When It's Over, It Isn't Over*

Before my Dad surrendered his life to Jesus in his late 80's, I had heard him say a few times, "There is no life after death. When you die, it's all over."

Not too long ago, a friend posted a priest's response to someone who said, "I can't believe in a god who allows such misery in the world." The priest said something like this… "I couldn't either, if I didn't also believe in Heaven." So who's right?

Solomon seemed to agree with my dad's pre-believer statement. In Ecclesiastes 9:2-3, he said this about the human condition, "It's one fate for everybody—righteous and wicked, good people, bad people, the nice and the nasty, worshipers and non-worshipers, committed and uncommitted. I find this outrageous—the worst thing about living on this earth—that everyone's lumped together in one fate. Is it any wonder that so many people are obsessed with evil? Is it any wonder that people go crazy right and left? Life leads to death. That's it."

Solomon's pessimistic view of life was the result of overindulgence. He had everything the world had to offer, and yet his conclusion was that death is all there is for all of us. Yes, we will all die. But is that the end, or the beginning?

Christians are familiar with the beauty and hope of Jesus's words in John 3:16, but there's more to what he said, "For God so loved the world that he gave his one and only Son, that whoever believes in him shall not perish but have eternal life. For God did not send his Son into the world to condemn the world, but to save the world through him."(V.16-17 NIV)

Solomon only saw part of the picture. He based his conclusions on his observations of mundane life. The hope of Heaven can only come through surrender to God's way of doing things, as Dad later learned.

The last time I saw Dad, I turned to him and said, "Daddy, you're about to embark on the greatest adventure of your life." My heart was breaking, but I knew I'd see him again in Heaven. Dad looked at me with love in his eyes and said, "I know."

My Dad was wiser than Solomon.

----------

## *It's Less Complicated Than I Thought*

Bill and I knew nothing about our business when we started it. Such ignorance would probably result in financial disaster in a conventional business, but we soon found that ours was different. If we followed the system and did what the successful people did, we would learn, grow and eventually teach others the same principles – and we'd become successful ourselves.

We humans like to complicate things. We make rules, and then add regulations to ensure we keep the original rules. Those, in turn, multiply into more detailed and stringent rules so that we obey the ones that were made to clarify the original ones. Before long, we don't leave ourselves room to breathe, much less enjoy any freedom.

It's a good thing that I started reading the Bible in the New Testament. I went from Matthew through Revelation, and then I decided to read it from the beginning.

The first time I plowed through Leviticus, I realized my life would have been very short in those days. Misfits don't do well with a lot of rules, so God's law would have been the death of me. Instead, I ran smack into God's amazing grace. I found complete forgiveness, extravagant love, a lifetime adventure, and unspeakable joy.

I met the Lord of Heaven, the Holy One of Israel, the One who gave his life for me and for all who place their trust in him. I met Wonderful, Counselor, the Mighty God, the Everlasting Father, the Prince of Peace foretold in Isaiah 9:6, and I found out that grace is where I fit in.

The Apostle Paul said in Ephesians 5:1-2, "Watch what God does, and then you do it, like children who learn proper behavior from their parent. Mostly what God does is love you. Keep company with him and learn a life of love. Observe how Christ loved us. His love was not cautious but extravagant. He didn't love in order to get something from us, but to give everything of himself to us. Love like that."

The prophets of old foretold his coming. Salvation was promised to all those who choose to believe in and place their trust in Jesus Christ, our Lord and Savior, our Hope and our Future. Instead of trying to fit ourselves in the box defined by the Law, we've been given a simple roadmap, nudged forward by the gentle hand of grace.

----------

## Questions

We watched horrific news reports of the devastating Typhoon Haiyan in the Philippines and elsewhere. Nearly every day, we watch storms shatter towns in the U.S.A. and around the world and wonder whether God is watching out for his people. We wonder the same thing when we see Jews and Christians being persecuted for their faith, children going hungry and thirsty, and people living in abject poverty.

Our heads say, "Of course, he is," but our hearts grieve, knowing that people are hurting. We're motivated to do something – anything we can – to alleviate just a little of the suffering. Why doesn't God do something? He can do anything and everything. He has unlimited resources.

David's worship leader, Asaph, asked the same question in Psalm 73:11, "What's going on here? Is God out to lunch?"

I imagine God grieves, too, but not in the same way. He sees the whole picture. He knows the effect of every event on the eventual realization of his plan and purpose. He grieves for each of us individually, for our humanity and brokenness, for our sin-sickness and sorrow.

He did do something. He sent his only Son to die in our place, so that we would have eternal life with him when we accept his unspeakable gift of pardon through Jesus Christ. We might suffer in this life, and we will die, but God has opened a door we can step through to a never-ending life of joy.

How does that help the victims of disasters? He uses us, normal everyday people, to minister to others. He strengthens us as we help others. He motivates us to do something. He gives us the joy of knowing we've made a difference to another human being.

Yes, he could do it all himself with his unlimited power and resources, but he's chosen to give us the blessing, instead. And he's waiting for us in Heaven, to give us the ultimate blessing of life with him.

Asaph ended Psalm 73 with this declaration, "You're all I want in heaven. You're all I want on earth! When my skin sags and my bones get brittle, God is rock-firm and faithful." Amen. Thank You, Lord!

----------

## *A Little Challenge*

God isn't afraid of a little challenge. If he can take a rebellious misfit like me and turn my heart so that I would fall in love with him and want to follow him forever, then he can handle any challenge.

The Psalmist said in Psalm 34:8, "Taste and see that the Lord is good." (NIV)

Some of our grandchildren were picky eaters. If there was a speck of green in the food, they'd turn their noses up and wouldn't try it. The trick was to challenge them, make a game of it, and let them try to win the game. Aren't we all like that?

I turned my nose up at anything smacking of Christianity. My concept of God was skewed by other people's opinions. When I finally stepped up to God's challenge and tasted (began to read the Word), he proved himself to be very good.

In Malachi 3:10, we're issued another challenge. "Bring the whole tithe (tenth) into the storehouse that there may be food in my house. Test me in this," said the Lord Almighty, "and see if I will not throw open the floodgates of heaven and pour out so much blessing that there will not be room enough to store it." (NIV)

He invites us to test him, the Living God, the Creator of the Universe! During the time I was a single mom and there was never enough money to cover expenses, I took this challenge and gave a tenth of every dollar that came into our house to the church. God delivered on his promise, and we saw miracle after miracle. We still don't have room enough to store his blessings!

Our Pastor challenged us to a thirty-day prayer initiative. Every day, we were to pray what the disciples prayed in Acts 4:29-30. Starting partway through verse 29, "...enable your servants to speak your word with great boldness. Stretch out your hand to heal and perform signs and wonders through the name of your holy servant Jesus." (NIV) God answers prayer!

Now to stay alert for opportunities to allow God to increase my boldness and help me to be quick to reach out and pray for miracles for people I encounter. Can you imagine if we ALL did this? I'm praying, and expecting God to answer. What about you?

----------

## *The Password*

"Me do yit! Me do yit!" Two-year-old Dyana whined when I lifted her down from the cabinet she'd climbed onto in order to get to the cookie she wanted. She was determined to do everything by herself. I knew what she couldn't do at that age, but I had to let her try some challenges or she'd never figure things out.

The instinct for independence is strong in us. We press beyond our limitations and grow. How many times did we fall before we learned to walk?

As adults, we've learned that we cannot do everything. I can't pilot a jetliner. The pilot may not be able to build tall buildings. Society works because we're interdependent.

There is one thing no human can do alone, no matter how much of an expert he or she is. No human can enter the Kingdom of God unless they go through the door, and the door only opens to those who know the password.

Jesus told his disciples a parable in John 10:6-10, "I am the Gate for the sheep...Anyone who goes through me will be cared for – will freely go in and out, and find pasture...I came so they can have real and eternal life, more and better life than they ever dreamed of."

He said it another way in John 14:6-7, after he'd told his disciples that he was going ahead of them to prepare their place in God's kingdom. "I am the Road, also the Truth, also the Life. No one gets to the Father apart from me. If you really knew me, you would know my Father as well."

We want to get to Heaven on our own, (Me do yit!) but we can't. We can't change our heart by ourselves. We can't sanctify ourselves. We can't find our way to our heavenly home by ourselves. As much as we want to believe there are many ways to get to Heaven, Jesus himself said there is only one way.

He isn't condemning anyone. He didn't come to condemn the world, but so the world might be saved from their inevitable end because humankind was already condemned by our own actions.

Why wouldn't we want to reach out and grab the hand of the One who gave his life for us; who loves us with an uncompromising, everlasting love; who knows the way and wants to lead us there? What is the password? I belong to Jesus.

----------

## *Raising The Dead*

When my kids were little, they attended Mustard Seed Christian School in Hoboken, New Jersey. Hoboken is at sea level, and we lived on the bluffs along the Hudson River. My friend Lynn drove her kids and mine to school every day in her old van. I went along in case she needed a push.

That thing popped and wheezed and rattled its way down the long hill with no problem. She shifted it to neutral and just let her roll. At the first intersection in town, she put it in gear and we waved at the dancing traffic cop, who moved us along with great enthusiasm and beautiful arm extensions. She always made us smile. Unfortunately, our cloud of oily smoke obscured the view of the folks following us, so the pleasure was all ours and they missed out.

Getting home was an exercise in prayer. Our friendly traffic cop gestured us through to a running start at the bottom of the hill. A quarter of the way up, Lynn had to shift down. No matter the weather, she had her arm out the window to wave people around us as we crawled up the last fifty yards of the hill in first gear. The car shook with backfires and the tailpipe belched black smoke. I prayed as it moaned and shuddered slowly upwards. Sometimes, it simply died.

We knew nothing about bringing a dead car to life again, but we knew the One who brought dead people back to life. It would be a simple matter for God to revive a dilapidated van. So we laid hands on the hood, thanked him for such a reliable car, thanked him for healing the van, and got back in.

Lynn turned the key. The old thing started right up, and we made it to the top – every time.

One thing we both learned during those daily adventures was that "Nothing is impossible with God." Luke 1:37 (NLT) Jesus himself said, "Humanly speaking, it is impossible. But with God, everything is possible." (Matthew 19:26 NLT) We had a very practical, first-hand lesson. If God can bring old vans back to life, what can't he do?

----------

## *Little Warrior*

My son was terrified of the dentist. When he was afraid of something, he became totally committed to fighting it off. One beautiful day, I put him on the back of my motorcycle, as if we were going for a ride in the country. What a nasty trickster I was! We went straight to the dentist.

Mike was about eight at the time. He refused to take off his full-faced helmet. There we sat, in the waiting room with other moms and kids; this mom with her defiant little biker, faceplate firmly in place, arms crossed and ready to fight. The dentist called him in and wouldn't let me come along.

I didn't hear any screaming. There was no commotion. I had just begun to actually relax when out marched my boy, helmet still on his head, faceplate up, and a grin on his face. The dentist, God bless him, worked on his teeth with the helmet on. He told me Mike had refused Novocain (a needle was involved), so he worked on him without it. Shudder....

In Ephesians 6:11-12 (NIV) we're told, "Put on the full armor of God, so that you can take your stand against the devil's schemes. For our struggle is not against flesh and blood, but against the rulers, against the authorities, against the powers of this dark world and against the spiritual forces of evil in the heavenly realms."

In the eyes of my little boy, the authorities were the parental units making him do what he didn't want to do, and the dentist who was bound and determined to make his life miserable. He didn't realize until later that we were motivated by love and determination to do the right thing for his welfare.

So what is the armor of God? It includes the belt of truth, the breastplate of righteousness, the shoes of the preparation of the gospel of peace, the shield of faith, the helmet of salvation, and the sword of the Spirit which is the Word of God. We might believe we're truth tellers or righteous, but what truth we know, or how righteous we think we are, are not enough. We put on these attributes because someone else is giving them to us. Every one of them describes Jesus.

Little Mike is now a grown man. He no longer needs the helmet for courage because he wears courage like a suit of armor. He wears the armor of God. He's grown into a mighty man of God (he'd be embarrassed to hear me say it), and I couldn't be any prouder now, or any more in awe, than I was when my little warrior took the drill without anesthetic. I am one blessed Mama!

----------

## *Passive Talent*

I like to think I helped birth our cousin John's rock music career. He was a member of the cast of Up With People, a stage production that toured the world bringing uplifting, joyful music to audiences everywhere. Their music was conservative, to say the least, and I wasn't. He may not even remember it, but I won't forget the look on his face the first time I let him listen to my Jimi Hendrix music. He's been a musician ever since.

I come from a musically gifted family. We have singers, song writers and musicians adept at a variety of instruments. My mom is so full of music it trickles out in a fountain of tunes whistled under her breath. She's usually unaware of doing it. It's a background of comfort we've gotten used to.

My musical gift is appreciation. I don't sing, play or write music, but I certainly do love it and appreciate my family's gifts.

In Psalm 68, David said, "Up with God!" There was nothing conservative about David. He entered into everything with full gusto and honesty.

He went on, "When the righteous see God in action they'll laugh, they'll sing, they'll laugh and sing for joy. Sing hymns to God; all heaven, sing out; clear the way for the coming of Cloud-Rider. Enjoy God. Cheer when you see him!" What enthusiasm! He could have been describing a rock concert starring God!

He continued, "Sing, O kings of the earth! Sing praises to the Lord! There he is; Sky-Rider, striding the ancient skies... Call out, 'Bravo!' to God, the High God of Israel."

What a spectacular show! Cloud-Rider makes an appearance, and the kings of the earth go wild with applause and shout their praise! Sky-Rider fills the sky with a display of his glory! That day is coming!

I am so grateful that God has given me the gift of appreciation, so I can join in with the crowd and shout, "Bravo, God! Yay, God! Awesome, God!" Haven't we all been given that gift?

----------

## *Big Dreams*

Our gifted niece Amber grew up in a musical family. My brother Dan's band played our high school dances, and he and his guitar were inseparable. When he married, he and Cindy had six children. Each of them learned to play an instrument or two, sang, and learned the mechanics of setting up a sound system, a stage, and recording their music. They made some wonderful CD's as a family, and have led worship in many different venues.

Amber and her husband Ewald have produced a CD with music they wrote and performed together. She plays keyboard and he, a master guitarist, gives his guitar voice. They both sing to honor and worship the Lord.

God gave her a dream that they would one day praise God in front of a vast audience. She's concerned that the dream is of her own making, and that her desire to fulfill it comes from pride. It seems God might have a different view.

"Good people, cheer God! Right-living people sound best when praising. Use guitars to reinforce your Hallelujahs! Play praise on a grand piano! Invent your own new song to him; give him a trumpet fanfare." (Psalm 33:1-3)

It sounds to me as if King David was speaking directly to her! Guitar, piano, writing your own song – it's all there. She and her husband are following God's directions. Wouldn't it be more prideful to refuse to use the gifts God gave them? His people need worship leaders!

"Worship God if you want the best; worship opens doors to all his goodness." (Psalm 34:9)

If God gave her that dream of leading the worship of multitudes, he will fulfill it. When it happens, I want to be in the audience to fully participate in cheering God. I can hardly wait!

----------

## *Hot Pink Haven*

Fourteen years ago, the Lord woke my mother-in-law up from sleep one morning and told her it was time for Bill and me to buy a house. Before we met, Bill owned a house in Florida, and I owned one in Pennsylvania – together with our respective pre-divorce spouses.

We ended up renting out both homes when we moved to Florida as a newly married couple. Things didn't work out well with the renters. One home was sold at a loss, and the other went to sheriff's sale. We figured it would be many years before we could buy another. Then God spoke to Mom.

She insisted we start looking. We decided on a neighborhood, but kept ignoring one house because of its bright color and the empty lot next door. Bill finally gave in and knocked on the door, and we discovered our house – painted garishly hot-pink outside, but perfect on the inside. It was a miracle that we were able to purchase it.

We dedicated this home to the Lord and asked him to use it for his glory. He has used it to minister to friends and family as a refuge, a place to call home for a while, and a place to just come and have some fun with Gramma and Grampa.

Occasionally, we host a fellowship meal with many of our Christian brothers and sisters. We invite people from our church and neighborhood to come and enjoy the food that they all bring, spend time getting to know each other and participate in a time of prayer for each other's concerns. God's hand is on us all.

God led Bill to Philippians 4:4-7 after the last fellowship, "Rejoice in the Lord always. I will say it again: Rejoice! Let your gentleness be evident to all. The Lord is near. Do not be anxious about anything, but in every situation, by prayer and petition, with thanksgiving, present your requests to God. And the peace of God, which transcends all understanding, will guard your hearts and your minds in Christ Jesus." (NIV)

Our hot-pink house has been a nice shade of blue for quite a few years now. It's still perfect for us. It was God's gift; one we didn't have to worry or fret over.

----------

## Flavor

When Bill's son Mike was little, he expressed his pleasure at something he ate by saying, "Mmmmmm. Flavor." Seasoning is flavorful. When someone politely asks me how I am, I often answer, "I'm blessed and highly flavored of the Lord."

Have you ever wondered what your purpose is here on earth? As a teenager, I questioned, "Who am I? Why am I here? What am I supposed to do with my life?"

Jesus said in Matthew 5:13-16, "Let me tell you why you are here. You're here to be salt-seasoning that brings out the God-flavors of this earth. If you lose your saltiness, how will people taste godliness? You've lost your usefulness and will end up in the garbage."

He continued, "Here's another way to put it: You're here to be light, bringing out the God-colors in the world. God is not a secret to be kept. We're going public with it, as public as a city on a hill. If I make you light-bearers, you don't think I'm going to hide you under a bucket, do you? I'm putting you on a light stand. Now that I've put you there on a hilltop, on a light stand – shine! Keep open house; be generous with your lives. By opening up to others, you'll prompt people to open up with God, this generous Father in heaven."

God wants us to be salt and light to those around us. If I had known about Jesus in those early days of my life, I could have avoided so much heartache.

Our purpose is to be highly flavored and to shine so others will be attracted by the seasoning and find their way to the Light.

----------

## Feel the Wind

Bill is not a great fan of windy days. It's tough teaching and playing tennis when the wind stirs up the clay on the court and wants to take the ball somewhere other than where you aimed it. The weather was a challenge the weekend of the National Father-Daughter Tennis Tournament, an annual event at the club where Bill teaches. It was too windy, and the occasional shower caused delays and cancellations.

I'm not a tennis player, so I don't feel too badly about loving windy days! I love the dance of the palm trees, and the way birds tack across the wind when they fly into it, and how they soar when they fly with it. I love the feel of it on my face and in my hair. It might have been a windy day when Paul wrote this portion of his first letter to the Thessalonians, chapter 4.

"We ask you – urge is more like it – that you keep on doing what we told you to do to please God, not in a dogged religious plod, but in a living, spirited dance." Like the palm trees! Like autumn leaves, up north!

"And then this: We can tell you with complete confidence – we have the Master's word on it – that when the Master comes again to get us, those of us who are still alive will not get a jump on the dead and leave them behind. In actual fact, they'll be ahead of us. The Master himself will give the command. Archangel thunder! God's trumpet blast! He'll come down from heaven and the dead in Christ will rise – they'll go first. Then the rest of us who are still alive at the time will be caught up with them into the clouds to meet the Master. Oh, we'll be walking on air! And then there will be one huge family reunion with the Master. So reassure one another with these words."

Can't you picture the millions of people rising, swirling in a "living, spirited dance" to meet Jesus in the sky? Walking on air, indeed! We'll be soaring, like birds with the wind behind them!

Wind stirs up my longing to be with God, and fills me with joy and anticipation of that amazing, indescribable day. Sorry about the tennis, Bill, but imagine what we have to look forward to.

----------

## Clark Kent or Superman?

I love some of the paintings I've seen of Jesus; like Jesus laughing, Jesus with the children, Jesus carrying the lamb, or Akiane's Jesus. I often think of him as a loving, gentle, mild-mannered Clark Kent type of person. I hate to think of him suffering on the cross for my sake, so I quickly picture him as someone like Superman, coming in the clouds riding a white horse on that wonderful day when he returns.

Yet, in Matthew 5, he was like the Old Testament God, and he said things I do not want to hear. Why? Because truth hurts, even when it's tempered by the knowledge that all sins are forgiven, and we are now new creations in Christ. Here's what I mean:

He said, "Let's not pretend this is easier than it really is. If you want to live a morally pure life, here's what you have to do…" Did he really say that we should blind one eye if we look at someone lustfully, or that we should cut off a hand when we raise it with threat to someone? Certainly he didn't mean that literally?

He continued, "Remember the Scripture that says, 'Whoever divorces his wife, let him do it legally, giving her divorce papers and her legal rights'? Too many of you are using that as a cover for selfishness and whim, pretending to be righteous just because you are 'legal' …You can't use legal cover to mask a moral failure."

"And don't say anything you don't mean … You don't make your words true by embellishing them with religious lace. In making your speech sound more religious, it becomes less true. Just say 'yes' and 'no.' When you manipulate words to get your own way, you go wrong."

Here we see a glimpse of the Old Testament God of judgment. According to these standards, it's impossible to live a morally pure life. After all, how often do our thoughts stray where they don't belong? We only have two eyes to blind and two hands to cut off – and who would do that to themselves anyway? How many of us are divorced? Who has always, without fail, done exactly what they said they'd do? So what hope do we have?

It's because of the picture of Jesus I hate to linger on that we have hope of redemption for our moral failures. He took those failures to the cross with him, so that we might have forgiveness and life everlasting. And he is coming, perhaps soon, riding that white horse, to call his people home.

----------

## *Prepare for Battle*

I turned the television off in disgust. A home invasion resulted in the victim's murder. A child was killed in a drive-by shooting. A fireman died when a car lost control and hit him as he was trying to change his tire. Someone is victimized every single day.

How about some good news? Try Psalm 103.

"God makes everything come out right; he puts victims back on their feet." We're all victims, in a sense. The enemy of our souls is constantly attacking us – in our emotions, in our circumstances, in our relationships, in our finances… you name it. Everything we hold dear is under attack. But we have nothing to fear, and everything to be thankful for! Why?

"God is sheer mercy and grace; not easily angered, he's rich in love. He doesn't endlessly nag and scold, nor hold grudges forever. He doesn't treat us as our sins deserve, nor pay us back in full for our wrongs."

This is the Old Testament God we're seeing here. Doesn't he sound just like the New Testament God? Surprise! He's the same, the One and Only God of Abraham, Isaac and Jacob.

"As high as heaven is over the earth, so strong is his love to those who fear him. As far as the sunrise is from the sunset, he has separated us from our sins. As parents feel for their children, God feels for those who fear him. He knows us inside and out, keeps in mind that we're made of mud."

This is why we love to go to church and join in worship with our brothers and sisters: "God has set his throne in heaven; he rules over us all. He's the King! So bless God, you angels, ready and able to fly at his bidding, quick to hear and do what he says. Bless God, all you armies of angels, alert to respond to whatever he wills. Bless God, all creatures, wherever you are – everything and everyone made by God. And you, O my soul, bless God!"

I bless God, with enthusiasm and gratitude and joy!

----------

## *Good Habits*

People are creatures of habit – some good and some not so much. For more than a year, I did an hour or more of Zumba nearly every day. Before that, I took regular tennis lessons with the best teacher on the planet – my husband. So what happened?

A pain in the heel interrupted tennis and a quick succession of trips and family visits interrupted the Zumba. I've heard it only takes 21 days to establish a habit, so why is it so hard to get back into it after an interruption?

Nature abhors a vacuum, so when one habit is broken, other activities fill up that time very quickly. The fact is I hate to sweat, so I didn't need much of an excuse to find something else to do.

One habit I pray will never stop is reading my Bible and spending time with the Lord every day. There's no sweating involved, so there's no excuse to quit. Right? I've also been reading and re-reading a little booklet entitled, "If My People…a 40-day Prayer Guide for Our Nation" by Jack Countryman. Forty days has grown into more than a year, so far.

Have you ever had a song run through your head all day? Today's scripture starts with one that my brother used to sing. I love the tune, and look forward to hearing it all day.

"Give ear to my words, O Lord, consider my meditation. Give heed to the voice of my cry, my King and my God, for to you I will pray. My voice shall you hear in the morning, O Lord; in the morning I will direct it to You, and I will look up." Psalm 5:1-3 (KJV)

Jack writes this prayer, "We beg you, O Lord, to hear our supplication. Do not let our words fall on deaf ears. Let us come to you each morning with a heart full of joy, for you are our Most High God, and everything we have comes from you. Bless us that we might bless others. Let us always look to you for every provision. Let us be an open vessel filled with your wisdom, that others might know your saving grace."

And may I add, O Lord, that you keep me on task and please don't let anything interrupt or stop our time together. It's one habit I want to keep for my lifetime. Amen!

----------

## *Bad Habits*

Yesterday "That Driver" stopped in front of me at a red light, in the right-turn lane, with no intention of turning right. You know which driver I'm talking about -- the one who bought her driver's license at Walmart.

I waited impatiently for the light to turn green. She waited to move until the people in the car behind me honked their horn, and then took off very, very slowly.

As a Christian, you'd think I'd have learned by now that "Those Words" should never issue out of my mouth. You know the words I'm talking about. After I said them, I repented and thought about how destructive "Those Words" are.

Back at home, I opened my Bible, and guess who was waiting for me to turn to the next passage in my daily reading? You know Who I'm talking about.

Here's what Jesus said, "You're familiar with the command to the ancients, 'Do not murder.' I'm telling you that anyone who is so much as angry with a brother or sister is guilty of murder. Carelessly call a brother, 'Idiot!' and you just might find yourself hauled into court. Thoughtlessly yell 'stupid!' at a sister and you are on the brink of hellfire. The simple moral fact is that words kill." (Matthew 5:21-22)

Guilty as charged. I'm so thankful that God has forgiven me all the times I've run into "That Driver" and said "Those Words." Every now and then, he reminds me how awful I can be, and that only he can change my heart. He's able to deliver me from my bad habits.

The day I've reached perfection is the day I have the right to criticize anyone else. When that day comes, I won't want to criticize anyone! I'll be busy in Heaven, worshipping God!

----------

## *Taxes*

It was getting too close to April 15, 2014. Not only were taxes due on that date, but it was also the day of the first of the four blood moons that were to begin in 2014 and fall on Jewish holy days. Perhaps events of Biblical proportions will occur over the next couple of years, but my biggest concern at the moment was taxes.

I am not a numbers person. No matter how many times I say it to myself and others, the job still has to get done, and I'm the one to do it. Thank the Lord we have a good accountant, but I have to pull it all together for her to make some sense of it.

Here's how I do it. I enter a few things into a spreadsheet, then get up for a bit of exercise. Note: I only get up for exercise when I'm doing taxes. I enter a few more things, and then get up to mop the kitchen floor. I enter more numbers and get up to grab a snack. Get the picture? I will do anything to avoid getting the taxes done.

As it happened, I read about the tax man in the Bible that day. Wouldn't you know, God will do anything to get my attention focused back on the task.

In Luke 18:9-14, Jesus told us of two men. One was a Pharisee, a religious, well-educated member of the upper class. The other was the tax man, whom nobody wanted to see, hear or have anything to do with. The Pharisee went to pray and thanked God that he wasn't like the tax collector. The tax man prayed with deep humility, asking for mercy and nothing else. One expected blessing, and the other hoped for it, against all hope.

Here's what Jesus had to say, "This tax man, not the other, went home made right with God. If you walk around with your nose in the air, you're going to end up flat on your face, but if you're content to be simply yourself, you will become more than yourself."

And there I was, nose not in the air, but on the grindstone, being myself and getting back to working on the taxes.

# SOUR LEMONS OR LEMONADE?

"We cannot change our past. We cannot change the fact that people act in a certain way. We cannot change the inevitable. The only thing we can do is play on the one string we have, and that is our attitude."

~ Chuck Swindoll, Pastor

## *The Free Will Dilemma*

After my first husband and I broke up, I turned away from God. I'm not proud of it. I felt as if God had abandoned me – that he honored the husband's free will to leave and ignored my free will to stay married.

Now I can almost hear God's exasperated sigh. What to do with this free will conundrum? What to do with these clueless, selfish children?

Solomon had this to say about the human condition in Ecclesiastes 9:11-12: "The race is not always to the swift, nor the battle to the strong, nor satisfaction to the wise, nor riches to the smart, nor grace to the learned. Sooner or later bad luck hits us all. No one can predict misfortune."

A broken marriage, and all the evils that followed, certainly qualified as "misfortune" in my book. I reacted in anger and disappointment. God didn't love me and never had – or so I tried to convince myself.

In spite of my pessimistic outlook, God broke through with many proofs of his unending love for me. When this surly child let go of the long, drawn-out tantrum and once again ran to my Father for comfort, he didn't reject me.

Paul said, in Galatians 6:8-10, "the one who plants in response to God, letting God's Spirit do the growth work in him, harvests a crop of real, eternal life. So let's not allow ourselves to get fatigued doing good. At the right time we will harvest a good crop if we don't give up or quit."

I gave up on God, but he didn't give up on me. As I learned to trust him to do the work he'd started in me, I began to see a good crop grow. Today, I can say that the husband I now have and all our children have been the best harvest anyone could ask for. Crops are still growing. I can't wait to see the harvest that's coming!

----------

## *Frenemies*

ARRGH!!! Why is it so hard to like someone you're having a conflict with? We know that some people light up a room every time they enter, and others light it up when they leave.

Jesus knows our nature. He knows that sometimes we're a friend, and sometimes we're an enemy. As always, he teaches us with great wisdom and empathy.

He said in Matthew 5:43-48, "You're familiar with the old written law, 'Love your friend,' and its unwritten companion, 'Hate your enemy.' I'm challenging that. I'm telling you to love your enemies. Let them bring out the best in you, not the worst. When someone gives you a hard time, respond with the energies of prayer, for then you are working out your true selves, your God-created selves. This is what God does. He gives his best – the sun to warm and the rain to nourish – to everyone, regardless: the good and bad, the nice and nasty.

"If all you do is love the lovable, do you expect a bonus? Anybody can do that. If you simply say hello to those who greet you, do you expect a medal? Any run-of-the-mill sinner does that.

"In a word, what I'm saying is, grow up. You're Kingdom subjects. Now live like it. Live out your God-created identity. Live generously and graciously toward others, the way God lives toward you."

The fact is we are that person who lights up the room, either by coming in or going out. Sometimes we're one, and sometimes the other. It's been said we don't like some people because we see ourselves in them. We share their failings. We are all complicated, and we fluctuate from happy to miserable, taking everyone with us on the roller coaster. Even the heroes of the Bible were less than perfect, with the notable exception of Jesus. Who are we to not forgive and love our enemies when God himself forgives and loves us?

----------

## *I Don't Want to Love My Enemies*

Why does God tell us to feed, or be good to, our enemies in Proverbs? Why did Jesus say we have to love our enemies?

I have to admit, I have struggled with this one. Bill reminds me that people are not our enemies – the dirty devil is ours and theirs, too. It's still hard to view people who hurt me or my loved ones as anything other than an enemy.

And then I read 2 Kings 6. In this story, Elisha, pursued by the army of the king of Aram, calmly asked God to open the eyes of his terrified servant. The servant saw God's army surrounding him and Elisha in fiery chariots. What a comfort that must have been!

Here's the rest of the story. God blinded the enemy hosts, at Elisha's request, and Elisha led them into a trap where they were surrounded by the king of Israel's army. Instead of asking for their slaughter, Elisha asked the king to prepare a feast for them. He did, they ate, and were sent back home. As a result, the raiding parties that had plagued the Israelites ended. Aram's army stopped bullying Israel.

So when we obey God and bless our enemies, He rewards us with peace. Sounds like a good idea to me. Now, if only I can remember that the next time some driver cuts me off.

----------

## *Mending the Shattered*

Can a relationship be so broken that nothing can fix it? Can the shattered shards be so far apart there is no possibility of a bridge between them, even if they end up glued elsewhere? How is reconciliation even possible?

Jesus said this in Matthew 5:23-26, "This is how I want you to conduct yourself in these matters. If you enter your place of worship and, about to make an offering, you suddenly remember a grudge a friend has against you, abandon your offering, leave immediately, go to this friend and make things right. Then and only then, come back and work things out with God."

Wait a minute. If my friend, or family member, has a grudge against me and isn't receptive to any overtures I make, how on earth can I be expected to make things right? The grudge is theirs, not mine. Was Jesus being unreasonable here? Is making the effort enough?

He went on to say, "Or say you're out on the street and an old enemy accosts you. Don't lose a minute. Make the first move; make things right with him. After all, if you leave the first move to him, knowing his track record, you're likely to end up in court, maybe even jail. If that happens, you won't get out without a stiff fine."

That seems a bit harsh. My enemy hates me, so I have to make the first move to reconcile with him or her. Got it. But doesn't it take two to make things right?

I may be wrong, but I interpret it this way: my actions are my responsibility. If I act in such a way that makes it clear that reconciliation is possible, then their actions, being their responsibility, don't matter – at least in context of my relationship with God. Clear as mud?

If a shattered relationship can be fixed at all, God is the only glue that can hold it together. He might create something completely different than the original relationship, but it will be beneficial to everyone involved.

Lord, make my heart and conscience clean before you, so that my offering is acceptable to you. Help me to forgive and make the first move toward reconciliation, in every case where someone has something against me. Amen.

----------

## *Troubles Are Temporary*

When it seemed as if everything was falling apart and God had turned his back on me, I found a scripture that carried me through until God showed up. I share it with loved ones going through trials. God has made it clear to me that he is true to his Word, even if it was delivered in a context other than our immediate needs.

"'For I know the plans I have for you,' declares the Lord. 'plans to prosper you and not to harm you, plans to give you hope and a future.'" (Jeremiah 29:11 NIV)

Jeremiah sent a letter to the exiles in Babylon. It was a message directly from God to them, telling them to make themselves at home in Babylon; to have children and thrive in that country. They were to work for their country's welfare and pray for its well-being, because they would prosper as Babylon prospered.

Then God said, starting in verse 10, "As soon as Babylon's seventy years are up and not a day before, I'll show up and take care of you as I promised and bring you back home. I know what I'm doing. I have it all planned out – plans to take care of you, not abandon you, plans to give you the future you hoped for." (MSG)

If we consider Heaven our home, then we're in exile here. God intends for us to grow in, thrive in and bless the country we now live in. When the time is right, and not a day before, God is going to show up, and this time, it will be Jesus riding a white horse, leading a vast army to deliver the world once and for all from evil and ugliness. Until we're called home individually, or until that day he returns, we're to be a blessing here.

Here's the rest of that message in verses 12-14: "When you call on me, when you come and pray to me, I'll listen. When you come looking for me, you'll find me. Yes, when you get serious about finding me, and want it more than anything else, I'll make sure you won't be disappointed."

That day won't happen until everyone who is looking for God has found him. He has awesome plans for every one of them – for every one of us!

----------

## *Stirring Things Up*

"Leave well-enough alone." "If it ain't broke, don't fix it." "Don't rock the boat." My dad was trying to teach us rebellious and cantankerous kids that life would be so much easier if we'd just stop stirring things up.

Maybe he was right. Perhaps life would be much calmer without the exercise of curiosity, limit-testing, opinion-sharing, and bucking the status quo. But what if the status quo is wrong? Are we justified then by our silence; by our leaving-things-be? The Jewish leaders of their time considered Jesus a radical rebel because he wouldn't stop rocking the boat.

Here's what he had to say about it in Matthew 5:17-20: "Don't suppose for a minute that I have come to demolish the Scriptures – either God's Law or the Prophets. I'm not here to demolish but to complete. I am going to put it all together, pull it all together in a vast panorama. God's Law is more real and lasting than the stars in the sky and the ground at your feet. Long after stars burn out and earth wears out, God's Law will be alive and working.

"Trivialize even the smallest item in God's Law and you will only have trivialized yourself. But take it seriously, show the way for others, and you will find honor in the kingdom. Unless you do far better than the Pharisees in the matters of right living, you won't know the first thing about entering the Kingdom."

The Pharisees were the experts in the law. No one knew it better than they did. What did Jesus mean when he said we have to do far better than the Pharisees in the matters of right living?

It seems that knowing the Law wasn't enough. The status quo needed shaking up. Unless we understand that the Law is all about loving God with all you are, and loving others as yourself, we've missed the boat. If you miss the boat, there's no boat to rock, is there?

----------

## *Memory Like A Steel Trap*

Bill and I saw a program featuring people who remember every moment of every day with complete clarity for all of their lives. One woman said it's a gift. I can understand that. I wish I could experience my babies' first smiles again. Another said it's not so great because they cannot forget the bad things they experience. I can understand that, too. Who wants to remember pain?

One boy has an identical twin brother who doesn't share his ability. Can you imagine being that closely linked with someone who does? That puts a whole new spin on the age-old argument, "I did not! – You did, too, at 10:13 am on Saturday, February 4, 2012!"

I'm thankful that my mind works normally. Of course, normal has no relevance to humanity. I'm simply grateful that I don't have that kind of recall. God knew I couldn't handle it, so he didn't let me have it. Instead, he gave me a multi-layered mind.

For example, I fix my breakfast shake, and think about what goes into it. As I reach for an ingredient, a thought of one of my grandkids leads to thoughts of his sister, and then another grandkid pops up and that leads to thoughts of her sibling and cousins and their parents, and that leads to thoughts of their siblings and their children, and so on. Meanwhile, I've fixed and drunk my shake and have washed the dishes.

I see my neighbor's car pulling out of her driveway, and then I mentally plan our next trip, which reminds me I have some calls to make, which makes me think of our grandsons and their new phone numbers, which makes me think of the new babies we're expecting to welcome into the family in the next couple of months, and so on. It's like the running news ticker at the bottom of the screen on Fox news -- all of it about our children and their children!

In Isaiah 55:8-9 we're told, "'For my thoughts are not your thoughts, neither are your ways my ways,' declares the Lord. 'As the heavens are higher than the earth, so are my ways higher than your ways and my thoughts than your thoughts.'" (NIV)

Bill and I agree that living in the moment is more satisfying than living in the past, and our minds are much too busy to hold total recall, anyway. God chose to give that gift to some for his own purposes, and their memory is limited to their own, individual experience. God's ability spans all space and time, and he can still focus on each of us individually and for our entire lives. Now THAT's amazing!

----------

## *Impatient for Answers*

I felt out of sorts for a few days, and had a conversation with the Lord about it. How possible is it to believe God is working on our behalf when we see no evidence of it? He's answered prayer many times in the past, but that was then, and this is now. Where are you, Lord?

Esther was a young Jewish woman in the Persian Empire who was groomed to become the king's bride. King Xerxes was the most powerful man in the known world. He didn't know, and most likely didn't care, that she was Jewish. He fell in love with her and made her his queen.

As the story unfolds, Haman, the evil advisor to the king, plotted to destroy all the Jews in Persia. He didn't know of Esther's background, either, or he might have chosen some other vendetta to pursue. In order to save her people, Esther had to be cunning and courageous. She could have lost her life just by approaching the king uninvited.

Her uncle Mordecai got word to her, "Don't think that just because you live in the king's house you're the one Jew who will get out of this alive. If you persist in staying silent at a time like this, help and deliverance will arrive for the Jews from someplace else; but you and your family will be wiped out. Who knows? Maybe you were made queen for just such a time as this." (Esther 4:12-14)

It seemed like everything was stacked against the Jews. In spite of the lack of evidence that God was working on their behalf, Esther did what she needed to do and saved the Persian Jews from slaughter. Even though he's never mentioned in the book, God was there.

Faith is a choice. We choose to trust God, or we choose to worry and fret. So right then, I chose faith -- again -- and suddenly my world centered, peace flooded in, and the worries shot out the door. Thank you, Lord, that we don't have to see you or touch you in order to believe you!

----------

## *Crisis after Crisis*

I answered the phone this morning, only to hear that some friends were experiencing another crisis. It seemed like catastrophes were like a storm cloud constantly raining over their heads. I got upset – not at them, but at the repetition of it.

I have a bad habit of venting and repenting. If I could control the first, I wouldn't need to do the second. I expected to get some justification for my indignation from the Word. Instead, I read Proverbs 21.

Here's what God showed me: "We justify our actions by appearances. God examines our motives." By all appearances, we've done enough and would be justified in washing our hands of it. Wait a minute. Isn't that what Pontius Pilate did? Lord, examine my motives and don't let me make a huge mistake here.

"Arrogance and pride – distinguishing marks in the wicked – are just plain sin." The Lord reminded me of the time in my life when

I lived from crisis to crisis. He provided for me and my family in miraculous ways. I have no grounds for pride or arrogance.

"Mixed motives twist life into tangles; pure motives take you straight down the road." On the one hand, we have plenty of needs among our own family, and we can't afford to do enough to help them. On the other hand, we're not destitute. The only solution is to ask God what he wants us to do. I say it often, and now I'm asked to live it -- you can't out-give God.

"If you stop your ears to the cries of the poor, your cries will go unheard, unanswered." Oh, boy. I'm getting, it, Lord.

"Whoever goes hunting for what's right and kind finds life itself – glorious life." Here's where I weigh being selfish against being kind and finding glorious life. Life wins.

"Sinners are always wanting what they don't have; the God-loyal are always giving what they do have." Am I self-loyal or God-loyal? My actions define my loyalty.

But, what about our friends, Lord? What are you doing about that situation?

"Nothing clever, nothing conceived, nothing contrived, can get the better of God." Leave it to me, God seems to be saying. Let me be the judge. You just do what I've called you to do.

I'm grateful that God doesn't let us get away with selfishness. He lets us vent, but then leads us to the repentance that clears the heart, brings peace to the spirit, and joy to the soul. Thank you, Lord!

# IT'S ALL ABOUT RELATIONSHIP

"Cherish your human connections – your relationships with friends and family.

~ Barbara Bush

## *The Power of Multiplication*

It seems just yesterday that after my husband and I introduced ourselves at a business presentation, he said, "We have twelve grandchildren." At the time we only had ten.

I said, "That's a prophetic statement," and everyone laughed good-naturedly.

Now we have twenty-two, including four who were recently added by marriage. Others are pre-existing, or newly added siblings of blood-related grandkids. We don't care. They belong to us, however they got here, and Gramma and Grampa belong to them.

Anthony and Ashley live near us, two others live three hours away, and the rest are spread out in different states. It seems to be uncommon for an extended family to live close together nowadays. We miss the ones we seldom get to spend time with, and we're grateful for God's kindness in planting a few nearby.

We're privileged to spend at least one afternoon a week with the local kids. I pick them up at school, bring them home for a while and, weather permitting, send them off to tennis with Grampa.

Once, I joined them and another girl in a tennis clinic for kids. Two were eight, one was six, and then there was Grammy. The kids invited me to share their lesson and games, and Grampa didn't mind teaching me right along with them. He's a wonderful coach, and their skill level is high for their ages. We might have some future champions there!

For a while, there was no age difference among us. We were just a bunch of kids having fun together. Who cares that Coach and Grammy are taller?

One day we rode our bikes to the park. I was grateful for the cool breeze and sunshine. We brought two basketballs and a friend along. Ashley challenged me to a game of catch with one of the basketballs. She said, "You can't catch it, Gramma. You're Old."

What, me? I caught it and threw it back, and the game began. Old is a matter of perspective. Proverbs 17:6 says, "Old people are distinguished by grandchildren." I'm not too distinguished to play a lively game of catch, especially with a ball that's big enough to see.

----------

## *A Misfit in the Kitchen*

God has a sense of humor. Since we're created in His image, so do we. We use a Magic Bullet to make our shakes. The grinder lid was stuck to the cup with the blended product inside; and I mean stuck. It sat on the counter for three days.

On the third morning, after I washed the windows and counters in the kitchen, I got the bright idea to hammer a hole in the plastic cup (it's very hard plastic), let the pressure out, and try to remove the lid again. About three hits on a nail did it.

The darn thing exploded! All over me, my face, my glasses, my hair, my clothes and all over the clean windows, counters, table -- you get the idea. I stood there stunned for a moment, and then started laughing. What a mess! I got my exercise this morning, both inner from the laughter, and outer from the double cleaning and second shower.

I never prepare the same thing the same way twice, so eating what I cook is a risky adventure. Recipes are a blessing, and I'm thankful to the generations of cooks who took the time to write down and measure the "pinch of this and dollop of that" that characterizes most of my cooking. I don't usually adhere to recipes.

My sweet husband will eat anything I make without making a face or complaining when it turns out weird. He's so easy to live with!

A culinary experiment sometimes turns out well. I made coconut rice, and it tasted great! I used rice, coconut milk, some shredded coconut, water, a dollop of olive oil, some honey, a little vanilla, and voila! Delicious! I mixed the leftovers with instant vanilla pudding (already mixed up), and that was even better! I'm so glad coconut is healthful.

For someone whose most used kitchen utensils are scissors and a can opener, I'm grateful that I didn't mess it up. No one has suggested we order pizza when I invite them over for dinner, yet. God is gracious!

----------

## Savory Friends

My friend and I love a local sushi place (Yu Mi - also love the name!) and we meet for a girls' night out whenever we have the chance. I don't eat raw fish, so we get some of their cooked rolls. The first taste makes me pray there's food like that in Heaven!

I thank God for the ability to savor such an amazing blend of flavors. Even better than the delicious food, though, is the wonderful company. Terri adds her own amazing flavor to life.

We enjoyed dinner at a local restaurant with Bill's mom and Connie, a long-time tennis friend. We caught up on family news, what's going on with mutual acquaintances, and had a great conversation about life in general. I imagine Heaven will be like that -- as if no time has passed and friendships are seamless.

Proverbs 18:24 tells us, "One who has unreliable friends soon comes to ruin, but there is a friend who sticks closer than a brother [or sister]." (NIV)

Our reliable friends are treasures, gifts from God and better than a perfectly prepared banquet!

----------

## The Work of Our Hands

Nearly every summer my husband and I get together with hundreds of friends involved in our business. The four days of our conference are packed with activity, teaching, and fellowship. As much as I enjoy it, I'm happy to get home after a weekend for which there are no adequate words of gratitude.

At the last conference, we met a lot of people in person for the first time. We'd been in contact with them by phone or social media. We basked in the lovely, loving culture of our company, and enjoyed the diversity of people from all over the world.

My heart often overflowed right out of my eyes -- sometimes in laughter! The company has a foundation that feeds tens of thousands of children around the world. Groups of distributors created songs and acts they performed at a rally for the kids. God blesses those who help others -- it's in the Bible! -- and the folks involved in our business give generously to the foundation.

I love our scientists and the way they discover, explore and reveal the intricacies of God's creation. I shook the hand of the scientist who discovered what could be the most important nutritional breakthrough of our lifetime. I hugged the scientist responsible for formulating nutrition that has transformed lives.

The Psalmist wrote in Psalm 90:17, "May the favor of the Lord our God rest on us; establish the work of our hands for us – yes, establish the work of our hands." (NIV)

A worship service on the morning after the Conference officially tied the richness of the weekend together in a package of gratitude and love, and presented it all back to God for his glory. Bill and I feel incredibly blessed to be a part of something that honors God, blesses people, and continues to be an answer to prayer for countless people.

----------

## *Unique Life Paths*

A tall, slim woman dressed in a colorful, flowing outfit, came late to a business presentation and sat next to me. We smiled and turned our attention to the speakers. My husband and I stood and shared our story with the group. When we sat down again, she whispered to me, "I've wanted to meet you."

Interesting people are among the best things about a business like ours. That day, we met someone who had been a sous-chef for Julia Child on the French Chef TV series. We met a woman who had been a commercial airlines pilot years before it became acceptable for women to fly in that seat. We met a congressional liaison and a retired college professor. We met a world famous artist, whose paintings hang at Universal Studios, at a bank in D.C., in three embassies and in private collections around the world. We met Ahlin, one woman who has achieved all of that! And she wanted to meet us.

God has a plan and purpose for everyone. We all have accomplishments that are unique to us. Everyone is interesting. If we're human, we have a story. Whether long or short, our lives are his story.

God gave us life and he leads us along our life-road and accompanies us as we live it.

King David nailed it in Psalm 139:14-16 when he said, "Body and soul, I am marvelously made!"

He went on: "Like an open book, you watched me grow from conception to birth; all the stages of my life were spread out before you, the days of my life all prepared before I'd even lived one day."

As I listened to Ahlin, I realized that she has lived some of my own dreams. My life took different turns, but I have no regrets. It makes me happy to know that someone wonderful did the things I would have loved to do, while I lived a life I love because it's where God led me. Our paths are uniquely ours.

Your blessings are no less than hers or mine. They're yours. Your life is valuable because you are infinitely valuable to your Creator. Live it in gratitude, and live it with gusto!

# A GATHERING OF MISFITS

"Come, now is the time to worship
Come, now is the time to give your heart
Come, just as you are to worship,
Come, just as you are before your God"

~ Brian Doerksen
Song: *Come, Now Is The Time To Worship*
From the album *Miscellaneous*

## *What is Heaven Like?*

Do you ever wonder what Heaven will be like? In church, I realized that we get to enjoy a taste of it right here! Our church is a multinational and multi-racial family. The love we sense when we walk in is palpable. Warm smiles, hugs, and kind words are freely passed around to visitors as well as old-timers.

I love the bemused look on a visitor's face when several people make a point of making them feel welcome. Many return time after time, until they're welcoming other visitors. Love draws them, and keeps them coming.

Some of our people came from the Caribbean islands, some from India, some from Africa and South Africa, some from Long Island or Pennsylvania, West Virginia or Arkansas and some came from right around here. They dress however they feel comfortable, and the result is colorful and fun. Every baby is beautiful and every child precious.

Pastor and Dolores are the heart of the church. They're pastors in every good sense of the word. They pray for, admonish, correct, encourage, help and love the people God has given to their care. They do everything with compassion and truth and without judgment.

The Holy Spirit visits us when we gather to worship God. Although he lives in us from the moment we surrender to Jesus and begin to walk by faith, not feelings, the sweet Spirit of God allows us to feel his presence. Imagine having that feeling all the time!

Here's how the prophet describes it in Isaiah 65:17-24, "Pay close attention now: I [God] am creating new heavens and a new earth. All the earlier troubles, chaos, and pain are things of the past, to be forgotten. Look ahead with joy. Anticipate what I'm creating: I'll create Jerusalem as sheer joy, create my people as pure delight. I'll take joy in Jerusalem, take delight in my people: No more sounds of weeping in the city, no cries of anguish; No more babies dying in the cradles, or old people who don't enjoy a full lifetime…For my people will be as long-lived as trees, my chosen ones will have satisfaction in their work…For they themselves are plantings blessed by God, with their children and grandchildren likewise God-blessed. Before they call out, I'll answer. Before they've finished speaking, I'll have heard."

That's what Heaven will be like. We have so much to look forward to!

----------

## *Clutter is Not Our Friend*

Oh, my aching back! We cleaned about 2/3 of our cluttered garage after an extended bout with procrastination. It's scary how much stuff we've accumulated in just fourteen years. I can remember when we first moved into this house, and the rooms echoed! It didn't take long to fill them. The overflow went into the garage, which is an extra-large version of the "black hole" I carry with me everywhere I go – my purse. No wonder my daughter is a minimalist!

When we go to church, we clean out the clutter of the week, without a complaining back afterwards.

Before my Dad knew the Lord, he said Christians work themselves into an emotional frenzy during worship and then live like the devil the rest of the week. That may have been true in his experience, until he surrendered to God himself. He knows the truth, now, of course. He lives in the presence of the Lord all the time, in Heaven.

Our church is lively, and we love it that way. Praise and worship is exercise for spirit and body. It's hard to stand still when the music is so good! We're moved by the rhythm and words of the songs, and our hearts are moved by the Holy Spirit, whose presence we feel. King David was so moved by worship that he danced in the streets of his city!

Here's what he said in Psalm 100 (NIV): "Shout for joy to the Lord, all the earth. Worship the Lord with gladness; come before him with joyful songs. Know that the Lord is God. It is he who made us, and we are his; we are his people, the sheep of his pasture.

"Enter his gates with thanksgiving and his courts with praise; give thanks to him and praise his name. For the lord is good and his love endures forever; his faithfulness continues through all generations."

Worship can range from deep sorrow to ecstatic happiness, but there is an underlying joy that doesn't come from our emotions. We send our love and devotion to God, outside of ourselves, and God sends his Holy Spirit to fill us on the inside.

We leave church with hope and a sense of expectation. God is going to do something marvelous today, tomorrow, and every day the rest of the week. He's already started! It helps to start the week uncluttered and ready for God's presence.

----------

## *Exotic Flavors*

Farmer's markets are fun. The larger ones have freshly made kettle corn, and all of them have wonderful veggies and baked goods. You can fill up on little tastes of things you'd never try otherwise – like chocolate bacon.

Yup. That's bacon covered in chocolate. And it is delicious! Before Reese's Peanut Butter Cups, I imagine most people grimaced at the thought of combining chocolate and peanut butter. Of course, peanut butter is more healthful than bacon, so I don't think Reese's will be signing on for Choco-Bacon anytime soon.

In church one Sunday, I was struck by the freedom we have in Christ and by the creativity of the song writers. They blend words and music like combinations of flavors. There was a time when people would have grimaced at some of the modern words and music, but I imagine the Lord saying, "Hmmm, Choco-Bacon.....delightful."

The Psalmist told us in Psalm 149:1-4, "Hallelujah! Sing to God a brand-new song; praise him in the company of all who love him."

"And why? Because God delights in his people, festoons plain folk with salvation garlands!"

I'm so grateful that the Lord delights in the worship songs of his people, no matter what type of music, as long as they're served up in love and adoration. After all, King David danced in the streets, and he was the apple of God's eye. See? Flavor.

----------

## *The Presence*

One recent Sunday, I felt the Spirit of God like the weight of a blanket falling over me. A refreshing flow of warmth spread from the top of my head to my feet. Tears leaked out of my eyes, even as I grinned with joy. In that moment, I understood why we can't live in Heaven in these bodies. We're too small to hold the magnitude of God's love. This was only a taste.

The Holy Spirit shows up in our church, and why not? The church is comprised of believers who, by virtue of having turned their lives over to Christ, carry the Holy Spirit around with them. Isn't it amazing that God allows us to feel his presence in a tangible way?

It's exciting enough that the Creator of the Universe gave us a written guide to life. For believers, the Bible lives and breathes and is completely relevant to whatever is happening in our lives.

Jesus told his disciples in John 14:26, "The Friend, the Holy Spirit whom the Father will send at my request, will make everything plain to you." To actually sense his presence is over the top.

I remained aware of him all day. I felt him in the breeze on the soccer field as we watched Anthony play. I watched him in the flight of birds soaring on the wind -- in the angle of their wings as they zigzagged across the sky. I saw him in the low puffs of racing clouds.

I touched him in Ashley's soft cheek as she snuggled with her mommy on the sidelines and I heard him in Mike and Jenn's voices as they yelled encouragement to their little boy.

I held his hand as Bill and I walked hand-in-hand back to the car, because he lives in my husband, as well as in our kids and grandkids. In spite of my own shortcomings, he has chosen to live in me, too. Just. Breathe.

----------

## *God's Family*

In light of the persecution of Jews and Christians in other countries, it's good to live where it's still legal to gather in Temple or church to worship God. We grieve and pray for our suffering brothers and sisters. They're family, and our hope is that one day, we'll get to meet them and spend eternity with them. We're God's people and he's always in control.

God told Moses, in Genesis 12:1-3, "I'll make you a great nation and bless you. I'll make you famous; you'll be a blessing. I'll bless those who bless you; those who curse you I'll curse. All the families of the Earth will be blessed through you."

"All the families of the Earth" includes those of us who weren't raised Jewish, but who have given our lives and love to the God of Abraham, Isaac and Jacob.

As flawed as we are, he loves us. He puts us in families -- whether biological, adopted, or united with a common purpose. We have others who care about us and about whom we care. We're not in this life alone. When we have trouble, or we're sick, or we need help, God has given us people who will give us a hand, who will pray for us.

Conversely, God has given us people to care for, to lend a hand to, and to pray for. I'm grateful for the system He's put into place for our success in life. I love our church and all our families.

My mom's and sister Margie's church is different from ours. Their pastor wears a white minister's collar and a formal stole draped over his shoulders to preach. At the same time, he wears sandals and blue jeans and keeps his long hair tied back in a ponytail. Our pastor dresses conservatively, has no ponytail and doesn't wear the formal collar or stole.

Both pastors share a passion for God and his people. They preach the Word, share from experience, don't take themselves too seriously, and let their emotions show. They enjoy modern music as well as old hymns, and they both shout as the Holy Spirit moves them.

The truth of God's Word gives us freedom that no one, no government, can ever take away. Whatever happens, God is still sovereign. God still loves us. God forgives us. God won't abandon us. And God is still full of surprises. Who knew that Mom, in her mid-eighties, would still groove to rock and roll worship music?

----------

## Four Reasons To Go To Church

I hate missing church. I love my church family, and nothing sets the tone for the week better than a good time of worship and hearing our pastor preach the Word. In Hebrews 10:25 we're told we should not neglect gathering together to worship, and especially not to make a habit of avoiding it. Why? What do we miss when we don't go to church?

Fellowship. We're huggers. I've watched people try to keep their distance and their dignity, but it doesn't last long. One of the few things that can keep me at home is the concern than I might infect someone else when I'm not feeling well. Every person is dear to me, and I love meeting new people and helping them to feel at ease among us. I leave feeling loved, cared for, prayed for, and ready to pray for them.

Worship. Worship transforms us. It ushers us into God's presence in a way that nothing else does. When we focus on God, our hearts and spirits expand to receive more of him. He energizes us, warms us, reassures us, heals us, lifts us up, approves of us, and prepares us to meet the world his way.

The Word. Our pastor preaches with passion and conviction. His knowledge, humor, and loving spirit open our eyes to the relevance of God's Word to us today. No matter how much we read and study the Bible on our own, Pastor's unique perspective opens up new ways of seeing things.

The Offering. We say an affirmation together before we give our tithes and offerings. We list things we're asking the Lord for, and thank him for the answers. We've heard testimony after testimony of how God has specifically answered many of those requests. We've all learned that you cannot out-give God!

When we were new in the area and looking for a home church, God made it clear to us both that he wanted us in this one. It's a joy to be a member of this body of believers! It's no wonder I hate missing church.

# WHAT IS THAT GIBBERISH?

"I pray that the Holy Spirit puts His Words in my mouth,
His movement in my heart and
His direction in my path."

~ Alisa Hope Wagner
*Eve of Awakening*

## Tongues of Fire

My baby girl would not stop fussing and crying. I'd fed, bathed and dressed her in a comfy sleeper, but she was still distressed. I held and rocked her, and sang words that just came to me. The tune was unfamiliar and the words, although beautiful, were not in any language I knew. Peace filled the room and she was soon asleep.

It was my first experience with tongues. I was a new believer in Jesus Christ, and had heard from my church that this was a gift from God. Some friends from another church said it was from the devil because the gifts mentioned in the Bible were only for ancient times. How easily we can confuse each other!

The next day, I asked God to show me the truth. I sat down to read my Bible as my baby napped, and a noisy wind started blowing outside. I thought a storm was about to break, so I got up to close the window. Not a leaf stirred outside. There wasn't a cloud in the sky. Yet the sound was still there.

I opened the Bible to the place I'd left off the day before – the beginning of the second chapter of Acts.

"When the Day of Pentecost had fully come, they were all with one accord in one place. And suddenly there came a sound from heaven, as of a rushing mighty wind, and it filled the whole house where they were sitting. Then there appeared to them divided tongues, as of fire, and one sat upon each of them. And they were all filled with the Holy Spirit and began to speak with other tongues, as the Spirit gave them utterance." (Acts 2:1-4 NIV)

I didn't see any tongues of fire, but then I wasn't looking in a mirror. My jaw dropped at the mention of the wind. I'd heard it!

Many years have gone by, but the memory of that sweet message from God to me has never faded. Neither has the lesson. When in doubt, go to the Source for the answer.

----------

## *Total Absorption*

Nothing penetrates and warms the heart more than a tiny infant totally focused on your eyes, or the baby talk of one interacting with you.

I recently came across some baby pictures of our grandkids. The most poignant photos capture a moment I remember well -- the wonder on Mommy's or Daddy's face as they gaze, completely absorbed, into the wide-open eyes of their baby. Now imagine we're the infants, and our gaze is captured by the most beautiful eyes in the universe – the eyes of our Heavenly Father.

Colton Burpo, whose story is told by his dad in the book *Heaven Is For Real*, said of Jesus, "He has the most beautiful eyes." Akiane Kramarik painted a stunning picture of Jesus when she was just eight years old. She also said, "He has the most beautiful eyes."

In the account of Colton's visit to Heaven, his dad showed him pictures of artists' paintings and drawings of Jesus. None of them matched the person Colton met in Heaven – until he saw Akiane's painting. He exclaimed, "That's him!" Look up Akiane's *Jesus: Prince of Peace*. Notice the eyes.

Are you aware that your voice goes up an octave or two when you talk to little ones? How does it feel when your interaction with a baby results in his or her excited laughter or nonsensical babble? Since we were made in God's image, isn't it logical that our interaction with him is met with that same delight?

What if we haven't learned Heaven's language yet? What if "speaking in tongues" is the same as a baby's babble? If that's so, then consider this: a baby may not know how to verbalize his or her delight in your attention, or know how to express hurt, anger, wants or needs, but we, as parents, get it.

When we, as God's kids, have more to say or ask than we have our own words for, we can pull up that gift of tongues and babble away – and God gets it!

The language I use when my heart needs more than English will be made clear to me when I pass into that next amazing life. In the meantime, I'm practicing the speech patterns and words I know are a real language, even though I don't understand it, and God is listening and answering the praise and prayers of my heart.

----------

## Barrier or Bridge

Our ship approached a solid cliff. I stood at the bow and watched a pod of dolphins leap and race toward shore. A crack in the wall widened as we closed in. We were heading into that crevasse. When we reached it, it seemed as if we could nearly touch the towering walls on either side of the vessel. We slid through the straits of Corinth to the islands beyond.

When I was 19, a friend and I traveled from Vicenza in northern Italy, to Bari at the heel of the "boot", where we bought cheap deck passage on a ship to Greece.

We stayed on the island of Corfu (Kerkyra) for a week, and then traveled to the mainland. We carried a small tent in one of the backpacks, and slept wherever we could find level ground when it got dark. One evening we pitched the tent in a field, and woke up to a shouting farmer.

The Greek people, like Italians, use their hands as much as their mouths to speak. We understood by his gestures that we were to follow him. We were pretty sure we were in trouble for trespassing on his property.

He led us to a covered patio at his home, where his smiling wife served us breakfast along with his family. We had misinterpreted his intent. He meant to bless us and not do us harm.

In Paul's first letter to the Corinthians, chapter 13, he said, "If I speak in the tongues of men or of angels, but do not have love, I am only a resounding gong or a clanging cymbal."

Language is both a barrier and a bridge. We didn't understand what our Greek friends said, but the love they showed helped us understand what they meant. What we thought was a clanging cymbal (or a warning siren) turned out to be an extravagant expression of unmerited love and generosity.

When we pray in tongues, the intent of the heart is much more important than the words we use. God has no trouble figuring out what we mean because he knows what we're thinking and feeling. He knows when we're grateful and full of praise, and he knows when we're sorry, have deep needs or are full of pain. The language that flows makes perfect sense to the One who gave it to us.

The people we encountered made the trip magical. We learned a few words of Greek, and taught some of them a few words of English. The most important lesson we all learned, though, is that love is a universal language.

----------

## *What is that Babbling?*

Anthony, Ashley and I sometimes play a game in the car during the drive home on the days I pick them up from school. One starts an animated "conversation" using nonsense words. We all join in, as if we're talking about the most exciting thing, or having a mock argument, or telling a scary story. The one who starts it, sets the tone. It always ends in wild giggles by the time we reach home.

So what's the difference between the gibberish of a made-up language and speaking in tongues? Consider the source. One of us starts the game, so we're the source of the gibberish. God is the source of the language we receive when we're baptized in the Holy Spirit.

In 1 Corinthians 14 Paul revealed the source of the language. "If you praise him in the private language of tongues, God understands you but no one else does, for you are sharing intimacies just between you and him."

Paul later said in that same chapter, "If I pray in tongues, my spirit prays but my mind lies fallow, and all that intelligence is wasted. So what's the solution? The answer is simple enough. Do both. I should be spiritually free and expressive as I pray, but I should also be thoughtful and mindful as I pray. I should sing with my spirit and sing with my mind."

And then he said, "I'm grateful to God for the gift of praying in tongues that he gives us for praising him which leads to wonderful intimacies we enjoy with him. I enter into this as much or more than any of you."

I just read an article in the *New York Times*, "A Neuroscientific Look at Speaking in Tongues" by Benedict Carey, published November 7, 2006.

The study found that those who spoke in tongues, whether in ecstatic, frenzied utterances or subdued and nearly silent, were more emotionally stable than those who did not. It's good to know that I'm not suffering from mental problems when I speak in tongues! When God is the source, He's protecting my brain, my heart, my soul and my spirit.

All young mammals play. It's practice for becoming an adult. Since the children start the game we play, perhaps they're practicing for the day the Holy Spirit fills them to overflowing, and the gibberish matures into their heavenly language. I surely hope so!

----------

## *Just One More Language*

In church one recent Sunday, my mom, who has never been shy, got up and reminded everyone about the time she received the baptism of the Holy Spirit.

Pastor had called her up for prayer. He said he felt the Lord telling him that he should pray for her to receive her gift of tongues, or speaking in a new language as the Holy Spirit enables. She was eager to get it.

When he laid hands on her head, she felt warm electricity flow from the top of her head to the tips of her toes. Then she started talking.

Mom talks with her hands as much as with her mouth. She turned to the congregation and spoke eloquently with graceful arm gestures and open hands.

We speak several languages in our family. It was obvious to us that this was a language, with intonations and words strung together. My sister and I shook our heads as Pastor asked if it was one we understood. We didn't.

Someone once asked me how many languages I speak. I listed them, and included Glossolalia. He said, "Oh yeah. I visited that island."

Glossolalia is the official term for 'speaking in tongues." I didn't have the heart to tell him that no such island exists.

My mom won the hearts of our church family that day, and we all laughed with her as she reminded us of that occasion.

----------

## *When Words Fail Us*

My daughter Dyana graduated High School a year before I met Bill. As a graduation gift, my dad sent her money to come visit him and Mom in Spain, and my brother and sister and their families in Germany. She went to Europe with her friend, Rachel.

One night, I woke up out of a sound sleep with the distinct impression that I needed to pray that they wouldn't be separated. I was overwhelmed with a sense of urgency. I didn't know what was happening, and didn't know how to pray, so I lapsed into my prayer language and didn't stop praying until I felt peace.

I may not understand the words, but I recognize that it's an actual language. I speak several, and this sounds like any language I don't yet understand. There's a pattern and rhythm, and reoccurring words and phrases. God, who certainly knows my heart, and who woke me up to pray, understood every word.

A few days later, Dyana called me from Spain. She and Rachel had been on a train traveling through France, and at some point realized they were going in the wrong direction. At the next stop, Dyana took her luggage and found someone who spoke English. The young man led her to different tracks to wait for the correct train. He stayed with her luggage while she ran back to get Rachel, who was still gathering her things. The problem was, their train was moving out of the station -- with Rachel still on board!

France is six hours ahead of us, so when God woke me up in the early morning dark, it was late morning there. At the last possible moment, Rachel threw her luggage off, and jumped onto the platform. That was about the time I felt peace and was able to stop praying.

Is the gift of tongues real? Is it something God gave for a short time and no longer? Is it something we make up as we go, like a child's game? I can only speak from experience. I recognize that it's a language. We don't have to understand a language for it to be real.

God confirmed it to me in a dramatic way. He knows my heart, and He answers prayer that I don't even understand myself praying. I feel His presence when I praise or pray in tongues, and the Word has plenty to say about it. That pretty much nails it for me.

# WHAT IS NORMAL FOR A MISFIT?

"There are more things in heaven and earth, Horatio,
Than are dreamt of in your philosophy."

~ William Shakespeare
Hamlet speaking to Horatio
In *Hamlet*

## *Different Viewpoints*

One lesson that's been hard for me to learn is that there may be more than one way to look at things. From my perspective, I'm always right. From yours, you are always right. So who is truly correct, and how do we reconcile this? Sometimes we think the loudest one wins, so we simply raise our voices more. Maybe the more logical one is the winner, or the one who feels most strongly about the issue. Or, maybe we're only seeing a part of the picture, and we're both right.

In Ecclesiastes, Solomon lamented that everybody, no matter what their background or status in life, is heading for the same end -- death. Was he right? Well, yes. From his perspective, that's all there was. He saw part of the story.

Paul told us more of the story in Ephesians 3:5-17, when he talked about the mystery of Christ. "None of our ancestors understood this. Only in our time has it been made clear by God's Spirit. The mystery is that people who have never heard of God and those who have heard of him all their lives stand on the same ground before God." Isn't that what Solomon said?

Then he went on to explain, "They get the same offer, same help, same promises in Christ Jesus. The Message is accessible and welcoming to everyone across the board."

In verses 14-17, he sent up this prayer for us, "I ask him to strengthen you by his Spirit – not a brute strength but a glorious inner strength – that Christ will live in you as you open the door and invite him in. And I ask him that with both feet planted firmly on love, you'll be able to take in with all followers of Jesus the extravagant dimensions of Christ's love. Reach out and experience the breadth! Test its length! Plumb the depths! Rise to the heights! Live full lives, full in the fullness of God."

While Solomon's understanding that all people are the same to God caused him to think life is futile because we all just die, Paul's understanding of the same thing gave him great joy, because he saw it from a different perspective. Who was right?

Both were. I'm very happy we now have a more complete picture than Solomon did. Yes, we all die, but for believers, it's the beginning, and not the end.

----------

## *God's Wardrobe*

I have a tendency to rile up some people in various discussions with my strong opinions and love of a good argument. My husband is a peace-maker and won't argue back, so I can really let loose on social media!

A recent discussion involved the self-made appearance of someone we would probably hesitate to make friends with – to put it mildly. I won't go into detail, but it involved a radical physical transformation. Some of the participants raised questions, some expressed outrage, some gave answers and some didn't like the proposed answers. It was fun!

So, what does the Bible have to say about our appearance? I love what the Apostle Paul said in his letter to the Colossians 3:12-17:

"So, chosen by God for this new life of love, dress in the wardrobe God picked out for you: compassion, kindness, humility, quiet strength, discipline. Be even-tempered, content with second place, quick to forgive an offense. Forgive as quickly and completely as the Master forgave you. And regardless of what else you put on, wear love. It's your basic, all-purpose garment. Never be without it."

He went on to say, "let the peace of Christ keep you in tune with each other, in step with each other…And cultivate thankfulness."

We don't know what motivated the person in question to radically alter their appearance that way. If we wore our inside on the outside, would we look any better? Is our inside dressed in the wardrobe God picked out?

The next time I engage in a challenging conversation, I hope to let the peace of Christ keep me in tune with my fellow combatants. Let the games begin!

----------

## *God In The Internet*

Elections happen every two years in the United States. It seems my voice and emotions grow more strident as we approach that critical time.

Did you know that God is fully aware of social media? He's also aware of me on social media. Here's how I know.

It's in Psalm 39:1-10: "I'm determined to watch steps and tongue so they won't land me in trouble. I decided to hold my tongue as long as Wicked is in the room. [think White House and Congress] 'Mum's the word,' I said, and kept quiet. But the longer I kept silence, the worse it got – my insides got hotter and hotter. My thoughts boiled over; I spilled my guts."

See? Me! There's more.

"What am I doing in the meantime, Lord? Hoping, that's what I'm doing – hoping you'll save me from a rebel life, save me from the contempt of dunces. I'll say no more, I'll shut my mouth, since you, Lord are behind all this. But I can't take it much longer."

God is in control of the outcome of all elections, whether they're fair or rigged. He has a purpose for the people in power, but we can't assume that his purpose won't include pain for a time. I can be vocal in my support of a candidate, and still believe that God's decision will be the right one for his purposes.

Having said that, I can't be silent about what I believe and hope for in the next elections. I might want to hold it in, but silence will only give me a bad case of heartburn. Maybe my words will give you one. I'm sorry about that.

----------

## *No Match For God*

During the last Presidential election, I'm pretty sure more than a few people unfriended me on Facebook. Those who opposed my stand and stuck it out anyway are dear friends indeed. I was impressed by the intelligent and thoughtful arguments of some, and became quite incensed that not everybody came around to my way of thinking.

Now that it's over, I've been able to cool my jets for a while. I'm so thankful that we serve God, who is above politics!

No matter how bad it gets as we approach this, or any, Election Day, the sons of Korah told us in Psalm 46 that "God is a safe place to hide, ready to help when we need him. We stand fearless at the cliff-edge of doom, courageous in sea storm and earthquake, before the rush and roar of oceans, the tremors that shift mountains." People in power are often called movers and shakers. They are no match for God.

"Godless nations rant and rave, kings and kingdoms threaten, but Earth does anything he says." Even the strange weather we've been having for a couple of years is no match for God.

I get so heated up over issues that I have to make a conscious effort to do as God says: "Step out of the traffic! Take a long, loving look at me, your High God, above politics, above everything."

The message to us from Psalm 46 is so important that it was repeated three times, in verses 3, 7 and 11: "Jacob-wrestling God fights for us, God-of-the-Angel-Armies protects us."

No matter who has power in the government; no matter what they do to or for our country, we can trust and depend on our High God, who has it all under his control. He's fighting for us. He's protecting us.

----------

## *Time To Start Over?*

Is our government controlled by toddlers prone to temper tantrums? It seems when things don't go the way the prevailing party thinks they should, they shut down the government in such a way that only hurts the citizens.

They say it costs too much to maintain, and yet they spend more money to hire security guards to keep war veterans away from their free, open-air memorials. They evict elderly people because their homes happen to be on government-owned land. They close down animal sanctuaries run by volunteers. They spend more money to shut it down than to keep it open.

I get angry at the insanity that is our government and the bullheadedness of our elected officials. I get angry at corruption and subversion, at lies and divisiveness, especially when it comes from those we entrust our country to. We elect them with hope that they will lead with integrity and intelligence, and they disappoint us.

Opinions vary about who's at fault and who is trustworthy. Your heroes might be my villains, and vice versa. Still, the thought of what goes on can set me off – if I let it.

When it really gets to me, God catches me up short. There is nothing new about the struggles of our government. Paul said something about it in 2 Corinthians 3:7-18.

He said, "The Government of Death, its constitution chiseled on stone tablets, had a dazzling inaugural." Every government is ushered in with hope for a better life to come. Paul referred to the bright glow on Moses's face after God gave him the Ten Commandments. He covered his face with a veil so no one would notice when the glow faded. What do our politicians do when their promises fade?

He went on -- "how much more dazzling, then, the Government of the Living Spirit?" When we face God, we "suddenly recognize that God is a living, personal presence, not a piece of chiseled stone. And when God is personally present, a living Spirit, that old, constricting legislation is recognized as obsolete. We're free of it! All of us! [There's] nothing between us and God, our faces shining with the brightness of his face."

This government is as temporary as they've all been. It isn't the first time it has 'shut down' and it won't be the last, until the day when all governments are swept away and only God's government remains. There will be nothing to be angry about that day – or in the days that follow.

----------

### Show Me The Eyes, Mom!

I believed my mom when she told me she had eyes on the back of her head. She always seemed to know when I did something I shouldn't have, or when I lied to her. Of course, there were no eyes covered by the curtain of her hair. She wasn't being truthful with me.

My grandkids hate it when I catch them doing something wrong. "Gramma, how did you know that?" Anthony asked after such an incident. I answered, "Maybe I have eyes in the back of my head." He knows I don't have an extra set of eyes.

Lies are unsustainable. As soon as the light of truth hits a tower of lies, it crumbles under its own weight. We're all guilty of saying things that aren't true, usually in the interest of self-preservation or to be in control.

I enjoy watching in-depth news programs like 20/20. The annual March for Life had just taken place in Washington, DC, and I hoped to see a report on it. In the episode that should have covered it, the BIG news they covered in depth was "Catfishing" and whether or not Beyonce lip synched the National Anthem. Oh, and that we are all liars by nature. That's news?

What happened to news about the March for Life in DC, where over half a million people stood up against abortion? In a world where the push for gun control trumps Benghazi, the economy, joblessness and jeeps being made in China, the truth is under-reported or not reported at all.

The light of the Truth of God not only tumbles the tower of lies we build in the mistaken belief that it's impenetrable, but he cleans house, forgives the lies, and builds a tower with himself as the foundation and walls. He is the true center of the universe.

Before the Crucifixion, Jesus spent some time instructing and comforting his disciples. They had no idea what was about to happen, but he knew. After telling them that he was going to leave them to prepare a place for them, Thomas questioned, "Lord, we don't know where you are going, so how can we know the way?" Jesus answered, "I am the way and the truth and the life. No one comes to the Father except through me." (John 14:5-6 NIV)

He said it. He's the truth.

----------

## *Love Letter*

When our daughter Tina and the love of her life planned to marry, Bill and I struggled with the question of whether we should attend their wedding or not. Several years ago, she had revealed to us that she was a Lesbian.

We didn't see it coming, but we weren't about to reject her or stop loving her. Then along came her partner Beth – a delightful, lovely young woman we fell in love with, in spite of her opposing political views. (I had to get that in there.)

Then we received a letter from Beth. She reminded us of the most important thing. God is Love.

Her letter made us think, do we take the path of condemnation, or do we walk the path of love? They don't believe their love for each other is wrong, so who are we to stand in judgment when we, ourselves, have done so much that the Bible says is wrong? We chose to walk in love. We're happy we did.

In Galatians 2:17-21, the Apostle Paul said, "Is it not clear to you that to go back to that old rule-keeping, peer-pleasing religion would be an abandonment of everything personal and free in my relationship with God? I refuse to do that, to repudiate God's grace. If a living relationship with God could come by rule-keeping, then Christ died unnecessarily."

Not long ago, a church kicked out the Boy Scouts because they'd changed their policy to allow homosexual boys to join their club. I'm sure the church had reasons that made sense to them, but were they sharing the love of God in the best way by doing that?

My mom once told me (often, actually, because of my temper), you attract more flies with honey than with vinegar. I ask you this, were the church or the Boy Scouts offering honey or vinegar?

Did they show the all-encompassing, extravagantly forgiving love of Christ, who said that "Whoever believes in him will have everlasting life."? (John 3:16 NIV) I don't read any exceptions there. Do you?

----------

## God's Voice

On a Sunday morning, years ago, I was enjoying the sermon when I heard it -- a whisper in my heart; words that left me a big tearful puddle, huddled in the pew with my face in my hands.

I had always wondered how people knew it was God talking when they said, "God told me…" I didn't know whether to believe them or not, especially when they claimed God told them something about me. Why didn't he tell me directly?

I learned to take their declarations with a grain of salt. After all, I knew he spoke to us through his Word, so I figured they'd surmised something from what they read.

I recently read Psalm 81:5, where Asaph said, "I hear this most gentle whisper from One I never guessed would speak to me." And I remembered.

The voice was gentle, full of love, and filled me with peace. I didn't think my heart could expand like that and still function. God claimed me before I was born, but in that moment, I knew it with every fiber of my being. My Father said simply, "My daughter."

The world went silent and all I could do was weep. I understood then why we can't go to Heaven in these limited bodies.

Sometimes God nudges us with the Holy Spirit. I've experienced the nudge much more often than I've heard his voice. I know it's him because he asks me to do something I don't normally do, and it always results in strong confirmation that it was exactly what he wanted me to do.

If I don't act, he keeps insisting until I'm really uncomfortable. I'm glad he does that. It means he's given me grace and allowed me the time to learn to listen. He does that for all of his children.

I've heard God say "My daughter" twice now, and the impact was the same the second time. If a whisper in my heart can fill me with such love and joy, what will it feel like when we see him face-to-face and feel his love and approval in person? I can hardly wait!

# A MATTER OF LIFE OR DEATH

"It is a poverty to decide that a child must die so that you may live as you wish.

~ Mother Teresa

## Called to Serve

My husband and I taught the training at one of our business meetings. A friend approached me afterwards and said, "You'd make a good counselor. I work with a ministry that needs volunteers. Would you be interested in finding out more?"

She had just practiced what she learned from us in training, only for a different cause than our business. She wasn't at all pushy. She gave me a sincere compliment, mentioned that she was working with a ministry that helps people, and asked if I'd be open to learning more. How could I refuse?

A few weeks later I went to interview with Suzette, the branch director of a family resource center. We hit it off immediately, and by the end of the interview she asked me when I could start. I didn't answer, because two young Hispanic women walked in at that moment. They spoke no English, and the volunteer receptionist spoke no Spanish. I do.

I jumped in, translated, and stayed to accompany the women through a counseling session. Afterward, Suzette and I looked at each other and laughed.

"I guess I already started," I told her. It was the beginning of a long and lasting relationship with First Care.

Ministries like First Care meet the needs of families and save the lives of babies with vision and excellence, courage and faith. Men and women in life-affirming ministries throughout the country are on the front lines fighting for the unborn. They are dedicated, courageous and determined to help moms choose life for their babies in the face of fierce and unwavering opposition.

The ones I know have warm, kind, loving hearts. They reach out with compassion to help frightened and hurting women. Both women and men have found the love of God through their ministry.

----------

## *Walk the Talk*

First Care, our local crisis pregnancy/family resource center, celebrated 30 years of saving babies at their annual Walk for Life. That's a long time for David to fight Goliath.

I walked with some friends from church, along with a huge crowd of friends I haven't met yet. Weather reports said that rain was expected all day, but there was no rain. It was a clear, sunny morning.

Kids played in bounce houses and mingled with goat-kids and lambs, chickens, ducks, ducklings, bunnies and a calf in the petting zoo. A pony pulled a cart loaded with children around a large circle. Butterflies, rainbows and painted-on eye patches decorated the faces of many of the children who slid down the slides or laughed on the swings in the playground.

A band played Christian music, and giant grills, manned and donated by a local church, cooked enough food for every person there.

"Speak up for the people who have no voice…" (Proverbs 31:8) It's interesting that this passage is found in the one chapter of Proverbs that addresses what constitutes a good woman. She takes care of her family; she's enterprising, creative, wise and generous. She earns her family's respect and love. When she speaks, people listen.

----------

## *Proverbs 31 Women*

The women who come to First Care for their pregnancy tests are usually young, frightened, unprepared and unmarried. Most have a terrible self-image and would never picture themselves as a Proverbs 31 woman, if they even knew what that was.

Each client meets with a compassionate patient advocate who shares the truth with her. She learns all about what to expect if she chooses abortion. Scare tactics are not used – just practical information. She also learns what First Care can help her with if she chooses to carry her baby to term. She is never made to feel guilty about her choice.

Whether pregnant or not, everyone is asked if they want to know more about the One who loves them the most. Those who say yes, hear the salvation message. Many place their trust in God, and the process of growing into the Proverbs 31 woman begins.

First Care provides a safe environment. The clinic provides pregnancy testing, STD screening, sonograms and early prenatal care – all free of charge to the client. They provide parenting classes and many practical things a new mom might need for herself and her baby. Most of all, they provide the support that many frightened young women are afraid they'll lose if they choose life for their babies.

First Care also has a program for those who have had abortions and are seeking healing and forgiveness from that trauma. Women don't need to feel any worse about aborting their child. Guilt comes naturally. We are not wired to hurt our babies. Even knowing that God forgives her, how does a woman forgive herself? First Care's program leads her through the process.

The crux of Proverbs 31 is in verse 30: "Charm is deceptive, and beauty is fleeting; but a woman who fears the Lord is to be praised."

For some, First Care is the first step to learning to love the Lord.

----------

## *After the Abortion*

Did you know that when a man gets a woman pregnant, he's a father? Of course you knew that. When a woman has an abortion, she doesn't stop being a mother, and he doesn't stop being a father. They are the parents of a child who has died and been denied the dignity of acknowledgement, a name, and a burial.

Whether they admit to it or not, they grieve – both of them. They can't grieve openly, because they've just gotten rid of a problem, and society doesn't recognize the personhood of that problem. They can't even acknowledge to themselves that they're grieving, and so it takes on self-punishing forms: low self-esteem; guilt like a low-grade fever, slowly burning up health and joy; emotional withdrawal; self-destructive behaviors, and the list goes on.

You might think the fathers of these babies never give it another thought. That may be consciously true, but the subconscious isn't fooled -- where God-awareness lives, where conscience lives. Nobody leaves an abortion unscathed. Babies die and parents are damaged.

First Care helps moms and dads deal with abortions they've had. Abortion is usually a result of fear and pressure. God forgives, restores and heals grieving hearts with no other outlet. The hardest thing is to admit the horror of what they've done, and to forgive themselves.

Society would like to make people think abortion is a quick and easy solution to a life-style-threatening problem. The fact is, by 2013, around 60 million lives had been snuffed out by an industry that uses our tax money and charges people for the privilege of killing their babies.

The population of New York, NY, was a little over 8 million people in 2010. 60 million lives would fill 7½ cities the size of New York. How many of those lives would have helped to make a better life for others? How many might have saved lives? Which baby might have grown up to find a cure for an incurable disease?

It takes money to help stop the bloody tide and restore hope and healing to people. God knows every child before they are born! We do what we can to see that they have the chance to fulfill His purpose for them.

To all of you who support ministries like First Care – to all those who help, in any way, to give tiny, voiceless boys and girls the choice to live – Thank You!

----------

## *We Are Winning!*

Janet Parshall spoke at First Care's annual banquet one year. She's an award-winning radio personality and the author of several books. She lives in D.C., where she's a strong voice and activist for Life. She's sharp, articulate and very knowledgeable, so when she announced, "We're winning!" we all sat up and took notice.

It certainly doesn't look like we're winning. Abortion has the weight of the government behind it. Planned Parenthood, the nation's largest abortion provider, is supported by our hard-earned tax dollars. The

President was the keynote speaker at their banquet, where they raised over 360 million dollars.

The press mostly ignored the trial of abortionist Kermit Gosnell, only reporting briefly that he'd been convicted of murder. So, how are we winning? Let's go back a few years to a time when it looked like Israel faced certain defeat.

In 2 Kings 19, Hezekiah and Israel were barricaded in Jerusalem, surrounded by Assyria's massive army. Assyria taunted the Israelites, intending to demoralize them.

Through the prophet Isaiah, God told Hezekiah, "Don't be at all concerned about what you've heard from the king of Assyria's bootlicking errand boys…"

The situation must have looked and sounded hopeless to the Israelites. They might have had a problem believing Isaiah's message, when he announced, in essence, "We're winning!" It looked hopeless. Then God sent a single angel to wipe out the entire Assyrian army.

Janet cited item after item of evidence that we are indeed winning the war for the life of American babies. Abortion providers are closing, stronger state laws are being passed and upheld, funding is being cut on the state level, opinion polls are showing that the majority of Americans are pro-life, and people are learning the facts about the barbarity of legal abortion and the damage it does to women, not to mention their babies. She had details to support everything she said – details you won't hear from the mainstream media.

I, for one, choose to believe the report of the Lord, and not listen to "Assyria's bootlicking errand boys." We are winning! Yeah, God!

# BREATHE GRATITUDE

"You simply will not be the same person two months from now after consciously giving thanks each day for the abundance that exists in your life. And you will have set in motion an ancient spiritual law: the more you have and are grateful for, the more will be given you."

~ Sarah Ban Breathnack
*Simple Abundance: A Daybook of Comfort and Joy*

## *Voices*

My friend Keturah C. Martin writes beautiful poetry. In her book *Jesus Never Wastes Pain; But Can Bring Eternal Gain*, she opens her heart and invites us in with a few well-chosen words. She leads us to the heart of God through her own path of pain and joy, darkness and light. She has experienced the worst of human life, and yet gives thanks for the saving, redeeming, and delivering love of God.

I recently read *One Thousand Gifts* where Ann Voskamp draws us in and lets us feel what it is to be a Christian. She shared her own valleys and hilltops, pain and joy. It's poetry in prose.

The way to joy, through the muck and madness of life, is to be grateful. How simple it sounds, and yet, as they so clearly express it, how difficult in bad times, and how often forgotten in good times.

Gratitude is a conscious choice, a verbalization from the heart, through the mouth or pen or keyboard. Gratitude opens the window and lets the breeze blow out the stale air. I have no words to compare with theirs. I admire and thank God for these courageous women who lay their souls open so others can find their way.

They write like a lyrical dance that brings me to tears. I can watch, but never move like that. I thank God that he gifted them so, but they've paid a price for their gift. They've suffered the pain of being human in a fallen world, maybe more than many of us. They speak in the voice that God has given them. I can only speak in my own voice.

One morning, one of our precious kids posted about being anxious, and God led me to Philippians 4:6-7. Later, I opened the little prayer book I've been reading, and there was the same passage! I have no doubt that God was saying this directly to me – and now to you.

"Do not be anxious about anything, but in every situation, by prayer and petition, with thanksgiving, present your requests to God. And the peace of God which transcends all understanding, will guard your hearts and your minds in Christ Jesus." (NIV)

With thanksgiving – I love God's voice most of all.

----------

## *For the Things We Take For Granted*

When my two oldest kids were little, we lived in an apartment on the third floor. I dragged my handcart full of dirty clothes down three flights of stairs and several blocks away to the Laundromat, usually with my little ones in tow. I took the same journey in reverse with the clean clothes. It is definitely more difficult to drag the cart up the stairs than down! I often longed for my own washer and dryer.

For many years now, I've taken those appliances for granted. It is wonderful to have a working washer, dryer and dishwasher. Most of the world isn't as blessed. In many countries, there's no running water, much less automatic appliances.

We have friends who routinely minister in locations in Africa with no amenities and very little food and water. One friend rides a mule to the remotest areas in South America to bring hope and healing to people whose lifestyle is so far removed from ours that we can't imagine how they live that way.

Paul said, in 2 Corinthians 9:12-15, "Carrying out this social relief work involves far more than helping meet the bare needs of poor Christians. It also produces abundant and bountiful thanksgivings to God."

In the United States, even the poorest among us can turn on clean, running water for hot showers, safe drinking and cooking. We have access to clean clothes and flushing toilets. Our grocery stores are a tourist destination because there is nothing that compares with the abundance of choices we have in a single store.

My Mom tells stories of Germany during WWII, when the children were sent to the Black Forest to live out the war in safe schools. Everything was rationed, and the adults often went without. She and her sister saved what they could for their mom and dad, including pats of butter. She doesn't take anything for granted anymore.

During our hardest times, God provided everything we needed. We saw his miraculous intervention, and experienced heavenly hugs, surprise gifts and sudden joy. I'm grateful for everything we have that makes our life comfortable, but I'm especially grateful that God often uses us to deliver his gifts to others who need them.

----------

## *Technology*

Technology is a wonderful thing. The internet makes it easy to find whatever we need online. A vast amount of information is available to us. It's easy to make friends and maintain connections, or find help when you need it.

I found a repairman for a snapped vertical blind cord, wished our beautiful granddaughter and a good friend Happy Birthday, and interacted with a couple of friends -- and I'd only been online for a few minutes.

I find coupons, advice, recipes, Bible verses, gifts, games, books, movies, directions, and catch up with what's happening in friends' lives.

Word processing and spreadsheet programs have given us amazing advantages. Not long ago, we routinely used typewriters. If you remember them at all, you remember how difficult it was to correct mistakes. Self-correcting typewriters still made a mess on the paper. What a relief is was to use an easy word processor complete with spell-checker!

My husband says I'm the techie in the family, but he has a gift for math, and I'm numerically challenged. Spreadsheets make life much easier when it comes to keeping records. A spreadsheet allows me to write a formula once and forget about it. The numbers are puzzle pieces to plug in until it's solved. Once done, I revel in a successful resolution.

Technology is nothing compared to what we have to look forward to. God knows all about the internet and all future inventions. In Ephesians 1:8-10, Paul said, "He thought of everything, provided for everything we could possibly need, letting us in on the plans he took such delight in making. He set it all out before us in Christ, a long-range plan in which everything would be brought together and summed up in him, everything in deepest heaven, everything on planet Earth."

God is the Father of all techies. Technology has, in some ways, simplified life, and I'm grateful for it!

----------

## The Downside of Technology

Does anyone really like those automated voices that answer the phone when you call a doctor or repair service? The day will come when every household will have one.

Press 1 for Bill, Press 2 for Patty. Then, for the next round, Press 1 if this is personal. Press 2 if it's business. The third round follows. Press 1 to complain. Press 2 to report a miracle. Press 3 to gossip – and so on.

Facebook has a "Like" button. We often click on it when we don't like something at all, but want to show that we've read the post. We use it to show care for someone who's hurting. We use it show our indignation against another unspeakable offense. We show that we're paying attention; that we're there; that we agree; that we disagree -- all by clicking "Like".

Why don't they have a "Love" button? We could use it to show we love a photo, or the person posting it. We can "Love" a video without making a comment about it. In fact, why doesn't Facebook have its own version of the automated voice? Press 1 if you "Love". Press 2 if you "Like". Press 3 if you "Agree". Press 4 if you're "Outraged".

The downside of technology is that we become used to taking shortcuts. In 2 Timothy 3:16, we're told, "There's nothing like the written Word of God for showing you the way to salvation through faith in Christ Jesus. Every part of Scripture is God-breathed and useful one way or another – showing us truth, exposing our rebellion, correcting our mistakes, training us to live God's way. Through the Word we are put together and shaped up for the tasks God has for us."

Thanks to the internet, we have access to any number of translations of the Bible online. There is a vast treasure to be found by reading the entire Bible.

I'd hate to have to press 1 for "Truth", or 2 for "Correction". I'm thankful that God's Word hasn't been modernized to the point where we can press a button to get a specific message from God. Of course, if it were available, I'd click on the "Love" button for every Scripture someone posts online.

# WHO ARE WE, REALLY?

"You're through. Finished. Burned out. Used up.
You've been replaced . . . forgotten.
That's a lie."

~ Chuck Swindoll, Pastor

## *Compared to the Universe*

I watched a short video of an experiment done by astronomers with the Hubble space telescope. Out of curiosity, they pointed the scope at a section of space that was completely dark and left it there for ten days.

The resulting photos showed countless galaxies billions of light years old in that dark spot. NASA scientists estimate there are well over 100 billion galaxies in the universe. Our galaxy alone has hundreds of billions of stars, enough gas and dust to make billions more stars, and at least ten times as much dark matter as all the stars and gas put together.

Proverbs 25:2 says this, "God delights in concealing things; scientists delight in discovering things."

There are several videos on YouTube that compare Earth to other planets in the Solar System, to the sun, and to increasingly massive stars. Next to our own sun, we're a dot on the page, as is our sun next to some of the stars. Humans are like molecules in comparison with the size of our Earth. You see where I'm going with us. We are miniscule.

The Psalmist was aware that the sky is full of mystery. In Psalm 19:1-2, he said, "The heavens declare the glory of God; the skies proclaim the work of his hands. Night after night they pour forth speech; night after night they reveal knowledge." (NIV)

Every bit of matter in the universe is made of atoms, which are, in turn, made of particles called quarks and leptons. Scientists expect that even smaller particles will be discovered in time.

I'm amazed at the sculptures people make out of Legos! Can you imagine creating something as vast as the universe out of quarks and leptons? What does that say about our Creator God?

Here we are: self-aware, God-conscious beings who occupy what might be an electron circling the nucleus of an atom (our sun). Our existence is mind-boggling, but having a God Creator who is not only aware of us but who LOVES us is miraculous!

Dr. Seuss nailed it when he wrote in *Horton Hears A Who*, "A person's a person no matter how small." I wonder if he knew how small we really are.

----------

## *How Does He Even See Us?*

Some days, I can't think of a single thing I'm thankful for. As soon as one thing comes to mind, another one replaces it; then another, and another. When that happens, I end up in tears -- not of frustration, but of deep gratitude.

The Creator of the entire universe -- suns, planets, quasars, galaxies, and everything we don't know about yet -- cares about you and me; about the smallest, most insignificant concerns we have. He knows each of us by name, and he knows the number of hairs on our head, and probably the number of quarks and leptons in our bodies.

The Creator of time loves us, even though our entire life is a blink of an eye to him. I can't wrap my mind around it.

The Creator who made Earth and said it was good speaks to us miniscule humans. Not only that, he loves us so much that he gave his own heart to make a way for us to be saved.

John 3:6 tells us, "This is how much God loved the world: He gave his Son, his one and only Son. And this is why: so that no one need be destroyed; by believing in him, anyone can have a whole and lasting life."

In the NIV, it reads, "For God so loved the world that he gave his one and only Son, that whoever believes in him shall not perish but have eternal life."

God allows us to live where we are, among people we love, tied by love to people who live elsewhere, in this moment, today. He has given us riches beyond imagining, and I'm not talking about stocks, bonds or money. We have every reason in the world to praise our God for his extravagant gift of life! I have no words to thank him enough or to praise Him enough, and no way to love him enough.

----------

## *Who Does God Say We Are?*

We recently visited our daughter Dyana and her family and went with them to Mellow Mushroom for dinner. The psychedelic posters and black light accents brought me back to my life in the 60's and 70's.

If I hadn't been an army brat living in Italy, I would almost certainly have joined a commune.

We talked, laughed, and ate some really good food, and then her sweetheart Billy said, "You're the hippiest Christian woman I know!"

Now that I'm in my own personal 60's, I got a kick out of that! His comment got me thinking -- who are we, really?

My young, hippie self was on a quest to find her own identity. My search ultimately led me to the One whose love defines me. What about you? Who do you believe you are? Is it an accurate assessment? Who does God say you are? Do your opinions match? If not, who's right?

Our Pastor posed this question to us one Sunday. Most of us are familiar with Psalm 23. It's a Psalm we often read as a declaration of hope. He asked us to read it as a declaration of who we are as followers of God.

"The Lord is my shepherd; I shall not want." (NKJV)

The Message puts it this way, "God, my shepherd! I don't need a thing," and the NIV puts it like this, "The Lord is my shepherd, I lack nothing." So what does that say about who I am – who we are?

We have a shepherd. We're protected. All our needs are met. We lack nothing. So, if we believe God and our inner voice is telling us we're broke, we don't have enough, or no one cares, then that voice is lying. The Bible is full of affirmations about our worth to our loving God.

----------

## *Not Sleep Deprived*

My firstborn baby had me in an almost constant state of panic. At first it seemed like all she did was cry, eat, dirty her diaper, and sleep – mostly sleep. Little did I know that I should have relished that first week when she slept so much, because everything changed when she developed colic. When "they" say colic is painful, but harmless, they aren't talking about the effect on the parents. It is not harmless!

The constant rocking, pacing, screaming – day and night – creates sleep-deprived zombies, incapable of any thought other than "Please Let Me Sleep!"

This parent was pretty much brain-drained, and when the baby was quiet for five minutes, I went unconscious until she started up again.

My heart ached for my hurting baby and I would have given my own life to make her more comfortable. Obviously, my life was better spent taking care of her. She and her parents survived just fine.

Sleep is vital. Our cells regenerate, our hormones balance out, and we heal during sleep. Kids grow as they sleep. Anyone who has ever had a teenager, or been one, knows that 20 hours of sleep a day are required to get through adolescence. Anyone going through menopause knows that sleep can be as elusive as the mythical unicorn.

In Psalm 23:1, we learned that we have a shepherd who protects us and provides for our needs. In verses 2 & 3, we learn that he values us enough to make sure we get some rest.

"He makes me to lie down in green pastures; he leads me beside the still waters. He restores my soul." (NKJV)

In this busy life of ours, our inner voice might be saying, "Keep going, you have so much to do, don't stop, you're lazy, you'll never succeed if you don't push yourself" – and other admonitions along this line. Here's what God says, "In vain you rise early and stay up late, toiling for food to eat – for he grants sleep to those he loves." (Psalm 127:2 NIV).

God loves you. You are loved. I am loved. So, sleep.

----------

## *Refreshed*

Our movie theaters offer two free movies a week through the summer for children of all ages. One rainy morning, I took Anthony and Ashley to the movies, and then to Chick-Fil-A for lunch and some indoor playtime. We didn't complain about the rain.

In fact, the kids and I pointed out how happy the grass, flowers and trees are, and how cool it looks when we see a curtain of rain stretch from a cloud to the ground ahead of us. Dramatic skies, tropical downpours, God's fireworks… it all makes for a lush and beautiful area to live in.

The first three verses in Psalm 23 remind me how blessed we are to live on a planet with a breathable atmosphere, weather changes, and interesting topography.

There's more desert than jungle in Israel, where the Psalm was written. Green pastures and quiet waters would have been wonderfully refreshing to David and his men.

Troubling times happen to all of us. My inner voice is quick to point out that my problems are entirely my fault. I'm no good. I've hurt someone. I'm worthless – and so on. In this Psalm, I find that I belong to God. He leads me to a place of refreshment. No matter how harsh the conditions of our locality or life may be, our God refreshes our soul.

Here it is again, and then I'll move on: "The Lord is my shepherd, I lack nothing. He makes me to lie down in green pastures; he leads me beside quiet waters. He refreshes my soul." (NIV)

----------

## Secure

When we move to a new place, I love to get lost. I'll drive down interesting streets just to see where they lead. It can be a challenge to find my way home without GPS, but that can be fun, too! I've met some wonderful people in my wanderings. There's a difference between "getting lost" as a deliberate adventure and being lost because of bad choices and circumstances.

Certain events have sent me into dark, scary mazes with no apparent exit. My inner voice gets very loud and insistent during those times. "Why do you always make such bad choices? You never listen to anyone. Look what you've done now! You'll never get out of this one!" Does anyone relate? How can God love someone who can be as rash and irresponsible as I've been?

In Psalm 23:4, God shows us that our negative inner voice is, once again, a liar. You and I are who GOD says we are.

"Yea, though I walk through the valley of the shadow of death, I will fear no evil; for you are with me; your rod and your staff, they comfort me." (NKJV)

"Even though I walk through the darkest valley, I will fear no evil, for you are with me; your rod and your staff, they comfort me." (NIV)

"Even when the way goes through Death Valley, I'm not afraid when you walk at my side. Your trusty shepherd's crook makes me feel secure." (MSG)

Can it be any clearer? You and I don't have to be afraid. God walks with us. God protects us with his shepherd's weapon. We are secure.

God's voice should be taping over the endless loops of self-condemnation we're prone to listen to. He loves you. He loves me. We are valuable to him.

----------

## In the Face of our Enemies

I felt like a cork in a whirlpool when my first marriage ended after 16 years. We had bought a lovely little townhouse and both of us were working at new jobs. It seemed as if we were finally financially stable, and then it ended. Prosperity suddenly turned to deficiency. I lacked money, confidence, and especially wisdom.

My mouth was one of my problems. That's not to say it hasn't been a problem at other times, too, but then it was particularly harmful. With my expenses far outweighing my income, I allowed fear to feed my negative inner voice and it spilled out audibly. When the kids needed something that cost money, I was quick to say we didn't have it and why. I'm sure I made my kids feel insecure. Who wants to hear that from a parent?

I allowed my fear to infect my children. What kind of a mother does that? Do you hear what I listened to every single day – not from anyone else, but from myself? "What kind of mother am I?"

Few of us get by without self-condemnation playing a loop of negativity in our heads. No one has to tell us that God's grace is undeserved favor. We know he loves us in spite of ourselves. I'm speaking in broad generalities here, but haven't you felt that way at some point?

In Psalm 23:5, David was talking about the kind of enemies who would run you through with a sword. We also have a real enemy – one who feeds the negativity we're already prone to with accusations.

"You prepare a table before me in the presence of my enemies; you anoint my head with oil; my cup runs over." (NKJV)

"You serve me a six-course dinner right in front of my enemies. You revive my drooping head; my cup brims with blessing." (MSG)

God has a banquet prepared for you, and he's serving it right in front of the liar's nose! He's filled your cup to overflowing with blessings, and the enemy has to watch him do it.

Lift up your drooping head and let God dispel the dark thoughts you might have about yourself. Only God speaks the truth about you. Enjoy your meal!

----------

## Friends for Life

I had imaginary friends when I was a kid. It was my "all things Irish" phase, and they were leprechauns. Then, like now, I had trouble remembering names, so I don't recall if any of them had one. They were real to me, though, and when I entered a room, I held the door open until all of them had gotten through safely. They followed me everywhere. For a long time, they were my only friends. I was very shy.

I've always been an introvert. An introvert is someone who gets energy from solitude, as opposed to an extrovert who is energized by being with other people.

I was also lonely, with an inner voice that filled me with self-loathing and made me fear what other kids might think of me. The voice has changed over the years. I can let it continue to escalate in condemnation, or I can listen to what God says about me.

Now when I hold the door for a moment longer than necessary, it's to let Goodness and Mercy follow me in. God says so! It's in Psalm 23:6.

"Surely goodness and mercy shall follow me all the days of my life; and I will dwell in the house of the Lord forever." (NKJV)

"Surely your goodness and love will follow me all the days of my life; and I will dwell in the house of the Lord forever." (NIV)

"Your beauty and love chase after me every day of my life. I'm back home in the house of God for the rest of my life." (MSG)

Who needs imaginary friends when God has given us Goodness, Mercy, Beauty and Love to be our companions? He's invited us to live with him forever!

The noise of my inner voice dies away to nothing as he ushers me in to his home. He wants me to be his friend. God wants to be friends with you! You must be someone really special!

# A MISFIT AND THE HOLIDAYS

"Blessed is the season which engages the whole world in a conspiracy of love!"

~ Hamilton Wright Mabie

## *Partners in Creativity*

It was snowing in some parts of the country on a late October day. I felt happy for those who loved it, and sorry for those who wished they were here, instead.

The heat and humidity of the day before had turned into a cool taste of fall. All the windows were open and a lovely breeze refreshed the air.

I took a long walk through the neighborhood in the morning. A neon green house with a bright yellow truck in the driveway sat next to a pale peach home. A sapphire house faced an olive drab one across the street. Sunny yellows, muted pastels, one or two greys with white trim – each home reflected the creativity and taste of its occupants.

The astounding creativity of our Creator thrilled and amazed me. We choose our plants and where to place them, but God created them and makes them grow into breathtaking works of art.

The Royal Poinciana trees had lost their fiery orange-red blooms, but feathery leaves continued to spread shade over lawns. The bougainvillea were heavy with hot-pink and purple flowers. Live oak trees provided cover over makeshift Halloween graveyards with clever sayings on the "headstones," while skeletal hands clawed out of the ground. People decorate like crazy around here.

How many types of palm trees are there? I'd lost count. Avocados and papayas hung over backyard fences, and front-yard coleus plants displayed their multi-colored leaves through drapes of fake spider webs.

I took pictures of spreading shade trees dotted with yellow flowers, a twenty-foot tall bird-of-paradise fan flanked with queen palm trees, and a beautifully landscaped yard in front of a stately lemon-yellow home. We are made in God's image, and we partner with him in creativity.

Psalm 89:11 tells us, "The heavens are yours, and yours also the earth; you founded the world and all that is in it." (NIV) I'm so grateful to God that we get to live on his beautiful earth!

----------

## *AAAH, Winter*

A sudden breeze set the palm trees dancing in the front yard. Our carpet of mismatched grasses and weeds waved as the wind brushed loose needles from the pine trees off the roof. Towering cumulonimbus clouds reflected the colors of the sun's passage – from brilliant white to glowing orange.

Winter in Florida means cool, breezy days with low humidity. Don't get me wrong. I'm grateful for Florida's humidity. It's good for the skin, keeps plants green, and can be avoided in air conditioning; but our late falls and winters -- aaaaaah.

The house filled with the smell of fresh-cut grass. Someone's house alarm went off. The noise of children playing, dogs barking, industrial-sized lawn mowers, leaf blowers and our neighbor's Harley are sounds of a family-friendly neighborhood. The occasional concert-level rap music from our neighbor's truck across the street brought me back to the days before our kids moved out.

Floridians go outside in the winter and hibernate all summer. We say hello as we work in the yard, stop to chat and catch up, and tease each other about our various Christmas decorations.

"You're so early!" "What are you waiting for?" "Didn't you have that thing the LAST ten years?" "What, ANOTHER blow-up Santa on a Harley?"

The weather this time of year is perfect for farmers to sell their produce at the local green market. There's no better way to get organic veggies than from the growers.

God reminded Job who's in charge of the weather in Job 38:36-38. "Who do you think gave weather-wisdom to the ibis, and storm-savvy to the rooster? Does anyone know enough to number all the clouds or tip over the rain barrels of heaven?"

We cook out and trim bushes and water flowers and shop outdoors. Thank You, Lord, for neighbors and farmers and open windows and cool, breezy, dry days.

----------

## It's Just Around the Corner

The closer we get to Thanksgiving, the more God reminds me of the people in our lives we're thankful for. We stay in touch with most of them on social media, but there are some family members and friends who don't participate online.

Most of our loved ones live a distance from us, and we see them infrequently or not at all, this side of Heaven. There are days and nights, when my heart aches with missing them. Still, it gives me great joy to love them and know that one day we'll all be together.

My heart echoes what Paul said in 1 Thessalonians 3:9-13. "What would be an adequate thanksgiving to offer God for all the joy we experience before him because of you? We do what we can, praying away, night and day, asking for the bonus of seeing your faces again and doing what we can to help when your faith falters."

Along with Paul, I also pray, "May God our Father himself and our Master Jesus clear the road to you! And may the Master pour on the love so that it fills your lives and splashes over on everyone around you, just as it does from us to you. May you be infused with strength and purity, filled with confidence in the presence of God our Father when our Master Jesus arrives with all his followers."

So, to all our friends and family, Bill and I are both immensely grateful for you, and we miss you deeply when we aren't with you, no matter where you live. We pray for you, trust God to answer your prayers and provide for all your needs, and we look forward to seeing you again.

----------

## Sweet Anticipation

I can still smell the spicy sweet aroma of baking gingerbread, also known as Lebkuchen. I can feel cold air biting my cheeks and tightening my forehead as I remember walking through the Kristkindlmarkt in Nuremberg, Germany, many years ago.

Brightly painted stalls decorated with twinkling lights and fresh evergreen branches lined the square, filled with gift items like wooden toys, Lebkuchen tins, nuts and fruit. A giant Christmas tree stood in the square, sparkling in tiny white lights. Sweet voices of children's choirs filled the market, singing Christmas songs we grew up with.

My memory conjures a post-card perfect picture of a winter evening, where the shopping and celebration of Christmas began shortly before the actual holiday. If it's embellishing the reality, I don't want to know about it. I like the memory as it is.

It isn't even Thanksgiving yet, and Christmas is already in full swing in the stores and on commercials. It seems to start earlier every year. One store displayed Christmas trees before Halloween!

As Paul said in Romans 8:21, "Meanwhile, the joyful anticipation deepens." He was talking about the Second coming, but in the meantime, why not Christmas?

The glitter, pomp, music, lights, and extravagance are unique to this season, but nothing in this country compares to the timeless atmosphere of old Germany.

----------

## *More Anticipation*

I love Christmas shopping when I have money. I anticipate the pleasure of our loved ones as they open their gifts. To give is better than to receive because, quite honestly, there really is more satisfaction in it. Receiving is fun, too, though, and I'm happy with the simplest things given in love.

I'm thankful that I woke up this morning to the gift of a new day. I'll write a list of what items to bring to Thanksgiving tomorrow, grind the herbs for the turkey and won't forget the baster!

We are blessed to have such an abundance of food that we can put the extra away for another meal or two after our feast. Turkey isn't half bad in sandwiches or combined with leftover gravy, stuffing and veggies over noodles.

My family calls me the "Leftover Queen" after Thanksgiving. I combine leftovers with herbs and spices and other leftovers to make truly delicious tasting dinners. They don't look as appetizing as they taste, but no one seems to care.

I keep exhaustive Christmas gift and card lists for our large extended family and friends. One is partially checked off, and the other will take a couple of uninterrupted days. I can hardly wait to enjoy the atmosphere of a Christmas-decorated house, but it will take some time and some work to get it done.

It's true that everything worth having requires work. Work is God's gift to us. It includes everything we're capable of doing that we put effort into, and it is valuable.

We learn in Colossians 3:23, "Work from the heart for your real Master, for God, confident that you'll get paid in full when you come into your inheritance."

I'm grateful for the work of prayer that others have done on our behalf and that we've done on theirs; the work of friendship which requires time to nurture; the work of sharing on our weekly conference call; and the work of sharing hope. Thank You, Lord, for keeping me busy until the day I meet you face to face.

----------

## *Thankful for Manifold Blessings*

Tomorrow is Thanksgiving Day! My heart is full of gratitude. I wouldn't know where to begin, so I'll share someone else's thoughts, instead.

On November 4, 1963, President Kennedy issued his annual Thanksgiving Proclamation. He died eighteen days later -- six days before Thanksgiving. That year, President Johnson urged all the nation's churches to share Kennedy's words in their Thanksgiving services. Here is an excerpt...

"Let us therefore proclaim our gratitude to Providence for manifold blessings – let us be humbly thankful for inherited ideals – and let us resolve to share those blessings and those ideals with our fellow human beings throughout the world."

"On that day, let us gather in our sanctuaries dedicated to worship and in homes blessed by family affection to express our gratitude for the glorious gifts of God; and let us earnestly and humbly pray that He will continue to guide and sustain us in the great unfinished tasks of achieving peace, justice, and understanding among all men and nations and of ending misery and suffering wherever they exist."

Amen! Let our gratitude become love in action. Happy Thanksgiving!

----------

## *T'was the Time Before Christmas*

Children have a wonderful ability to live in the moment. Their anticipation of Christmas is made more impatient because they live in the now and the future seems so very far away. At my age, the future seems to be rushing toward me, too quickly, and too forcefully.

I want to hold on to this moment, to now, and to live fully in it. In 2 Corinthians 6:2 we're told, "For he [God] says, 'In the time of my favor I heard you, and in the day of salvation I helped you.' I tell you, now is the time of God's favor, now is the day of salvation." (NIV)

We aren't guaranteed any more than now, this moment.

The outdoor lights are up, presents are wrapped, boxes are packed and the cards are finished. I love getting Christmas cards and letters, and I love sending them. We pray for each family as they share a bit of their lives with us, and as we send them a bit of ours. I keep the photo cards to see the year-to-year growth of their families.

Christmas is definitely a labor of love, but it's nothing compared to that of the baby in the manger, who grew to live among us, gave himself for us, and ascended to sit in glory on his throne at the right hand of the Father.

He is the wonder of Christmas, the awe we feel in the deep night stillness after the shopping, baking, decorating and wrapping are done. He is the peace before opening gifts, before the meal, before the party. I treasure that moment, sitting by the tree, having done all, when I imagine Mary cradling her baby while Joseph stands guard.

I'm reminded that God also has an almost-completed project. His Kingdom come, his will be done on Earth as it is in Heaven. His project for Earth will be completed one day, as will his project for each of us.

----------

## The Non-Baker Bakes

It was baking day number one! I admire people who love to bake and make an art form out of it. They come up with these beautifully perfect concoctions – prize-worthy gourmet delights that melt the heart before they ever hit the palate and melt in the mouth. Sigh! I make two kinds of Christmas cookies, and it takes me two or three days to do it.

I can generally follow a recipe, but I've been known to substitute baking soda for baking powder (there's a difference?) and forget the sugar. I've tried using the cookie dough I bought from our grandkids' school in place of actually mixing ingredients. Peanut blossoms are supposed to be like little exquisite mounds topped with partially melted chocolate kisses. Mine were flat. The pictures of the artistically painted vanilla cookies you see in cookbooks – picture Jackson Pollock or Picasso on mine.

What Paul told James in his letter became very real to me while I was baking. "Consider it pure joy, my brothers and sisters, whenever you face trials of many kinds, because you know that the testing of your faith produces perseverance. Let perseverance finish its work so that you may be mature and complete, not lacking anything. If any of you lacks wisdom, you should ask God, who gives generously to all without finding fault, and it will be given to you." (James 1:2-5 NIV)

Although my little kitchen looked like the aftermath of a flour explosion, I thanked the Lord that it would, indeed result in joy. Who cares if the Christmas tree cookies looked like orange blobs on a brown background? The taste was sweet (when I didn't forget the sugar).

----------

## More Baking for the Baking-Challenged

It was break time in the cookie factory, and I prayed, "Help me, oh, help me God, my God, save me through your wonderful love; then they'll know that your hand is in this, that you, God have been at work." (Psalm 109:26)

Along those lines, here are some hints from this cookie baking Gramma.

Do not try to mix the dough for 16 dozen cookies in one bowl, unless you're using a bathtub. I'm a "more is better" kind of person, so I doubled a quadrupled recipe.

When measuring ingredients, write everything down and have a system. Years of experience have finally taught me to tally the cups of flour and sugar. I used to sing the numbers out loud, until I realized the words were morphing into a song about random numbers and not about keeping count. I'd have to go back and re-measure – every time. Thank God someone invented pencil and paper!

What I hadn't learned was to separate the bowls far enough apart so I remember which one I just added the sugar to. Next year, I'll do it right – if I remember.

If you divide one batch between two bowls, do it before you measure the ingredients. When you eyeball the dough, it can result in two different consistencies. Trust me. I did both -- one quadruple batch not so neatly divided into two bowls, and one batch in one bowl and all over the counter.

The term "hand mixer" is appropriate when using one that's 40 years old. When the smoke clears, expect to mix, literally, by hand.

Our friends and family who were obligated to eat the cookies should not be concerned if they bit into a few little lumps. It's flour, not fingernails. I sanitized my hands before playing with (mixing) the gooey dough, and I had no fingernails to start with.

----------

## *Cookie Art for the Baking Challenged*

I rolled out the dough, roughly in the shape of Africa – every time – and, like the continent, there were thin places and thick places and I have no idea how it all happened. Maybe it's a brain thing.

The cookie cutters made perfect stars and Christmas trees, and it was beginning to look like we might have some nice cookies after all.

Then somewhere between the dough and the cookie sheet, the stars became dancing starfish with oddly shaped arms of uneven length. Some of the trees looked as if they'd been in a hurricane, and others would have been at home in Whoville.

The oven did its magic. Some cookies came out white and others were brown.

Psalm 147: 4 tells us, "He counts the stars and assigns each a name." I consoled myself with the thought that, within the next couple of days, our grandkids and I would work our own modern art magic and cover the stars and trees with unique and unintelligible designs. We'd have our own creativity party.

Bill took one look at some Dr. Seuss-worthy trees and said, "You always did like pizazz. Nothing is ordinary for you." I love that man!!

----------

## Cookie Proverbs

Proverbs are "a manual for living, for learning what's right and just and fair; to teach the inexperienced the ropes and give our young people a grasp on reality. There's something here also for seasoned men and women, still a thing or two for the experienced to learn." (Proverbs 1:3-5) Here are some Cookie Proverbs from yours truly:

When a rubber spatula with a plastic handle gets caught in the beaters, don't speed them up. Those sturdy, bendable spatulas make the journey without mishap – if you don't speed up the mixer.

I tallied the flour and dry ingredients as I added them to one bowl. Then I put all the sugar and mushy ingredients in the other bowl I use for mixing. And then I read the directions. Always read the directions first.

When it says to gradually add the sugar and eggs, you should do so. Did you know that each box of dark brown sugar has exactly two firmly packed cups of sugar? I figured it out with the first box, and then just dumped the second box in the other mushy bowl. Who knew it would be rock hard?

Once the old hand mixer gives out (at about two cups of flour for mine), fold in the additional flour by hand. Do it gently, unless you want a face full of it. I speak from experience.

If you cannot get your wedding/engagement rings off, let the dough dry thoroughly before using a toothpick to clean the rings. Gently pry the dough out, rinse, count your diamonds, and enjoy the added luster from the peanut butter.

God reminded me of some life lessons in the process of mixing the batter. Life is full of unexpected challenges, and we can make a real mess of it. Clean up the mess as you make it, or you'll face a huge cleanup later.

Be patient. Eating raw cookie batter might be bad for your health. Eating baked cookies is not much better – just less likely to give you salmonella.

Enjoy the bloopers. You'll laugh about them one day.

Don't be afraid to get your hands dirty. Hand mixing cookie dough is the adult equivalent of playing in mud. Soap and water are your friends.

Be grateful for the ingredients God has given you to make a life with. Shortening is pretty awful by itself, but the cookies would be awful without it.

----------

## *Kitchen Mishaps*

We had Turkey Surprise, Pineapple Ham I Hope, and Cross-Your Fingers Cherry Ham for our family Christmas dinner. A word of caution to all of you who, like me, can't make turkey without those lovely cooking bags – things happen.

My turkeys usually turn out great. I generously rub the bird with fresh herbs I'd ground the day before, smear lots of butter on it, pack it full of stuffing and hold it together with skewers. I pour a bottle of white cooking wine and some water into the bag, seal it up, cut a few holes on top, pop it in the oven for a few hours – and out comes a perfect turkey every time.

This time, after I confidently prepared my 20+ pounder, I had to transfer it from one pan into an open bag in another pan. Bill was teaching tennis, so I was all by myself.

With the Lord's help and a lot of grunting on my part, the trussed turkey went into the bag, but not before smearing the outside of it with generous gobs of herbed butter. I sealed it up, wiped down the bag, and noticed wine leaking out into the pan. That would not do.

This is why they include at least two cooking bags in the box. I was going to pop the turkey, bag and all, into a freshly prepared bag, and remove the first bag once it was safely settled. The problem was, the skewers ripped the first bag in transit and all the wine, water and most of the herb butter went down the drain.

I had a little white wine and a lot of Marsala in the pantry. I'd never used Marsala with turkey, but there's always a first time. I sprinkled a variety of seasonings all over the bird (all the fresh herbs had gone down the drain), patted it affectionately, sealed it up and popped it into the oven. Turkey Surprise, anyone?

My kitchen is very small, so I decided to prepare the ham in a crock pot for the first time. Of course it didn't fit in one, so I cut it into two pieces, rubbed brown sugar all over them, and then remembered to take the lids off both of my crock pots so I could put them in. I'd never washed my hands that often! One cooked with pineapples and the other with cherry pie filling. I crossed my fingers and hoped for a good outcome.

The best part of the day was yet to come – our friends and family! They were hungry enough not to care how the turkey and ham turned out, and they loved my dancing starfish and Whoville tree cookies! Good times!

----------

## *The Mayan Apocalypse*

We started a new tradition in 2012. There was a lot of hoopla that year about the end of the Mayan calendar, which had accurately marked the days for at least 5,000 years.

Newscasters spoke about the coming apocalypse with a great deal of humor and some sarcasm. Others seemed afraid of the possible meaning of it all. UFO programs gained new popularity as people wondered what the end of the calendar signified.

We decided to have our Christmas party on that final Mayan date: December 21, 2012. Since no one knows for sure exactly when Jesus was born, I figured the 21st was close enough to celebrate his birthday.

We had a great meal (Thank you, Lord for crock pots and turkey bags), played a hilarious gift exchange game, and had a lot of fun with family and friends. After dinner, and before we opened gifts, I went outside to check out the sky. After the game, I did it again, and, as we said goodbye to everyone, I glanced at the sky once again.

In Mark 13:21-37, Jesus told his disciples what to expect concerning his return. He admonished them, "But the exact day and hour? No one knows that, not even heaven's angels, not even the Son. Only the Father. So keep a sharp lookout, for you don't know the timetable."

I'm happy to report that no alien spaceships filled the skies that night. No tsunami inundated Florida; no worldwide earthquake knocked our cities down; and no global electro-magnetic pulse took out all our electronics. We would all know it if Jesus had returned.

The party was so successful; we decided to continue the tradition on the weekend before Christmas every year. It frees our kids up to spend Christmas day with their children or their other in-laws, and gives us a peaceful day together to thank the Lord for Jesus.

Bring it on, you alien invaders! My God knows the day and the hour of His return. I choose to trust Him and I'm not afraid of you.

----------

## *Christmas in the Neighborhood*

A little, spotted goat contentedly nibbled a shepherd's shoelace. The shepherd stretched out the crook of her staff to nab the elbow of one of the wise kings. He held candy canes to dole out to kids in passing cars, and she wanted one. Another shepherd stretched out on the grass, his robe hiked up around his knees, exposing his jeans and sneakers.

Santa Claus tenderly cradled the baby Jesus on his arm in his rocking chair under a sign that read, "Even Santa Gets It!"

Mary and Joseph chatted as they rested on bales of hay. A large star illuminated the scene, and the angel kept walking away from his wings, which were tacked to the back of the stable. Who wants to carry heavy wings around?

Every year, Bill and I take a tour of the neighborhood Christmas displays. I like to count the nativities, and am happy to report that the number increases every year. So how have we consistently missed this one?

A Living Nativity was played out one block over from our own, and this was the first time we saw what they were doing.

This was youth group night. The teens were dressed in costume, unashamedly sharing the Good News with every passer-by, and enjoying each other's company. Isn't that the way it should be all the time -- perhaps without the costumes?

We listened to the gift of Christmas music our neighbor gave us. Joy, peace and love filled my heart, and I was refreshed. Unless the Lord returns, we're leaving our world to a generation being raised by godly men and women.

The angel said to the shepherds, "Do not be afraid! I bring you good news that will cause great joy for all the people!" (Luke 2:10) That's good news for all of us!

----------

## Christmas Eve

The last month of pregnancy is specifically designed to make us women want to birth our baby as soon as possible. Fear and anxiety about the birth process is tamped down by our desperate need to deliver the baby so we can sleep again, walk normally, and not have to pee every fifteen seconds. We are exhausted carrying the extra weight, and we want our normal appetite back.

Mary was on a donkey (ouch) and there were no facilities along the highway to Bethlehem. The bed she was so looking forward to wasn't available anywhere.

Had I been on that donkey, (thank God he was wise enough to choose Mary) I would have grumbled an earful to hapless Joseph, who was doing his best to make his miserable, pregnant wife happy. Being Mary, she probably didn't grumble.

I imagine that by the time they found the stable to bed down in, she didn't care where she was, as long as it was off that donkey's back!

Suddenly, her water broke, and labor began. She became totally focused on what was happening to her -- the contractions, the pain, the need to push.

A human baby was coming into the world. The Son of God, the King of Kings, the Savior of mankind -- a divine baby was about to make his appearance. He was wholly man, wholly God, Holy Jesus.

Thank you, Lord, for Mary, a willing human woman, and Joseph, whom you chose to be your only Son's foster dad. It was Christmas Eve. Immanuel, God with us was born.

An angel of the Lord said to the shepherds in the field, in Luke 2:11-12 (NIV), "Today in the town of David a Savior has been born to you; he is the Messiah, the Lord. This will be a sign to you: You will find a baby wrapped in cloths and lying in a manger."

Oh, come let us adore Him together! Merry Christmas, dear ones!

----------

## *The Gift of Christmas*

Years ago I asked God to help me truly love others. My favorite Christmas present this year was a heart full of warm, gooey, mushy love for my family and friends.

Love was given in every gift we received and gave this Christmas. We are blessed beyond measure.

Chris and Veronica came to celebrate Christmas with us. Our granddaughter Autumn went straight to the toys and spread them out all over the guest room, just as our local ones do. Then she crawled into a box and did somersaults in it, trying to find her foot.

The giggles from the box kept us all laughing. It became her spaceship, so she and her toes went on a long journey, laughing all the way.

Our brand-new grandson Austin slept through most of it -- his calmness in contrast to her energy, at least for now. Mom and Dad can take some time to breathe with this sweet baby.

Every one of our grandchildren is perfect and brilliant. What can I say? Good genes.

All that love points us to the One who loves us the most -- the One who knows our thoughts, our feelings, our hurts, our failures, our strengths, our needs, our desires, our hearts, our spirits, and everything about us – and yet still loves us unconditionally.

Jesus was born, and we celebrate his birth. More importantly, Jesus lived among us. He was as human as you and I. He knows us from experience, not theory; and even knowing all that we are and aren't, he gave himself in total, sacrificial love for us.

That's the miracle of Christmas: not just his birth, but his entire life, death and resurrection.

"For God so loved the world that he gave his one and only Son, that whoever believes in him shall not perish but have eternal life." (John 3:16 NIV)

And now we wait to open the best present of all -- his return! Now that will be a celebration! Merry Christmas!

----------

## *Reflecting on the Old*

On New Year's Day, I reflected on all the blessings, challenges, surprises, and even sorrows of the ending year.

Challenges kept us in prayer. God met some needs and furthered his agenda toward a world where his kingdom takes over. The rough journey will end in wonder someday. We look forward to the fulfillment of prophecy in the coming year or years.

Sorrows are the valleys that make the mountaintops so wonderfully attractive. The deeper we grieve, the higher our joy. We grow in the valleys, and we're grateful for them. As painful as it is, sorrow is a part of a full, complete life.

I'm thankful that God allows us to participate in his creativity. I watched the dazzling colors of the Rose Parade floats and wondered how many flowers, seeds and foliage were carefully placed on each float to create each masterpiece.

I think of the care, skill, artistry, and creativity that God puts into the creation of each one of us -- so much more than a float in a parade. God allows us to interact with and impact others, to grow and glow, to be filled with color and life and his Spirit. Wow, God! Beautiful work!

I love that God continues to surprise us no matter how old we get. The number of our grandchildren jumped from under a dozen to over twenty in no time flat. Some came by birth, some were related to those new ones, and some were added by marriage. All are welcomed and loved.

I'm thankful for the constants: for our God, our faith, our church; for the love of friends and family; for my faithful, strong, generous, warm-hearted husband; for our home and creature comforts; for our business and the friends we've made there -- too many blessings to count!

The Psalms close with Psalm 150. "Hallelujah! Praise God in his holy house of worship, praise him under the open skies; praise him for his acts of power, praise him for his magnificent greatness. Praise with a blast on the trumpet, praise by strumming soft strings; praise him with castanets and dance, praise him with banjo and flute; praise him with cymbals and a big bass drum, praise him with fiddles and mandolin. Let every living, breathing creature praise God! Hallelujah!"

Praise is a fitting transition from the old year to the new. Bring it on, Lord! Hallelujah!

----------

## *Resolutions*

A new year is like Baptism, in a way. Paul said in Romans 6:3, "When we went under the water, we left the old country of sin behind; when we came up out of the water, we entered into the new country of grace – a new life in a new land!" The first day of January presents us with a clean slate, an opportunity for new life.

In the United States, it's customary for people to make a list of New Year's resolutions. Most of us break them pretty quickly, especially the one declaring "I will lose weight." I avoid that one. Are there resolutions we can keep? Here are mine:

I will continue to be grateful because it keeps me focused on our
    Father in Heaven, the Source of every good and perfect gift.
I will speak out against injustice in my own small way.
I will speak for the unborn.
I will ask the Lord to forgive me every day because I screw up at
    least once a day.
I will do all I can to bring honor and glory to God.
I will forgive everyone who hurts me.
I will pray for my enemies.
I will pray for those I love and those who God lays on my heart to
    pray for, and I'll trust that someone prays for us, too.
I will ask God to save every one of our friends, neighbors and family
    members who still haven't met or received their Savior Jesus
    Christ. Heaven wouldn't be the same without them.

Paul gave us a list we can keep in Colossians 3:15-17, "Let the peace of Christ keep you in tune with each other, in step with each other. None of this going off and doing your own thing. And cultivate thankfulness. Let the Word of Christ – the Message – have the run of the house. Give it plenty of room in your lives. Instruct and direct one another using good common sense. And sing, sing your hearts out to God! Let every detail in your lives – words, actions, whatever – be done in the name of the Master, Jesus, thanking God the Father every step of the way."

May this New Year be your most blessed year ever!

----------

## *Holiday Aftermath*

The sad job of putting away Christmas was done. I loved the way the house looked and felt with all the decorations up and the tree full of a lifetime of ornaments lighting up the corner of the living room.

Now that the tree was gone and the decorations were packed away, I also liked the way the house looked and felt without it.

Why do we put so much work into putting it all up, and then taking it all down, year after year? It isn't the decor that makes the house feel like home.

Mike and our grandson dropped in for a few minutes, and Bill's mom came over, had a nap and kept me company until we shared dinner and he took her home.

The house was emptier when they left than it was without the tree. It filled up again when Bill came home.

In 2 Corinthians 5:1-10, Paul assured us the cycle of putting up and taking down will end. "We know that when these bodies of ours are taken down like tents and folded away, they will be replaced by resurrection bodies in heaven – god-made, not handmade – and we'll never have to relocate our 'tents' again…The Spirit of God whets our appetite by giving us a taste of what's ahead. He puts a little of heaven in our hearts so that we'll never settle for less."

That little bit of Heaven in our hearts is the secret. I'm grateful for the people who make our home feel like home with or without Christmas.

# IS JESUS THE MESSIAH?

"As I read, my suspicion that Jesus might really be the Messiah was confirmed."

~Jay Alan Sekulow

## *What Are the Odds?*

Every now and then we'll buy a lottery ticket. Bill likes to tell me the odds of winning are a gazillion to one, but I feel the odds are more like 100%. If you win, you win. If you lose, you lose. It's 100% either way. So far we've lost 100% of the time, but we have fun dreaming about what we'd do with the winnings.

Numbers and I live in different worlds. I did better at algebra than any other math because it included letters. However, I can recognize the staggering improbability of what mathematicians have figured out – that the odds of one person fulfilling just 8 of the Messianic prophecies is 1 in 100,000,000,000,000,000.

I had to count the zeroes as I typed them; to be sure I wasn't putting in too many. To put it in perspective, one trillion has only twelve zeroes. The possibility of one person fulfilling 48 prophecies is 1 chance in 10 to the $157^{th}$ power. If I understand that correctly, that is a 10 followed by at least 157 zeroes, but I could be wrong. Not a numbers person, remember?

So I wonder, which prophecies actually pertained to the Messiah? Since I'm not a Bible expert, I defer to others who've done the research. I'm sure there's room for interpretation, and that some might not agree with others – but that's for them to duke out. Every morning I read from both the Old and the New Testaments. I'm still amazed that I can find the birth, life, death and resurrection of Jesus written centuries before he was born.

Isaiah said, in Isaiah 53, "Who believes what we've heard and seen? Who would have thought God's saving power would look like this?" Those of us who have read the story of Jesus in the New Testament are astonished at the accuracy of Isaiah's description of the Savior.

The chapter ends with, "Because he looked death in the face and didn't flinch, because he embraced the company of the lowest. He took on his own shoulders the sin of the many, he took up the cause of all the black sheep."

He took up the cause of all misfits, everywhere. What other prophecies might point to Jesus as the Messiah?

----------

## *Was He the One Moses Prophesied?*

As Bill and I were getting to know each other in the months after we had met in church, I was bothered by the question that kept popping up in my mind. Is he the one I'll want to spend the rest of my life with? Instead of a prophetic word to reassure me, the Lord filled me with peace and love for the man I would marry and be happy with.

It was a bit more complicated for the Lord to let Israel know about their coming Messiah. He spoke through prophets like Moses, and the prophecies were often vague.

In Deuteronomy 18:15, Moses said, "God, your God, is going to raise up a prophet for you. God will raise him up from among your kinsmen, a prophet like me. Listen obediently to him."

Okay, granted, there were many prophets after Moses, and I'm sure God wanted Israel to listen to each of them. How many of them led their people to the Promised Land like Moses did? And if Jesus is the one he was talking about, did Jesus lead his people to the Promised Land, too? Or will he?

Listen to this, from John 7:40-42, "Those in the crowd who heard these words were saying, 'This has to be the Prophet.' Others said, 'He is the Messiah!' But others were saying, 'The Messiah doesn't come from Galilee, does he? Don't the Scriptures tell us that the Messiah comes from David's village?'"

The Jews of that day knew where the Messiah would be born, but they forgot that Isaiah prophesied the Messiah would also come from Galilee. (Isaiah 9:1)

The Apostle Luke wrote about the second coming of the Messiah in Acts 3:20-23. "Turn to face God so he can wipe away your sins, pour out showers of blessing to refresh you, and send you the Messiah he prepared for you, namely, Jesus. For the time being he must remain out of sight in Heaven until everything is restored to order again, just the way God, through the preaching of his holy prophets of old said it would be. Moses, for instance, said, 'Your God will raise up for you a prophet just like me from your family. Listen to every word he speaks to you. Every last living soul who refuses to listen to that prophet will be wiped out from the people.'"

It sounds like Jesus will, indeed, lead his people to the Promised Land. I say the odds are 100%. Jesus is or he isn't the prophesied Messiah.

----------

## Family Tree

Several members of our family had decided to explore our roots. They researched our family tree and compiled a history of where we came from. I admire them for doing that. I have enough trouble remembering the names of our children and grandchildren, and yet, our ancestry is important. Much of who we are has been handed down through the generations.

It seems logical, then, to find out what the ancestry of the Messiah would be, according to the prophecies. That way, people would know what family he'd be born into.

We know his mother will be human. In Genesis 3:15, God said to the serpent, who had just deceived Eve and caused Adam to fall, "I'm declaring war between you and the Woman, between your offspring and hers. He'll wound your head, you'll wound his heel."

He'll be a descendant of Abraham, Isaac and Jacob. All the nations of the earth will be blessed through Abraham (Genesis 12, 18 and 22). God's covenant with Isaac (Genesis 17 and 26) was passed to Jacob (Genesis 28) and down to Judah, from whose line the rightful ruler would come (Genesis 49 and 1 Chronicles 5). He'll be a descendant of Boaz and Ruth and their grandson Jesse (Ruth 4).

Isaiah prophesied a lot about the coming Messiah. In Isaiah 11, he said, "A green Shoot will sprout from Jesse's stump, from his roots a budding Branch ... On that day, Jesse's Root will be raised high, posted as a rallying banner for the peoples. The nations will all come to him. His headquarters will be glorious."

Isaiah lived after David had already reigned, so he wouldn't have been talking about King David in the future tense. Jesse was David's father. The Root of Jesse would be a descendent who would rally his people and all the nations in the future.

----------

## *Unraveling the Lineage*

My dad once told me, convincingly, that William Tell was one of our ancestors. He was a legendary character in Austria and Switzerland who lived in the early fourteenth century. My mom is a descendent of the Astor family. John Jacob Astor, one of the wealthiest men in the United States, went down with the Titanic. Our human ancestry has little bearing on world events, but that isn't the case with the Messiah.

The Messiah would be a descendant of David. Samuel prophesied that David's throne would be established forever in 2 Samuel 7. Nathan succeeded Samuel, and told David the same thing in 1 Chronicles 17. Ethan prophesied in Psalm 89 that the David's line would continue forever because of God's covenant with him.

Isaiah told the house of David that the Lord would give them a sign in Isaiah 7. In Isaiah 9:7, he said, "Of the greatness of his government and peace there will be no end. He will reign on David's throne and over his kingdom, establishing and upholding it with justice and righteousness from that time on and forever." (NIV)

Jeremiah said, "'The days are coming,' declares the Lord, 'when I will raise up for David a righteous Branch, a King who will reign wisely and do what is just and right in the land.'" (Jeremiah 23:5-6 and 33:14-15) (NIV)

In Ezekiel 34, God told the prophet Ezekiel, who lived about 400 years after King David, "I'll appoint one shepherd over them all: my servant David. He'll feed them. He'll be their shepherd. And I, God, will be their God. My servant David will be their prince. I, God, have spoken." He was obviously referring to a descendant of David, since David was long gone.

Did Jesus follow this line of descent? Here is what we're told in Matthew 1, "The family tree of Jesus Christ, David's son, Abraham's son:"

Matthew wrote, "There were fourteen generations from Abraham to David, another fourteen from David to the Babylonian exile, and yet another fourteen from the Babylonian exile to Christ."

That included Abraham, Isaac, Jacob, Judah, Boaz and Ruth, Jesse, and David. Finally, in verse 16, we're assured that Jesus was, indeed, born of a woman, Mary.

Wait a minute. Does Jesus's ancestry determine that he's the Messiah? Not necessarily. Many people descended from David. This is only the beginning.

----------

## *Beyond the Lineage*

I can't imagine the complexity of figuring out a family tree, especially with a family like ours. I often say we have a family bush, or a hedge. We have branches grafted in all over the place. It reminds me of the immense grace of God who grafts us into his family simply because we choose to love him.

We know that Jesus could be the Messiah because he fits the lineage requirement, but what sets him apart from others who could make the same claim? How many Davidic descendants can claim to be the son of a virgin mom -- or the son of God? Let's see what the prophets said.

Messiah would be born of a virgin. The prophet Isaiah said to the house of David, "Therefore, the Lord himself will give you a sign: The virgin will conceive and give birth to a son, and will call him Immanuel. (Isaiah 7:14 NIV)

He also said, "For to us a child is born, to us a son is given." (Isaiah 9:6 NIV)

Messiah would be the Son of God. The Lord told Samuel to assure David that he would establish David's throne forever through his offspring. He told him, "I will be his father, and he will be my son." (2 Samuel 7:12-14 NIV)

God repeated the message through the prophet Nathan in 1 Chronicles 17:13-14.

In Psalm 2, the Lord prophesied to Israel that he's installed his king on Zion. He said, "you are my son; today I have become your father." He then exhorts the rulers of the earth to serve him with fear and take refuge in him.

In Proverbs 30:4 (NIV) we're asked a question, "Who has gone up to heaven and come down? Whose hands have gathered up the wind? Who has wrapped up the waters in a cloak? Who has established all the ends of the earth? What is his name, and what is the name of his son? Surely you know!"

Messiah would be God's "firstborn." In Psalm 89:19-29, Ethan recounted a vision God gave him about the Messiah. In verses 26 and 27, he said, "He will call out to me, 'You are my Father, my God, the Rock my Savior.' And I will appoint him to be my firstborn, the most exalted of the kings of the earth." (NIV)

We know who the Messiah's Father is. Who would his mother be?

----------

## *The Virgin Mom*

When I struggled through adolescence, I often wondered why I was born into my crazy family. Every time my parents laid down the law and I lost an argument, I wanted to be someone else and live somewhere else. I didn't choose my parents, and neither did Jesus.

Mary was a simple girl -- a virgin, engaged to be married to Joseph. One day an angel appeared to her. In Luke 1:31-35, the angel told her, "You will become pregnant and give birth to a son and call his name Jesus. He will be great, be called 'Son of the Highest.' The Lord God will give him the throne of his father David; He will rule Jacob's house forever – no end, ever, to his kingdom." Does that sound like any of the prophecies?

Mary asked how it could be possible, since she was still a virgin. He answered, "The Holy Spirit will come upon you, the power of the Highest hover over you; therefore the child you bring to birth will be called Holy, Son of God."

In Matthew 1:20-23, an angel later appeared to Joseph and told him that Mary's baby was conceived by the Holy Spirit. "'She will bring a son to birth, and when she does, you, Joseph, will name him Jesus – 'God saves' – because he will save his people from their sins.' This would bring the prophet's embryonic sermon to full term: Watch for this – a virgin will get pregnant and bear a son; they will name him Immanuel (Hebrew for "God is with us")."

Twice in the life of Jesus, a voice from the sky was heard by the people around him. The first time, in Matthew 3:16-17 when Jesus was baptized by his cousin John, and the second in Matthew 17:5 when he was on the mountain with some of his disciples. Both times, the voice said, 'This is my Son, chosen and marked by my love, delight of my life. Listen to him."

It's conceivable that Mary concocted this elaborate story because she cheated on her fiancé, and it's also conceivable that the prophecies relate to someone else or another time. The voice could have been an auditory hallucination. We believers are convinced it's true, of course, but does it prove that Jesus is the Messiah?

----------

## *You Can Choose Your Friends, But Not Your Family*

My poor mom listened to me complain throughout my teen years, "I didn't choose to be born in this family!" I heard it from my children when they disagreed with me, or I laid down the law. It's possible their own children have said it to them. It's a fact. Babies do not choose their parents.

I didn't choose where my Dad would be stationed, where I'd go to school, how many countries I'd live in, or any other circumstances beyond my control. So it stands to reason that Jesus didn't choose his virgin mother, or to be born in a stable. What else was going on that the prophets foretold about the circumstances surrounding Messiah's birth?

Isaiah foretold the birth of Messiah in Isaiah 9:6: "For to us a child is born, to us a son is given, and the government will be on his shoulders. And he will be called Wonderful Counselor, Mighty God, Everlasting Father, Prince of Peace." (NIV)

When Jesus was born, a bunch of shepherds were watching their sheep when "An angel of the Lord appeared to them, and the glory of the Lord shone around them, and they were terrified. But the angel said to them, "Do not be afraid. I bring you good news that will cause great joy for all the people. Today in the town of David a Savior has been born to you; he is the Messiah, the Lord. This will be a sign to you: You will find a baby wrapped in cloths and lying in a manger." (Luke 2:9-12 NIV)

Messiah would be born into a poor family, not a royal one. Isaiah said "He grew up before him like a tender shoot, and like a root out of dry ground. He had no beauty or majesty to attract us to him, nothing in his appearance that we should desire him." (Isaiah 53:2 NIV)

Jesus was born to a pair of travelers who couldn't even find a decent room for the night. He was born in a stable. "She wrapped him in cloths and placed him in a manger." (Luke 2:7 NIV) His first bed was a feeding trough for livestock.

Baby Jesus probably slept through the angelic display that awed the shepherds. He didn't care where he slept as long as he was fed and warm. He thought baby thoughts and dreamed baby dreams because he was a human baby, born to a human mommy. Yet, we'll learn that there's more to him. His little family was about to face great danger, and it was all foretold. Was he the Messiah? It's beginning to look more and more plausible.

----------

## *Tumbleweeds*

We traveled a lot because Dad was a military man. I was born in Germany, moved to Kentucky at age two, went to elementary school in Texas, and continued school in Germany and Italy. I didn't plan any of it, and certainly didn't choose it. Neither could little Jesus choose where his family took him. The prophets saw glimpses of Messiah's life and travels. Could they have been seeing Jesus?

Messiah would be born in Bethlehem. The prophet Micah said, "But you, Bethlehem, David's country, the runt of the litter – from you will come the leader who will shepherd-rule Israel ... His family tree is ancient and distinguished." (Micah 5:2)

Jesus was born in Bethlehem, during the time of King Herod. Wise men from the east came to Jerusalem and asked around, "Where can we find and pay homage to the newborn King of the Jews? We observed a star in the eastern sky that signaled his birth. We're on pilgrimage to worship him." King Herod was pretty upset when he heard that, so he asked the chief priests and teachers of the law where the Messiah was to be born. They told him, "Bethlehem, Judah territory." Then they cited the very words Micah had said. (Matthew 2:1-6)

Messiah would be protected by God. "He gave me speech that would cut and penetrate. He kept his hand on me to protect me. He made me his straight arrow and hid me in his quiver." (Isaiah 49:2) Angels repeatedly appeared to Joseph in dreams to warn him of impending danger.

Messiah would come out of Egypt. Hosea prophesied, "When Israel was only a child, I loved him. I called out, 'My son!' – called him out of Egypt." (Hosea 11:1)

The wise men found Jesus and brought him expensive gifts, including gold. By now, Herod was searching for this usurper. The family of Jesus was in jeopardy. An angel appeared to Joseph in a dream and warned him to "get up. Take the child and his mother and flee to Egypt. Stay until further notice. Herod is on the hunt for this child, and wants to kill him." (Matthew 2:13-15) The gold must have come in handy as they fled.

----------

## *Herod Was Convinced*

It's ironic that King Herod was one person who believed Jesus might be the Messiah. He wasn't happy about the possibility that the prophesied King might have appeared on his watch.

Jeremiah prophesied that there would be great tragedy following the Messiah's birth. "Listen to this! Laments coming out of Ramah, wild and bitter weeping. It's Rachel weeping for her children, Rachel refusing all solace. Her children are gone." (Jeremiah 31:15) Ramah was where Rachel died on her way to Bethlehem.

When Matthew wrote this account, he was convinced it was the fulfillment of prophecy, "Herod, when he realized that the scholars had tricked him, flew into a rage. He commanded the murder of every little boy two years old and under who lived in Bethlehem and its surrounding hills. (He determined that age from information he'd gotten from the scholars)." (Matthew 2:16-18)

Messiah would live in Galilee. Isaiah wrote, "... in the future he will honor Galilee of the nations, by the Way of the Sea, beyond the Jordan—"(Isaiah 9:1 NIV) After Herod died, an angel told Joseph he could return with his family to Israel. Herod's son was now king in Judea, and Joseph was afraid of him. "But then Joseph was directed in a dream to go to the hills of Galilee. On arrival, he settled in the village of Nazareth. This move was a fulfillment of the prophetic words, 'He shall be called a Nazarene.'" (Matthew 2:19-23)

I don't know about you, but we kids lived where our parents lived, and we had no choice in the matter. Is it coincidence that little Jesus was moved from Bethlehem to Egypt and then to Nazareth, and that the prophets had foretold the Messiah making this journey many ages before? Was he able to manipulate Herod into fulfilling the prophecy concerning the slaughter of innocent children in Bethlehem?

Remember those odds the mathematicians came up with? The odds of one person fulfilling just eight of the Messianic prophecies are 1 in 100,000,000,000,000,000. We've already seen more than eight prophecies fulfilled just by the birth and early childhood of Jesus. Is he the Messiah? I'd say yes, 100%.

# A WALK THROUGH SEASONS

"Harvest dance, got me running like a kid throwing leaves up in the air. I see them falling everywhere. Harvest dance, got me playing in the sun, finding wonder after wonder in your world of red and gold. Harvest dance."

~ Amber and Ewald Sutter
Song: *Harvest Dance*
From the album *Collecting the Past*

Lyrics and music by
Amber and Ewald Sutter

## *A Nice Change of Weather*

When we moved to Florida, I never dreamed I'd be happy about turning on the heat in the house. We came in February, the day after an ice storm hit the Philadelphia area. The first breath of warm, muggy air sold me. We had come home! We moved down six months later.

It's difficult for me to refrain from making comments about our wonderful winters when the rest of the country is freezing (note that I just did). My sister Sharon lives in Minneapolis. The temperature was 50 degrees below zero with the wind chill. We had a high of 85. That's a difference of 135 degrees.

Her daughter lives in Alaska, where the temps reached 35 above zero. That's an 85 degree difference from 50 below. It surely seems topsy-turvy, doesn't it? Minneapolis is south of Alaska.

The arctic blast blew into our area overnight. We woke up to temps in the low 40's, with a wind-chill factor in the 20's. Bill canceled his early morning lessons. He'll stay bundled up on the tennis courts all day. It won't reach 60 degrees today.

I'm grateful for the cold! Perpetual summer sounds good in theory, and I'm not complaining about warm weather. God made the seasons for many reasons. I'm convinced that one of them is to help us appreciate the others more.

Those who have seasons, also have spring to look forward to. Our spring arrives right after the cold snap passes through. Summer is back the next day – until the next strong cold front comes in.

In Psalm 147:15-18, we're told, "He sends his command to the earth; his word runs swiftly. He spreads the snow like wool and scatters the frost like ashes. He hurls down his hail like pebbles. Who can withstand his icy blast? He sends his word and melts them; he stirs up his breezes, and the waters flow."

Whatever weather you're enjoying or enduring right now, know that God is in control, that he loves you and that the warmth of his love will never end. Meanwhile, I'm going to enjoy the cool spell.

----------

## *Joyful Noises*

It was our turn to get our street resurfaced, and what a great day for it! The weather was perfect. I had the windows open, and the noise penetrated into every corner of every room right along with the fresh air. How was that good?

It was January, and the windows were open! That was enough to make me want to shout for joy to the Lord! Psalm 100 exhorts us to worship God with gladness and joyful songs.

"Know that the Lord is God. It is he who made us, and we are his; we are his people, the sheep of his pasture. Enter his gates with thanksgiving and his courts with praise; give thanks to him and praise his name." (NIV)

The noise outside gave me the freedom to make a joyful noise inside, even with the windows open! Who could hear me over that din? God did.

I didn't sing very loudly, because my voice was still hoarse from a week of fighting a bad cold. And yet, I praised God because I have a voice, no matter how squeaky or faint or out-of-tune.

The big freeze was over, and our northern loved ones began to enjoy some warmth. They were dealing with a new set of problems because of the thaw, but they didn't freeze to death that winter.

Dyana and Billy completed their move to a new place without incident, in spite of nearby tornadoes, 85 mph straight line winds, and a migraine.

Our kids' homes weren't flooded in spite of more than a foot of rain that fell in just a few hours. I'm thankful that the God we serve hears and answers prayer!

He loves us! Why? "For the Lord is good and his love endures forever, his faithfulness continues through all generations." We're his, our children are his, their children are his, and he faithfully loves us all.

Street-repairing machinery isn't in the same category as praising God, of course, but it reminded me that he's listening to billions of people praying and praising in their own language, and the noise would probably deafen us. His windows are always open, and our noise fills every nook and cranny of his house. Let's make it a joyful noise today!

----------

## *Valentine's Day*

My husband wore a silly grin and kept looking at me as I put on my makeup, as if he anticipated something. I took my time, because I knew he had a surprise for me. It was Valentine's Day. He gave me a colorful bouquet of flowers and a card.

Bill's sweet card was perfect, and completely made my day. He wrote loving words in addition to the printed words that were, somehow, exactly right.

When he shops for a card, he searches and searches until he finds one that says precisely what he wants to express. He does it for everyone he gets a card for. I appreciate and love his thoughtfulness. It's as much a reflection of his generous, loving spirit as his smile. I love you forever, Bill!

The book of John is God's love letter to mankind. Jesus is God's greatest expression of his love and generosity. In fact, the entire New Testament can be distilled into God's reason for sending his Son to us – John 3:16-17.

"For God so loved the world that he gave his one and only Son, that whoever believes in him shall not perish but have eternal life. For God did not send his Son into the world to condemn the world, but to save the world through him." (NIV)

Our belief in Jesus Christ doesn't give us license to condemn others, because he didn't come to condemn anyone. God gave us a way to receive forgiveness and salvation by giving his Son to bridge the gap between God and humanity. Then he told us to show others the way.

God loves you and me forever, and he's given us forever to love him back. Now that's a Valentine!

----------

## *St. Patrick's Day*

To this day, I believe I saw my leprechaun friends help me clean my room and move things around for me when I was a little girl. I saw faeries dancing in the moonlight on the lawn beneath my window.

Perhaps I've always loved Irish music, Irish dancing, and Irish myths because I was named after St. Patrick.

My family is not Catholic, but I'm happy to share a name with the man who brought Christianity to Ireland. Of course, my name is gender-specific, but Pat is Pat in any gender. Did you know Patrick was not Irish?

St. Patrick was born in Britain around 390 A.D. to an aristocratic Christian family. He didn't profess to be a Christian until after he was kidnapped at age 16 and brought to Ireland as a slave. That's where he had an encounter with Christ that changed his life.

He escaped back to Britain, and there felt the Lord leading him right back to Ireland. In spite of many trials he experienced as a missionary to the Irish, he planted the seeds of Christianity throughout the country.

Since there never were any snakes in Ireland because of the cold waters surrounding the island, the "snakes" that St. Patrick drove out would have been symbolic of the pagan practices of his time.

When he died on March 17, 457 A.D., he was mostly forgotten, but God didn't forget him. Centuries later he was honored as Ireland's Patron Saint.

Wearing green is an American custom. The color green is considered unlucky in Ireland since it's the favorite color of the "Good People", or faeries, who supposedly steal children who wear too much green. The faeries I saw as a child weren't interested in stealing me because they were having too much fun dancing.

Isn't it wonderful how much information you can find when you Google "Why do people wear green on St. Patrick's Day?"

I wish you all a very happy St. Patrick's Day. "May the road rise up to meet you, may the wind be always at your back. May the sun shine warm upon your face and the rain fall soft upon your fields, and until we meet again, may God hold you in the palm of his hand." (Irish blessing)

----------

## *April Fool's Day*

Rumor has it that April Fool's Day started as a political joke sometime between 306 and 337A.D. A group of court jesters and fools told Emperor Constantine that they could do a better job of running the empire than he did. The amused emperor allowed a jester named Kugel to be king for a day. Kugel passed an edict calling for absurdity on that day, and it stuck. Apparently, so did the practice of allowing fools to run the government.

*The Merriam-Webster Dictionary* defines a fool as (1) a person who lacks good sense or judgment, or (2) one with a marked propensity or fondness for something. The Bible has a lot to say about both kinds of fools.

Here are some examples: In Proverbs 10:18 "Liars secretly hoard hatred; fools openly spread slander."

In Proverbs 12:15-16: "Fools are headstrong and do what they like; wise people take advice. Fools have short fuses and explode all too quickly; the prudent quietly shrug off insults." I don't know about you, but I have, on occasion, been this kind of a fool.

Here's one we can see openly operating in our society today: "Lady Wisdom builds a lovely home; Sir Fool comes along and tears it down brick by brick." Proverbs 14:1

In 1 Corinthians 1:18-25, we're given a different take on foolishness. "For the message of the cross is foolishness to those who are perishing, but to us who are being saved it is the power of God." Christians look like fools to unbelievers. We're the second kind of fool, with a "marked propensity" and "fondness" for God.

"Where is the wise person? Where is the teacher of the law? Where is the philosopher of this age? Has not God made foolish the wisdom of the world?"

"For the foolishness of God is wiser than human wisdom, and the weakness of God is stronger than human strength."

I'd much rather be considered a fool because I love and follow God, than to be considered a fool for all the wrong reasons, or to be thought of as smart and wise by people who don't know him.

With that, foolish me wishes you fun and blessings on April Fool's Day!

----------

## *Springtime*

Happy Spring! I can feel our northern family's joyful anticipation of warmer weather from here! My bragging rights days will soon be over, as they enjoy the freshness and relief of balmy air and new growth.

When you live in perpetual spring-summer-fall, the coming of spring isn't as sweet as it is up north. I am not complaining! I love it here all year, and I'm genuinely happy for them.

In fact, we suffer through our "allergy" season which peaks in the spring. We sneeze and rub our itchy eyes during the last days we can comfortably open all the windows and air out the house. It smells so fresh between sneezes! Are environmental allergies an indication that we are not in the environment we're created for?

I like how Hebrews 13:14 is worded in the New Living Translation: "For this world is not our permanent home: we are looking forward to a home yet to come." In Philippians 2:30 we're reminded, "But we are citizens of heaven, where the Lord Jesus Christ lives."

I imagine every day in Heaven will be like springtime should be here – with sweet warm breezes, the scent of flowers everywhere – and no sneezing or itching.

----------

## *Palm Sunday*

Some of the neighborhood kids came home from church one Sunday waving palm fronds. I was jealous. We lived in Kentucky where there were no palm trees, so I wanted to know where they got them. It was Palm Sunday, and not one of the few days we attended church.

Palm Sunday is the day we celebrate the triumphal entry of Jesus into Jerusalem before the Passover, where the excited crowd waved fronds and shouted praise. It was a meager foreshadowing of his triumphant return to Earth as King of Kings and Lord of Lords. It's good to be in church to celebrate and anticipate and shout our praise to the coming King.

As I read the Bible one Palm Sunday morning, the Lord impressed on me that it was Psalm Sunday! Here's what I read in Psalm 66:1-6.

"All together now – applause for God! Sing songs to the tune of his glory and set glory to the rhythms of his praise. Say of God, 'We've never seen anything like him!'

"When your enemies see you in action, they slink off like scolded dogs. The whole earth falls to its knees – it worships you, sings to you, can't stop enjoying your name and fame.

"Take a good look at God's wonders – they'll take your breath away. He converted sea to dry land; travelers crossed the river on foot. Now isn't that cause for a song?"

I'll say! I'm so glad we attend church regularly now. Every Sunday is Psalm Sunday, where we can worship and sing and raise our arms and wave the palms of our hands toward God and clap them together in the delight of His presence among us!

Hallelujah! God Rocks! God rules! The King is coming!

----------

## *Easter*

It was Easter weekend, and what better time to read again God's love letter to mankind – the book of John. John introduced us to the Word who was God in John 1:1-18.

"Everything was created through him; … what came into existence was Life, and the Life was Light to live by. The Life-Light blazed out of the darkness; the darkness couldn't put it out."

"The Life-Light was the real thing! Every person entering Life, he brings into Light. He was in the world, the world was there through him, and yet the world didn't even notice. He came to his own people, but they didn't want him. But whoever did want him, who believed he was who he claimed and would do what he said, he made to be their true selves, their child-of-God selves. These are the God-begotten, not blood-begotten, not flesh-begotten, not sex-begotten."

"The Word became flesh and blood, and moved into the neighborhood. We saw the glory with our own eyes, the one-of-a-kind glory, like Father, like Son, generous inside and out, true from start to finish."

"We all live off his generous bounty, gift after gift after gift. We got the basics from Moses, and then this exuberant giving and receiving.

This endless knowing and understanding – all this came through Jesus, the Messiah."

"No one has seen God, not so much as a glimpse. This one-of-a-kind God-Expression, who exists at the very heart of the Father, has made him plain as day."

In John 1:19-34, John the Baptizer recognized who his cousin Jesus really was.

"The very next day John saw Jesus coming toward him and yelled out, 'Here he is, God's Passover Lamb! He forgives the sins of the world! ... I knew nothing about who he was – only this: that my task has been to get Israel ready to recognize him as the God-Revealer ... This is the Son of God."

I pray that you and yours all come to know the One who became God's Passover Lamb, who forgives the sins of the world.

Make him your own, and he will make you his own. Salvation is a free gift from a loving God to a dying world. Believe and receive the Life-Light that dispels and defeats the darkness. Jesus is the Christ, the Messiah, and one day, even the scoffers will know it.

----------

## *When the Time Comes*

Why is the Bible divided between the Old and New Testaments? In my opinion, it should be divided this way: History, Prophecy, Fulfillment, and Future. It's all in there! I read both Old and New Testaments at the same time, because I've found so many links from one to the other. For example:

In Jeremiah 31:31-34 (Old Testament), God said, "'the time is coming when I will make a brand-new covenant with Israel and Judah. It won't be a repeat of the covenant I made with their ancestors when I took their hand to lead them out of the land of Egypt...This is a brand-new covenant that I will make with Israel when the time comes. I will put my law within them – write it on their hearts! – and be their God. And they will be my people. They will no longer go around setting up schools to teach each other about God. They'll know me first-hand, the dull and the bright, the smart and the slow. I'll wipe the slate clean for each of them. I'll forget they ever sinned.' God's decree."

Now jump to the New Testament. You'll find this in all four Gospels, when Jesus met with his disciples for the Passover meal. It would be their last supper together. Here's what he said, in Matthew 26:26-28: "During the meal, Jesus took and blessed the bread, broke it, and gave it to his disciples: 'Take, eat. This is my body.' Taking the cup and thanking God, he gave it to them: 'Drink this, all of you. This is my blood, God's new covenant poured out for many people for the forgiveness of sins.'"

In Jeremiah, God said "When the time comes." That time came when Jesus shed his blood as the sacrificial lamb to atone for our sins, once and for all time. That's the new covenant.

From that day forward, God would write the law of his overwhelming love on the hearts of those who receive his Son as their Savior.

----------

## *Mother's Day*

The grandkids and I love to go to the drive-through animal park in the spring. We get excited about baby giraffes, baby zebras, and baby rhinos. Babies are everywhere! Is it any wonder that we celebrate Mother's Day in the spring?

We wish a Happy Mother's Day to every woman who has ever loved a child, whether hers or not. We know and love precious women who weren't blessed with kids of their own. Instead, they've poured their love into other kids, and in that way, they made them their own.

My aunt and her husband left their life in Germany to follow her sister to the USA because of us children. She wouldn't have loved her own kids more, had she had any. She later married a man with children, and loved them, too. Today, I honor her along with my mom. She's a delight and owns a huge part of my heart.

My dear friend pours her love into children she cares for as their parents go to work. God knows how much her light will influence those kids, long after they've left her care. She won't have to go through adolescence with any of them, so, in a way, I almost envy her. Don't worry, moms of teens, you will survive and thrive, and so will they.

Another dear friend has helped her nieces and nephews through childhood and adolescence. You'd better believe those kids will always love their Auntie.

I've had teachers who were childless, but the children they trained are now making a difference in the world because of their influence. I love and appreciate them and I'm forever grateful to them.

Although some women simply don't want to have their own kids, I believe God intended for all women who do to have children to nurture. "He [the Lord] gives the childless woman a family, making her a happy mother. Praise the Lord!" (Psalm 113:9 NLT)

So Happy Mother's Day to all Foster Moms, Adoptive Moms, Teachers, Aunties, and all women who give their love to children everywhere. And to you Moms who are blessed with your own children, Happy Mother's Day to you, too!

----------

## *Feathered Critters*

Bachelor mockingbirds sing to attract mates. One unattached bird likes the telephone pole in the front yard. He sings his little heart out, one melody after the other. If he were on the reality show, *The Bachelor*, he'd have females flocking around him. If I were a mockingbird, I'd certainly be attracted by his beautiful music.

A red-headed woodpecker attempted to hammer a hole in our metal rain gutter. I can imagine the headache that poor little guy ended up with. He eventually found a nice telephone pole to work on.

Jesus used birds to remind us that God is our provider in Matthew 6:26. "Look at the birds, free and unfettered, not tied down to a job description, careless in the care of God. And you count far more to him than birds."

Ibises are some of my favorite Florida birds. Their long, delicate, pointed beaks aerate the soil while they peck for delicious (pesky) insects. They hunt in flocks, and are mostly white. Our neighborhood flock more closely resembles a bunch of dark and spotted sheep.

They're big birds and look ungainly when they line up on the telephone wires, but they're perfectly balanced and seem delighted to view the world from that high vantage point.

I discovered that we cannot park our minivan directly beneath the wires over our driveway. The Ibises covered the van with white splatter. The only splatter around it appeared to have splashed off the van as it was being used for target practice. I must say, they had good aim. I wonder if they congratulated each other?

----------

## *Four-Legged Critters*

I challenged a squirrel to a territorial battle one morning. He was pretty upset with me. Orchids and other bromeliads thrive in Florida because of our high humidity. It's also great for the skin. During the winter and early spring, humidity can be very low, which is much more comfortable for humans, but not very healthy for orchids. One dry spring day, I took my spray bottle and misted the flowers on the lanai.

Suddenly, a squirrel sat up on a nearby branch of our towering ficus tree and started scolding. It dawned on me that the sound I made squeezing the spray trigger was the same sound squirrels make when they're angry. Pfft, pfft, pfft. The sounds, along with sharp tail twitches, are their way of warning rivals off. Instead of twitching my tail in response, I laughed.

Our resident lizard peeked out from a flower pot and I obliged him with a quick shower. Who knew that God would give me a glimpse of his indescribable greatness in the sound of a squirrel, the scurry of a lizard and a spray bottle?

In Proverbs 8:22-31, we're told that Wisdom was there with God as he created the world. In verses 30-31, Wisdom says, "Day after day I was there, with my joyful applause, always enjoying his company, delighted with the world of things and creatures, happily celebrating the human family."

This member of the human family is, in turn, happily celebrating the God who created such a delightful world. Thank you, Lord!

----------

## Scaly Critters

A critter rustled the papers on Bill's desk behind me. The poor little guy had been there for three days, hidden in Bill's piling system. I have the same system. No one can ever accuse us of having an uncluttered office.

Lizards are as common as birds in Florida. Sometimes, they hide out between our screen door and front door, and we miss them when we come inside, so they scurry in with us.

In Proverbs 30:24-38, we're told, "There are four small creatures, wisest of the wise they are – ants – frail as they are, get plenty of food in for the winter; marmots – vulnerable as they are, manage to arrange for rock-solid homes; locusts – leaderless insects, yet they strip the field like an army regiment; lizards – easy enough to catch, but they sneak past vigilant palace guards."

The writer obviously didn't try to catch a Florida lizard inside the house. They may be wise, but there's nothing for them to eat here, and so we eventually find their remains. I feel sorry for them, and hope to catch them when they're too weak and slow to run away.

Sometimes, God has to wait until we're too weak and slow to run in order to catch us, too. Life is busy and time is short. We scamper around and often hide in fear of whatever we imagine attacking us, and forget to feed on the Word. We starve ourselves until God can cradle us and draw us back to the safety of his presence.

The poor little lizard was stuck in a trash can and couldn't get out, so I caught him and released him under the bushes. He'll eat and survive, and I'll sit down to a satisfying meal in the Word of God.

----------

## All In One Day

It was hot and muggy today. I looked to the east and saw a few puffy clouds laze in a clear, sunny sky. Then I turned to face northwest to see a black and ominous shelf cloud speeding towards me.

Sixty mile-per-hour gusts tore down the street, separating trash cans from their lids and tossing basketball hoops across the road. Horizontal rain soaked lawns and flooded the streets.

In another few minutes, the black sky was east of us. A brilliant double rainbow stood in contrast to the darkness behind it. It was as if the storm had never happened.

This time of year, trees with bare branches are weighed down with clusters of bright yellow spring blossoms. The ground around the thinning sea grape hedges is littered with leaves the colors of fall. Trees clouded with the pale green of new leaves sway next to the dark green trees of full summer. Orange trees blossom and bear fruit at the same time. Hibiscus bushes look like a child's drawing of a tree trunk topped with a perfectly round green circle dotted with large pink flowers.

Although we live near the beach, we rarely go. I don't like sand; but we had visiting family, so we drove along the beach and stopped for a while. The jewel-like aquamarine was almost painfully beautiful - breathtaking. If I can pick the colors of my dream mansion, the floor would be that stunning shade of blue-green.

We watched four kite-boarders race through and jump the waves. As one came back to shore, he launched off an incoming wave and let the kite keep him airborne for about thirty feet. He flew to shore. How joyful that must have felt.

In Psalm 64:9-10, we're told, "Be glad, good people! Fly to God! Good-hearted people, make praise your habit."

I want to fly over aquamarine seas like that young man on his kite-board, only without limits – without tethers. Wings would be okay, Lord. Meanwhile, I'll let my spirit take flight in praise, and wait for that day to come.

----------

## The Scent of God

Our rainy season has finally begun. In this subtropical climate, the seasons are more "dry" and "rainy" than the four seasons most of the country enjoys. I love our dry season (late fall through early spring, normally), with the dry air and cooler temperatures; but it's the rainy season that keeps Florida green and blooming throughout the year.

More rain means less chance of drought and wild fires. More rain makes crops, fruit and farmers happy. Yet, we see the sun every day, even during hurricanes.

The rains come with drama in the afternoons - thunder, lightning, wind, sheets of rain - after it has become almost unbearably hot and humid. They break the heat for a short spell, and clear out quickly, leaving rainbows and a few sun showers behind.

I think of the Creator of these quick Florida storms. In Psalm 97:2, "Bright clouds and storm clouds circle 'round him; right and justice anchor his rule." Beauty and drama surround the God who created them – bright clouds and storm clouds alike.

I love the ozone scent of approaching rain that we get every day. I read a story, once, of a little boy who had gone to Heaven and returned. When he smelled on-coming rain, he exclaimed, "That's what God smells like!" Of course he does.

# A FAMILY OF MISFITS

"Rejoice with your family in the beautiful land of life."

~Albert Einstein

## *From Parents to Grandparents*

Babies, unfortunately, don't come with an instruction manual. We grow in wisdom as they grow in stature, as long as we love them and are willing to learn. Parenting can be the most frustrating job in the world. We don't know what we're doing; we hope we're helping and not hurting; and we want so much for our kids and get impatient with them and with ourselves. Does anyone else relate?

Getting to be grandparents is the reward we've earned for helping our kids to survive childhood and adolescence – and for surviving along with them.

A lot of people have written books on raising children, and there's some wisdom in many of them. I've read a few, but when the kids refused to follow the instructions, I had to rely on the only things that worked.

I cried, prayed, and read the Bible. I shared with friends, relied on my church family, and prayed some more. I made tons of mistakes, did very few things well, and loved, loved, loved my kids – joyfully, painfully and hopefully. God did the rest.

Self-help books aren't the answer to life's challenges, although they can be helpful in letting us know we're not the only ones who behave like that. Only God knows all the answers. He knows our children from before they were born. He knows every moment of their lives, even before they live it. He has a plan and a purpose for each of them, and He'll be with them to carry it out.

"Before I shaped you in the womb, I knew all about you. Before you saw the light of day, I had holy plans for you." (Jeremiah 1:5)

"You saw me before I was born. Every day of my life was recorded in your book. Every moment was laid out before a single day had passed." (Psalm 139:6)

The hope we have is offered to our children and grandchildren, as well. We can trust God. We must trust God. He has a plan for us!

----------

## *Sleepovers and Gram Camp*

Every now and then, Mike and Jenn have a date night, and their children get to enjoy a sleepover at Gramma's and Grampa's.

We get the kids fed and watered, exercised at the park, popcorned and movied, showered and teeth brushed, jammied and settled in for a good sleep. Ashley cries a little, missing her parents, and Anthony comforts her. I remind her that morning comes faster when we're asleep. They eventually drift off, and I'm usually right behind them.

When you have eight children who live in different states and live their own full lives, it isn't easy to coordinate schedules for visits. We manage to get to them, but their visits to us are pretty staggered throughout the year. Bill and I can visit them all in one long trip, but we never expect them to come see us all at the same time.

We know from Proverbs 16:3, to "commit to the Lord whatever you do, and he will establish your plans." (NIV) We made plans to have some of the grandchildren stay with us for a week, and we committed our plans to the Lord.

Dyana and Billy drove all four kids living in one state down to Florida. They left the kids and their minivan here, drove my car home, and I drove the minivan back to them and picked my car up a week later. It was our first Gram Camp.

----------

## *Gram Camp*

I'm amazed at how much God can fit into a week. Here's a recap: Bill had surgery the same day four of our grandkids arrived from up north. Anthony and Ashley joined them at our house and we had our first six-grandkid sleepover, while Grampa tried to rest.

We had pasta fest Friday, a cookout at Mike and Jenn's house on Saturday, pot roast here on Sunday, and then Dyana and Billy started back and left Julian, Gabe, Emery and Bella here for the rest of the week.

The boys spent one night with Mike and Jenn while the girls stayed with us. Then the next night they switched, and then they switched back. What a blessing our kids are! The last night, all six stayed here.

The boys were delightful -- generous and loving and rough-and-tumble with their cousins. The two girls were inseparable, more like sisters than cousins. They wore look-alike bathing suits, played with little dolls that look like them, and sang and danced their way through endless showings of *Teen Beach Movie*.

Bill, who was still recovering and in some measure of pain, took the younger children to see one movie and I took the two older ones to see another at the same time.

Before they came, Bella's step-dad Jeff proposed first to her and then to her mom Andrea. It was the sweetest thing ever! Both accepted, and, while we had the kids, they wasted no time in getting married. Big party to follow!

At the same time, our daughter-in-love Missy lost her father. We grieved with her and prayed together for her family.

We look forward to that day described in Revelation 21:3-5, "Look! Look! God has moved into the neighborhood, making his home with men and women! They're his people, he's their God. He'll wipe every tear from their eyes. Death is gone for good – tears gone, crying gone, pain gone."

We experienced God's strength, love, mercy, healing and comfort -- all in one too-short week for me and too-long week for our loved ones whose dad went home to Heaven. It's a good thing he's given us resilient hearts that can handle love, joy, pain and grief, until that day comes when he moves into the neighborhood.

----------

## Gram Camp Trip Home

It was a sad day when we started the journey north with the four kids who live there, and Gram Camp ended. We girls cried and the boys tried to look tough.

We encountered some torrential tropical downpours through Jacksonville during rush hour, had gray rain and drizzle all day, and passed three accidents where traffic was stop-and-go and maxed out at ten miles per hour for miles and miles. The four kids were amazing!

The twins Julian and Gabe took turns sitting up front with me, and kept me entertained with great conversation about the stories and characters in their video games. We discussed politics, friends, school, and they told me endless jokes and factoids. Emery and Bella shared ear buds to listen to the same music. They talked, laughed, and never complained.

Emery had a bottomless pit that needed constant filling, so we were never without food or water and we took plenty of potty stops. They were delighted with the hotel, which made me delighted with it. I love seeing the world through fresh eyes.

As I drove the long miles, I remembered what I read in Proverbs 3:21-23, "Dear friend, guard Clear Thinking and Common Sense with your life; don't for a minute lose sight of them ... You'll travel safely, you'll neither tire nor trip."

I wonder which of the twins is Clear Thinking, and which is Common Sense? They certainly kept me from getting tired along the way.

I sorely miss them all when I don't have them with me, and I treasure the times we have together. My cup is full. I am so proud of them all.

----------

## *Happy Hearts*

Every child is a beacon of love, joy and hope. I can't imagine life without them, and Bill and I are overjoyed with each and every one of them.

Ashley asked me once about the day I was born. I told her that it was a Sunday and the church bells announced my arrival – not on purpose.

She asked what day she was born. When I told her the date, she gave me an astonished look and said, "Gramma! That's my birthday!" Yep, Sweetheart, it certainly is.

She was deftly playing with a hula-hoop one day. She stopped suddenly, looked at me solemnly and said, "Gramma, you're old." Oh, yes, Darling. From your perspective, I am, indeed.

Anthony is easy-going, with a mischief-maker in there that peeks out of his eyes every now and then. He can push her buttons and get her going until the word "Stop!" drives their Gramma up the wall.

They can so easily make my husband and me laugh, and they'll do the same thing over and over again to keep it going. It was funny the first time. They try so hard because we're easy marks.

Isaiah was describing the coming new Heaven and new Earth when he wrote Isaiah 65:17-25. In verse 23, he said, "For they themselves are plantings blessed by God, with their children and grandchildren likewise God-blessed."

All of our children are doing a wonderful job raising our grandchildren, and Bill and I get to enjoy the fruits of their labor. We love those kids!

----------

## Loyalty is a Mark of Good Parenting

We know our children are raising their kids well when the grandkids are quick to jump to the defense of someone they love.

Bill and I took Anthony and Ashley to the movies to see *Rio 2*. Talking birds and animals were fun for the kids, but Bill and I were impressed with the bright colors and beautiful artistry of the animation.

In the story, two blue spix macaws, who believed they and their chicks were the last of their kind, took their family and set out to find another blue spix rumored to live in the Amazon jungle. They found family, including the little birds' grandfather.

I thought the old bird looked familiar. There was something about the facial expressions; and then he saw the little ones and said, "Call me Pop-Pop!"

I had to laugh! The resemblance to our grandkids' real Pop-Pop was uncanny! I have photos of their other grandfather with many of the expressions the animators captured in their version. Did they use him as a model?

On the way home, I mentioned how much the bird Pop-Pop looked like theirs. Our grandson was occupied by a video game, but Ashley immediately said, "He does not!"

I pointed out the similarities in their faces and expressions. She would have none of it. She was insistent, "That bird does not look like my Pop-Pop!"

I told her I like Pop-Pop, and I wasn't saying anything bad or critical about him.

She then said, rather forcefully, "But Gramma, POP-POP IS NOT BLUE!" Indeed he isn't.

In Proverbs 17:6 we learn, "Children's children are a crown to the aged, and parents are the pride of their children." I'd add to that, "Children who raise loving children are a pride to their parents." We are so blessed!

----------

## *The Prayer of Jabez*

Children are a gift from the Lord. When we're given that gift, it's up to us to love, nurture, train, comfort, and accept them with joy. Families like ours are bushes and hedges rather than trees. They accept and love kids from all backgrounds, races and countries, giving no thought to their bloodlines, or what other people might think.

God loves the variety of his children, or he wouldn't have made them that way. Not one of us is exactly like any other -- not even identical siblings. How amazing is that?

In 1 Chronicles 4:9-10, I bumped into the prayer of Jabez. He was one of many children with a long list of ancestors. What made him unique? I've read it in three versions of the Bible, the NIV, the New King James and my favorite, The Message.

In all of them Jabez was more honorable than his brothers. His mother named him Jabez, which means "Oh, the pain!" because she had a hard labor. She was obviously not thinking clearly. I'll bet his less honorable brothers teased him unmercifully about it. "You're a pain, Jabez!" So what did he do? He cried out to God.

Jabez asked for four things. He asked God to bless him. When we pray, we ask the Lord to bless our loved ones, but how often do we ask him to bless us?

He asked God to expand his tent, or territory – to give him large tracts of land. Today, that would translate into expanding our business, our income, our livelihood, or our homes.

He asked that God's hand would be with him, that he would provide his personal protection. I see that as asking God to do what he does best, while I stay out of the way. When I pray for something specific, I have to work at trusting God to answer in his own way. My tendency is to jump in and try to make it happen, and that is often a recipe for failure.

Finally, he asked God to keep him from harm -- and here is where the versions differ a little. In the NIV, his motive is to be free from pain. In the New King James, he asks to be kept from evil so that he won't cause pain. In The Message, he asks God to keep evil from hurting him.

God gave him what he asked for, just as He gave us what we asked for. I laugh when I see how God has expanded our territory – by adding to our family! Our hearts, not our tents, have grown to a much bigger capacity to make room for them all. Keep them coming, Lord!

# A MISFIT HITS THE ROAD

"Travel not for the destination, but
for the joy of the journey."

~ Sir Joseph Fresco

## *On the Road Again*

If you could choose an age to be forever, what would it be? Many friends post fun tests on Facebook – like what animal would you be, or what color are you, or what mental age are you? I take them for fun. I'm a 12-year-old purple dog who lives in Maine. But if I could choose an age to spend eternity in, it would have to be nineteen.

At nineteen, I took a year off to bum around Europe. I saw the full moon rise over Mount Olympus in Greece. I woke up one morning on a beach surrounded by a flock of warm, smelly sheep, and I hiked up a mountain every day for a week to buy the day's sustenance in a pristine village whose white walls reflected the colors of the sun from sunrise to sunset. I stood at the bow of a ship as dolphins leapt and sped alongside, leading us into the Straits of Corinth.

In London, strangers became good friends. A homeless man led me from pub to pub and introduced me to people who spoke a form of English I did not understand. I shopped at a bazar in Istanbul, admired the gnarled trees under the Eiffel Tower, spent a night at Frankenstein's castle, and experienced much more.

I had no car and very little money, and used my thumb and wits to get around – sometimes with friends and sometimes alone. I was healthy, strong, and fearless, and yet, something significant was missing.

The true richness of life developed after I surrendered my life to Jesus. No adventure is as fulfilling and intriguing as that of following the Lord. The unexpected is all around for us to discover – like this truth I found in Psalm 84:10-12:

"One day spent in your house, this beautiful place of worship, beats thousands spent on Greek island beaches ... All sunshine and sovereign is God, generous in gifts and glory. He doesn't scrimp with his traveling companions. It's smooth sailing all the way with God-of-the-Angel-Armies."

My life-road has dipped into very dark valleys and climbed onto beautifully clear peaks, winding through tangled woods, along fresh streams and through arid deserts. So I choose nineteen, but with all the life-experience God has given me and will continue to give me until he takes me home. Will I look that age in Heaven? It doesn't matter. I'll be with God and my loved ones, and we'll have some whopper stories to share!

----------

## *Still Cruising*

I sat at my kitchen table, on solid ground, and my body thought it was still on board the ship. We had just finished a cruise to the eastern Caribbean, and apparently it was not quite over with. I loved the gentle rocking and slept wonderfully at sea.

We've enjoyed three cruises along with dear friends and family, and have loved every one of them. This time we went by ourselves on the longest cruise, so far. Bill was concerned he'd spend the last few days longing to get home and get active. I didn't know what to expect, but was determined to live in the moment and be thankful for whatever God sent our way.

As it turned out, we met wonderful people and loved hearing their interesting stories. Conversation flowed around the dining table each evening. I learned to say a few words in Turkish from our table attendant.

Bill learned how to play Bocce and won two out of three games against experienced and enthusiastic players. He played a table tennis tournament partnered with an Indian pediatrician who wore a black turban. They won the silver medal in a final nail-biter game. We enjoyed a Salsa lesson and he learned Cha-Cha with another partner because I had lost track of time and forgot to meet him there.

At night we saw some wonderful dance, acrobatic and musical performances. They have the best entertainers on cruises! I sat on the veranda and looked at more stars than we can see in our sky. God sent a few meteors streaking through the night for me. As we entered and left the ports, I watched the land slide smoothly by and enjoyed the sensation of effortless movement.

We're told in Psalm 89:8-9, "God-of-the-Angel-Armies, who is like you, powerful and faithful from every angle? You put the arrogant ocean in its place and calm its waves when they turn unruly." We watched it happen. We were blessed with rough seas the first day and calm seas thereafter. We headed into an ominous dark squall line, had ten minutes of rain, and sailed right back into sunshine.

More often than I could keep track of, I'd pause and think, "I can't believe we're here, in this moment. Thank you, Lord!" Back at my solid, steady kitchen table, I remembered the week, and said again, "I can't believe I'm here, in this moment in time. Thank you, Lord!"

----------

## *An Island Divided*

Memory is a funny thing. The first thing that came to mind one morning was our recent visit to St. Maarten, where we had stopped on our last cruise.

"Leon the Lover" was our tour guide. He was a handsome man, tall and strong-looking with dark chocolate skin and kind eyes. No one asked him how he got his name.

We boarded the blessedly air-conditioned bus, and he deftly maneuvered through traffic and narrow roads from the Dutch side of the island to the French side. He talked all the way about the evolving political situation involving the French (in France) and their ignorance of island ways. It seemed he needed to vent, and we, a busload of tourists, were all ears.

We admired the views from the hilly road, tried to capture the multiple shades of blue and aquamarine in the water down below with our cameras, and thought about the people living on the island. We passed houses of many hues with gardens and yards in various states of beauty and disrepair. We stopped at a flea market spread out at a port filled with sailboats and yachts.

I wanted to dance through the abundant colors of dresses, scarves, shawls, shirts, paintings, crafts, jewelry – but it was oppressively hot. I watched the faces of the vendors as they hawked their wares, and sensed unhappiness. Perhaps it came from heat and exhaustion or perhaps it was their concern over the future of the island and the depressed economy on the French side.

Back in the air-conditioned bus – sometimes it's awesome to be a tourist – we learned that it was Leon's 72nd birthday. We wished him

Happy Birthday, and prayed that God works everything out for his benefit and for the good of all the islanders.

"Among leaders who lack insight, abuse abounds, but for one who hates corruption, the future is bright." Proverbs 28:16. I want to say to Leon, "Love God! Look up! You hate corruption and your future is bright!"

----------

## *Traveling Eyebrows*

A recent television commercial mentioned little-known facts. By now, everyone who watches TV knows that honey does not spoil and Mona Lisa has no eyebrows. Call me Mona Lisa.

Since my eyebrows seem to have migrated south, I've been learning to draw in the shapes I like where they once sat firmly above my eyes. On some days, I manage perfectly arched eyebrows, just the width I like them. Usually I'll get one higher, one straighter, one thicker or one curved, and that's just in one try. The other usually doesn't match, and I end up trying again. It continues to be a learning process.

So there we were, on a slightly rocking bouncy ship, buffeted by heavy seas and a strong wind. First, one eyebrow crawled crookedly up towards a sudden drop, while the other curved drunkenly toward the apex. Wipe off – start over. One was finally the way I liked it. The other stubbornly wandered into my ear.

Would it matter if the rocking stopped for a minute? I don't think so.

Half a tissue box later, I finally achieved two matching streaks atop my eyes – as long as you didn't look too closely. Bangs cover a multitude of defects. I'm grateful to God that I don't wear lipstick!

Who said growing old can be fun? Oh, wait. I did. In the words of King Solomon in Ecclesiastes 1:2: "Vanity of vanities," says the Preacher; "Vanity of vanities, all is vanity." (NKJV) I agree. Mona Lisa looks just fine without eyebrows. Why not me?

----------

## *The Floor In My Mansion*

The color of the shallows in the Caribbean seemed impossible. The sea looked as if it was illuminated from below, and the jewel-brilliant aquamarine almost hurt my eyes, even as I couldn't get enough of it!

The sea around the islands is God's living stained-glass window. Depending on the topography below the water, the colors are sharply outlined and contrasted. A beam of green brilliance is framed by streaks of purple that fade to royal blue. I've asked God to design the floor in my mansion with those colors. You're all welcome to visit me there!

In Revelation 21:12-27, we're given a glimpse into the New Jerusalem that will descend out of Heaven. Here's what the Apostle John saw:

"The City shimmered like a precious gem, light-filled, pulsing light…The wall was jasper, the color of Glory, and the City was pure gold, translucent as glass. The foundations of the City walls were garnished with every precious gem imaginable: the first foundation jasper, the second sapphire, the third agate, the fourth emerald, the fifth onyx, the sixth carnelian, the seventh chrysolite, the eighth beryl, the ninth topaz, the tenth chrysoprase, the eleventh jacinth, the twelfth amethyst. The twelve gates were twelve pearls, each gate a single pearl. The main street of the City was pure gold, translucent as glass." I'd like to see the oysters that made those pearls!

Here's the kicker: "Only those whose names are written in the Lamb's Book of Life will get in."

The Book of Life is mentioned in the Old Testament as well as the New. (Psalm 69:28, NIV) (Daniel 12:1-2, MSG)

I believe the brilliance of Caribbean waters is a mere shadow of the life to come. When we get there, our eyes will be able to handle it, because the Light of God will illuminate every part of our hearts and spirits. Jewel-bright chrysoprase aquamarine floors shot through with emerald, amethyst and sapphire…. I want my name in that Book!

----------

## *Off To See The Family*

No road is as lovely as the one that leads to loved ones. The road that leads home after a long trip is a close second! In one trip we had the pleasure of seeing eighteen of our widely-spread-out grandkids – from the newest to the oldest, who will graduate high school next year. Where does the time go?

We arrived home last evening, and I was itching to see Anthony and Ashley again. I should have been frantically trying to catch up. The washer and dryer were going, bags were unpacked and the mail was sorted and waiting for my attention. Around 400 photos needed cropping and red-eye removal before I posted some of them. Yet, there I was, back at the keyboard, happily remembering our dear friends and family and our beautiful, brilliant and endlessly amusing grandkids.

Our first stop was in North Carolina, where some of our best friends always welcome us like family. "Just as lotions and fragrance give sensual delight, a sweet friendship refreshes the soul." (Proverbs 27:9)

We met our newest grandson Jack, and later our new granddaughter Rosy, and my heart officially melted into a puddle.

We have five grandchildren in North Carolina: one girl and four boys. Bella has skipped ahead in school and will be attending an engineering school where she'll be able to simultaneously get a middle to high school education and earn college credits. Her baby brother Jack has an amazing big sister to look up to.

Julian and Gabe are learning Japanese together, from the computer. They can read one of three sets of symbols used in Japanese writing. When Gramma was obsessed with James Cameron's *Avatar*, they taught themselves the fictional Navii language.

Emery isn't interested in learning a new language. He's an artist, and we bought one of his paintings from an art auction. It hangs in our living-room gallery, and I point it out to everyone. Did I mention our grandchildren are brilliant?

"I'm thanking you, God, from a full heart. I'm writing the book of your wonders. I'm whistling, laughing and jumping for joy; I'm singing your song, High God." (Psalm 9:1-2) Technically, I can't whistle, and there is no book written that can hold God's wonders. The whistle is there in my mind, and God's wonders fill my heart.

----------

## *Heading to Philly*

We recently traded a sedan for a mini-van. My husband's back is much happier with his driving now that he has a seat that's right for him. He did all the driving through several traffic backups and over the pot-holed, ridiculous roads around Philadelphia.

I can hardly wait until someone figures out how strange socks show up in clothes dryers at the same time single socks disappear. Once they do that, they'll know how teleportation works and we can visit our loved ones without the torture of pot holes or long exhausting drives. But then, we'd miss the beauty of the trip, too.

Mike and Missy graciously put us up, right in the middle of the kids' end-of-school-year activities and packing to move a week later. We have three families and our favorite water ice cafe in the Philadelphia area.

Getting together with everyone was a miracle, considering their crazy work, school and sports schedules. We enjoyed two park days, one with the entire gang, and three trips to get treats we can't get here. Megan graduated into middle-school, Jayna played a softball game, and all six grandkids swam in Renée's and Gary's tropical oasis pool. Jane, Jayna, Jennica, Julia and Megan acted more like sisters than cousins. The only boy JayJay, the baby at 18 months, was a little motor on legs. Every time his mom, Lana, set him down, his legs started running!

Grand-parenting is absolutely the best stage of life there is! I almost envy the long-lived folks in the Old Testament, who had hundreds of years to enjoy the generations of kids in their family. I say "almost" because we do look forward to the life to come, where we won't have to drive to see everyone, and where teleportation is probably commonplace.

God invented grand-parenthood because he loves us. "As high as heaven is over the earth, so strong is his love for those who fear him. As far as the sunrise is from sunset, he has separated us from our sins. As parents feel for their children, God feels for those who fear him." (Psalm

103:11-13). I'm convinced he didn't intend to leave out "As grandparents feel for their grandkids..." in that passage. Our hearts are full.

----------

## To The Nation's Capital

The traffic around Washington, D.C. was as bad as Philadelphia traffic. Did I ever mention that I don't care for big cities? If our hearts weren't there, we'd probably never go. Yet, there we were, following our hearts, and were pleasantly surprised when we arrived at our daughters' home. We hadn't visited since they moved in.

Tina and Beth live in a stately old neighborhood, surrounded by a monastery, a convent, and the nearby Catholic University. Trees, flowers, lawns and Victorian style houses line the streets. They are doing a beautiful job restoring their home; and they're doing a great job parenting their sweet little girl.

My heart melted again when I held our baby granddaughter Rosy for the first time. What is it about the solemn look and sudden smiles that draw and keep our attention focused on our little ones? A baby smudges the lines that define us by our choices and beliefs and builds bridges of understanding and care. Love takes on a deeper, more expansive meaning for us. We come closer to understanding God's extravagant, generous, inclusive love. What a gift!

We thank the Lord for our kids. Our conversations -- with humor, understanding and acceptance -- proved we share a lot of common ground. We have different approaches to the concerns we share, but we care deeply for others and for each other.

I took dozens of photos around the monastery grounds, surprised to find such a wealth of nature in the city. We ate at a tiny Italian restaurant, where four adults and a baby sat around a table the size of a chess board. Delicious! We're sad that we had so little time to spend with them, but they had to get to work the next day, and we had more family to see.

This one's for Tina and Beth: "Is there anyone around who can explain God? Anyone smart enough to tell him what to do? ... Everything comes from him, everything happens through him; everything ends up in him." (Romans 11:34-35) Sometimes we just have to take that leap of faith.

----------

## *Into the Mountains*

The trip to Knoxville, Tennessee took us over a road winding around mountains and through valleys – a little like life. It was beautiful, with some traffic obstacles along the way.

Our firstborn grandchild Cayla was also the first to be heading into her senior year in high school. Their mom Laura home-schools Cayla and her brother Kyle. They belong to to a co-op of multi-talented parent-teachers who have provided a rich and varied educational experience for all the kids. We caught them between summer camp activities and a mission trip.

She is full of grace; he is perpetual motion. They get along better than any siblings I've ever known! We went with Laura, John and the kids to a remote little church where they performed three dances they'll be doing in street ministry. During one jump, Kyle jumped so high we thought he'd fly off the stage, and all the kids gasped! He has springs for legs!

When we arrived at our home after two weeks of traveling, my husband took one look at me and said, "You're all tripped-out, aren't you?"

I wonder, sometimes, whether God gets all "tripped-out?" In Psalm 84:5-7 we learn, "…how blessed all those in whom you live, whose lives become roads you travel. They wind through lonesome valleys, come upon brooks, discover cool springs and pools brimming with rain! God-traveled, these roads curve up the mountain, and at the last turn – Zion! God in full view!"

Our lives are roads that God travels! For humans, it's as exhausting as it is exhilarating. Thank God he never tires of traveling with us! As you travel your own roads, we wish you safety on the trip, and God's presence with you always.

----------

## *On the Road with Mom*

As usual, I prayed for traveling mercies as I headed out to visit Mom. To get to her house, I take the Florida turnpike south to Alligator Alley (only once have I seen any gators along there, and then there were hundreds of them!), cross the state and head up I75 heading north. It takes from two and a half to three hours, and it's usually a pleasant trip, other than an occasional thunderstorm along the way. That day's weather was unusual. I had non-stop rain all the way across.

I like rain. It makes the grass and trees and flowers happy. This rain fed the Everglades and probably made a lot of aligators happy. There were no tropical downpours, no lightning storms, no wind storms, and no flooding; just rain. That is a traveling mercy I'm grateful for!

Mom and I took a short road trip together. First, we headed a few miles north, where some friends gathered for a business event. Mom enjoyed meeting everybody. We stayed at the hotel and went to bed after the event.

Sometime during the wee hours of the morning, I heard repeated slamming and saw a light turn on and off near the door to the hallway. I sat up, disoriented, and heard my mom's voice saying, "Ach, du lieber Zeit...." which is her expression of extreme annoyance.

I jumped up and found her trying to open the door over and over again. The safety bar was engaged and wouldn't let her out, but she was making quite a racket trying!

"Are you attempting to escape, Mom?" I asked, as I pushed the door closed and stood in front of it.

She glared at me and said, "Why won't the bathroom door open?"

"It's the wrong bathroom, Mom," I answered. Life with my mother is never dull.

----------

## *Crossing the Everglades*

Mom and I drove along the Tamiami Trail, a two-lane road that crosses the Everglades. With swamp on the left and swamp on the right, interrupted by an occasional air-boat or gator exhibit, it cuts across the Miccosukee Reservation.

We stopped at a chamber of commerce building to get out and stretch a little. An information desk curved along the far wall, and postcards and travel brochures sat in a display on the side.

A man sat at a card table in the corner, painting flowers on sand dollars. He wore a bracelet full of claws and sharp teeth and looked a little gruff, so my curiosity compelled me to strike up a conversation. I bought a painted sand dollar and asked if he was the artist who created the stunning drawings and water-colors tacked up on the wall. "Yes, Ma'am," he said quietly.

I wish I had taken a photo. One was a panther on the hunt, yellow laser-focused eyes, muscles bunched for the attack, coming directly at me. The power of the cat made my heart pound. A water color of an African Grey and a Macaw on a branch was taped next to it. I asked about the bracelet and his drawings. Then, as if my interest sparked something in him, he pulled out a portfolio.

I gasped when I saw his pen and ink drawing of Jesus, head bowed under a crown of thorns. "Are you a believer?" I asked.

"I saw him," he said softly. He told me he'd died in a severe car accident. He found himself walking along a beach, with Jesus walking next to him. Jesus talked to him for a while and then said, "Son, you have to go back." He woke up in the hospital.

"That's when I drew this," he said. And then he gave it to me. I wasn't going to accept it if he hadn't told me he had the original at home. I offered to buy the beautiful print from him, but he refused. Mom and I left that stop feeling exceedingly blessed. We felt God's watchful eye on us, and thanked him for the gift of meeting James.

"Come, bless God, all you servants of God! You priests of God, posted to the night watch in God's shrine, lift your praising hands to the Holy Place and bless God. In turn, may God of Zion bless you – God, who made heaven and earth!" (Psalm 134) Praise God, who made the Everglades and everyone in them!

----------

## *Know When To Stop*

There are two things I've learned from Mom, Dad and God: God blesses those who help others; and you'd better listen to those in authority over you. Mom exemplified a life of generosity. Bill's mom, too, is a giver. Neither will ever amass any wealth on earth, but I can't wait to see their mansions in Heaven! As for the "listen" part, Mom and Dad were no slouches in the discipline department. Neither is God. I've learned to hear and obey.

Mom and I continued along the Tamiami Trail and were soon praying that there might be a restaurant somewhere along the way. It was pretty desolate and devoid of any food establishments along that stretch.

We passed a man bent under a loaded knapsack walking in our direction on the opposite side of the road. As soon as I drove past, God told me to offer him some water.

"But, Lord, he's way back there and there's no place to turn around!" I said, thinking I should be excused because the swamp bumped right up against the road. Oh, boy. My insides began to quake and the voice in my head became very insistent. "Give water to that guy! Now!"

The road suddenly widened after a narrow bridge, and I flipped the minivan around and headed back. The young man graciously accepted the water Mom handed to him out the window and then I knew. "Water" is God's code word for "Ride". When he settled in the van, he told us the most amazing story!

"I'm on a Faith Walk," he announced. "I'm a minister, and God has kept me on the road for quite a while. I've just walked from Naples, and it's taken me two and a half days to get this far." You can imagine the conversation that took off from there. What a launching point!

Zachary Smith started his walk in Seattle, Washington. He hasn't had to walk the whole way, because God told him He'd give him divine appointments with people who would help him. God told Zach he was never to hitchhike or to ask anybody for anything. He was to learn to depend solely upon the Lord for all his needs.

When God leads someone along that difficult a road, there's a strong purpose behind it. Zachary Smith may very well be a prophet (although you won't hear that from him).

"They wandered from country to country, camped out in one kingdom after another; but he didn't let anyone push them around, he stood up for them against bully-kings: 'Don't you dare touch my anointed ones, don't lay a hand on my prophets.'" (1 Chronicles 16:22)

----------

## *God Wasn't Finished With The Water*

Mom, Zach and I were happily talking about the Lord and Zach's journeys when we passed a man trudging, barefoot, along the road. He was shirtless with a deep tan and mussed black hair. Guess what the Lord told me to do? "Offer that man some water."

I pulled over and waited for him to catch up. I got out of the car with a bottle of water in hand and asked where he was going. He smiled and pointed forward. By now, I understood God's code, and offered him a ride.

The tanned guy looked like a Native American and didn't seem to understand much – or at least, he wasn't sharing much. Mom whispered to me, "He's running away from his family." Her whisper is more like a stage whisper – loud and clear. We found out his name is Ray, he has four kids, was baptized and "respects" Jesus. Perhaps "respect" means more in Miccosukee than it does in English. When we asked where he was going, he mumbled something unintelligible. We discovered later that he'd been walking in the wrong direction for the destination he had in mind.

After ten miles or so, we found the one and only eatery along Tamiami Trail. We stopped for lunch at the Miccosukee Restaurant. Zach ate heartily, sampled some gator bites, and carried on a great conversation with us. Ray drank a soda and went outside to wait. Mom treated us all and we piled back in the van for the last twenty miles.

As soon as we got to the gas station at the turn-off, Ray took off. We prayed he found a ride back to the town he was trying to get to, and back to his family. We prayed with Zach, loaded him up with more water and a few provisions, and parted ways.

We're told in Hebrews 13:2: "Be ready with a meal or a bed when it's needed. Why, some have extended hospitality to angels without every knowing it!"

"Do not forget to show hospitality to strangers, for by so doing some people have shown hospitality to angels without knowing it." (NIV)

My Mom taught me the meaning of hospitality when I was young and brought countless hitchhikers home with me for a meal and a place to sleep. I have no doubt some were angels. This time, we might have helped a prophet of God along the way. God is amazing!

----------

## Mysteries Abound

Mysteries are all around us. When we told Zach we were heading to Coral Castle, he asked why. I told him I had seen a program about it on *Ancient Aliens*. He asked me why I, a Christian woman, would watch such a program. He opened a can of worms, and worms started crawling out faster than I could stuff them back in.

First I assured him that what I was about to say in no way negates my belief in Creator God and in his Son Jesus Christ. The Word of God is full of mysteries. Visitations from the Angelic realm were common. Ezekiel's visions; the Nephilim who were the offspring of the "sons of God" and the "daughters of men"; New Jerusalem descending from the sky – are some of the examples of mysteries and visitations we have no real explanation for.

I believe God is far bigger than we can imagine him to be. Isaiah 55:8-9 says this: "'I don't think the way you think. The way you work isn't the way I work.' God's decree. 'For as the sky soars high above earth, so the way I work surpasses the way you work, and the way I think is beyond the way you think."

In the NIV it goes like this: "'For my thoughts are not your thoughts, neither are your ways my ways,' declares the Lord. 'As the heavens are higher than the earth, so are my ways higher than your ways and my thoughts than your thoughts.'"

I never believed the Pyramids were built by a gazillion slaves hauling tons of rock up to place in the exact spot, with the exact measurements needed to create the monument we see today. I don't believe the Aztecs built their pyramids in the high Andes using llamas and primitive tools, and I don't believe a 100 pound, five-foot guy built the Coral Castle by himself with hand-made tools, at night, without some knowledge we've either lost or haven't been given the secret to.

Did aliens give humanity the secret of anti-gravity? Did God? Who knows for sure, other than Ed, who built Coral Castle and took the secret to the grave with him?

God telling me to "offer water" to Zach and Ray is a mystery. Who am I to hear such clear direction from God? Why and how did God put them in our path at that exact place and time? I'm no different from you. It's not about you and me. God has mysterious ways.

----------

## Many Gifts

Zach told us about his travels and the people who have helped him along the way. Some were Christian, some not. Among the Christians, some were charismatic, some not. Some held doctrines that he wasn't familiar with or doesn't agree with. He's kept an open mind and allowed God to help him discern what's true and what isn't. He said he'd never heard anything like what I was telling him! I wonder how he'll classify it.

I love what Paul said in 1 Corinthians 12:4-11, especially the way it's worded in The Message:

"God's various gifts are handed out everywhere, but they all originate in God's Spirit. God's various expressions of power are in action everywhere; but God himself is behind it all. Each person is given something to do that shows who God is: Everyone gets in on it, everyone benefits.

"All kinds of things are handed out by the Spirit, and to all kinds of people! The variety is wonderful: wise counsel, clear understanding, simple trust, healing the sick, miraculous acts, proclamation, distinguishing between spirits, tongues, interpretation of tongues. All these gifts have a common origin, but are handed out one by one by the one Spirit of God. He decides who gets what and when."

What God opens my mind to may be different from where God is leading you. He knows the plans he has for you, and they're not the same as mine. In Zach's case, God has a purpose for his life that may be far greater than his purpose for mine. I'm fine with that! Zach doesn't watch *Ancient Aliens* because it's irrelevant to his walk.

People think I'm crazy for my wandering imagination, and that's fine with me because this is my walk – and I'm enjoying it. God is with me. So walk with God, and enjoy the journey he has you on!

# A MISFIT'S JOURNEY THROUGH FEAR

"You gain strength, courage, and confidence by every experience in which you really stop to look fear in the face. You must do the thing which you think you cannot do."

~ Eleanor Roosevelt

## *Fear*

Lightning struck outside the house. There were few clouds around, no rain, no storm that I was aware of, and yet, there it was! Lightning. That close. I nearly jumped out of my own skin. Was it frightening? Naturally!

One Sunday, Pastor talked about fear. How many times is "fear not", or something along those lines, mentioned in the Bible?

Some say it's 365 times, or one per day. Does it matter how many times we find "fear not" in the Bible, or is it enough that God cares enough to assure us that we need not fear anything as long as we fear him?

I've been afraid many times. The lightning struck a little fear into my heart. I was afraid each time the kids got hurt, when someone I love was gravely ill, and when I didn't know how I'd pay the bills.

What is fear? I've heard the acronym: False Evidence Appearing Real. For most of us, fear might show up as worries about something that hasn't happened yet. Aren't we wired to fight or flee when confronted with real danger? Aren't there things we should be afraid of? The Bible says we should fear God! Why?

Paul told us in Romans 11, "Make sure you stay alert to these qualities of gentle kindness and ruthless severity that exist side by side in God." God is generously extravagant in love with qualities of gentle kindness, but he is also ruthlessly severe. He's the Judge as well as the Father, and so to fear God is to have a healthy respect for and awe of the One who created the universe and keeps it going.

So what happens when God reaches down and confronts us? I wonder how I'd react if he or one of his warrior angels suddenly appeared in front of me. I imagine I would freeze and be unable to breathe, much less move, but, if the first thing he said to me was "Don't be afraid," everything would change. What did others do when they were in that situation?

----------

## *Don't Be Afraid*

I was in the passenger seat of a two-seater Cessna, piloted by a friend who'd logged many hours in small planes. A cross-wind buffeted the tiny aircraft as we came in for a landing. It appeared to me that we were about to hit the runway sideways, and my side would be the first to make impact. I visualized doing cartwheels when the wingtip made contact with the ground.

"Don't be afraid," my pilot friend said as I prayed out loud. He skillfully straightened out the plane at the last possible second for a smooth landing.

The first time I read those words was in Genesis 15, before Abram's name was changed to Abraham. He'd had some adventures up to that point. "After all these things, this Word of God came to Abram in a vision. 'Don't be afraid, Abram. I'm your shield. Your reward will be grand!'"

This is where God told Abram he would have a son. He told him his descendants would be as numerous as the stars. God would give him the lands he'd mapped out for him. This was where God made his covenant with him and his descendants. Because Abram believed him, God declared him "Set-Right-With-God." I imagine as soon as God said, "Don't be afraid, Abram," the fear just drained out of him.

God has, in fact, spoken the same words to each of us. We have the same Word that appeared to Abram in the vision.

The Apostle John described Jesus in John 1:1-2, "The Word was first, the Word present to God, God present to the Word. The Word was God, in readiness for God from day one."

So today, because of Jesus, we don't have to be afraid, either. I hear you, Lord!

----------

## *Fear of What God Might Do*

My firstborn was just a baby when the doctor discovered an abnormality in her eye. He scared me to death with dire predictions of what it could be and that she might lose the eye.

Her first surgery, at age four months was unsuccessful, so she went in again four months later. My fear and sense of helplessness overwhelmed me. I knew nothing about God, but I was convinced he was going to take my baby away.

Can you imagine the fear that the Hebrews felt when the well-armed Egyptian army came after them? They were convinced that God led them out of Egypt just to kill them off. In Exodus 14, God had not yet given them the Law, so they knew nothing about him.

Moses knew him, though, and he told the people, "Don't be afraid. Stand firm and you'll see the deliverance the Lord will bring you today… The Lord will fight for you; you need only to be still."

God's angel, who'd been leading the Israelites, moved to their rear and kept the Egyptians at bay until the next day, when God parted the sea for the Hebrews and drowned the pursuing army. "And when the Israelites saw the great power the Lord displayed against the Egyptians, the people feared the Lord and put their trust in him."

After my daughter's second surgery, she and I were alone in her hospital room on the third floor, cuddling in a chair near the only door into the room. I glanced up toward the windows on the wall opposite the door, and two men sat on chairs under the window. They nodded, smiled and didn't speak, but my heart heard "Do not fear." I glanced down at my daughter's sweet face and then back to the men, but they had vanished, leaving a sense of deep peace and calm.

Her eye was saved, and the hospital zeroed out the huge medical bill. I didn't meet the Lord until nearly two years later, but I placed my trust in him the moment he sent two angels to reassure me that my baby would be fine.

God loves us even before we know who he is. Sometimes, we're powerless to change our circumstances and all he asks is that we be still and let him be God.

----------

## Surrounded by God's Army

I saw angels when my baby had surgery. I saw a swirling orb of color when my Dad died, and had the distinct impression it was his angelic escort to Heaven. On the Sunday we first entered the building that would become our home church, I sensed giant angels lining the walls, worshipping God with us. I might have doubted my sanity, too, had it not been for Elisha and his servant in 2 Kings 6:8-23.

You could say Elisha was the ultimate source of intelligence for the king of Israel when the king of Aram waged war against Israel. Aram's king was convinced there was a spy in his ranks, because Israel knew about Aram's every move. One of his men told the king it was Elisha, who even knew what the king had talked about in private.

When Aram's king found out Elisha was in Dotham, he sent horses, chariots and many men to surround Dotham at night. The next morning, Elisha's servant was shocked to see the forces arrayed against them.

In verses 16-18, Elisha told his servant, "Don't worry about it – there are more on our side than on their side." Then he prayed, "O God, open his eyes and let him see." And God showed the servant what Elisha saw by faith – the whole mountainside full of horses and chariots of fire surrounding him and Elisha.

Elisha, like the Pied Piper, led the enemy army into a trap. He didn't let the king of Israel harm any of them. He fed them a huge feast and sent them home. Aram didn't bother Israel any more.

This story reminds me of something Jesus said. After his resurrection, he appeared to some of his disciples, who later told Thomas he'd been there. Thomas, like Elisha's servant, wanted to see Jesus with his own eyes. He wanted proof it was really Jesus and not some imposter. Jesus later came to him and said, in John 20:29, "So, you believe because you've seen with your own eyes. Even better blessings are in store for those who believe without seeing."

Not everyone sees or senses angels, and it's been a couple thousand years since anyone has physically touched Jesus. Nevertheless, Elisha showed us, as well as his servant, that we are surrounded by God's angel armies. Jesus assured us that we're blessed because we know him by faith. So, what do we have to be afraid of?

----------

## *Moving Into the Unknown*

Our military family moved every time Dad got orders to report to a new post. Dad went ahead of us and began his new duties, and Mom followed with the family and furniture. They obeyed those orders without question.

My parents rode herd on five kids. We had no idea how difficult it was to uproot, pack quickly, and move to an unfamiliar location with all our worldly goods. Mom did a great job of helping us see it as an adventure and involving us in the process. I have the greatest admiration for the spouses of military people, who have to think of countless details every time they move and still carry on with parenting, work and life.

In Genesis 46, Jacob, a.k.a. Israel, was faced with moving his family to Egypt at Joseph's insistence. That included his sons, their wives, the children, all his servants, herds, tents and goods. By this time, he was getting old, and it's doubtful that he wanted to make the journey.

God spoke to him, "Jacob! Jacob!" I imagine he was a bit hard of hearing by then, so God had to call his name to get his attention. "I am the God of your father. Don't be afraid of going down to Egypt. I'm going to make you a great nation there. I'll go with you down to Egypt; I'll also bring you back here. And when you die, Joseph will be with you; with his own hand he'll close your eyes." It all happened just as God had promised.

Mom didn't hear God tell her to not be afraid to go somewhere new, at least not then. He didn't promise to make her kids a great nation, but he did promise her that he would never leave her nor forsake her.

Her kids have all become members of the body of Christ. Dad died peacefully with Mom and a couple of his children at his bedside. Mom is still alive, and ready to go wherever God leads her, and we kids have learned that life with God is an adventure to be involved in, and not something to fear.

----------

## *Strangers In Strange Lands*

My first husband and I were married in Germany. I'd been in Europe around fifteen years. I loved it there, and wasn't looking forward to moving to the United States. His family lived in New Jersey, directly across the Hudson River from Manhattan. There was nothing in my experience to prepare me for the big city, and everything I'd ever heard of it frightened me. I very nearly let him go without me.

Imagine how the Israelites felt, in Numbers 14, when the twelve leaders were chosen to explore Canaan, and came back with tales of giants and well-fortified cities. Joshua and Caleb tried to turn the tide of fear when they said,

"The land we walked through and scouted out is a very good land – very good indeed. If God is pleased with us, he will lead us into that land, a land that flows, as they say, with milk and honey. And he'll give it to us. Just don't rebel against God! And don't be afraid of those people."

We know the story. The people didn't listen. The luscious grapes and stories of beautiful, rich land did nothing to allay their fear of the obstacles they faced. They wandered in the wilderness until their generation died off -- except for Caleb and Joshua. Those two faithful men led the Israelites into the same land they could have been living in for the past forty years, if they'd only listened.

I'm happy to report that I listened to my husband and moved to New Jersey. The New York skyline was stunning from our side of the river, and New York City had much more to offer than I'd ever imagined. We lived in a Cuban barrio, and I learned Spanish and fell in love with the people, the culture, the music and the food.

Best of all, I met the Lord Jesus Christ in a little church a few blocks from our apartment. If I had chosen to stay in Europe, I might have had to wander in the wilderness much longer before I found my way to God. Only he knows.

Fear can paralyze us, if we let it. I've found that life is an adventure, and whether we know him or not, God is there, leading us on pathways that just might have a few delightful surprises along the way. Don't be afraid. God has this.

----------

## *Leave the Judgment to the Lord*

It's been years since my first husband and I split up. We've both found happiness since then, and all the garbage from those terrible days has been flushed out. I learned much about God's faithfulness while we were in the middle of it, but the lessons were hard.

Divorce is terrible, even when it's amicable, especially where children are involved. I will always regret the pain and damage we did to the kids. There are repercussions, even today, and yet I see God move in their lives and lead them on their own paths to life in him, and I trust him with them.

In Deuteronomy 1, Moses reminded the Israelites of their history. He retold the story of how the judges were assigned to mitigate disputes among the people, and he said to the judges, "Don't be impressed by big names. This is God's judgment you're dealing with."

Later, he retold the story of how God led them to the land in front of them, and how Caleb and Joshua were the only ones with faith to take the land. Now there they were again, forty years later, at the same place.

Moses said, "Look, God, your God, has placed this land as a gift before you. Go ahead and take it now. God, the God-of-Your-Fathers, promised it to you. Don't be afraid. Don't lose heart." He said it again, "Don't be terrified of them. God, your God, is leading the way; he's fighting for you." They saw the miracles of God, and still had trouble believing him.

While we fought our battle in court, those scriptures brought me a lot of comfort. I had no idea how the custody situation would work out, or whether I could support the kids on whatever the court awarded us. I was terrified and discouraged much of the time, but, like the Israelites finally did, I placed my trust in God, who fought for me as he'd been doing all along.

I didn't like some of the judgments, but God knew they were the best for all of us. Judgment belongs to the Lord.

In retrospect, I'm grateful it worked out the way God knew it would. Even in the worst of times, in the midst of battle, we can trust the Lord and don't have to be afraid.

----------

## *Power We Can Count On*

One day not long after the divorce, my daughter called me at work. I could barely understand her as she told me the power company had shut off our electricity. She was frantic. It was mid-March and still cold outside. We had electric heat, not oil, so the heat shut off, too. I left work and came home to try to console the kids.

As a single mom, paying bills was a game of "borrowing from Peter to pay Paul". Apparently, "Peter" wasn't willing to wait any longer.

The kids spent the night with friends, but before they left, I assured them that God would get the power back on the next day. Where did that come from? All I knew was the fear I'd left work with was gone, and in its place was a calm assurance.

In Genesis 21, Sarah and Abraham were the proud parents of a brand new baby boy, Isaac. Hagar was the mother of Abraham's fourteen year old son Ishmael. Sarah didn't want Hagar around anymore. Abraham reluctantly sent Hagar and their son Ishmael on their way to wander in the desert, with nothing more than the food and water she could carry.

When that ran out, she was in despair. God heard her son crying and an angel spoke to her from Heaven, "What's wrong, Hagar? Don't be afraid. God has heard the boy and knows the fix he's in. Up now; go get the boy. Hold him tight. I'm going to make of him a great nation."

Then God opened her eyes and she saw a well of water. We know that Ishmael didn't die that day, and his descendants fill the Middle East today.

We didn't freeze that cold March, either. By midnight that same night, several friends had stopped by and said that God had told them to give me money. I hadn't said a word to any of them. The total amount they gave me was just what I needed to pay the bill the next day and get the power restored.

Frankly, the real Power had already warmed my heart with his message, "Don't be afraid. By tomorrow it will be taken care of." My ears heard no voice from Heaven, but my heart had heard him loud and clear.

God cares. He provides, and there is no problem he doesn't have the solution for. We can trust him. We don't have to live in fear.

----------

## *Everyone Needs Compassion*

We're born selfish. A hungry baby won't stop crying until you feed him. A toddler wants her own toys and everyone else's, too. Compassion may be just as necessary as selfishness for survival, and seems to be instinctive, as well. Children reach out to other crying kids long before they learn to talk. So when we do something that is completely selfish, to the point of hurting others, aren't we glad that compassion often mitigates our well-deserved punishment?

I'm guilty of having done great harm in my lifetime. I was sure God was planning a particularly painful and appropriate punishment. Then I read what Joseph's steward said to his brothers in Genesis 43:23.

Joseph's brothers, if you remember, threw him into a pit and then sold him into slavery. They told their father that he'd been mauled to death by a wild animal, and presented his many-colored cloak soaked in goat's blood as evidence. There was no way to prove it wasn't human blood, and Jacob, a.k.a. Israel, mourned deeply for his favorite son.

Years later, Joseph was the number two man in Egypt, in charge of selling food during a terrible famine. Jacob's family needed food, so all the brothers except for the youngest, Benjamin, went to Egypt. They had no idea who this powerful man was. He gave them what they asked for and sent them home, but held Simeon hostage until they brought Benjamin to him. He also had their money secretly placed back into their sacks of food.

When they finally returned to Egypt -- along with Benjamin, the money they found in their sacks, and more money to buy more food with -- they were afraid of retaliation. I find it interesting that, even though they didn't know Joseph was their brother, they blamed their current predicament on what they did to him years before. Guilt is powerful and long-lasting.

When they went to Joseph's servant, the steward, to try to explain how they found the money in their sacks, he told them, "Everything's in order. Don't worry ... I was paid in full." Then he brought Simeon out to them, unharmed and probably well-fed.

They deserved punishment and knew it. So did I. What they found was compassion and a new relationship with the one they had tossed away. So did I.

Don't we all deserve punishment for something we've done in our lifetime? And yet, there is an unlimited source of compassion available to each of us, and we do not have to live in fear of retaliation. Thank you, Lord!

----------

## *Who Cares What They Think?*

I worked for a division of a large pharmaceutical company in New Jersey. I had a new boss, Arlene, who couldn't stand me and made my life miserable at the office. The feeling was mutual.

One morning, I felt the Lord tell me to buy Arlene some flowers. It had to be his voice my heart heard, because it surely didn't come from me! Still, I didn't do it.

Every day thereafter, the impression became stronger and stronger until I finally gave in and bought the flowers. I handed the bouquet to her and said, "God wants you to know that he loves you." I was surprised to see tears in her eyes before she turned her back on me.

The story of Joseph is full of intrigue. His brothers sold him into slavery, and through a series of events engineered by God, he became the Pharaoh's right-hand man. Famine drove the brothers to Egypt to buy food for their aging father. They didn't recognize Joseph, and he tricked them into bringing him his youngest brother, who was born after their treachery.

Even after Joseph revealed who he was and treated them with great kindness, they feared retaliation. In Genesis 50, verses 19-21, the brothers again threw themselves on Joseph's mercy, expecting him to finally exact revenge after their father's death. Here's what he told them,

"Don't be afraid. Do I act for God? Don't you see? You planned evil against me but God used those same plans for my good." God took what they intended for harm and turned it into great good, and he calmed their fears.

So, did things improve with Arlene at work? No. But when Bill and I decided to move to Florida, God moved Arlene to eliminate my position, which allowed me to be laid off with a very generous severance package. I found the pink slip on my desk the same day I was going to give my two-week notice, which would have prevented me from getting any severance package. No one understood why I was so delighted to be laid off!

We sometimes have to set aside our fear in order to obey God. He shows us his mercy when we're obedient, even when we do it reluctantly. We have no idea what blessings are in store for us, or what good will come of it. Don't be afraid. Just do it!

----------

## In Harm's Way

Our son joined the U.S. Air Force after the first Gulf War. I figured he'd serve his time, learn a lot, and get out – all during peacetime. He did it all, but he didn't exactly get out. He transitioned from the military to being a civilian contractor, doing the exact same job.

By then, the second Gulf War was already set in motion. The Air Force sent him to Qatar just before the war began with Shock and Awe. His base was targeted by enemy missiles and, civilian or not, he was in as much danger as everyone else.

We have friends whose children are deployed in harm's way, even today. We worry about them and pray for their safe return while they courageously go about doing their jobs, which is exactly what their commander tells them to do.

In Deuteronomy 3, Moses was about to send his loved ones into danger. He reminded them of the time in the desert when they encountered two hostile kings. One of them was Og, king of Basham. The Lord had told Moses, "Don't be afraid of him; I'm turning him over to you, along with his whole army and his land." God gave Israel victory over Og and his army.

Moses would have led his people himself, but God had forbidden him to enter the Promised Land, so he commissioned Joshua to take the people across the Jordan. He said, "You've seen with your own two eyes everything God, your God, has done to these two kings. God is going to do the same thing to all the kingdoms over there across the river where you're headed. Don't be afraid of them. God, your God – he's fighting for you."

We can't be with our loved ones in war zones, but we can send them off with the same kind of encouragement that Moses gave to Joshua. "You have seen God at work in your life. He will always be with you, fighting on your behalf. Don't be afraid of the enemy. God has your back."

Moms and Dads, whatever happens, God has your kids' backs. Our son came home. We pray your child does, too. We can all be encouraged because life is much, much more than the little bit we see on this side of Heaven. There's a Promised Land waiting for all of us. We don't have to live in fear.

----------

## *Surrounded by Enemies*

When I was very young, my Dad was deployed to Korea for a year. Mom had three little ones at home and was pregnant with the fourth when he left. North and South Korea were at war, and the Americans were fighting for the South.

Dad had survived the horrors of World War II, only to have to face another enemy determined to wipe him out, along with every other American and South Korean. Mom faced her own giants, worried whether he'd come home or not while she raised four small children by herself.

Today, we have friends who live in a country surrounded by powerful enemies. Other friends have children deployed to war zones. Still others fight enormous battles right here at home, with diseases attacking their bodies. How do they face it?

Here's what Moses told the Israelites in Deuteronomy 7, "You may say to yourselves, 'These nations are stronger than we are. How can we drive them out?' But don't be afraid of them. Remember well what the Lord your God did to Pharaoh and all Egypt." (NIV)

Later, he said, "When you go to war against your enemy and see horses and chariots and soldiers far outnumbering you, do not recoil in fear of them; God, your God, who brought you up out of Egypt is with you."

He directed the priests to give the people a pep talk, saying "In a few minutes you're going to do battle with your enemies. Don't waver in resolve. Don't fear. Don't hesitate. Don't panic. God, your God, is right there with you, fighting with you against your enemies, fighting to win." (Deuteronomy 20:1-3 MSG).

Dad came home from Korea, Mom survived the year and they went on to have yet another baby. It doesn't always work out as well, but when we're facing impossible opposition, we can take comfort by reminding ourselves that God, our God, is with us, fighting our enemies, fighting to win. With God on our side, what do we have to fear?

----------

## From Dependent to Leader

Seeing the power of multiplication in action is both life-changing and life-affirming. We have eight kids, and 22 grandchildren. It's exciting to see that third generation from us expand and grow, and eventually multiply into an even larger number of great-grandchildren!

When our children were young, they depended on us to know enough to take care of them. We tried to impart our knowledge to them so that they would eventually be able to care for themselves and later, pass it on to their own children. Our hope has always been that they learn to depend on God and that they trust him and follow him.

We see a great example of that transition from dependent to independent and then to leader of the next generation in Deuteronomy 31.

Moses was 120 years old. He knew he was about to die and would never enter Canaan himself. He had led the Israelites out of bondage, through the desert, and now they stood ready to lose him and move forward on their own. He addressed his "children".

"Be strong. Take courage. Don't be intimidated. Don't give them [the giants in the land] a second thought because God, your God, is striding ahead of you."

Then he handed the baton of leadership to Joshua. In front of all Israel, he addressed Joshua, "Be strong. Take courage. You will enter the land with this people...God is striding ahead of you. He's right there with you. He won't let you down; he won't leave you. Don't be intimidated. Don't worry."

Finally, in acknowledgment that Joshua was now responsible for himself and all of Israel, God spoke to him directly, "Be strong. Take courage. You will lead the People of Israel into the land I promised to give them. And I'll be right there with you."

God hasn't changed. He's still right here with us. He hasn't let us down and won't leave us. Parents and Grandparents, his words are still true today. "Be strong. Take courage. Don't be intimidated. Don't worry." Okay, Lord!

----------

## *Leaving Friends*

Military brats are used to moving from place to place on very short notice. I dealt with it by not getting close to anyone – until high school, when I met my best friend and partner in mischief.

Together, we were fearless. Our parents and teachers never suspected the escapades we got ourselves into. We were honor students by day, adventurers by night and on weekends. We didn't get into anything seedy or dangerous (in our opinion), and so we were able to pull it off, and pull the wool over everyone's eyes.

Then her dad got the dreaded orders, and she was gone, moved to another country. I felt as if life ended that day. I had no idea that God had more adventures in store for me, because I didn't yet know him.

In Joshua 1, the Israelites had just lost their leader, Moses – the one who had brought them through some pretty amazing adventures of their own. Joshua lost his best friend and mentor, and now he was the one who had to lead these people. I can imagine how devastated he must have felt. Unlike me, though, Joshua knew his God, and heard his voice when he gave him his orders to go take the land for Israel.

God told him, "In the same way I was with Moses, I'll be with you. I won't give up on you; I won't leave you. Strength! Courage! You are going to lead this people to inherit the land that I promised to give their ancestors. Give it everything you have, heart and soul."

God said it again, "Haven't I commanded you? Strength! Courage! Don't be timid; don't get discouraged. God, your God, is with you every step you take."

I imagine Joshua felt less alone when the Israelites affirmed him as their new leader and echoed God's words back to him, "Strength! Courage!"

Even though I didn't know God during high school and college, he knew me! I thank him every day that he was with me, protected me, and led me to find him when the time was right. My best friend had moved to another base, but God never left me.

The good news is, my God is also your God, and his exhortation to have courage and be strong is for all of us.

----------

## A Pause In Time

There are moments with our grandchildren, when I wish God would stop time for a little while. I want to enjoy them right where we are just a little longer. I felt like that as a Mom, too, when our kids were little.

Sometimes, I wish I could go back in time and do something over again. I wonder if I would have the life God has given me if I had done things differently. I'll never know.

The fact is, God doesn't stop time… or does he? He did once, in Joshua 10.

The Israelites had fought and won battles to get to an area near Gibeon, where Israel allied with the Gibeonites. Gibeon was soon under attack by five Amorite kings and their armies. Joshua and his army went to Gibeon's aid and God told him, "Don't give them [the Amorites] a second thought. I've put them under your thumb – not one of them will stand up to you."

Not only did Israel rout the enemy, but God hurled giant stones on them from the sky! I know which side I want to be on in a conflict! Then God did something that had never been done before – something so impossible that it could only have come from the creator of time himself.

In front of all Israel, Joshua said, "'Stop, Sun, over Gibeon; halt, Moon, over Aijalon Valley.' And Sun stopped. Moon stood stock still until he defeated his enemies."

"The sun stopped in its tracks in mid-sky; just sat there all day. There's never been a day like that before or since…" Joshua had the gall to ask God to stop time, and God did it.

Isn't that scientifically impossible? Either God stopped the machinery of the universe for one earth day, or he stopped the rotation of the earth and kept everyone from flying off at the sudden stop. Either way, it was impossible, but God did it anyway.

With God on our side, what do we have to be afraid of? He may not stop time for us, but there's no enemy in the universe that can stand against us when God fights for us. Take courage. Be strong.

----------

## *Consequences*

I just turned a year older than last year. Since I'm still a year younger than next year, I'm not concerned about growing older. There's more of life to come! Every birthday, every anniversary, is a celebration because I've reached it! And every one brings me closer to the eternal life I've been given as a free gift when I placed my trust in God. In Joshua 23, the leader of Israel was 110 years old. Happy Birthday!

Israel had been enjoying peace in their God-given land for a number of years. Joshua gathered them together for one last time, to remind them that God had driven out superpower nations so they could claim and inhabit their land.

He said, "I'm an old man. I've lived a long time. You have seen everything that God has done to these nations because of you. He did it because he's God, your God. He fought for you."

Then he told them to stay alert, steady and strong, and to remain obedient to God. "Now vigilantly guard your souls: Love God, your God. Because, if you wander off and start taking up with these remaining nations still among you (intermarry, say, and have other dealings with them), know for certain that God, your God, will not get rid of these nations for you."

God knew the Israelites would disobey him. Although Joshua exhorted them to remember all the good God had done for them, they shrugged it off, forgot it, and went their own way. I imagine the mess in the Middle East might have started right there.

You could say we are all like Israel. I, for one, have put God on the back burner, gone my own way, disobeyed him, rebelled against him, and all the while giving no thought to the consequences of my actions. There have been consequences, just as God said there would be. Israel learned that truth the hard way – just as we all do.

As long as we walk with and trust in God, no super-powered enemy can stand in our way. Let's stay alert, be steady and strong, and remain obedient to the One who is fighting and winning our battles for us!

----------

## Rooting For The Underdog

Don't you love it when the underdog wins? One news program I like to watch does a feature every week about someone who has overcome impossible odds. They have something heart-warming and encouraging every day. The Bible is full of underdog stories, but one I particularly like is the story of Gideon in Judges 6.

Gideon was the weakest member of the weakest clan in Israel during a time of severe oppression by the Midianites. He was the underdog of underdogs. God sent an angel to Gideon, who was threshing wheat in an old winepress out of the oppressors' sight. The angel said, "God is with you, O mighty warrior!"

Was God mocking him? Gideon was a bit skeptical, to say the least. He started asking questions we often hear today, "If God is with us, why has all this happened to us? Where are all the miracle-wonders our parents and grandparents told us about, telling us 'Didn't God deliver us from Egypt?' The fact is, God has nothing to do with us – he has turned us over to Midian."

Sound familiar? I often hear, "If God is so good, why is there so much evil in the world?" and variations of that same question. God didn't explain himself to Gideon. He simply said, "Go in this strength that is yours. Save Israel from Midian. Haven't I just sent you?"

Gideon had just finished telling the angel that he has no strength, but here was God saying he does. Is it any wonder he was skeptical? So he did what any reasonable person would do. He asked for a sign. The angel burned up the meal Gideon had prepared for him, and then disappeared. It convinced him the visitation was from God, but he still had trouble trusting.

Later, he asked for two more signs. One night he laid a fleece on the ground and asked that God would make dew appear only on the fleece. It happened, but it wasn't enough for Gideon. The next night he laid the fleece out and asked that dew appear everywhere except on the fleece. I can imagine God's exasperation with Gideon, but he didn't give up on him. He made it happen. Then Gideon and 300 men (of the 32,000 men he started out with) defeated the entire Midianite army.

God isn't intimidated by questions and skepticism, and we shouldn't be, either. We may not have the answers, but we have a God who takes action, who gives us direction and signs when we need them, who can overcome overwhelming odds with few resources, and who can make an unlikely hero out of the least of the underdogs. So, what do we have to be afraid of?

----------

## War Against Women?

One thing that raises my hackles is when people say Conservatives are waging a war against women. It's one thing to rail against a non-existent "war", and another to lay one's life on the line to fight a real war against women – and against all civilized people.

Malala Yousafzai is a Muslim from Pakistan who recently won the Nobel Peace Prize. A Taliban soldier shot her in the head on her way to school when she was fifteen, because she was outspoken in her belief that everyone deserves an education.

Here's what she said when she addressed the United Nations recently, "They thought that the bullet would silence us. But they failed. The terrorists thought that they would change my aim and stop my ambitions. But nothing changed in my life except this: weakness, fear and hopelessness died. Strength, fervor and courage were born."

Malala has inspired millions to rise up for human rights. Her recovery from the Taliban bullet was miraculous. Yet, she's a woman and a Muslim. What does God think about that?

We might get a hint in Judges 4. "Deborah was a prophet. She was judge over Israel. The people of Israel went to her in matters of justice." A woman prophet? A woman judge?

The king of Canaan and his commander Sisera had oppressed Israel for twenty years. God made it clear to Deborah that Barak would command the Israelite army that would defeat Sisera. Barak wasn't willing to go without Deborah. She said to him, "Of course I'll go with you. But understand that with an attitude like that, there'll be no glory in it for you. God will use a woman's hand to take care of Sisera." Indeed, a woman, Jael, killed the general in his sleep.

Women are as valuable as men in the Bible, and their background and religious upbringing are irrelevant to God.

In the genealogy of Jesus Christ, Tamar was a woman who deceived her father-in-law, Judah, so she could have a son; Rahab was a prostitute; Ruth was a Gentile; Bathsheba was an adulteress, and only one, Mary, was a virgin. (Matthew 1)

I, for one, am very glad that God is not waging a war against women. In fact, He lifts us all up, and raises up women like Deborah, Jael and Malala to bring about great good in the world. Where would the world be without women?

----------

## *Fear Mongering*

"Looming fiscal cliff" …. "Default" …. Scary verbiage punctuated by a "shutdown" that victimized WWII veterans who fought against the tyranny that seems to be taking over their country and evicted elderly people out of their homes on government land.

Bear with me, liberal friends, because I'm not playing a blame game here. I've been exploring what God's word says about fear, and you have to admit, there's a lot of fear going around. Psalm 46 is a Psalm of extreme contrasts.

It starts out with an assurance that counteracts our concerns about politics and the crazy dangerous weather plaguing the country. "God is a safe place to hide, ready to help when we need him." Do we need him?

"We stand fearless at the cliff-edge of doom" (there's your fiscal cliff and default), "courageous in sea storm and earthquake, before the rush and roar of oceans, the tremors that shift mountains." You could add to that, raging floods or killer snowstorms and tornados.

"Godless nations rant and rave, kings and kingdoms threaten, but Earth does anything he [God] says." This verse follows a picture of God's Kingdom, where "river fountains splash joy" and "the streets are safe" because "God lives here."

We're told, "Attention all! See the marvels of God! He plants flowers and trees all over the earth, bans war from pole to pole, breaks all weapons across his knee." What a contrast with the world we live in. On the one hand, we have a marvelous life with God. On the other hand, we're living in this world with its problems. How do we deal with that?

God says, "Step out of the traffic! Take a long loving look at me, your High God, above politics, above everything." He might as well have said this directly to me.

Finally, this next verse is repeated three times in this Psalm, like the chorus in a song, "Jacob-wrestling God fights for us, God-of-the-Angel-Armies protects us."

When we feel overwhelmed by what's happening in our country and our world, we can get out of the "traffic", focus on our loving God who is above politics and everything else, and find our safety and rest in him. Thank you, Lord. I needed that.

----------

## *God's Hand in Wartime*

My friend and I were on a train heading somewhere in Italy, on one of our adventures. A pleasant young Israeli woman sat in the seat across from us.

She had been one of the soldiers fighting in the Six-Day War, and described how it felt to be surrounded by enemies with more soldiers, more tanks, more fighter jets, and more combined firepower than all of Israel.

What she told us was simply miraculous. I didn't know God then, but after her account of what she and many other soldiers witnessed, I knew that I wanted to be on his side in any battle. This was nothing new for Israel. In 2 Chronicles 32: 6-8, Hezekiah and his people faced the massive army of the King of Assyria.

"Hezekiah rallied the people saying, 'Be strong! Take courage! Don't be intimidated by the King of Assyria and his troops – there are more on our side than on their side.'" Humanly speaking, that wasn't true, and everyone could see it. Israel was outnumbered.

But here's what Hezekiah said, "'He only has a bunch of mere men; we have our God to help us and fight for us!' Morale surged. Hezekiah's words put steel in their spine." God sent one angel – just ONE – who wiped out everyone in the Assyrian camp, both warriors and officers.

The Six-Day War ended June 11, 1967. The outnumbered Israel Defense Forces rolled over the Arab coalition and more than doubled the amount of territory under Israel's control.

Yitzhak Rabin shared his reasoning behind the victory, (taken from Wikipedia) "Our airmen, who struck the enemies' planes so accurately that no one in the world understand how it was done…; our armored troops who beat the enemy even when their equipment was inferior to his; our soldiers…who overcame our enemies everywhere, despite the latter's superior numbers and fortifications – all these revealed not only coolness and courage in the battle…but an understanding that only their personal stand against the greatest dangers would achieve victory for their country and for their families, and that…the alternative was annihilation."

The young Israeli soldier added something beautiful to that. On the sixth day of the war, in the very early morning, her unit saw the hand of God appear in the sky. If one single angel can wipe out an army, what can the hand of the Almighty God accomplish? Rabin named the Six Day War in honor of the time it took God to create the world. What do we have to fear?

----------

## *Baggage Handlers*

"Everybody carries baggage. Everybody needs the Lord." My husband reminded me of this today. I know I qualify as a baggage handler. I have a checkered past that has resulted in painful consequences. I have no one to blame but myself, but that doesn't mean I have to wallow in guilt or self-pity. I've been forgiven, delivered, empowered by the Holy Spirit, and clothed in blessing – even in the midst of the trials.

King David also suffered consequences resulting from his affair with Bathsheba and the killing of her husband. God told him that violence would never leave his family. Absalom, his firstborn son, killed another of his sons out of revenge for what he did to his sister. Consequently, David banished him from the kingdom. He later forgave him and brought him back. Later, Absalom plotted to oust David from the throne and succeeded in having himself crowned king. David and his household fled for their lives into the wilderness. That's where he wrote Psalm 3.

"God! Look! Enemies past counting! Enemies sprouting like mushrooms, mobs of them all around me, roaring their mockery: 'Hah! No help for him from God!'"

Imagine being surrounded by a mob of people out to get you, who are fueled by your own child's hatred. Every mocking word must have seemed to have come from his son. The heartache must have been overwhelming. Yet, David knew who to turn to.

"But you, God, shield me on all sides; you ground my feet, you lift my head high; with all my might I shout up to God. His answers thunder from the holy mountain."

God was David's shelter, his place of safety. No mockery or curses would be able to touch him there.

David said, "I stretch myself out. I sleep, then I'm up again – rested, tall and steady, fearless before the enemy mobs coming at me from all sides."

I have cried myself to sleep sometimes, longing for the day God restores what's broken, but when I place my trust in God alone, I can sleep like David slept. I have learned, as David said, "Real help comes from God. Your blessing clothes your people!"

So, today, we can get up, get dressed in God's blessing, and stand fearless, knowing God is in the business of restoration, and everything will turn out well in the end.

# SURVIVING STORMS

"We cannot stand through the storms of life based on someone else's faith. We must be fully assured in our own hearts and minds."

~ Joyce Meyer

## Trust Trumps Fear

It struck me again this morning that the Creator of the Universe not only knows our names, but cares about what happens to us. He was present in church, with us at lunch, and watched over us as we rested this afternoon. I am so grateful that He answers our prayers, comforts or corrects us when we need it, and provides for us in often miraculous ways.

I watched coverage of the storms that have been sweeping across the country, and I'm grateful that God is in control of the weather. A man took a video of a fireball racing along power lines right outside his house. No one was hurt. Two airplanes collided in midair, and the one carrying a bunch of skydivers broke apart. The other crash landed. Even the pilot of the broken plane got out safely, parachuting to the ground. No one was killed. I'm thankful that God was there with those folks.

Not every story ends as well. People do get hurt, and people die. It would be a platitude to say that God has a plan and a purpose even for the hard things in life if we didn't have the hope of salvation and a new life with God following this one. God is there, even when everything is falling apart.

This morning I read one of my favorite verses in the Bible. It has sustained me through many difficulties. It works as well for blessings as for problems. I've been able to pass on its wisdom to many others, and it's as valid for them as for me. It's one of the few verses I've actually memorized because I use it so frequently.

"Trust in the Lord with all your heart. Don't lean on your own understanding, but in all your ways acknowledge him and he will make your paths straight." Proverbs 3:5-6 (NIV)

No matter what happens, we can be sure that God knows what is happening, why it's happening and how to get us through. We have no reason to fear when we're leaning on God.

----------

## *Super Hero Strikes Again*

I was a devout comic book fan until well into my teens. Maybe that's why I still love movies about super heroes wielding their powers to vanquish evil super-villains and save the world. Now that I know the ultimate Super Hero, I enjoy seeing him in action – especially in stories like this one.

In 2 Kings 1, King Ahaziah fell off his balcony and severely injured himself. He sent messengers to ask Baal-Zebub, the god of Ekron (and an arch villain), whether he'd recover or not. God sent Elijah the prophet to intercept the message and deliver bad news back to the king. Ahaziah wasn't happy with Elijah's news and sent a 50-man platoon of soldiers with their captain to find him and bring him back.

Elijah was calmly sitting on a hilltop when the soldiers arrived. The captain called out, "O Holy Man! King's orders: Come down!"

Elijah didn't like his tone and replied, "If it's true that I'm a 'holy man,' lightning strike you and your fifty men!" Notice the super-power here: a bolt of lightning shot out of the sky and incinerated all fifty-one of them.

The king must have thought it was a fluke, because he sent out another platoon. This time, the captain was even more belligerent when he said, "O Holy Man! King's orders: Come down. And right now!"

Why do villains always taunt and antagonize the super heroes? Don't they read the comics? The same thing happened again! Lightning, incineration; so Ahaziah sent a third platoon of men. This time, the captain fell on his knees and begged Elijah to spare his life and the lives of his men.

God's angel told Elijah, "Go ahead; and don't be afraid." I wonder what Elijah had to fear after that display of power? He went with the soldiers to Ahaziah.

When the prophet faced the king, he said, "God's Word: Because you sent messengers to consult Baal-Zebub" [Arch-Villain] "as if there were no God in Israel to whom you could pray" [Ultimate Super Hero], "you'll never get out of that bed alive."

There is one thing I've learned from reading stories like those in the comics and this one in the Bible – don't mess with God's hero! God has his back! And when God has your back, be careful where you toss that lightning!

----------

## God's Drum Roll

This morning I woke up thinking of the folks in California and the huge Pacific cyclone that generated flooding rain bands in southern California. Did the cyclone even have a name? Wasn't it the wrong season for cyclones?

Weather has been strange for a few years now, and, although I'm not a proponent of "global warming," I do believe that God controls the weather and he's sending a message. I prayed for our California friends and then got up and read Psalm 29.

"Bravo, God, bravo! Gods and all angels shout, 'Encore!' in awe before the glory, in awe before God's visible power. Stand at attention! Dress your best to honor him!" What does that have to do with the storm? Notice that King David said that gods, along with angels, are shouting "Yay, God!"

"God thunders across the waters, brilliant, his voice and his face, streaming brightness – God, across the flood waters." Here we go…

"God's thunder tympanic, God's thunder symphonic." Thunder is the drum roll of the heavens.

"God's thunder smashes cedars, God topples the northern cedars. The mountain ranges skip like spring colts, the high ridges jump like wild kid goats." Mudslides, anyone?

"God's thunder spits fire. God thunders, the wilderness quakes; he makes the desert of Kadesh shake. God's thunder sets the oak trees dancing a wild dance, whirling; the pelting rain strips their branches. We fall to our knees – we call out, 'Glory!'"

Sometimes, that is all we can do. Bill and I have lived through hurricanes, and there is no way we can do anything but pray in the height of the storm.

"Above the floodwaters is God's throne from which his power flows, from which he rules the world. God makes his people strong, God gives his people peace."

I pray that God makes everyone in wild weather to be strong and at peace. Place your trust in him, and he'll turn the craziest weather and all its consequences to your good. We got a new roof out of the hurricanes, and the sure knowledge that God is in control, no matter how bad things seem. Be blessed!

## *Rough Waters*

Tornados and damaging hail cut swathes of destruction and rip up lives along the way. People – many of them God's own – suffer the loss of loved ones and all their property. Where is God when these things happen?

We were at sea in rough waters when this passage came up in my daily reading, "Ocean saw you in action, God, saw you and trembled with fear; deep Ocean was scared to death. Clouds belched buckets of rain, sky exploded with thunder, your arrows flashing this way and that. From Whirlwind came your thundering voice, lightning exposed the world, Earth reeled and rocked. You strode through Ocean, walked straight through roaring Ocean, but nobody saw you come or go." (Psalm 77:16-19)

God is there, unseen but powerful. The teenaged daughter of a family that was interviewed at the location of their tornado-splintered home said this, "We held each other tightly in the closet and Daddy yelled out, 'God, spare my family! Spare my family!', and God did." He will provide everything they need to start again.

He took some of his dear ones home during the storms, and miraculously spared others whose purpose on Earth is not yet completed. We don't know God's mind. We only know he IS, even during the worst of the worst.

----------

## *Firenados and Hurricanes*

If you've watched the news lately, you've seen videos of an amazing and terrifying sight – a towering twister of fire. It may be nothing new to the incredible heroes who fight wild fires.

When I see footage of the frightening super cell storm clouds and tornados sweeping across the country, I remember how terrifying it is, and pray for everyone in the storm's path.

Bill and I were here when Hurricanes Frances and Jeanne targeted us in 2004, the same year Hurricanes Charlie and Ivan also hit Florida farther north. Hurricane Wilma went directly over us in October 2005, not long after Katrina did so much damage in the Gulf and New Orleans.

During Frances, we camped out in our walk-in closet – Bill, his mom and me. We had the radio on low. The newscasters gave us moment by moment reassurances and news of exactly where the storm was all night long. They're heroes! We prayed, slept, and rejoiced when it was over. Then we went outside and began the cleanup.

Just about a month later, Jeanne took the same track and passed directly over us. Again, we huddled as the wind screeched and branches banged into the roof. We got a new roof out of that one! Blue tarp-covered roofs all over the state made us the butt of many jokes and cartoons. Recovery was slow, but people are amazingly resilient.

By the time Wilma came over, we kept the storm shutters off the back and watched the hedge bend almost in half, and the tall pines bow low before the strength of the wind. It was cool to see, and we praised God who controls the weather and kept us safe.

Is God still our loving God when disaster strikes and people lose everything? Here's a hint in Psalm 97:1-6, "God rules: There's something to shout over! On the double, mainlands and islands – celebrate! Bright clouds and storm clouds circle 'round him. Right and justice anchor his rule. Fire blazes out before him, flaming high up the craggy mountains. His lightnings light up the world; Earth, wide-eyed, trembles in fear. The mountains take one look at God and melt, melt like wax before earth's Lord."

And then the good news: "The heavens announce that he'll set everything right, and everyone will see it happen – glorious!" Our loving God will set everything right in the end. This life is simply a prelude to the glorious life to come for those who surrender to the sovereignty of our God who controls the weather.

----------

## God Is In Control

We spent the weekend visiting Chris and Veronica to celebrate our granddaughter's fourth birthday. Her baby brother was due to arrive in about a month. Mike and Jenn and their kids were there, too.

I admire Veronica who, along with her mom and sister, prepared some amazing food and baked and decorated a beautifully artistic cake, even with her advanced pregnancy. She even made gluten-free, soy-free cupcakes for one little friend with food allergies. I'm amazed at her thoughtfulness and loving heart.

Bill and our sons Chris and Mike rode herd on a bunch of rambunctious, playful kids who raced from a castle bounce house to a half dozen other activities. I later broke away to visit a dear friend who lives nearby, and Bill bonded with the guys over a Gators game.

The next day, we got to visit with the family in a much calmer atmosphere. It occurred to me as I observed and interacted with them…. love is contagious, and love is courageous.

Here's what the Apostle John says about love in 1 John 4:17-18: "God is love. When we take up permanent residence in a life of love, we live in God and God lives in us. This way, love has the run of the house, becomes at home and matures in us, so that we're free of worry on Judgment Day – our standing in the world is identical with Christ's. There is no room in love for fear. Well-formed love banishes fear." In the NIV we read, "There is no fear in love. But perfect love drives out fear."

We girls chatted about all sorts of things while the boys watched another game. We shared our concern about current events and came to the conclusion that with God in control, we have nothing to fear. Let me make it perfectly clear… God Is In Control. He is perfect love. We have nothing to fear.

----------

## *Why Can't I Keep My Mouth Shut?*

I could hardly see the road. Tears blinded me. My heart was too heavy to bear. What would we do now? I was a single mom, and my big mouth had just gotten me fired. Never mind that the people I worked for were corrupt, and that they were in violation of numerous safety issues that could have hurt any of my co-workers. I didn't have to say anything, did I?

People who know me, understand that I couldn't have kept my mouth shut if my job depended on it. Oh, wait. It did.

I got home before the kids were out of school. I made myself some tea, sat down, and opened the Bible. I read what Jesus said in Matthew 5.

"You're blessed when you're at the end of your rope. With less of you, there is more of God and his rule." Blessed? You call being in this pickle blessed?

"You're blessed when you feel you've lost what is most dear to you. Only then can you be embraced by the One most dear to you." I'd lost an income, but God was waiting to hug me.

"You're blessed when you're content with just who you are – no more, no less. That's the moment you find yourselves proud owners of everything that can't be bought." That meant I had to stop beating myself up for getting fired. The problem was, we needed the stuff that has to be bought – like food and electricity.

"You're blessed when you've worked up a good appetite for God. He's food and drink in the best meal you'll ever eat." So much for needing food… I decided to stop worrying about buying groceries, and instead paid attention to what God was trying to tell me.

"You're blessed when you care. At the moment of being 'care-full,' you find yourselves cared for." I just got fired because I cared about the safety of my co-workers.

"You're blessed when you get your inside world – your mind and heart – put right. Then you can see God in the outside world." At the moment, my outside world was a mess. How could I see God in the fact that I just lost the income that would put food on the table? I couldn't control that, though, so I had to work on my faith and trust.

If this were all I read that day, it would have inspired me to depend on God to help me out of the mess. Jesus had more to say.

----------

## *Too Close For Comfort*

The Lord wasn't finished talking to me about the job I lost because of my big mouth, so I continued reading Matthew 5.

"You're blessed when you can show people how to cooperate instead of compete or fight. That's when you discover who you really are, and your place in God's family." I didn't need God to remind me that I'm the troublemaker in the family. How could I possible show people how to cooperate when I just blew it with my boss? Yet, here I was with a family of my own, and my kids were wonderful. We'd cooperate, as we always did, and everything would work out.

"You're blessed when your commitment to God provokes persecution. The persecution drives you even deeper into God's kingdom. Not only that – count yourselves blessed every time people put you down or throw you out or speak lies about you to discredit me. What it means is that the truth is too close for comfort and they are uncomfortable. You can be glad when that happens – give a cheer, even! – for though they don't like it, I do! And all heaven applauds. And know you are in good company. My prophets and witnesses have always gotten into this kind of trouble."

Okay, now I was in tears again, but for a different reason. God was telling me it's okay to lose a job over speaking out at injustice. My boss knew when he hired me that I was a Christian. When I brought up the violations, the truth must have been too close for comfort. Instead of correcting the problem, he fired the voice bringing it to his attention.

I soon found another, better job. I also learned that trust in God is never misplaced. He always comes through for his children. Every hardship brings us closer to the One most dear to us.

----------

## Hurricanes

In 2004, we were directly impacted by two hurricanes, one after the other, just a few weeks apart. We huddled in our closet during the height of Hurricane Frances, and again a month later as Hurricane Jeanne took the same track and blew through. Two more hurricanes hit Florida that year, Charlie and Ivan; and all four caused extensive damage. Florida became the blue-roof state as blue tarps covered damaged homes everywhere.

One cartoon showed the entire state huddled between Montana and the Dakotas saying "Enough is enough!" Another showed a bruised and battered Florida tightly curled up and clinging to Georgia as Hurricane

Ivan approached. Since we have bragging rights during every winter, it's okay for the rest of the country to make fun of us once a century or so.

We saw pictures of even greater devastation in the Philippines, where blue tarps were scattered among mountains of debris after a typhoon. People lined up for food, water and evacuation flights. Teams of men bagged the bodies of the dead, and makeshift hospitals treated the wounded without adequate medications or equipment. It must have been overwhelming and hopeless to those needing aid and those giving it.

David's worship leader, Asaph, expressed what many must have felt in Psalm 77,

"I found myself in trouble and went looking for my Lord. My life was an open wound that wouldn't heal. When friends said, 'Everything will turn out all right,' I didn't believe a word they said. 'Just my luck,' I said. 'The High God goes out of business just the moment I need him.'" I know that feeling. So what did Asaph do? He opened the door to God by remembering all the good God had already done. "I'll ponder all the things you've accomplished, and give a long loving look at your acts."

One picture that stuck in my mind was that of a Latter Day Saints missionary leading a line of people hand-in-hand, with the caption that all those in his care were safe. I heard that everyone in a Catholic orphanage was also safe. Every fear-filled, tear-filled face in every photo was someone who was saved from the fury of the storm. Where there is life, there is hope.

Asaph concluded with this, "…You led your people like a flock of sheep." Sheep don't know what the Shepherd is doing. They follow him in complete trust that he'll care for them, no matter what. Lord, help us to trust you that completely. Where there is trust in the Lord, fear has no standing.

----------

## *What Happens Here, Stays Here*

The twenty-something son of my sister's friend suddenly stopped breathing. The ambulance crew performed CPR and worked hard to save his life, without success. The hospital kept him on life support, until his mom made the heart-wrenching decision to donate his organs. It was what he wanted. He was her only child.

Another friend's young nephew reached his ninth birthday in the hospital. He was in a coma from which he never recovered. His organs gave new life to four children whose parents had been praying for a miracle. His eyes gave a little girl her sight. He was the miracle in the storm of his family's grief.

A friend we knew through our business died. She and her husband have made a real, healing difference in the lives of countless people. Earth is poorer because she's gone, and Heaven is richer.

In John 14, Jesus said, "Don't let this throw you. You trust God, don't you? Trust me. There is plenty of room for you in my Father's home. If that weren't so, would I have told you that I'm on my way to get a room ready for you? And if I'm on my way to get your room ready, I'll come back and get you so you can live where I live."

We live in the ante-room of Heaven. What happens here, stays here when we move on to the place God has prepared for us. Meanwhile, God has not left us to grieve alone.

"I'm telling you these things while I'm still living with you. The Friend, the Holy Spirit whom the Father will send at my request, will make everything plain to you. He will remind you of all the things I have told you. I'm leaving you well and whole. That's my parting gift to you. Peace. I don't leave you the way you're used to being left – feeling abandoned, bereft. So don't be upset. Don't be distraught."

Another friend lost her son in a car accident. He was a young husband and father whose future on Earth was cut short. She grieves, but her faith and trust that he's waiting for her in Heaven has uplifted everyone who knows her. We pray that all the families of those who've passed on find the peace of God.

----------

## *No Zombies*

Jesus might raise the dead, but he doesn't make zombies. Sorry, *Walking Dead* fans, but those raised up by the power of God are not going to start the zombie apocalypse.

I've met, talked with, hugged, and loved one of those people who had died and been brought to life by God's power alone. Before she moved, she always sat in the front row of our church, giving everyone who spoke with her an encouraging word and a reminder that Jesus is coming back really soon.

She was our pastor's mother-in-law, a sweetheart in her late 90's who has since gone to be with the loves of her life – her husband and Jesus. Her husband, a pastor and missionary, witnessed and participated in the miracle of people coming back to life several times. He laid hands on them, prayed, and they came back. She was one of them.

Jairus was the leader of a local synagogue. His daughter was gravely ill, so he went to Jesus to ask for his help. Jesus was, as usual, surrounded by a crowd of people who all wanted his attention. As they were slowly making their way to Jairus' home, his servant came to him and said, "Your daughter is dead. Don't bother the teacher anymore." (Matthew 8 NIV)

When Jesus heard that, he said to Jairus, "Don't be afraid; just believe, and she will be healed." They arrived at the house, where everybody was wailing and mourning for the young girl.

"'Stop wailing,' Jesus said. 'She is not dead, but asleep.' They laughed at him, knowing that she was dead. But he took her by the hand and said, 'My child, get up!' Her spirit returned, and at once she stood up."

Lazarus had been dead for three days when Jesus called him out of the tomb. After the crucifixion and before Jesus was resurrected, many graves opened up and people who had been long dead came back to their families. Raising the dead is something God does – and they are not zombies. So why doesn't he do it all the time? Why do we have to grieve the loss of someone we love?

I don't know the answers, but I believe the Bible gives us a big picture full of hope. This is not our home. Pastor's mother-in-law enjoyed her time on earth with her family, following her first death many years ago. She was ready to go when God called her home. She wasn't afraid. She'd been there, and knew there was nothing to fear. We have an amazing future ahead of us!

# A MISFIT'S MONTH IN PROVERBS

"The Christian does not think God will love us because we are good, but that God will make us good because He loves us."

~ C.S. Lewis

## Start With God

Years ago, a friend challenged me to read one chapter of Proverbs each day for one month. It wasn't my favorite book of the Bible because it seemed there were as many negatives as positives sprinkled throughout the chapters.

I accepted the challenge, and have never stopped reading through Proverbs every month. In months of less than 31 days, I read the remaining chapter(s) on the final day. I go through Proverbs twelve times every year. Why?

I'm learning how to "live well and right, with understanding." (Proverbs 1:1-7) The book of Proverbs is "a manual for living, for learning what's right and just and fair." Verse 7 sums it all up in one phrase. "Start with God."

That seems simple enough, but it isn't easy. Putting God first means self has to sit in the back seat. God has every right to interrupt my day with his plans, as much as I might want to shove through my own agenda.

It's amazing to think that the Creator of the Universe takes such an interest in us. He speaks to us plainly. Wisdom is a free gift from God, who is "plainspoken in knowledge and understanding. God is a rich mine of Common Sense for those who live well; a personal bodyguard to the candid and sincere. He keeps his eye on all who live honestly and pays special attention to his loyally committed ones." (Proverbs 2:6-8)

What does he want from us in return? Verse 21 tells us! "It's the men who walk straight who will settle this land, the women with integrity who will last here."

It seems that everything we need is a gift that God is willing and eager to give us: Wisdom, Common Sense, Understanding, Knowledge, and Protection. From us, he wants loyalty, commitment, honesty and integrity.

The reward of submitting to God is covered by Proverbs 1:20-33 -- Wisdom. Would I trade the illusion of control for the solid reality of wisdom? Yes. In a heartbeat. In a lifetime of heartbeats.

----------

## *Rewards*

Another student received the scholarship I thought I had earned in my senior year of high school. It was disappointing, and I nearly walked out of the awards assembly until I saw our English teacher Miss Elkins stand up. The auditorium grew silent. She walked to the podium, cleared her throat and said, "I haven't given this award to anyone in three years. I felt no one has earned it until now. I present this Senior English award to…" And she said my name!

Proverbs 3 is chock full of how God rewards those who follow him. Verses 5-6 have sustained me through many troubles. God asks us to remember what he teaches us.

We're to love and remain loyal to God, trust him wholeheartedly, run to him and away from evil, honor him with our tithes, accept his discipline, use wisdom and insight, guard clear thinking and common sense, be generous and live wisely. Whew!! Seems like an awful lot, doesn't it?

So, what can we expect if we live this way? The rewards include a long life, lived full and well, guidance, a body glowing with health and bones that vibrate with life. He gives us overflowing abundance.

We'll know his love and delight in us; his recognition and blessing. We'll have a soul that is alive and well. We'll stay fit and attractive and enjoy safe travel. We'll live with energy and balance and get great sleep. We'll enjoy safety, have no reason to worry or panic, live in a blessed home and live with honor.

The scholarship money would have been nice, but the Senior English award meant more to me. Miss Elkins, someone I loved and respected, presented me with an award she rarely gave anyone because I had earned it.

God's rewards far outweigh the little we contribute! Isn't that the way it always is with our Lord God?

----------

## *I Repeat*

As we grew, my parents taught us largely through repetition. They freely gave advice which we generally ignored, especially as we entered adolescence. It usually didn't end well for us.

In Proverbs 4, God essentially said, "I'm giving you some fatherly advice. Listen carefully!" And then He did what our parents did. He repeated what He told us yesterday.

Proverbs 4 also includes some warnings. We're to avoid actions like entertaining wickedness, perversity, and violence. Lies and gossip result in restlessness, trouble and sleeplessness, and make everyone miserable. Living that way results in an increasingly darker life.

On the other hand, the pursuit of wisdom and understanding results in a glorious life, full of grace and beauty, with years added on and a clear direction for living.

How easy life would have been, if I'd only listened to Mom and Dad the first time they spoke to me. My husband and I gave those same words of wisdom and warning to our kids, and they pass them on to our grandkids.

Because we love them, we kept repeating what we knew to be the best for them. God does that for us – in Proverbs – because he loves us.

----------

## *X-Rated*

I was a teenager during the 1960's. It was the Vietnam War era, and we were determined to break out of the moral restraints we felt our parents imposed on us.

The cast of the musical *Hair* were among my friends, and I was determined to live life my way. Our motto was "Make Love, Not War." It was the era of the Sexual Revolution.

Proverbs 5 is all about sex. Actually, it's about choices we make, and there's a good reason for the warnings about extra-marital affairs. God wants to keep us out of trouble. There are rewards or consequences to every choice we make.

This is a tough one, because our natural tendency is toward self-indulgence. To choose discipline over temptation goes against our baser nature.

So here we're admonished to avoid temptation – to stay out of the neighborhood. Why trade enduring intimacies for cheap thrills or dalliance with a stranger? The consequences are that we'll ruin, squander and waste our life if we allow strangers who care nothing about us to take advantage of us -- to exploit us.

Remember that God is aware of everything we do. We can choose to listen to those who love and care about us, or reject a disciplined life, stumble around in the dark and end our life full of regrets, "nothing but sin and bones." (I love the wording in The Message).

The freedom we sought during that time was an illusion. We have watched society change from one based on absolute truths to one in which everything is relative. It seems good to us to think we can do anything that feels good, until we hurt others in the process.

God's way is more challenging, but the rewards are immeasurable.

----------

## *Adultery Again?*

God is persistent, even in the face of human stubbornness. Proverbs 6 starts out with a warning to get out of debt, because it's a trap. Do you remember the fable of the ant and the grasshopper? Proverbs 6 is the origin of that! The common sense result of laziness is poverty.

In verses 16-19, we learn that there are seven things God hates. What? The God of Love has things he hates? Yep.

Here they are: arrogance, lies, murder of the innocent, plotting evil, taking the wicked track, lying under oath and a troublemaker in the family. I see myself in there. What would I do without his forgiveness?

From verse 20 on, there are some strong warnings against adultery. Why? It's a brainless act, soul destroying, self-destructive, and it really makes the spouse mad. I love the wording in The Message, verse 27: "Can you build a fire in your lap and not burn your pants?"

Why does God devote three whole chapters and one Commandment to adultery? There it is again in Proverbs 7.

Remember King David and Bathsheba? Now there was some temptation. David forgot everything he knew about how to behave and jumped at the chance to be with beautiful, married Bathsheba. He even had her poor, hapless husband killed so he wouldn't find out what was going on. But God knew.

As a result, they lost their first son and there was violence in David's house until he died. Every action has consequences.

God knows our weaknesses. It's amazing that he loves us anyway. In Proverbs, he gives us ample, repetitive warning to stay out of that neighborhood.

He tells us that obedience is taking action. Do what God says. Focus on getting wisdom and insight. Treasure his instructions. Stay away from temptation.

It sounds easy enough. Rely on God's grace, take the right actions, and reap the rewards of a life well-lived. Once again, we're admonished to listen and to follow the advice of our parents and, of course, our Heavenly Parent.

----------

## *Help, Lord!*

Do you write in the margins of your Bible? My margins have been filling up over the years, particularly with pleas for God's help with something. I found a couple of those today, in Proverbs 8, that I'll share with you because they're on-going. But first let me say that I'm grateful for God's persistence in trying to get our attention. And I love how it's worded in The Message.

Lady Wisdom stood at the busiest intersection in town and shouted, "Listen, you idiots -- learn good sense! You blockheads -- shape up!" It doesn't get much clearer than that. And in the margin, I wrote, "Trying! Help, Lord!"

Wisdom said, "You'll only hear true and right words from my mouth...You'll recognize this as true -- you with open minds; truth-ready minds will see it at once." Here, I wrote, "Keep me open-minded and truth-ready, Lord!"

This chapter compares wisdom to wealth. Living a disciplined life is better than the pursuit of money, and God-knowledge is way better than a lucrative career. Wait a minute. Are we supposed to live in poverty? Not if we love wisdom. The rewards are wealth, glory, honor and a good name.

This chapter also talks about politics! God doesn't leave any stone unturned, so watch out, grubs and spiders! Wisdom is the key to good leadership, to lawmakers legislating fairly, to governors governing. Fear-of-God means to hate evil, pride, arrogance and crooked talk. Our government should listen to Lady Wisdom shouting in the streets!

It ends with this.... "Blessed the man, blessed the woman, who listens to me, awake and ready for me each morning, alert and responsive as I start my day's work." May we all start each day with the Lord God, and enjoy the blessings he has in store for those who love him.

----------

## *Welcome to the Banquet*

God's Word is practical. In Proverbs 9, we're invited to a feast by Lady Wisdom. She's set the table, the food is ready, and she's inviting everyone in the streets. "Leave your impoverished confusion and LIVE! Walk up the street to a life with meaning."

Who wouldn't want to live such a life, to enjoy the rich foods offered to us? We're told not to waste time with those who don't: the scoffers and the arrogant who think they know it all. "Tell good people what you know -- they'll profit from it."

Proverbs 10 is where the recipe for a good life begins! God starts a list of ingredients to make a delicious, exuberant, full and satisfied life. I'll be sharing some nuggets that I particularly like, or don't like. You'll enjoy mining for your own gold, as God speaks to you through these short, simple verses.

It starts out like this, "Wise son, glad father; stupid son, sad mother." We pray that all our kids, and our parents' kids, turn out to be wise. That includes yours truly, who so often struggles with her own attitudes.

"Make hay while the sun shines -- that's smart; go fishing during harvest -- that's stupid." How often have I 'fished during harvest'?

Maybe I'm the only one who plays computer games instead of following up with our customers. I can choose to watch television, or write. See? Choices.

"The wage of a good person is exuberant life; an evil person ends up with nothing but sin." Jesus says no one is good except the Father, so I'm assuming "good" here is in the context of human experience. In order to choose life, I have to behave myself. Thankfully, I'm learning how to do that.

"God's blessings make life rich; nothing we do can improve on God." Whew! That lets me off the hook for trying to behave all on my own. I can never be good enough on my own efforts. I need God's grace!

"The Fear-of-God expands your life; a wicked life is a puny life." Who wants a puny life? See what I mean? Every time I read through this book, I pick up more nuggets. By the time I get to Heaven, I'll have amassed a fortune there! And I'll gladly give it all back to the Lord, who wrote the Book.

----------

## *Light and Shadow*

When the palm trees are silhouetted against a flaming sunset sky, the contrast between light and shadow is stunning. In Proverbs 11, God uses contrasts to teach us how to live.

For example: cheating is one thing God hates, but he blesses a business that's above-board, or run fairly.

As I read through these verses, God reminded me that there have been times when I've chosen badly. Thankfully, we're given choices until the day we die -- choose abundant life by living for God, or choose a miserable life by following evil.

Have you ever heard people say, "God helps those who help themselves"? I challenge anyone to show me where it says that in the Bible. In fact, right here in Proverbs 11 we're told that God helps those who help others! "When you're kind to others, you help yourself." And again: "The one who blesses others is abundantly blessed."

This is how I want my life to be: "a God-shaped life is a flourishing tree." I want to flourish. "A good life is a fruit-bearing tree."

My knotty tree might have some twisted branches, and some of the fruit may be bruised and battered because of choices I've made and some I might still make, but I'm forgiven, I love the Lord, and my life is a tree!

Proverbs 12 is a smorgasbord of wisdom: from sex (God approves!) to what our treatment of animals says about our character.

Character is measured by what we do when no one is watching. God is always watching. That should encourage character-building behavior!

The chapter begins with discipline, which I see as an elongated four-letter word related to work, study, and self-control. I may not like it, but it certainly makes life easier.

Speaking of words, did you know we can influence life and death in the words we speak? Several verses sprinkled throughout this chapter address the power of words!

"The words of the wicked kill; the speech of the upright saves." That's heady stuff. Words can hurt, cut, maim, and get us into a boatload of trouble -- or they can bring healing, satisfaction, illumination, and encouragement. It's all there, in Proverbs 12.

----------

## Grandchildren

Our local movie theaters have free kids' movies during the summer. I get to take the grandkids to the theater twice a week, where we share a bag of popcorn and plenty of laughs. Our grandchildren have made this the best time in our lives. Proverbs 13 mentions grandkids!

"A good life gets passed on to the grandchildren; ill-gotten wealth ends up with good people." I like the second half of that verse as much as the first half! The good guys win!

How is the wise person different from the foolish person? Intelligent children listen to their parents (are you listening, kids?), and foolish children do their own thing. I've been that foolish child more often than I can count.

Listen to this, parents! God has something for you here, too! "A refusal to correct is a refusal to love; love your children by disciplining them." The root word of discipline is "disciple" or student. In other words, teach your kids!

Here are a few of my favorite things from Proverbs 13: Honor God's commands and grow rich (yeah!); make a lifestyle of good sense; follow your hearts and thrive; keep company with wise people and your appetite for good will be satisfied.

Here are some of my not-favorite things, mainly because I can see myself here, too: foolish people ignore the Word, litter the country with silliness, are bent on evil, despise matters of the soul, hang out with other fools until life falls to pieces, and always want more.

Again, at least four verses talk about the power of our speech and the words we say. These words tie it together for us in verse 6: "A God-loyal life keeps you on track; sin dumps the wicked in the ditch." Life gets better as we learn to stay out of the ditch. I want to be one of the good guys. I'm working on it.

----------

## *A Many-Course Meal*

Our family of seven went to a wedding in Italy. We children dressed in our best clothes and were warned to use our best manners. We didn't know what to expect, and still hadn't learned to speak Italian.

We made short work of a tray of delicious appetizers. Waiters brought out soup as the next course. By the time we'd finished that, I thought I might manage some pasta, thinking it was the main meal.

I found out the hard way that pasta is followed by meat and veggies, then the salad, and then dessert. A formal dinner in Italy consists of several courses, beginning with antipasto and ending with dessert. I thought the tiny scoops of sorbet served in-between courses were the dessert. I could barely move!

That's how it is with Proverbs 14. We're getting into the main course here -- or maybe just the pasta. It's filling! And there's more to come!

The contrast between the wise person and the foolish person is made very evident in these verses. I can relate to both, but prefer to be considered among the wise. Who wouldn't?

The wise person is honest and wise. He isn't afraid to work. He has an open mind and is moral, gracious, prudent and even-tempered. He is warm-hearted, realistic, compassionate and thoughtful. He is truthful, loyal, slow to anger, kind and understanding. Diligent and confident, he fears God, has integrity, and lives a holy life. Wow. That describes my husband! It applies as much to women as men.

God has a lot of work to do in me. It's one of the reasons I read through Proverbs every month -- and still learn!

Here's a bit of wisdom our government should pay attention to: "God-devotion makes a country strong; God-avoidance leaves people weak." Actually, it's a good word for all of us. Enjoy the feast!

----------

## *Spacious Living*

I recently posted a few things that really bother me about what's going on in our country -- and then realized how much I need the lessons in Proverbs 15 today! Several verses deal with hot-tempered people.

I'm the daughter of a Scots-Irish man and a German woman, and I spent my formative years in Italy, where people speak loudly and eloquently and with much gesturing. Temper is no stranger to me! It's no wonder I wrote "Help with this, Lord!" in the margin!

I'm grateful that God gave me my peacemaker, Bill, and that Proverbs shows me how to make the needed attitude adjustment. Bill often (too often) says, "You can choose to be miserable, or you can choose to be cheerful. It's up to you." Proverbs 15 says the same thing!

Who wouldn't want to choose to be this kind of person: gentle, knowledgeable, kind and teachable? What about flourishing, perceptive, prayerful and genuine? Wouldn't everyone like to be determined, cheerful and eager for truth; simple, calm, diligent and intelligent; congenial, thoughtful, humble, generous, disciplined, and joyful?

Not when I'm furious -- even knowing how foolish I am. And then I read this: "An undisciplined, self-willed life is puny; an obedient God-willed life is spacious." I prefer spacious to puny. Begin attitude adjustment...

We cannot hide from God. He's everywhere we are. That's a good thing, even when we don't feel like it is. I read Psalm 103 this morning.

"O my soul, bless God. From head to toe, I'll bless his holy name! O my soul, bless God; don't forget a single blessing!

I'd rather have God love me enough to correct me when I'm wrong, than hang on to self-willed misery. Here's to spacious living -- and Proverbs 15.

----------

## It's Only Water

Anthony, Ashley and I went to the park. The sky was clear, with no hint of a cloud as far as we could see. A half hour later, we ran home laughing and drenched from a sudden downpour. Our mantra for those wild sudden storms has become, "It's only water. We'll dry quickly."

I love what Proverbs 16 says about God's creation. "What a wildly wonderful world, God! You made it all with wisdom at your side; made earth overflow with your wonderful creations."

God made everything with a plan and a purpose; even the wicked, only for judgment. Who knew? When we put God in charge of our work, he makes our plans succeed. We can plan our life, but God makes us able to live it.

In this chapter, God shows us that life, business and even politics are really pieces of the same pie. Character shows in all aspects of life. Good leaders (people of good character) motivate, don't mislead and don't exploit. They're honest; they hate wrongdoing and they have a moral foundation. They cultivate honest speech and love advisers who tell them the truth. They're good tempered and they're not prideful.

Here's what he says about politics: "Moderation is better than muscle, self-control better than political power. Make your motions and cast your votes, but God has the final say."

In Proverbs 17, I found out that "Old people are distinguished by grandchildren." Old People?!? I prefer elegant, self-confident and powerful. Isn't that what distinguished means?

God sees us as we are, and loves us anyway, like friends and family. "Friends love through all kinds of weather, and families stick together in all kinds of trouble."

"A cheerful disposition is good for your health; gloom and doom leave you bone-tired." I know this is true because I always feel better after a laughing fit with our grandkids, who make us distinguished. Elegance flies out the window when you're doubled up in laughter.

Here's a nugget I should take to heart, if at all possible, especially during election cycles. "The one who knows much says little; an understanding person remains calm." Hmph.

"Even dunces who keep quiet are thought to be wise; as long as they keep their mouths shut, they're smart." Hmph again.

Oh, well, I'm grateful for friends and family and my ever-patient God who love me anyway, because my keeping quiet is not going to happen.

----------

## Words Matter

Growing up in my tumultuous family, I soon learned that the loudest kids got the most attention. It was negative for the most part, but we didn't get lost in the crowd. Notice I included myself in that number.

We made arguing an art form. The more clever and sarcastic we were, the more we won. Our opponents simply lost their temper and went off to plan revenge. Sometimes I won, sometimes another did, but the result was never pretty. It was also not a healthy environment for growing children.

Before I learned that a peaceful life is much happier than one in constant turmoil, I enjoyed besting my opponent. I identify with both the fool and the wise person in Proverbs 18.

God points out the difference between talk and trash-talk, between listening to gossip and listening to good conversation. "Fools are undone by their big mouths; their souls are crushed by their words." Ouch.

"Words satisfy the mind as much as fruit does the stomach; good talk is as gratifying as a good harvest." The words that come out of our mouth make a difference to us and to those listening to us, whether good or bad.

Speech is only one half of the equation in this chapter. What we listen to, and entertain, are just as important to God. "Listening to gossip is like eating cheap candy; do you really want junk like that in your belly?" I like candy sometimes, but it doesn't do me any good. It keeps me from being hungry for nourishing food and it hurts the waistline. Gossip is hurtful.

"Answering before listening is both stupid and rude." I've been guilty of this, but didn't realize it was important enough to warrant a verse in the Bible!

This is where I want to be: "Wise men and women are always learning, always listening for fresh insights."

There are more treasures in this chapter of Proverbs. Some of my favorite passages are here. Two of them back me up in my stance for life. "Contempt for life is contemptible." A country will destroy itself when it sacrifices its children.

"Words kill, words give life; they're either poison or fruit -- you choose." I choose life, and then I run to God's Name -- to my place of protection. See you there!

----------

## Savory and Unsavory Tidbits

We occasionally host a fellowship meal at our house. People in our church congregation come from different locations within the United States, from the Caribbean Islands, and even from as far away as India. We often have ethnic dishes to enjoy. At times like that, I lament our limited ability to fill up on good food.

Proverbs 19 is like a pot-luck meal, with small servings of many different dishes. Some taste awesome and I want the recipe, and others are not to my taste.

Take these verses about parenting, and being the child of parents, for example: "Discipline your children while you still have the chance; indulging them destroys them." That's pretty strong. Nope, I don't like the taste of that.

"Kids who lash out against their parents are an embarrassment and a disgrace." I've been guilty of this. Mom and Dad disciplined and I lashed out. It still leaves a bad taste in my mouth. Sorry, Mom and Dad!

There are more dishes that don't taste very good, in the verses about lying and how we can ruin our lives by our own stupidity and blame God for the mess we've made.

But what about the good stuff; the food we savor, the recipes we want?

How about this: "Grow a wise heart -- you'll do yourself a favor; keep a clear head -- you'll find a good life." Yummy. And this: "Mercy to the needy is a loan to God, and God pays back those loans in full."

All in all, I'd say Proverbs 19 is a balanced meal. Enjoy!

----------

## *A Hodgepodge of Nuggets*

I don't know about you, but before breakfast every morning random thoughts already clutter my brain. I think about what I have to do that day. I wonder how our children and their children are doing. I lose my keys and find them. I get so distracted I put the milk in the pantry and the box of cereal in the refrigerator.

In Proverbs 20, I realize I'm not alone, and read with delight that my mind was created in God's image after all.

What a hodgepodge of nuggets we have here, with one thought that leads to another, in no evident linear path. It starts with a few thoughts on quarrels, with admonitions against drinking, mad-dog leadership and foolishness.

Life would be so much easier for us and our children if we'd only live for God and put foolishness behind us. Yes, that thought is in there, too, in verse 7. Here are a few more:

Young people, don't think for a minute you're fooling anybody. Laziness leads to poverty. Good leaders care about their business, ask for good counsel and help, and sweep out the rebels and dolts. Whatever a dolt is, it isn't good for business. God hates cheating.

There are plenty of "don'ts" in this chapter. Don't make impulsive promises you can't keep, don't loan to a stranger without collateral, don't confide in a gossip, don't steal, and don't be vengeful -- leave it to God.

And here is the "do" list, the one that wakes me up in the morning and pesters me all day: avert quarrels, do what's right, shop for bargains (I like that one), drink in knowledge, ask for counsel and help, and lead with love, truth and integrity.

God directs our steps. He's in charge of our lives and knows everything we think and do, so we can't escape his scrutiny. We can trust that he loves us and won't let us down.

By the time you get to be my age, you'll be prestigious. "Youth may be admired for vigor, but gray hair gives prestige to old age." How nice to be both distinguished and prestigious.

Now it's time to get knee deep in closet cleaning. What to do with the clutter in my mind? Maybe I'll write some proverbs.

----------

## Cool Water Leadership

The pools in Florida are open all year for good reason. Hot days are not relegated to summer here. We've gone swimming on Christmas and made sure our freezing northern family heard about it. Cool water is a luxury on hot days, and there is plenty of it in our state.

Proverbs 21 begins with splashes of cool water. "Good leadership is a channel of water controlled by God; he directs it to whatever ends he chooses." Send some this way, Lord!

God doesn't care about appearances, or how "religious" we are. He examines our motives, and helps us explore our own motivations. I wrote "Help with this, Lord" in big letters in the margins of my Bible.

I get a slap on the wrist when I read that it's better to live alone than with a cross, petulant and nagging spouse. I don't nag! I merely suggest over and over again until the job gets done. Poor Bill. Help, Lord!

There are some good things about being a God-loyal person. Careful planning gets you ahead. You see right through the plots of the wicked and have the power to undo their plans. You can expect to be helped when you need it because you help others. You soothe anger with a quietly given gift. You celebrate when justice is served, while the evildoers have a bad day. You find glorious life because you're looking in the right places. You're respected because you speak the truth. Now there's some sunshine to bask in.

All you preparedness folks will like this ending to the chapter! "Do your best, prepare for the worst -- then trust God to bring victory." I'm trusting you, Lord! And I'm going to splash around in the sprinkler on this typical Florida day.

----------

## Cleaning Closets

Reading Proverbs 22 is a little like cleaning out a closet you haven't touched in thirteen years. I'm describing myself, here. Some nice clothes will fit someone else better, at least for now. Some are keepers because I wear them all the time. Some are like treasures -- the ones hiding at the back of the closet -- so old, they're like brand new! Here are a few of those treasures: old, but relevant; worn, but still elegant:

"A sterling reputation is better than striking it rich; a gracious spirit is better than money in the bank." I've experienced a tarnished reputation, but God shined it up for me as I learned to live his way. A gracious spirit means you're willing to extend that kind of grace to others.

We're all equal, rich and poor alike. Living God's way leads to plenty, honor and a satisfying life.

"Generous hands are blessed hands because they give bread to the poor." My hands may show my age, but I'll take blessed over young and smooth.

God and good leaders love people who are pure-hearted and well-spoken.

Here is one of my favorite treasures -- the one I bank on and pray I've paid enough into: "Point your kids in the right direction -- when they're old they won't be lost." Take heart, parents. God didn't say they'd straighten up in your lifetime, but they will by the time they're old. Never stop praying for them.

Beginning here, and in the next couple of chapters, we're given a list of 30 tested guidelines to live by. Start your list!

1. Do not mistreat the poor just because they're poor!
2. Temper, temper! Stay away from hotheads. Bad temper is contagious.
3. Don't gamble -- you'll lose your shirt.
4. Don't move the boundary lines. In other words, don't cheat.
5. Watch what successful people do. In our business, we say, "do what the successful people do."

I pray you find your own treasures among these proverbs. Happy hunting!

----------

## *Guidelines for a Good Life*

I'm not fond of rules and regulations. I've always been something of a rebel, a cause of concern and worry for my parents. When I had children of my own, I got some of that back.

God knows who we are and what it takes to rein us in. He gives us more guidelines to protect us from the minefields of life in Proverbs 23. I can relate to too many of them.

6. Don't pig out. Mind your manners. My parents taught me this, and it still applies..
7. Don't wear yourself out by chasing after money. It can disappear in an instant. We've all experienced this in the last few years.
8. Don't accept a meal from a stingy person. (How would you know?)
9. Don't try to talk sense to foolish people. They'll only mock you.
10. Don't move the boundary lines. There it is again! In this case, it's in order to cheat someone else. I like this part: "for they [the cheated] have a powerful Advocate who will go to bat for them." Yay, God!

11. Pursue disciplined instruction. Listen to your teachers. Do your homework.
12. Correct your young ones. You'll be saving them from a ton of misery later if you nip the problem in the bud early. Earlier in Proverbs, I read that you don't love your kids if you don't discipline them.
13. Become wise and make your parents happy. Mom and Dad, this one's for you.
14. Don't envy careless rebels. They end up with nothing, probably because they've stepped on too many mines in the minefield. Living God's way is where your future lies.
15. Control your appetites. Drunks and gluttons (and drug addicts) end up on skid row.
16. Respect your father and take care of your mother. Pursue truth, become wise, and make your parents proud.
17. Avoid temptation. Illicit sex will drag you down and steal everything you have.
18. Drunks and addicts are full of self-pity and live pitiful, beat-up lives.

God loves us enough to reach into our sometimes pitiful lives and save us out of the pit we dig ourselves into. He turns negatives into positives when we allow him to. I, for one, have become really grateful for the boundaries. The list goes on.

----------

## *Don't Forget*

My mom did this to me, and I, in turn, did it to our children. She gave me advice, and then kept on reminding me of it. Remember to do this...remember to do that...don't forget. Apparently we come by it honestly, because here, in Proverbs 24, God does the same thing. First, we get the completed list of 30 principles to live by, and then the reminders begin.

19. Avoid and don't envy people who like to make trouble.
20. The building blocks for a beautiful home are wisdom, understanding and knowledge.
21. Wars are won by wisdom and intelligence. They outrank brute strength.
22. Wise conversation is over the heads of foolish people.
23. Foolish people incubate evil. Cynical people desecrate beauty. Skepticism is not cynicism, in case you happen to be skeptical. It's just being cautious. Cynicism is ugly.
24. Don't let a crisis get the best of you. Find your strength, or rely on God's.
25. Rescue the dying. Don't hesitate to step in. God isn't impressed with lame excuses.
26. Knowledge and wisdom are like nourishing honey. They secure your future and give you hope. Sweet.
27. Don't interfere with the lives of God-loyal people. No matter how often they're knocked down, they keep getting back up, unlike the wicked (not the Broadway play) who fall flat on their faces.
28. Don't gloat at your enemy's defeat. You'll provoke God.
29. Don't envy bad people, no matter how successful they seem. They have no future.
30. Fear God, respect your elders, don't be defiant or rebellious. Your life can turn upside down in an instant, without warning.

Here's where I hear my mom's voice: Don't forget -- never go along with injustice. Whoever exposes evildoers will be thanked and rewarded (this is for you whistle-blowers -- God will bless you!). An honest answer is like a warm hug. (I like hugs!) Do everything in its proper order. Don't gossip. Don't seek revenge, and don't be lazy or you'll end up in the poorhouse!

Okay, Mom. I'm on it.

----------

## *God's Delight*

A day spent with Anthony and Ashley is a little like reading Proverbs. They tackle every event with enthusiasm and energy -- from the movies to the splash pool in the front yard to the park. They even eat their snacks with gusto!

They equally energize and exhaust me, and they always delight me. Did you know that God takes delight in playing hide and seek? It's right here, in Proverbs 25!

"God delights in concealing things -- scientists delight in discovering things." Science is the discovery of things God has created and hidden just for them to find!

He tells us that good leaders don't promote themselves to prominence. Unless they're promoted based on their merits, it will end in humiliation. Good leaders have broad and deep understanding. When bad leaders are removed from office, then authority will be credible and God-honoring. That's one I often pray for!

He tells us that friends keep confidences. They don't jump to conclusions; they say the right words at the right time and they reprimand in a loving manner. Good friends do what they say they'll do. They're patiently persistent, speak gently and don't wear out their welcome.

He has this to say about our enemies: "If you see your enemy hungry, go buy him lunch; if he's thirsty, bring him a drink. Your generosity will surprise him with goodness, and God will look after you."

Compassion is rewarded by God's caring for us. Lord, make me a more compassionate person! And thank you for days with our grandkids!

----------

## *Foolishness*

I have a love-hate relationship with Proverbs 26. When I was in rebellion, as I have been at certain times in my life, I hated and avoided this chapter. God speaks strongly to fools here, and you could have substituted my name in just about every verse. When people I love fall into this category, I go into some serious prayer for them.

I love this chapter when it makes me feel justified, but when I pat myself on the back because I'm anything but the fool, God has a way of taking me down a peg or two. Foolish me.

As you read it, remember that we're all in this life together, so we all struggle with behavioral issues of one kind or another, at one time or another. Hopefully, we grow into wisdom and maturity and leave foolishness behind.

Sometimes, our only option is to trust God. The first verse in Proverbs 27 reminds us that we don't know what tomorrow will bring. Our job is to trust God and do what we know is right today. We learn by repetition, which is why much of this chapter repeats what we've already heard. The nagging spouse is mentioned here, but I have a question for God.

If you have to repeat these proverbs until we get the message, does that mean we aren't nagging when we do the same thing? The answer, I believe, lies in the final verses…but I'll get to that.

Bill and I like to buy a lottery ticket when we travel. Call it a little dream indulgence. We certainly don't make a habit of it, but it's fun to wonder 'what if?' We've noticed over the years that fame and fortune don't change people. They only make them more of what they already are. We all know the infamous stories – the athletes gone wild, the fallen stars.

We also know the Tebows, the Grahams, and others who have used their fame and wealth to bring about great blessing. "The purity of silver and gold is tested by putting them in the fire; the purity of human hearts is tested by giving them a little fame."

Our prosperity, our living a good life, is dependent upon our taking responsibility for those entrusted to us. We are mandated to care for them, and not to take them for granted.

Doesn't that include teaching them? And if it takes constant repetition to get the point across…well, doesn't God set the precedent in Proverbs? I'm not nagging, Honey. I'm investing in our good life.

----------

## *Bunny Trails*

Proverbs is written very much like the way my days go – at least the days I can stay home to get 'stuff' done. After breakfast and time spent with the Lord, the fun begins. I throw a load in the laundry and head to the office. I see the pile on my desk and remember that I have a project in the living room. I start that project and see something that distracts me, and so on.

Imagine the bunny trails you find in the depths of a closet you're trying to clean! Proverbs 28 seems to jump from topic to topic, but it all makes sense.

I think of many of you as I read the first part of this chapter. "Honest people are relaxed and confident, bold as lions." I have lions for friends. No matter which side of the political fence they're on, they believe strongly and aren't afraid to speak out. God has some things to say about politics, too. I hope we can all agree with Him!

"When a country is in chaos, everybody has a plan to fix it – but it takes a leader of real understanding to straighten things out." Lord, raise up that leader!

"Justice makes no sense to the evil-minded. Those who seek God know it inside and out."

"When good people are promoted, everything is great, but when the bad are in charge, watch out!"

"Among leaders who lack insight, abuse abounds, but for one who hates corruption, the future is bright. When corruption takes over, good people go underground, but when the crooks are thrown out, it's safe to come out."

Here's one we all need to take to heart. "God has no use for the prayers of the people who won't listen to him."

I wrote in the margin, "Lord, open my ears!" Listening, like love, is an action word. Lord, help me do what you tell me to do. And keep repeating it until I get it.

----------

## *Balanced*

I've had days when it seemed as if I needed to be two people at the same time. I worked about an hour away, and then dealt with the challenges of being a single mom to three kids at home. That hour's drive was my time to pull the plug on the day's concerns and change my focus to the kids. The reverse happened every morning. Mom brain was replaced by business brain. Mom concerns had to take a backseat to work until the drive home.

Life has become so much simpler now that I'm happily married and all of our children have their own families. Still, the best days are the ones where I feel everything is in balance. A little sunshine, a little rain, a little work, a little play – I'm sure you've had days like that. I'm impressed with the balance in Proverbs 29.

Each verse is like a battery, with the positive and negative poles, except for the first one. Proverbs 29 starts with a dire warning. "For people who hate discipline and only get more stubborn, there'll come a day when life tumbles in and they break, but by then it'll be too late to help them." Lord, help me be less stubborn!

I get the impression that God is beginning to sum up the lessons he's been teaching. Rather than go through the dos and don'ts, I'll list the people he mentions here: rulers and leaders; children, parents and neighbors; the poor and the rich; cynics and sages; murderers and moral folks; fools, degenerates and right-living folks; workers and outlaws; victims, and some I might have missed. In short, we're all in here somewhere!

The dos and don'ts are summed up in verse 27: "Good people can't stand the sight of deliberate evil; the wicked can't stand the sight of well-chosen goodness."

Most of us fall somewhere between the two, leaning one way or the other at different times. Proverbs helps us to develop habits resulting in right-living. The rewards are worth it.

----------

## *The Fours and the Ideal Woman*

Lists are my lifesavers. I keep lists of names and birthdays. How else would I remember all of our kids and grandkids? With the help of Christmas gift lists I've kept over the years, I haven't knowingly duplicated presents. I keep Christmas card companies in business, and for that, I need lists.

In Proverbs 30, we're given five lists of fours: four insatiables, four mysteries, four intolerables, four small wonders, and four dignitaries. Billy goats and adolescents are listed. Is the billy goat insatiable? Intolerable? What about the adolescent? I'll leave that up to you to find.

The first part of Proverbs 31 is one I've taken seriously. "Speak up for the people who have no voice." Millions of aborted babies had no voice. The infants whose mothers are going to choose abortion cannot speak for themselves. I feel compelled to speak up for the babies.

I have mixed feelings about the second part, only because I find this ideal wife to be difficult to live up to. Thankfully, I have a loving, forgiving family and God. After all, "a good woman is hard to find."

Here are some of the attributes I'd love to live up to. A good wife is trustworthy, generous and never spiteful. She's a good shopper, a hard worker, a bargain hunter, an early riser, a good cook, an organizer, and a gardener.

She's eager to get things done and senses the worth of her work. She's unhurried, skilled in home care, quick to help those in need and reaches out to help the poor. She keeps the family clothing clean and in good repair, makes her own elegant clothes and turns her skills into a cottage industry.

She dresses well, is optimistic, kind, intelligent and a leader in her home.

She's rewarded by the respect and praise of her husband and children. "The woman to be admired and praised is the woman who lives in the Fear-of-God. Give her everything she deserves! Festoon her life with praises!"

Quite frankly, all I want is a little nap. Be blessed today!

----------

## *And Repeat!*

Bill says, "You can't become a tennis-pro by taking one lesson. It takes training, repeating the basics over and over, in order to become good at it." It's the same with any skill. Learn the basics and drill. They say it takes twenty-one days of repetition to develop a good habit.

Training turns head knowledge into muscle knowledge, so that when we're tested, we know what to do. Life is challenging, and with all the training we have available, we still handle some challenges badly.

When that car cuts you off at the intersection, do you bless the other driver or say some colorful words you later have to ask forgiveness for?

He also reminds me often that life is about choices, and so is Proverbs. We can choose wisdom, which results in a good life, prosperity, peace and joy, or we can choose foolishness which leads to trouble, poverty and a miserable life.

We can choose the way of love, life and God, or choose to live in hate, greed and emptiness. Proverbs shows us how to choose wisdom in a variety of scenarios.

I need more training, so, here I am, back to the basics, beginning with Proverbs 1. If you're doing the same, allow God to sink His life lessons deeply into your spirit and enjoy the fruits of a life well-lived.

As God said in Deuteronomy 30:19, "I place before you Life and Death, Blessing and Curse. Choose life so that you and your children will live. And love God, your God, listening obediently to him, firmly embracing him."

Read Proverbs. Choose Life!

# THAT MISFIT DAVID

"When the Spirit of the Lord comes upon my heart
I will dance like David danced"

~ Fred Hammond
Song: *Spirit of David*

## Many Hats

I had a long list of chores to do and errands to run, and by the end of the day I had accomplished what I set out to do and got my walking exercise in. I admire and empathize with all my women friends who, like me, manage to cram an amazing amount of activity into each day.

The next morning, God brought me up short with the story of Obed-Edom, a man who wore at least as many hats as moms do. Did you know that men also get an amazing amount of activities done each day? His story is in 2 Samuel 6 and 1 Chronicles 13, 15, 16 and 26.

King David and his soldiers were tasked with bringing the liberated Ark of the Covenant back to Jerusalem on a cart. They exuberantly celebrated their victory, until the oxen that pulled the cart stumbled. Uzzah impulsively reached out to steady the Ark, and God struck him instantly dead. It seems harsh, doesn't it?

It brought the celebration to a very quick end. David was afraid to go any farther, so he left the Ark at the house of a Levite, Obed-Edom. If I were Obed's wife, I think I might have had a few objections at that point. "That thing KILLS people, Obed, and you want to keep it here? What are you thinking?"

What choice did he have? The King asked him, a Levite, to protect the Chest of the Covenant. He obediently kept the Ark for three months, during which God blessed his family and everything around him.

When it was time to take the Chest to King David, Obed-Edom packed up his family and moved to Jerusalem with the Ark. Here's where he got busy.

He became a security guard and was later promoted to lead the guards. He was a member of the choir and marching band. He was one of the men allowed to carry the Ark on poles. He and his eight sons and sixty other relatives were assigned to help Asaph and his co-workers with the work of worship around the clock. He was a very busy man.

Why was he mentioned so many times in these passages? Because God blessed him and his family as he committed his life to God's service. Obed-Edom was a true servant-leader, a man who wore many hats and probably ended each day a little worn out. I can empathize.

----------

## *The Zest of Life*

It was mid-winter in Florida, and the air had finally turned cool enough to open all the windows and wear long pants. We'd had summer weather for far too long. I love Florida winters precisely for the cool, dry air. There hadn't been enough of it that year, and I was grateful for whatever we were blessed with.

King David must have had the windows open when he wrote Psalm 27. Perhaps it was a cool evening in the desert. I can picture the breeze blowing diaphanous curtains as he sat with pen in hand and wrote.

"Light, space, zest – that's God! So with him on my side, I'm fearless, afraid of no one and nothing."

David was a man after God's own heart. As King of Israel, he had everything he wanted or needed, except this: "I'm asking God for one thing, only one thing: to live with him in his house my whole life long. I'll contemplate his beauty; I'll study at his feet. That's the only quiet, secure place in a noisy world, the perfect getaway, far from the buzz of traffic."

We know David's story. Quiet moments must have been a rare luxury for such a busy man. Between wives and wars, David had little peace. He was realistic enough to know he wouldn't get to live in God's house his whole life long – at least not in this life. Yet, he remained positive.

"I'm sure I'll see God's goodness in the exuberant earth. Stay with God! Take heart. Don't quit. I'll say it again: Stay with God." Amen!

----------

## *In Hiding*

When I was little and did something bad, I'd run and hide in the closet. It was my cave, my place of safety, and it was an illusion. My real safety was in the care of my parents. I didn't know at the time that the punishment I had, no doubt, earned was, in fact, a part of my training.

Our parents showed us love by teaching us what behavior is acceptable, and what is not. We learned respect and empathy, and we now look back and laugh at our antics and remember the pain on our parents' faces when they disciplined us.

God disciplined King David through pain. When he had the affair with Bathsheba and had her husband killed, God took their firstborn son and told David that violence would never leave his house. He'd already been hounded by King Saul, and would later be hunted by his son Absalom.

In Psalm 31, David was running and hiding. "I run to you, God, I run for dear life…You're my cave to hide in, my cliff to climb. Be my safe leader, be my true mountain guide. Free me from hidden traps, I want to hide in you…I hate all this silly religion, but you, God, I trust."

Wait a minute. Don't only religious people trust God? David understood that religion originates with humans. Relationship originates with God. David had a living, loving relationship with his God. That's why he trusted him, even as God meted out punishment for David's sin.

Throughout this Psalm, we hear David's pleas. "Be kind to me, God – I'm in deep, deep trouble again. Desperate, I throw myself on you; you are my God."

And then David's tone changed. "What a stack of blessing you have piled up for those who worship you, ready and willing for all who run to you to escape an unkind world. Blessed God! His love is the wonder of the world."

"Love God, all you saints; God takes care of all who stay close to him. Be brave. Be strong. Don't give up. Expect God to get here soon."

I crawled out of the closet to face the music. I was disciplined, and then Daddy or Mommy got down to my level, and hugged me tightly. I quickly forgot the punishment and enjoyed the security of knowing my parents loved me. I didn't forget the lesson, though, and avoided the behavior that resulted in the discipline. I imagine David did, too.

----------

## *Spin Cycle*

Have you ever felt like you're in a washing machine, both drowning and being beaten up by the agitation? I've been there many times, most often because I've done something that brought it all down on my own head. That's where David found himself after he was confronted by

Nathan about his affair with Bathsheba. He wrote Psalm 51 from inside a washing machine.

"Generous in love – God give grace! Huge in mercy – wipe out my bad record. Scrub away my guilt, soak out my sins in your laundry. I know how bad I've been; my sins are staring me down." There he was, in the washer.

We can't hide anything from God. He sees everything we do and he knows how awful we can be. He doesn't expect perfection from us. He wants us to be truthful. That's why David was the apple of God's eye, even after he got Bathsheba pregnant and had her husband killed in a futile attempt to hide the fact that the baby she carried was his.

"Soak me in your laundry and I'll come out clean, scrub me and I'll have a snow-white life. God make a fresh start in me, shape a Genesis week from the chaos of my life."

In the NIV, it reads like this: "Create in me a pure heart, O God, and renew a steadfast spirit within me."

"Going through the motions doesn't please you; a flawless performance is nothing to you. I learned God-worship when my pride was shattered. Heart-shattered lives, ready for love, don't for a moment escape God's notice." (MSG)

I also love how verse 17 is worded in the NIV: "My sacrifice, O God, is a broken spirit; a broken and contrite heart you, God, will not despise."

Thank God he's made that washing machine available to us! It's no fun to suffer the consequences of our actions, but we don't have to stay in the muck. He'll throw us in the wash, and make us fresh and clean, as often as we need it.

----------

## *A Father's Heart*

One winter day in New Jersey, I took a walk along the Palisades overlooking the Manhattan skyline across the Hudson River. I was pregnant with my second child, and my marriage was falling apart. Alone, frightened, envious of every couple I walked past, I cried out to God, *Don't you love me anymore?*

My walk led me past a small garden in front of a dull gray building. The plants were withered and brown, naked in their winter sleep; except for one. One solitary rose, barely opened, its branch full of dark green leaves, nodded on an otherwise leafless bush.

I suddenly felt warm. *For me?* I whispered. I sensed God smile and knew he really did love me.

Is it any wonder that King David was close to God's heart? He was an adulterer, conspired to commit murder, and had way too many wives and concubines, but he loved God wholeheartedly. Here's what he wrote when he was in the wilderness of Judea, in Psalm 63:

"God – you're my God! I can't get enough of you! I've worked up such a hunger and thirst for God traveling across dry and weary deserts.

"So here I am in the place of worship, eyes open, drinking in your strength and glory. In your generous love I am really living at last! My lips brim praises like fountains, I bless you every time I take a breath; my arms wave like banners of praise to you."

God's presence has never left me in all the years I've belonged to him. It's a privilege and joy to go to our place of worship, to sing and dance and wave my arms like banners of praise!

----------

## Moon Stroke

I love it when the moon is full and the night is cool. I went outside to enjoy the full moon on one clear night and saw a moonbow completely encircling the moon. I saw the muted colors, like a rainbow through a filter, and wondered at the complete circle it made.

I never knew moonbows existed until then, or that there is such a thing as moon stroke. Do you know anyone who has suffered from moon stroke? It's mentioned in Psalm 121 in The Message.

The medical term for it is Selenoplexia, from the Greek selene, 'the moon', and plexis, 'stroke'. Sun stroke is a highly dangerous condition that can be fatal. Apparently, there is some evidence that moon stroke can also kill. Some experts doubt its validity. The wording is a little different in the NIV, but the implication is still that the moon can be harmful. Let's start from the beginning.

Many of us are familiar with the first two verses. "I lift up my eyes to the mountains – where does my help come from? My help comes from the Lord, the Maker of heaven and earth." (NIV)

Have I mentioned that I love the wording in the Message? I have friends who believe in a Supreme Being, but call it the Universe. The Message addresses that in verses 1-2:

"I look up to the mountains; does my strength come from the mountains? No, my strength comes from God, who made heaven, and earth, and mountains." Why worship the created when you can go straight to the One who created it?

The rest of the Psalm is about our Guardian God who never sleeps, who stays by our side, guards us from every evil, guards our very life, and, in verse 6, shields us from sun stroke and shelters us from moon stroke. Why would God shelter us from something that isn't real?

I take great comfort from this Psalm. Whether we're awake or asleep, God is watching over us. I love the last verse, "He guards you when you leave and when you return, he guards you now, he guards you always."

There is no better bodyguard in the universe...not even the universe itself. So tonight, I will sleep without fear of moon stroke.

----------

## *Music on the Wind*

The grandkids and I were outside one day, when our granddaughter came running up to me yelling, "I hear it! I hear it!" Since I heard it, too, I knew what she meant.

A carillon tower plays tunes about five miles away. When the wind blows in the right direction, we can hear it from our house. Five miles is quite a distance, and it makes her happy that the music travels all the way to us. It's a smile from God. Like Psalm 67.

"God, mark us with grace and blessing! The whole country will see how you work, all the godless nations will see how you save. God! Let people thank and enjoy you. Let all people thank and enjoy you."

God's wind blows and carries his grace and blessing to us, like the music of the carillon. I pray that our nation and all the nations of the earth hear the music and respond like our granddaughter, "I hear it! I hear it! Isn't it beautiful?"

At the *Academy Awards* ceremony in 2014, one of the winners, Darlene Love, gave glory to God and spontaneously burst into song – *His Eye Is on the Sparrow.*

The actors, actresses, film makers, song writers – all the elite of Hollywood – jumped to their feet in a standing ovation. I wonder if they knew they were also giving glory to God because they affirmed her in her praise. Psalm 33 makes me want to stand and applaud God!

"Good people, cheer God! Right-living people sound best when praising. Use guitars to reinforce your Hallelujahs! Play his praise on a grand piano! Invent your own new song to him; give him a trumpet fanfare."

What a wonderful Psalm of praise to Creator God. Here are a few of my favorite verses;

"Blessed is the country with God for God; blessed are the people he's put in his will."

"Watch this: God's eye is on those who respect him, the ones who are looking for his love. He's ready to come to their rescue in bad times; in lean times he keeps body and soul together." God's eye may be on the sparrow, but it's also on you and me! And finally,

"We're depending on God; he's everything we need."

"Love us, God, with all you've got – that's what we're depending on." How can we not rejoice when the Creator and Maintainer of the universe has his loving eye on us and sends music on the wind?

----------

## Take a Deep Breath

Sometimes, reading the Bible is like taking a deep breath of the sweetest, freshest air. I pray for friends and family members who are going through unimaginable troubles. My heart is heavy, I cry easily, and I want so badly to see God turn things around for them. Then he gives me a jewel like Psalm 34.

"I bless God every chance I get; my lungs expand with his praise. I live and breathe God; if things aren't going well, hear this and be happy: join me in spreading the news; together let's get the word out." Breathe in and be happy, even when things are not going well. Isn't that just like God?

"God met me more than halfway; he freed me from my anxious fears. Look at him; give him your warmest smile. Never hide your feelings from him."

"When I was desperate, I called out, and God got me out of a tight spot. God's angels set up a circle of protection around us while we pray."

One thing I appreciate about growing older is perspective. God has saved me out of many desperate situations, so I can be confident that he won't let me down now.

"Open your mouth and taste, open your eyes and see – how good God is. Blessed are you who run to him. Worship God if you want the best; worship opens the door to all his goodness."

The rest of the Psalm is for our instruction. How do we worship him? Read it and see. Just remember this, "Is anyone crying for help? God is listening, ready to rescue you."

Take deep breaths and relax. God is watching out for all my friends and family, and for yours. How sweet it is to know that he cares when things get really tough.

----------

## *Cleansing Confession*

Our parents had planned a trip to Rome for my best friend and me. They bought the train tickets, booked hotel rooms, and gave us the itinerary. As soon as we arrived at the first stop, in Venice, we hopped off the train, cashed in our tickets and hitch-hiked the rest of the way to Rome.

We stayed in cheap hostels and saved the hotel money for the dance club where we intended to dance all night, every night, until we left for home. We bought a guidebook so we could tell our parents about the sights we never saw. We had the best time, but we had both lied to our families.

Even before I came to know the Lord, I had heard the expression, "Confession is good for the soul." Yeah, right. Confession can get you into a lot of trouble if you've been up to no good, and I was always up to no good in those days.

So why is confession good for us? Maybe David can shed some light on that in Psalm 32.

"Count yourself lucky, how happy you must be – you get a fresh start, your slate's wiped clean. Count yourself lucky – God holds nothing against you and you're holding nothing back from him."

"When I kept it all inside, my bones turned to powder, my words became day-long groans. The pressure never let up; all the juices of my life dried up."

"Then I let it all out; I said, 'I'll make a clean breast of my failures to God.' Suddenly the pressure was gone – my guilt dissolved, my sin disappeared. These things add up. Every one of us needs to pray."

Confession releases the pressure that sin builds up. I don't remember all the times I lied to my parents, but I distinctly remember the guilt that felt like a weight around my heart. I just recently shared our adventure in Rome with my mother. I had stubbornly kept her in the dark all these years.

"Don't be ornery like a horse or mule that needs bit and bridle to stay on track. God-defiers are always in trouble; God affirmers find themselves loved every time they turn around."

After I told her, I felt like I'd had Alka-Seltzer for the soul. What a relief it was! Mom just laughed, but that didn't make it right. God made it right. He always will, when we come to him and tell him what we've done.

----------

## *I Love You This Much*

A game I played with the grandkids on the days I picked them up from school started with my saying "I love you."

Anthony said "I love you this big," and Ashley countered with "I love you 100." That was followed by "I love you 200" and I would answer, "I love you to the moon and back."

They were much younger and had no concept of amounts, so 100 or 200 was a HUGE number. My favorite, though, was, "I love you sebenty thirty hundred!" Now that's a lot of love!

King David tried to describe God's love in Psalm 36:

"God's love is meteoric, his loyalty astronomic, his purpose titanic, his verdicts oceanic. Yet in his largeness nothing gets lost; not a man, not a mouse, slips through the cracks."

"How exquisite your love, O God! How eager we are to run under your wings."

"You're a fountain of cascading light, and you open our eyes to light."

Easter week is the culmination of thousands of years of prophecy in the death, burial and resurrection of Jesus Christ. For those of us who believe, it's the saddest and most joyful of all our celebrations.

What Jesus did for us was the ultimate demonstration of God's immeasurable, meteoric, astronomic, titanic, oceanic love. We have very little comprehension of the immensity of it.

Like our grandkids, we can only say, "I love you sebenty thirty hundred" while our hearts feebly attempt to hold the universe that God has given us because He loves us.

----------

## He Always Provides

One day, when I was a struggling single mom, I didn't know how I'd feed the kids that week. My paycheck wasn't due for a week, and I had run out of money because other bills had to be paid. I wasn't worried, though. I had faith that God would take care of us – at least that's what I kept telling the kids.

I found an envelope stuck in the front door. There was no name on it, so I opened it and found a check made out to me that would cover groceries for a couple of weeks! It was from a local church we had never attended. We didn't know anyone who went there, and still have no idea how they knew – unless God told them.

I had been tithing for a long time – even when there was so little it seemed crazy to give any of it away. I figured the tenth belonged to

God, not me. I have found it to be true that you cannot out-give God! His extravagant love is a generous love. He admonishes us over and over again throughout the Word to give, give and give more. That's what he does!

Psalm 37 is much like Proverbs. Here are some nuggets:

"God keeps track of the decent folk; what they do won't soon be forgotten. In hard times, they'll hold their heads high; when the shelves are bare, they'll be full." I watched it happen many times!

"Wicked borrows but never returns; righteous gives and gives. Generous gets it all in the end; stingy is cut off at the pass."

"I was young, now I'm gray-haired – not once have I seen an abandoned believer or his kids out roaming the street. Every day he's out giving and lending, his children making him proud."

"The spacious, free life is from God, it's also protected and safe. God-strengthened, we're delivered from evil – when we run to him, he saves us."

Hard times are inevitable in this life. Everyone has some problem or another. Yet, God gives us a spacious, free life right in the midst of it, and we can see his hand at work everywhere. So keep giving! You'll never out-give God!

----------

## Roses in the Desert

Did you know that Israel is the world's largest exporter of roses? God has turned the desert into fertile lands, full of crops and flowers!

Psalm 65 starts out, "Silence is praise to you, Zion-dwelling God, and also obedience. You hear the prayer in it all." Praise can certainly be boisterous, but God hears it in our silence, too. Obedience is praise! He hears our silent prayers, even when we don't know we're praying. That tells me he hears our hearts, even in our busyness.

"We all arrive at your doorstep sooner or later, loaded with guilt, our sins too much for us – but you get rid of them once and for all." Even in David's time, he knew there is life after death and our God forgives sins!

Our God is "Earth-Tamer, Ocean-Pourer, Mountain-Maker, Hill-Dresser, Muzzler of sea storm and wave crash, of mobs in noisy riot." God IS all that! Who wouldn't want to serve that God!

And this: "Oh, visit the earth, ask her to join the dance! Deck her out in spring showers, fill the God-River with living water. Paint the wheat fields golden. Creation was made for this!

"Drench the plowed fields, soak the dirt clods with rainfall as harrow and rake bring her to blossom and fruit.

"Snow-crown the peaks with splendor, scatter rose petals down your paths, all through the wild meadows, rose petals.

"Set the hills to dancing, dress the canyon walls with live sheep, a drape of flax across the valleys. Let them shout, and shout, and shout! Oh, oh, let them sing!"

The Psalmist wasn't thinking about the deluges that cause floods or horrific storms that bring ruin and pain. God is present in all of that. He turns disaster into blessing in his good time, and in his way. He works all things together for good -- after the flood, after the fire, after the wandering in the desert. Blessing is on the way.

I received a report of God's answers to very specific prayers. All I could do was raise my hands, say, "I love you, Lord!" and rejoice in the roses that are blooming in lives that have been in the desert. I'm singing, Lord! Hallelujah!

----------

## *Wanderers*

My dad used to say we were a family of gypsies. When we moved to someplace new, we parked our bags and took off to explore. You couldn't nail us down. We never lived on base, so we got to know the people and the language of our location. It was great training for life.

It resulted in all of us settling in different places in the world – at least until God moved us somewhere else. God has opened us up to adventure and opportunities to go wherever he wants us and whenever he moves us.

Dan and Cindy live in Germany with their tribe of kids and grandkids. They travel all over the world with their ministry.

Margie, in Florida, has kids and grandkids in Germany. They cross the Atlantic as often as they can to visit each other.

Mark and Patty are leaving the States and embarking on a mission to parts unknown and probably dangerous. They can't wait!

Sharon and Steve spent a great part of their life in a remote village in high mountains in another country, teaching them to read and write their language and giving them the Word.

Our sister Mary didn't live with us, but travels to see us when she can.

My mom sold her home in Spain and moved here because she heard God tell her it's time; and he blessed her with miracle after miracle to make it happen! He did the same for Margie when she moved to Florida from Germany.

This morning I read Psalm 84. "How blessed all those in whom you live, whose lives become the roads you travel; they wind through lonesome valleys, come upon brooks, discover cool springs and pools brimming with rain! God-traveled, these roads curve up the mountain, and at the last turn – Zion! God in full view!"

Way back in the time of King David, the Psalmist recognized that God lives in us. He directs our paths, and wherever we go, he goes – even in the valleys of loneliness.

Whatever road you take, when you know God, the last view, the one we're all traveling toward, will be of God in full view. Wow!

----------

## *Circle of Life*

When we first moved to Florida, with five of our eight kids in tow, we drove a mini-van. It was great for hauling kids and stuff, but the air conditioner was broken, and it became a daily trial to drive in Florida's heat and humidity. I could not wait for some of our children to get their own cars so that we could graduate to a newer model sedan. When that day finally arrived, I blasted the air conditioning until I felt icicles form on my nose!

We've been driving nice, well-maintained cars ever since. Now that we're grandparents, we sometimes have a bunch of grandkids come visit. How much nicer it would be to have them all in one car, rather than have to take two everywhere. So we got a mini-van! I believe it's called the "Circle of Life," at least in *The Lion King*.

Having watched our babies grow up to be wonderful men and women, we're acutely aware of our life-cycle. We start out as helpless, dependent infants, grow into our strength, have our own babies who have their own babies, and meanwhile, if we live long enough, we decline with age and will someday be helpless and dependent again.

It seems a bit dreary when you leave out all the good stuff in the middle. Here's what the Psalmist said about that, in Psalm 103:1-5:

"O my soul, bless God. From head to toe, I'll bless his holy name! O my soul, bless God, don't forget a single blessing!

"He forgives your sins – every one.

"He heals your diseases – every one.

"He redeems you from hell – saves your life!

"He crowns you with love and mercy – a paradise crown.

"He wraps you in goodness – beauty eternal.

"He renews your youth – you're always young in his presence.

"God makes everything come out right; he puts victims back on their feet."

From mini-van to mini-van, from childhood to grand-parenthood, God never changes! Life is full and rich and wonderful because God is in it all!

----------

## *Laying Their Lives Down*

I watched a *World News* report on Moore, Oklahoma, one year after an F-5 tornado devastated the town. The storm flattened two schools and killed 24 precious people. The report showed footage from the classrooms during and right after the storm, where teachers covered their students with their own bodies and assured them over and over that it's almost over while the kids screamed in terror. As terrified as they were, the teachers were willing to lay their lives down for the kids in their care.

A year after the disaster, new schools were ready for the next school year, with safe storm shelters built in. New homes stood where there had been nothing but rubble. Building continued. People recovered. We are a resilient humanity. So where was God?

Psalm 103 is one of my many favorites. You may be familiar with how it opens: "Bless the Lord, O my soul…" Verses 15-18 can easily apply to Moore, and to everyone who's lost property or loved ones in a disaster.

"Men and women don't live very long; like wildflowers they spring up and blossom, but a storm snuffs them out just as quickly, leaving nothing to show they were here."

"God's love, though, is ever and always, eternally present to all who fear him, making everything right for them and their children as they follow his covenant ways and remember to do whatever he said."

God's love is eternally present. This life is temporary for all of us. He told us, in John 3:26-17, "This is how much God loved the world: He gave his Son, his one and only Son. And this is why: so that no one need be destroyed; by believing in him, anyone can have a whole and lasting life. God didn't go to all the trouble of sending his Son merely to point an accusing finger, telling the world how bad it was. He came to help, to put the world right again. Anyone who trusts in him is acquitted."

The door to Heaven has been opened for us by the Hero who sacrificially gave his own life for us. If we acknowledge him and receive the gift he's given us, we have access to a wonderful eternity. Why would anyone refuse such a gift?

----------

## *What a Wonderful World*

Our double hibiscus bush was loaded with bright pink blossoms, and dozens of bulbs were about to bloom. The explosion of growth was as close to Spring as we get, since the bush blooms all year.

I watched a squirrel lay across a few branches, grab a bloom in his paws, and chirp happily as he ate the flower. I'm sure he smiled! I know I did! Who knew that squirrels love hibiscus flowers? The flowers only lasted as long as it took for the squirrels to eat them.

Psalm 104 is King David's anthem of appreciation for God's creation. It starts out: "O my soul, bless God! God, my God, how great you are! Beautifully, gloriously robed, dressed up in sunshine and all heaven stretched out for your tent."

David's joy is summed up in verses 24-27: "What a wildly wonderful world, God! You made it all with Wisdom at your side, made earth overflow with your wonderful creations...All the creatures look expectantly to you to give them their meals on time. You come and they gather around; you open your hand and they eat from it."

The hibiscus bush was the hand of God feeding the squirrels. I imagine his pleasure as that squirrel lost himself in the enjoyment of his meal.

"The Glory of God – let it last forever! Let God enjoy his creation! O my soul, bless God!" Let the hibiscus bush continually bloom for the squirrels to feast on. Amen!

# THE LONGEST PSALM

"Knowledge is love and light and vision."

~ Helen Keller

## *How To Eat An Elephant*

How do you eat an elephant? No offense to elephants, which happen to be among my favorite animals – and not because I've ever tasted one. The answer is: one bite at a time.

I love reading the Psalms, except for one. Assuming King David wrote this one, I can't help but think how human and flawed he was. And yet, God considered him the apple of his eye and loved and blessed him all his life. David suffered the consequences of his actions, as we all do, but it didn't change how God loved him.

So which Psalm do I keep bumping up against, read with reluctance, and can't wait to get through? It's the longest one: Psalm 119. The only way I can read and digest it is one bite at a time.

If I hadn't double checked, I could easily have mistaken verses 1-8 as a chapter in Proverbs. Doesn't this sound familiar? "You're blessed when you stay on course, walking steadily on the road revealed by God. You're blessed when you follow his directions, doing your best to find him."

David determined to live for God so he wouldn't have to live with regrets. He boldly told God, "I'm going to do what you tell me to do; don't ever walk off and leave me." As we know, he didn't do what God told him to do (bad news), and God never walked off and left him (good news).

Regardless of David's failings, his heart was in the right place. I'm no King David, but I'm the daughter of the King of Kings, and I'm eager to know him better, so I'll savor each bite.

----------

## *Fireworks*

On the Fourth of July, Bill and I wish you a joyful celebration of the founding of our wonderful country. We've been blessed in America, and have an incredible list of things to be thankful for – in part, because the United States was begun by a band of men who exercised wisdom, laid out a map for the future, and did not veer off course.

Those of you who travel that weekend will follow a map, whether on paper, in your head, or on GPS. How fitting that Psalm 119:9-16, tells us that the Word of God is a map, and that if we follow the road signs, we won't get lost.

Proverbs 4, oddly enough, also tells us that God's Word is a road map and that we should follow the road signs. I love the harmony in the Bible.

Our neighborhood is lit up with fireworks on this mid-summer holiday. People spend thousands of dollars on them, and then burn up all that money in one night. They provide a spectacular show for themselves, their families, and the rest of us who just like to stand outside, turn in a circle, and watch the skies light up.

Here's some good news, in case you're concerned about burning up all your money. David said, in this Psalm, "I've banked your promises in the vault of my heart, so I won't sin myself bankrupt." The promises of God will stave off the bankruptcy of a damaged, empty soul. You're on your own with the fireworks.

When we're excited about something, what do we do? We tell our friends and family about it! David ended this section by saying he delights in God's instructions for living. He promised to retain every word, and share what he learned with others.

Here's a little more harmony for you. Daniel 12:3 says this, "Men and women who have lived wisely and well will shine brightly, like the cloudless, star-strewn night skies. And those who put others on the right path to life will glow like stars forever!" We can be God's very own fireworks display! Light me up, Lord!

----------

## *Hungry*

Since long before I became a believer, I've longed for a home I know is out there somewhere -- especially while stargazing. I've always felt a pull toward my heart's home, so far away I'd never be able to reach it. The feeling grew less after I surrendered myself to the Lord, but it's never completely gone.

Don't get me wrong. I love my family and have lived in some pretty cool places, so it isn't discontent. Have you ever felt like you didn't belong here?

In Psalm 119:17-24, David called himself a stranger on earth. Is it possible that we're all strangers, here?

David asked God for some clear directions. Wouldn't it be amazing if, when we ask for help making a decision, God would speak to us audibly?

King David longed to hear from God. "My soul is starved and hungry, ravenous! – insatiable for your nourishing commands." He didn't wait for God's audible instructions.

He looked to his Word for the answers. If we're hungry to hear from God, we don't have to wait, either.

----------

## *Does He Love Me?*

The telltale pain started in the back of my neck and spread to cover the entire right side of my head, from neck to brow, like half a helmet full of spikes. I suffered with migraines. Each one gave me three days of misery at a time. I wrapped myself up in self-pity and begged God to take away the pain. I asked him, *Don't you love me, anymore?* Can anyone relate?

In Psalm 119:25-32, King David was sick. In his misery, he also questioned God, but in a different way. He wanted God to help him understand his ways. "My sad life's dilapidated, a falling-down barn; build me up again by your Word. Barricade the road that goes nowhere; grace me with your clear revelation."

Where I couldn't think about anything but myself until the misery passed, David sought revelation, in spite of how badly he felt. He said, "I choose the true road to Somewhere ..." Who wants to go Nowhere?

He finished by saying "I'll run the course you lay out for me if you'll just show me how." What a guy!

David was right. I've learned that God does still love us when we feel abandoned, sick and alone; and he has a way laid out for us that leads to healing and purpose. If we ask him, he'll show us the true road to Somewhere, and he'll show us how to follow it. Wait up, King David! I want to go Somewhere, too!

----------

## *Distractions*

When the finals of Wimbledon were on, we recorded the match, which freed us up to go to church, shake off every distraction, and focus on worshipping our amazing God. David had a problem with distractions, too. Imagine his responsibility as king: his wealth, his wives, and his critics.

In Psalm 119:33-40, he asked God to keep him focused on the course God had set out for him. He said, "Guide me down the road of your commandments; I love traveling this freeway!"

He admitted to being distracted by loot, toys and trinkets. How susceptible we all are to the same kinds of diversions. Video games, Facebook, Wimbledon – what is it that captures your attention?

The discipline it takes to focus on God requires having a hunger for God, and a disregard for the critics who think they know what's best for us. David reminded God, "see how hungry I am for your counsel; preserve my life through your righteous ways!"

After church, we watched Andy Murray give his entire focus to a big win for Great Britain. He and his nation were hungry for it. You can believe he was focused! Win or lose, he gave it his all – and he won. Lord, help me to give you my all.

----------

## *Love, Truth, Wisdom and Harmony*

Love, truth, wisdom, harmony – who wouldn't want a life filled with these attributes? Love? Oh, yeah. Songs have been written about wasting a lifetime looking for love in all the wrong places. Truth? What a surprise when we discover it is not relative. Wisdom? Don't you have to be old to be wise? Harmony? Most of us experience plenty of discord in life. So how does one go about finding these elusive elements? Ask King David.

In Psalm 119:41-48, he started by saying, "Let your love, God, shape my life with salvation, exactly as you promised; then I'll be able to stand up to mockery because I trusted your Word."

Here's some news for you -- mockery of our faith is nothing new. It predates Christianity! What is our defense against it? God's love.

David dedicated his life to guarding what God taught him. He was constantly searching for truth and wisdom. He cherished and loved God's counsel, and he wasn't afraid to tell everyone what he learned. "Then I'll tell the world what I find, speak out boldly in public, unembarrassed." So, if you want to know, ask David. He'll tell you.

You've probably figured out by now that this section doesn't mention harmony. Harmony is found by reading other parts of the Bible at the same time. In Proverbs 8, wisdom and truth existed before the creation of the world. The benefits are worth more than riches. Those who love truth and wisdom find armloads of life! They are blessed!

Conversely, in Hosea 4:6, God can't find anyone who loves or is faithful. "My people are ruined because they don't know what's right or true."

Maybe David was motivated to speak out in public, in order to educate his people. The best definition of love I've ever found is in 1 Corinthians 13. Love encompasses truth, wisdom, harmony, and every good attribute of life. May you all find love in the right place!

----------

## Mockers

Our family battles escalated when my youngest sister Sharon became a Christian. The battleground was our dinner table. With the exception of Mom, the rest of us were heathens, and we turned up the volume on sarcasm and mockery of our little sister. Why? She dared to bring Someone to the table who convicted us. She brought the Holy Spirit to dinner, and we wanted nothing to do with him. We thought she was easy prey, but God put a rod of steel in her backbone, and she never backed down in her faith. As a result, each of us came to know the Lord. She won us over to the One who saved us all.

Can you imagine someone making fun of King David for his faith in God? Hadn't God proven over and over again that he was real and active in David's life? Yet, there were mockers. Nothing has changed since then. In Psalm 119:49-56, David showed us how he dealt with them.

"These words hold me up in bad times; yes, your promises rejuvenate me."

David knew his strength came from God's words. He put them to music and sang them. He meditated on them and treasured them. "Still, I walk through a rain of derision because I live by your Word and counsel."

As much as he sought after God and tried to live according to his ways, he wasn't perfect. No one is. If people look to us as the experts on God and his ways, they're sure to be disappointed.

All we can do is follow David's example. Trust God. Allow him to saturate our lives more and more until, like David, we live in the music of God's Word.

David danced in worship. Who cares what people say? Let's dance!

----------

## *In a Pickle*

There have been times in my life when I did not see how God could possibly get me out of the dilemma I was in. Sometimes, circumstances put me there, and other times, my own bad choices resulted in overwhelming problems.

In Psalm 119:57-64, I empathize with King David. My cry was his cry, "I beg you from the bottom of my heart; smile, be gracious to me just as you promised." David was surrounded by people who wanted to take him down.

I've learned over the years that it doesn't help to curl up in a blubbering ball in a corner. Raging, feeling sorry for myself, complaining – none of it helps. I've learned to do what David did. "I get up in the middle of the night to thank you."

When I roll up my worries and hand them to God, telling him (and myself) that I trust him, and then thank him for the answers he'll come up with, I can, like David, say, "I can't wait till morning!"

David chose to be a friend and companion to like-minded believers. He chose to ignore the naysayers and mockers and to trust God to handle them. What he found was this, "Your love, God, fills the earth! Train me to live by your counsel."

We're in training. When we ask God to train us, be ready to learn to trust him! If his love fills the earth, aren't we included, after all?

----------

## *Spreading Rumors*

Other than three of my siblings, Sharon, Mark and Margie, I didn't know any Christians. When my friends in college told me that God-followers have to obey all these rules and never have any fun, I believed them.

Why did I trust people I barely knew more than I trusted the ones I grew up with? I made false assumptions and believed downright lies about Christ-followers like my own brother and sisters. Godless as I was, I even spread the lies. I didn't know I was following an ancient pattern.

In Psalm 119:65-72, people were saying stuff about King David. "The godless spread lies about me."

You can imagine how much trouble that caused David. Rumors and lies still ruin lives today, but here's something David learned from it, "My troubles turned out all for the best – they forced me to learn from your text book."

I was an unbeliever before God found me. David said, "Before I learned to answer you, I wandered all over the place, but now I'm in step with your Word."

Those who don't go after God, wander around clueless. I once thought that God followers lead boring lives. Now that I know better, I agree with David when he said, "They [the godless] are bland as a bucket of lard, while I dance to the tune of your revelation."

Who's having fun now? Move over David. I'm done being bland, and I'm ready to dance.

----------

## *In God's Lap*

I went through a particularly painful time in my life when I was expecting my second child. One night, I cried out to God with all I had. I wanted nothing more than to know that he would never desert me. I suddenly felt as if he'd gathered me onto his lap, wrapped me in his arms, and rocked me like a baby. I sobbed out my distress, and breathed in his peace.

It was a turning point in my faith, and a moment I will treasure forever. King David, a warrior and mighty king, had moments just like that.

In Psalm 119:73-80, David was talking to his Dad. "With your very own hands you formed me; now breathe your wisdom over me so I can understand you."

Here's that moment of complete vulnerability, "Oh, love me – and right now! – hold me tight! Just the way you promised. Now comfort me so I can live, really live; your revelation is the tune I dance to." I love the heart of this warrior king, and fully understand why, in spite of his glaring sins, God loved his heart, too.

David knew the influence he had as king over his people, and that those who feared God would take heart as he waited, expectantly, for God's Word. Yet, he didn't pretend to be anything more than an obedient son. "I can see now, God, that your decisions are right; your testing has taught me what's true and right."

He understood that his strength came only from God, and that he was the example his people looked up to. "Let those who fear you turn to me for evidence of your wise guidance. And let me live whole and holy, soul and body, so I can always walk with my head held high."

Me, too, Father God! Me, too!

----------

## *Homesick*

Have you ever been homesick? When I first came to the United States with my first husband, after having lived in Europe for fourteen years, I longed for the life and family I'd left behind. Homesickness brought me to tears many times, in spite of the life I was building in the States.

King David was homesick in Psalm 119:81-88. What did he have to be homesick for? He lived in a palace, had a huge family with his wives and children, was waited on hand and foot by many servants, and he lacked for nothing.

And yet, he said, "I'm homesick, longing for your salvation; I'm waiting for your word of hope. My eyes grow heavy watching for some sign of your promise; how long must I wait for comfort?" David sensed there was more – a home he hadn't seen yet.

I wept when I read the next verse, thinking of the brave team of firefighters who lost their lives attempting to save other people's homes, and the brave men and women who put themselves in the line of fire every day. "There's smoke in my eyes – they burn and water, but I keep a steady gaze on the instructions you post."

I can't help but believe the prayers of those men crying out for rescue were answered, and that they're enjoying their true Home in the presence of their loving Father. King David is undoubtedly there, too – no longer homesick.

In these verses, David complained. How long would he have to put up with the arrogant godless who tried to throw him off track with lies – constantly pushing to get their way, ignorant of God and his ways? How long until God hauled these tormentors to court? Does it sound familiar? He could have been talking about our times.

When we're feeling homesick – grieving for the lost and longing for a home we haven't yet seen, we can say with David, "In your great love revive me so I can alertly obey your every word." God's Word leads us home.

----------

## *Ignore the Law?*

In a recent, highly publicized court case, the prosecution asked the women in the jury to use their emotions to decide their verdict. In other words, ignore the evidence, ignore the law, and go with your feelings.

Isn't that the prevailing atmosphere of our times? Truth is relative – it's only true if you feel it's true. That, my friends, is the foundation for chaos.

I love King David's proclamation in Psalm 119:89-96. "What you say goes, God, and stays as permanent as the heavens. Your truth never goes out of fashion; it's as up-to-date as the earth when the sun comes up. Your Word and truth are dependable as ever; that's what you ordered – you set the earth going."

God's Word and his truth are absolutes. They don't change. Everything we do is measured against that truth.

Is that a bad thing? David didn't think so. He delighted in God's revelation, his wisdom, his Word. The truth kept him going when hard times came. His life was saved by God's truth. "Save me! I'm all yours. I look high and low for your words of wisdom. The wicked lie in ambush to destroy me, but I'm only concerned with your plans for me."

Some would say we believers live a restricted life because we trust that God's Word is true. Here's what King David, who had access to every human pleasure imaginable, had to say about that, "I see the limits to everything human, but the horizons can't contain your commands!" The heavens cannot contain the limitless power of God's truth!

The women who were so disrespected by that prosecutor ignored his bad advice and did exactly what they were capable of doing – they followed the law, weighed the evidence, and rendered their verdict based on the truth.

Good for you, women! I feel like dancing a little bit. That's the truth.

----------

## *Super Hero*

In my teens, my favorite superhero was "Faster than a speeding bullet! More powerful than a locomotive! Able to leap tall buildings in a single bound!" His power came from our yellow sun. As far as fictional superheroes go, he's still my favorite.

Since then, I've found a real-life Super Hero, who, in a single act, gave the whole world hope for salvation. King David hadn't met him, yet.

In Psalm 119:97-104, we see that David's source of power, the Word of God, gave him some extraordinary abilities. It gave him the edge over his enemies, made him smarter than the smartest teachers, wiser than the wisest sages. He loved God's commands, which never become obsolete.

God's word was sustenance to him. "Your words are so choice, so tasty; I prefer them to the best home cooking." David understood life because of what God's Word taught him.

Superman had a weakness – kryptonite. Remnants of the life he'd left behind weakened him and made him vulnerable to his enemies. David knew that to stray off the path God laid out for him would have that same effect on him. "I watch my step, avoiding the ditches and ruts of evil so I can spend all my time keeping your Word. I never make detours from the route you laid out; you gave me such good directions."

The truth of God's word was David's yellow sun. Lies and false propaganda were his kryptonite. Our yellow sun, our kryptonite – nothing has changed. We have the same source of power David did, and the same challenges. Lord, I'm plugging in for more of your powerful Word!

----------

## God's Flashlight

I haven't always wanted to do what God says to do. In fact, after the divorce I experienced what some have described as the "dark night of the soul." I turned away from God and wanted nothing to do with his people. I refused all offers of prayer and didn't want to listen to advice that included God in any way.

Did he turn away in disgust, as I would have done? Did he condemn me, cast me out, throw me away, or desert me? Absolutely not! God handed me a flashlight! Ancient, battle-dented, often reviled and mocked, it will never lose its light.

In Psalm 119:105-112, King David was given that same old flashlight. "By your words I can see where I'm going; they throw a beam of light on my dark path."

I remember it by a song we sometimes sing in church, "Thy Word is a lamp unto my feet, and a light unto my path." The tiniest light can dispel the darkest gloom. This beam of light is not tiny, as David found out.

God's Word kept his life from falling apart and kept him on course even when others tried to throw him off track. God sent glimmers of light into the darkness I'd wrapped myself in. He sent hugs and surprises until I was ready to get back to the beacon of his Word. We can't get lost if we follow the light.

----------

## *The Tenderizer*

My mom had a secret. We took it for granted that the meat she prepared for the family was always tender. She used seasonings, so we assumed it was something she sprinkled on the meat. Vegetarians, you may skip the next part.

Then one day I heard this banging in the kitchen and discovered her beating the stuffing out of a steak with a heavy metal-studded mallet. Hoo, boy, was I glad she never chased us with that thing!

Sometimes it seems as if the older we get, the more God allows us to be tenderized. The tough parts of us give way to the pounding, while what's left is nourishing and useful. The result, in my case, was more compassion, more emotion and more tears. Things I once considered gravely important, weren't, and things I had little time for became vital.

The process can be painful, like a deep tissue massage, but it draws me closer to the source of life, and I'm grateful for it.

King David, in Psalm 119:113-120, saw that the consequences of rejecting God's instructions were deadly. "Expose all who drift from your sayings; their casual idolatry is lethal."

David understood that in order for God to do the work in us, we have to submit to the process, commit to the path, and embrace God's instructions. The more we know God's Word and follow his instructions, the less tenderizing we need!

God loves us, so He gives us rest, as well. "You're my place of quiet retreat; I wait for your Word to renew me." The result of David's submission was this, "I shine in awe before you; your decisions leave me speechless with reverence."

Come enjoy some time at God's spa. After the tenderizing deep tissue massage, we can shine, too!

----------

## *Nothing's New*

It was King Solomon who said there is nothing new under the sun.

The more I read the Bible, the more convinced I am that politics were around since the devil offered Adam and Eve incentives to disobey God.

The political climate of King David's day was much like ours, only the lines were drawn according to God followers or those in opposition to God's principles. In Psalm 119:121-128, David laid out his platform.

"I stood up for justice and the right; don't leave me to the mercy of my oppressors. Take the side of your servant, good God; don't let the godless take advantage of me. I can't keep my eyes open any longer, waiting for you to keep your promise to set everything right." We are still waiting for God to fulfill that promise. Will he?

"Yea-saying God, I love what you command; I love it better than gold or gemstones. Yea-saying God, I honor everything you tell me, I despise every deceitful detour."

God says "Yes." God's truth stands firm. When that day comes, I want to be found on God's side of the issues.

----------

## *Good Boy!*

We grew up with dogs, cats, hamsters, rabbits, lizards, snakes, birds -- you name it. If it was smaller than the pony I always wanted, we had it. We loved them all, but the dogs expressed their love for us the best.

When they greeted us with their hopping dance, energetic tails, flopping ears and complete body enthusiasm, we knew they were happy to see us. The feeling was mutual.

In Psalm 119:129-136, King David expressed his devotion to God and his Word in a way that reminded me of the trust our dogs had in us.

"Mouth open and panting, I wanted your commands more than anything. Turn my way; look kindly on me, as you always do to those who personally love you." Now I'm not comparing David to a dog. In fact, some of the other verses make me think of a toddler.

"Steady my steps with your Word of promise so nothing malign gets the better of me. Rescue me from the grip of bad men and women so I can live life your way." Humble King David trusted God like his parent. His own considerable strength was like a child's compared to the challenges he faced.

David cried out to God to open his words so that ordinary people would see the light. He wanted people to see what he saw, "Every word you give me is a miracle word – how could I help but obey?" His disappointment in them was acute, "I cry rivers of tears because nobody's living by your book!"

Hungry, humble, passionate King David knew he needed God's strength and the truth of his Word. Don't we all?

----------

## Conscience

A few years ago, millions of dollars were spent on a study to determine when children begin to show compassion. Anyone who has ever had or known a child could have answered that question free of charge. Babies show compassion to each other.

I wonder if the same attention and tax money has ever been dedicated to the study of conscience. When our kids and grandkids were still in diapers, we always knew when they did something wrong – and so did they. We didn't have to tell them or catch them at it. They just knew. How? What sets the standard against which right or wrong is determined, even in very young children?

King David told us in Psalm 119:137-144. "You are right and you do right, God; your decisions are right on target. You rightly instruct us in how to live ever faithful to you."

He said something revealing about himself. "I'm too young to be important, but I don't forget what you tell me." Too young to be important? King David?

Once again, he showed that his relationship with God was like that of a little child with a loving parent. He affirmed that God sets the standard for conscience to work properly. "Your righteousness is eternally right; your revelation is the only truth."

David accepted God's instructions, knowing that the path to a full and happy life is to keep a clear conscience. "The way you tell me to live is always right; help me understand so I can live to the fullest."

I've suffered the consequences of doing wrong because I ignored the nagging voice of my conscience telling me to stop. Is there anyone who hasn't ignored it? Like David, though, I've found that the richest, fullest life comes from doing what's right according to God's plan. Thank you, Lord, for keeping me and King David on the right track.

----------

## Worrier or Warrior?

I like to think I'm a warrior, not a worrier, but when our children began to drive cars, I knew I was deluding myself. When they went out at night, I stayed up until they came home. When a child was sick or hurt or facing danger, I worried. When our son was deployed in a war zone, I stayed up all night at times praying for him. It's comforting to know I'm in good company.

King David was surrounded by people whose opposition was life-threatening. A king couldn't be voted out. He could retire, after appointing a son as successor, as David did, or die by natural causes, in battle, or by treachery. Imagine living under the pressure of that threat. In Psalm 119:145-152, David described how it kept him awake.

"I call out at the top of my lungs, 'God! Answer! I'll do whatever you say.'" My inability to keep that promise also keeps me awake at night.

"I was up before sunrise, crying for help, hoping for a word from you. I stayed awake all night, prayerfully pondering your promise."

He appealed to God's love and justice to keep him alive and safe from those out to get him. Then he shared his source of comfort and strength. "But you're the closest of all to me, God, and all your judgments are true."

God's closeness is the buffer between us and everything that threatens us and our loved ones. As David said, "I've known all along from the evidence of your words that you meant them to last forever."

So, if God's word lasts forever, and he's the buffer that stands between us and our troubles, why do we worry? I am looking forward to a really good night's sleep.

----------

## *Unlimited Mercies*

I did not grow up in a Christian home. My mom was a closet believer, who knew and loved the Lord but didn't talk about him, and my dad didn't believe in an afterlife, or that Adam and Eve could have populated the world. When you live nearly a thousand years and there's no TV, what else is there to do, Dad? I digress.

There I was, in my early twenties, oblivious to the dimension of God. I longed for any friend, knew that something was missing and felt homesick for somewhere in outer space. My brother and sister were saved by that time and tried to get me to listen, but their vocabulary made no sense to me and, frankly, turned me off.

In Psalm 119:153-160, I read that King David knew all about that. He said, "'Salvation' is only gibberish to the wicked because they've never looked it up in your dictionary."

God's dictionary is his Word, and it only made sense to me when I gave up and gave in to what he wanted me to do – surrender. Then, like David, this is what I found to be true: "Your mercies, God, run into the billions; following your guidelines revives me."

Billions!! Unlimited mercies – unlimited favor – unlimited love. The older I get, the more I appreciate what this means. I cannot out-give, outlive, outsmart, outdo, outwit, or hide from God – and He loves me anyway.

I had racked up frequent-quitter miles up to that point in my life, but knew that if I cashed them in and quit this, I'd go back to an empty, lonely life. King David knew about that, too. "I took one look at the quitters and was filled with loathing; they walked away from your promises so casually."

Who knows why we humans quit so easily? When I found the truth, the impulse to walk away, walked away. I find, with King David, that "your words all add up to the sum total; truth. Your righteous decisions are eternal."

We have unlimited eternity to enjoy our unlimited God. My mom came out of the closet and now speaks freely about her loving God, and my dad gave his heart to the Lord before he went home to Heaven. He's probably talking to Adam and Eve and wondering how he ever doubted. Is there anything better than the Truth?

----------

## Uncommon Sense

One of my pet peeves is a lack of common sense. When kindergartners are punished for pointing their fingers at each other in play, or chewing their toast into the alleged shape of a gun, or even punished for an innocent kiss or bringing mom's nail file to school, it just burns me up. What have the adults in this world become?

Some of you will agree with me that our current government sets the bar very, very low for common sense. My own occasional common sense lapse irks me even more than seeing it in others. Is there a cure? Are our times any different than King David's times?

It might surprise you, as it did me, to know that nothing has changed -- not even politics.

In Psalm 119:161-168, King David described the climate of his times, and gave us the only answer that makes sense: "I've been slandered unmercifully by the politicians, but my awe at your words keeps me stable."

He was ecstatic over what God said – as if he'd won the lottery. Lies feed stupidity and cause those without discernment to stumble around in the dark. Common sense drains out when people believe the lying fodder coming from common sense killers.

David said, "I hate lies – can't stand them! – but I love what you have revealed. For those who love what you reveal, everything fits – no stumbling around in the dark for them."

David lived in active expectation of God's salvation and deliverance, doing what he knew God wanted him to do. He stopped and praised God seven times a day because God keeps everything running right. How often do we stop and praise him?

I would love to have had King David running our government. Common Sense would have thrived under his leadership. "My soul guards and keeps all your instructions – oh, how much I love them! I follow your directions, abide by your counsel; my life's an open book before you."

No wonder the politicians slandered him. He didn't play by their rules. What is the cure for a lack of common sense? What God has revealed! The Truth!

----------

## *Personal God*

During my single years, I worked for a company that employed scientists and engineers to develop solar technology. A visiting scientist from Israel invited me to dinner one evening. It didn't take long for me to share my faith with him. He was surprised. "Do you actually believe in a personal God?"

He was skeptical but honestly curious, and we talked about it all evening. When he dropped me off at home, he expressed his own longing to believe that God would take a personal interest in him. He was in good company. The king of Israel expressed that same longing a few centuries ago, but with a difference. He knew, and told us about it in Psalm 119:169-176.

"Let my cry come right into your presence, God; provide me with insight that comes only from your Word. Give my request your personal attention; rescue me on the terms of your promise." He asked God for his personal attention, and knew he would get it!

"Put your hand out and steady me since I've chosen to live by your counsel." God's presence was as real to David as his own father.

I remember my Dad coming to comfort me after another move when I thought I would die from homesickness for the friends I'd left behind. David knew that comfort, "I'm homesick, God, for your salvation; I love it when you show yourself!" Only a personal God would show himself.

Like me, David didn't keep his relationship quiet. "Let praise cascade off my lips; after all, you've taught me the truth about life! And let your promises ring from my tongue; every order you've given is right." David found that the more we share our faith, the stronger we get. "Invigorate my soul so I can praise you well; use your decrees to put iron in my soul."

I'd like to say I led my scientist friend to the Lord, but I can't. I didn't keep in touch with him, either. I do know that the seed was planted, and that our personal God won't let him go. He's our Daddy, our Shepherd and his love never, ever fails us. "And should I wander off like a lost sheep – seek me! I'll recognize the sound of your voice."

I believe he sought and saved that curious scientist, just as he sought and saved King David – and you and me. You can't get more personal than that.

# A MISFIT ON THE ROMAN ROAD

"More of you, less of me
Make me who I'm meant to be"

~ Colton Dixon
Song: *More of You*
Songwriters: R. Ortolani, N. Oliverio;
Ital. Lyric: M. Ciorciolinis, N. Newell

## Clear Sight

A police officer shot a man he believed was reaching for a weapon at a routine traffic stop. The man was actually reaching for his driver's license, which the officer had requested. Tensions around the country had been high following a tragic event involving police officers, and the policeman was exceptionally nervous. His interpretation of what he saw resulted in a wounded man, the officer's suspension and an investigation.

There are some pretty controversial statements in the book of Romans, and the way I read them is not always the way they've been interpreted by much more highly educated people than I. It's so rich that I hesitate to add my uneducated comments to Paul's eloquence.

Here's a little background on the Apostle Paul. His Jewish name was Saul. He was born a Roman citizen, and later used the name Paul, so that's how I'll refer to him.

Paul was a well-educated Pharisee, a young man being groomed for the Sanhedrin, or council of Jewish priests. He was fanatical about ridding Israel of the upstart followers of Jesus. He was on his way to Damascus to arrest the heretics there, when Jesus himself blinded him with a bright light and asked him, "Saul, Saul, why are you out to get me?" (Acts 9:4)

He told Paul to go into the city and wait for God's instructions. Then Jesus appeared to Ananias and told him to go and pray for Paul and he'd regain his sight.

Paul's reputation preceded him. Jesus-followers were terrified of him. They hadn't learned yet that he had encountered Jesus, whom he knew had been crucified. Meeting Jesus changed his life forever. After Ananias prayed for him, he became one of the Apostles and spread the news about Jesus everywhere he went.

Paul's highly trained and well-educated interpretation of the Gospel would naturally stem from his background, as the police officer's interpretation of events stemmed from his. They both chose to serve others, yet, their resulting actions were vastly different.

One didn't see clearly and acted impulsively. The other had his eyes opened and began to see things from a misfit's point of view.

"We don't yet see things clearly. We're squinting in a fog, peering through a mist. But it won't be long before the weather clears and the sun shines bright! We'll see it all then, see it all clearly as God sees us, knowing him directly just as he knows us!" (I Corinthians 13:12)

----------

## *Ouch*

I love Paul's letter to the Roman Jews, with the exception of parts of chapters one and two. I wish I could skip them and go right into the best part of the letter, but there's some real value in getting our hands slapped now and then.

He started out by relating the Jewish prophecies of the coming Messiah to Jesus, in Romans 1: "His descent from David roots him in history; his unique identity as Son of God was shown by the Spirit when Jesus was raised from the dead, setting him apart as the Messiah, our Master." Those were strong words from a highly educated Jewish leader who actively persecuted Christians until he met Jesus.

Now there he was, spreading the same news he'd hated earlier. "It's news I'm most proud to proclaim, this extraordinary Message of God's powerful plan to rescue everyone who trusts him, starting with the Jews and then right on to everyone else!"

God has a plan to rescue everyone who trusts him. "God's way of putting people right shows up in the acts of faith confirming what Scripture has said all along: 'The person in right standing before God by trusting him really lives.'"

So what don't I like about that? Nothing. It's what comes next that I'd rather not read or write about. As in Proverbs, the positive is coupled with the negative.

What happens to people when they refuse to believe God and turn their backs on him? "They traded the glory of God who holds the whole world in his hands for cheap figurines you can buy at any roadside stand." Cheap figurines can be taken literally or they can stand for anything we allow to turn us away from God.

Then God said, "If that's what you want, that's what you get." Uh, oh. God turned his back on them, and "all hell broke loose".

The last verses described some of the things that happen to people who are left to their own devices. It's a scary world, and one we're all familiar with.

So, does that make us superior? If you think so, be prepared to get slapped down in chapter two. I don't like that one, either.

----------

## Our Common Humanity

I enjoy having an occasional lunch with a dear friend who isn't like me. We don't share the same faith. We have different occupations and different education levels. She's much more educated than I, and I've lived in different countries than she has. Why point this out? We have much more in common than not.

We love and appreciate each other for who we are, regardless of, and because of, our differences. I cannot be her and she cannot be me, and we're both glad of it because it makes for good conversation.

Paul reminded us of our common humanity in Romans 2. It started with a continuation of the first chapter. "Those people are on a dark spiral downward. But if you think that leaves you on high ground where you can point your finger at others, think again. Every time you criticize someone, you condemn yourself."

Strong words, Paul! Why? "Judgmental criticism of others is a well-known way of escaping detection of your own crimes and misdemeanors." Someone once told me that when you point a finger at someone else, three are pointing back at you. Try it.

If you have kids, or you've ever been one, you know that they learn early on to direct your attention elsewhere when they've done something wrong — usually by blaming another kid. But God is a parent, and parents see through that stuff.

Paul reminded us that God is kind, but he's not soft. "In kindness, he takes us by the hand and leads us into a radical life change." Did you know that God is a radical? He's also not fooled by our shenanigans. The day is coming when we'll all get what's coming to us. Those who choose to live for God can look forward to real life, and those who choose not to, will face God's judgment — not ours.

God doesn't care what our background is or where we came from. He doesn't care if we're Jewish or not. Paul was taught that God was the Hebrew God and Gentiles were outsiders, without hope of salvation. He said, "Being a Jew won't give you an automatic stamp of approval.

God pays no attention to what others say (or what you think) about you. He makes up his own mind." That's good news for both Jews and non-Jews – or is it?

----------

## *How Much We Know*

The book of 1 Chronicles is a genealogist's dream-come-true, and a nightmare for the rest of us. I tend to skim it, but there are a few surprises I'm glad I didn't miss. Ephraim and his family were cattle rustlers. Ephraim's daughter, Sheerah, was an engineer/builder who built two cities. Joshua, the right-hand man of Moses and a strong man of God, descended from criminals.

A prostitute, a Gentile, and an adulteress were in the lineage of Jesus. How God must laugh when we get self-righteous. Paul had something to say about that, too, in Romans 2.

He made it clear that God isn't interested in our background or how much we know. He cares about what we do with it. Action determines our outcome. "Doing, not hearing, is what makes the difference with God."

What happens to all those people who haven't heard about God? Anthropologists might tell us that isolated tribes live by their own moral code. They love, interact, live by rules, make friends, teach their children – just like 'civilized' people who know of God and his law. Paul said that, by this evidence, God's law is a part of the fabric of human life. "There is something deep within them that echoes God's yes and no, right and wrong." God takes it all into account.

Did you know that religion cannot save you? "I have a special word of caution for you who are sure that you have it all together yourselves and, because you know God's revealed Word inside and out, feel qualified to guide others through their blind alleys and dark nights and confused emotions to God. While you are guiding others, who is going to guide you?"

He said, "You can get by with almost anything if you front it with eloquent talk about God and his law." Fancy talk, extensive Bible knowledge, being an 'insider' to God's revelation -- none of it matters to God.

In the final verses of Romans 2, Paul said that circumcision, the surgical ritual that marks Jewish men, is great if they follow God's ways. The reverse is also true. "The uncircumcised who keep God's ways are as good as the circumcised." Since he spoke directly to Jews here, we non-Jews can extrapolate that we're included in this if we have chosen to follow God.

"It's the mark of God on your heart, not of a knife on your skin that makes a Jew. And recognition comes from God, not legalistic critics." Have we Christians become legalistic critics?

God forbid. In the next chapter, Paul said it does make a difference who's a Jew and who isn't, but not in a way you might assume.

----------

## *It's Not My Fault!*

Dyana wrote a blog about how she suddenly realized she sounds just like her mother. I laughed and felt my heart expand with love for this young woman of incredible insight. I wonder if she knows that she sounded like me before she reached adolescence. So did her brothers.

Have you ever used an argument similar to this? "I didn't ask to be born! You made the stupid rules just so I'd break them. It's not my fault, it's yours!" Maybe I'm the only kid who said this to my folks, but Paul said otherwise in Romans 3.

"So what difference does it make who's a Jew and who isn't, who has been trained in God's ways and who hasn't? As it turns out, it makes a lot of difference – but not the difference so many have assumed." The difference is that God entrusted them with writing down and keeping the Holy Scriptures. Have you heard of the 80-20 rule? 20% of the people do 80% of the work. It seems that hasn't changed since ancient times.

Some abandoned their posts, dropped the ball, were distracted by life, and were faithless to the God who had proven himself over and over again. In spite of them, His faithfulness is not dependent on theirs. "God keeps his word even when the whole world is lying through its teeth."

Paul then used logic to make the same argument I made to my parents. "But if our wrongdoing only underlines and confirms God's right doing, shouldn't we be commended for helping out? Since our bad words don't even make a dent in his good words, isn't it wrong of God to back us to the wall and hold us to our word?"

As a kid, it made perfect sense to argue that we can't live up to our parents' standards, so they must want us to fail. Right? As a parent, I say with Paul, "The answer is no!" How else is God going to straighten us out if he doesn't hold us to his standards?

Adults can take that argument to the depths of depravity. In Paul's day, they accused him of spreading this lie, "The more evil we do, the more good God does, so let's just do it!" It was pure slander then, and it's pure slander now.

"So where does that put us? Do we Jews get a better break than others?" This may be where people mistakenly believe the difference between Jews and non-Jews lies. They have the inside track because of their history with the God who chose them. Paul said otherwise. Scripture makes it clear that we're all in the same sinking boat. We are all sinners.

----------

## *The Sinking Ship*

Sin is such an archaic word. I'm a good person, you're a good person; why would we be considered sinners? The *World English Dictionary* defines sin as transgression of God's known will or any principle or law regarded as embodying this. Every society has a moral code, whether Jew, Gentile, Aboriginal or Secular. I've heard it said that sin is anything that separates us from a holy, perfect God.

Paul was speaking to Roman Jews in this letter. By extension, he spoke to all of us who believe in God. In Romans 3, he said, "Our involvement with God's revelation doesn't put us right with God. What it does is force us to face our complicity in everyone else's sin." It doesn't sound like there's much hope of rescue from this sinking ship.

It seems I'm always trying to get ahead of myself, and usually just find myself farther behind. Don't we do that with God, too? How many blessings would we have missed out on if God had answered our prayers the way we wanted him to?

I'm learning to trust him to do it his way. We would all miss the lifeline God has thrown to our sinking ship if we insist on our own way. Many do miss it. So how do we catch it?

Paul reported that what Moses and the Prophets were given glimpses of has happened. God has given the Jews a way out of the sin ship – not only the Jews, but also everyone who believes! Since no one is capable of living the glorious life God wants for us, God made the way for us. "Out of sheer generosity he put us in right standing with himself. A pure gift. He got us out of the mess we're in and restored us to where he always wanted us to be."

Did you get that? It's a gift, not something we can earn, but only something we can accept or reject. "And he did it by means of Jesus Christ." That's our lifeline!

----------

## Perfect Sacrifice

Almost all of the earliest Christians were Jews, many of them in the priesthood. They understood the concept of sacrifice. They had been sacrificing animals to atone for their sins for centuries. They kept sinning, and kept sacrificing.

Why is this important for us to know? Because what we do imperfectly, God does perfectly. Paul said so, in Romans 3.

"God sacrificed Jesus on the altar of the world to clear the world of sin." The world includes everyone in it.

"Having faith in him sets us in the clear. God sets things right and makes it possible for us to live in his rightness." We don't have to go down with the ship! We can live on solid ground and enjoy the blessings of God!

Remember that Paul addressed his letter to his Jewish friends. They might have taken offense at this next part, "So where does that leave our proud Jewish insider claims and counter-claims? Canceled? Yes, canceled." Say, what?

"And where does that leave our proud Jewish claim of having a corner on God? Also canceled." I can see where this might have caused an uproar.

Paul suffered imprisonment and beatings at the hands of his fellow Jews, and reading this, I can see why. He was as bold in speaking to them as he was in writing to them. Brave man, Paul! He didn't leave it there, though!

"God does not respond to what we do; we respond to what God does." Does that sound familiar? He sets the standards, he does things his way, and we'd better follow along.

"God is the God of outsider non-Jews as well as insider Jews. How could it be otherwise, since there is only one God?"

The question that must have plagued his readers is this: Does this negate the careful observance of the Law?

Here's what Paul said about that, "What happens, in fact, is that by putting that entire way of life in its proper place, we confirm it." How is that?

----------

## *Abraham as the Father of Israel*

Ladies, what would you do if an angel appeared to you and said, "You're going to have a son by this time next year."? Let me narrow that down. You are 89 and your husband is 99.

I would probably die of a heart attack right then and there, but when it happened to Sarai, she laughed! No way was that ever going to happen!

God, who gave us our sense of humor, probably laughed with her in delight, and then he told Abraham to name their son Isaac, meaning laughter. He changed Sarai's name to Sarah, which means princess, because she would be the mother of many nations. Can you imagine

Abraham's reaction to all this? You waited until now to fulfill your promise, Lord?

In Romans 4, Paul asked a few good questions regarding Abraham's role as the Father of Israel. "So how do we fit what we know of Abraham, our first father in the faith, into this new way of looking at things? If Abraham, by what he did for God, got God to approve him, he could certainly have taken credit for it. But the story we're given is a God-story, not an Abraham-story."

What did Paul mean by that? "Abraham entered into what God was doing for him, and that was the turning point. He trusted God to set him right instead of trying to be right on his own." Isaac happened because Abraham trusted God to invigorate him.

Paul assumed that all his Jewish friends agreed that Abraham was declared fit before God because he trusted that God would do something that was beyond Abraham's capability, something he couldn't have done on his own. That's the faith that set him right with God.

And then Paul quoted King David. "Fortunate [blessed] are those whose crimes are carted off, whose sins are wiped clean from the slate. Fortunate [blessed] the person against whom the Lord does not keep score."

Then he asked, "Do you think for a minute that this blessing is only pronounced over those of us who keep our religious ways and are circumcised? Or do you think it possible that the blessing could be given to those who never even heard of our ways, who were never brought up in the disciplines of God?"

We Christians should be asking that same, very good question. Is the blessing limited to those of us who practice our religion, or is it for everybody?

----------

## *Religion is a Crutch*

I've heard it said that belief in God is a crutch for those who can't think for themselves. I have two things to say about that. Firstly, I'd rather lean on God, who knows everything, than on my own intellect any day, so bring on the crutch.

Secondly -- I'll let Paul tell you what I think, in Romans 4. One of my favorite things about this letter is Paul's logic.

"Now think," he said. "Use your mind -- not your emotions; not your gut; not your religious dogma. Was that declaration [that God declared Abraham was right with him] made before or after he was marked by the covenant rite of circumcision? That's right, before he was marked."

Circumcision was the evidence and confirmation of his faith. His faith didn't depend on it and he didn't have faith because of it.

In this next section, we're getting into the good part of Paul's letter to the Romans. "And it means further that Abraham is the father of all people who embrace what God does for them while still on the 'outs' with God, as yet unidentified as God's, in an 'uncircumcised' condition."

This, my friends, is the reason that people like me can be saved! It's the reason anybody, in any condition, belief system or lifestyle can be saved. Go back and read John 3:16. But wait a minute. What about the Jews who are already circumcised?

"Abraham is also, of course, father of those who have undergone the religious rite of circumcision, not just because of the ritual, but because they were willing to live in the risky faith-embrace of God's action for them, the way Abraham lived long before he was marked by circumcision."

Here's the part we all need to chew on for a while. "If those who get what God gives them only get it by doing everything they are told to do and filling out all the right forms properly signed, that eliminates personal trust completely, and turns the promise into an ironclad contract! That's not a holy promise; that's a business deal. A contract…only makes sure that you will never be able to collect. But if there is no contract in the first place, simply a promise – and God's promise at that – you can't break it."

Does this mean there is hope for misfits like me and for my family of misfits and independent thinkers?

----------

## *Trust Is An Action Verb*

When Dyana and Billy brought four of our grandkids to us from another state, they left home after work in a van with nearly 160,000 miles on it and drove all night. My husband went in for minor surgery the same day. I rediscovered that trust is an action verb.

We trusted God to get the kids here safely and to take care of Bill in the operating room. On a daily basis, we choose to trust him to act on our behalf, and we trust him to enable us to do what he wants us to do while we're doing it.

I'm convinced that life is the training ground for eternity. How would we learn to trust our God if we didn't have any challenges? Here's what Paul said in Romans 4.

"This is why the fulfillment of God's promise depends entirely on trusting God and his way, and then simply embracing him and what he does. God's promise arrives as a pure gift."

It's so simple, but is it easy? What about when everything seems overwhelming or impossible?

Paul referred back to Abraham. "When everything was hopeless, Abraham believed anyway." Then he acted on his faith, and that is what made him right with God.

What about the rest of us? Abraham is held up as an example to us, but not everyone knows about Abraham. God didn't forget the rest of the world. He gave us a way to become acceptable to him.

We become right with God when "we embrace and believe the One who brought Jesus to life when the conditions were equally hopeless. The sacrificed Jesus made us fit for God, set us right with God."

We don't have to earn right-standing with God. In fact, we cannot make ourselves good enough for God -- but we can accept his free gift of salvation through his Son, Jesus Christ. I have a feeling Heaven will be filled with misfits and independent thinkers.

----------

## *Joy in Chaos*

Why is it that God followers keep living with joy even when everything is falling apart around them? How do the Coptic Christians in Egypt smile and hold up signs that say, "You can burn down our churches, but you can never touch our faith," even as they're persecuted and humiliated?

I've been thinking about our loved ones, and the loved ones of friends who've recently gone home to Heaven. How do we survive the grief when our loved ones die?

Paul made it plain in Romans 5. The hope he spoke of is not only for those who die, but for all of us who live.

Paul said that we do what God has always wanted us to do through faith. God wants us to be right with him and fit for him. He sent us Jesus to make that happen. What a surprise to find that when we open ourselves to God, he's already there!

"We find ourselves standing where we always hoped we might stand – out in the wide open spaces of God's grace and glory, standing tall and shouting our praise."

I can picture our loved ones looking around in awe at the new world they see – wide open spaces of God's grace and glory. The same grace and glory are available to us right here, in this life.

What about persecution? Trouble? Hardship? How do they fit in with God's grace and glory? Paul told us, "We continue to shout our praise even when we're hemmed in with troubles, because we know how troubles can develop passionate patience in us." I'm familiar with Barely Tolerable Patience, but Passionate Patience?

Do you remember the story of Elisha and the widow's oil? (2 Kings 4:1-7) Paul referred to her experience with the prophet, when she and her son were on their last bit of oil and getting ready to starve. Elisha told them to collect every vessel they could find and, from the near empty bottle, filled all of them with valuable oil. This not only staved off starvation, but provided enough to sell and keep them during the entire famine.

In Romans, Paul redefined patience as being alert expectancy. This is a lesson I really need to take to heart. "We can't round up enough containers to hold everything God generously pours into our lives through the Holy Spirit." Wow. Be passionately patient.

----------

## Not Enough Time

I had a talk with the Lord about time. "I don't have enough of it," I complained loudly, as I drove to the store to find out what was wrong with my brand new phone.

"I need an uninterrupted day to get things done, Lord." As I wallowed in it, he suddenly reminded me that it's not about my agenda. It's about his, and maybe there was a purpose in sending me on this errand that should not have been necessary.

I took a few deep breaths and acknowledged that my times are in his very capable hands. Then I was caught in a tropical thunderstorm and got thoroughly soaked, only to find it was a very simple fix I could have done at home. Maybe the purpose was to teach me some of that passionate patience I want nothing to do with. Maybe it was to remind me that God is always on time when we leave the timing to him.

Paul found that out and reminded us, too, in Romans 5. "Christ arrives just in time to make this happen. He didn't, and doesn't, wait for us to get ready."

Thank God, he didn't leave our salvation up to us. We're too weak and rebellious to ever be ready for God. Yet, Jesus presented himself as the ultimate sacrifice for us – even while we were in that condition of rebellion.

We can understand and admire those who put their lives on the line, and often lose them, in service to others. We can understand someone giving up their life for a good and noble person or cause, or for someone they dearly love. What motivated God?

"But God put his love on the line for us by offering his Son in sacrificial death while we were of no use whatever to him." We were useless – worthless – self-centered – rebellious – and God still made a way for us to come to him and be saved.

The consummate blood sacrifice is what set us right with God. Remember how God commanded the Israelites to sacrifice animals in order to cover their sins? Consummate means perfect. God gave his Son to be the one sacrifice that covered all sin for all time for all people.

It was nothing we did, and there is nothing we can do that will give us access to a perfect God except to receive this sacrifice as a free gift. "Now that we have actually received this amazing friendship with God, we are no longer content to simply say it in plodding prose. We sing and shout our praises to God through Jesus, the Messiah!" Amen! Who can turn down a gift like that? Not me, Lord. I'm forever grateful for your timing!

----------

## Undeserved Favor

During the years before my Dad chose to become a believer, one obstacle he couldn't seem to overcome was his skepticism that Adam and Eve populated the earth. Knowing how long they lived, and how lacking they were in electronics, movies, and other amusements, I never had a problem believing it. What else did they have to do for fun?

Neither of us understood that Adam and Eve had, indeed, thrown up an obstacle to belief in God, but it wasn't about how many kids they might have had. Paul talked about it in Romans 5, with one notable exception. Paul never mentioned Eve.

He said, "You know the story of how Adam landed us in the dilemma we're in – first sin, then death, and no one exempt from either sin or death." Death is the chasm separating us from God. We have no hope of crossing it on our own. "But Adam, who got us into this, also points ahead to the One who will get us out of it."

Here's more of that logic I love so much. "If death got the upper hand through one man's wrongdoing [notice...no Eve mentioned here], can you imagine the breathtaking recovery life makes, sovereign life, in those who grasp with both hands this wildly extravagant life-gift, this grand setting-everything-right, that one man Jesus Christ provides?"

Who wouldn't want a wildly extravagant life? I love this about Paul. He kept it simple. "Here it is in a nutshell: Just as one person did it wrong and got us in all this trouble with sin and death, another person did it right and got us out of it. But more than just getting us out of trouble, he got us into life."

This is for those who want more laws and bigger government, "All that passing laws against sin did was produce more lawbreakers." Whether guns or sin – laws made against them will be broken!

Here is the best part, the best news for all of us: "But sin didn't, and doesn't, have a chance in competition with the aggressive forgiveness we call grace. When it's sin versus grace, grace wins hands-down."

Grace -- undeserved favor, undeserved forgiveness -- is an aggressive act of God! "Grace…invites us into life – a life that goes on and on and on, world without end."

WooHoo! Name one thing that can top that!

----------

## *Why Baptism?*

I've known people who have rejected Christianity only because they perceive Christians as hypocrites. I can understand that. Some people piously pose in church on Sunday and live like the devil the rest of the week. I haven't met a perfect Christian yet, and that starts with me. So what does becoming a Christian do for us?

Is it simply fire insurance, or is there really hope for a better life, even before we die? If we have freedom and forgiveness, does it matter how we live? If we want to live for God, how do we go about doing that? In Romans 6, Paul shared some answers.

"So what do we do? Keep on sinning so God can keep on forgiving? I should hope not!" Paul assumed that new believers are baptized into their faith. He was talking about full-immersion baptism, not water sprinkled over a forehead. The decision to receive God's gift of salvation is followed by the act of baptism. Why full-immersion?

"When we are lowered into the water, it is like the burial of Jesus; when we are raised up out of the water, it is like the resurrection of Jesus. Each of us is raised into a light-filled world by our Father so that we can see where we're going in our new grace-sovereign country."

We've moved from the country of sin to the country of grace. When I was baptized, I didn't feel a zap or zing of any kind. I just felt wet. It isn't about feelings. My heart was changed the second I received Christ as my Savior, and my life began to fit into my new heart.

Okay, it's still in the process, but I am a different person today than I was then. Baptism was the confirmation of my commitment. We believe that, "If we get included in Christ's sin-conquering death, we also get included in his life-saving resurrection."

Do you know what that means? "Never again will death have the last word." Death is not the end, folks! And that death-ending life starts now. So what do we need to do?

"Throw yourselves wholeheartedly and full-time [not just on Sundays] into God's way of doing things. Sin can't tell you how to live. After all, you're not living under that old tyranny any longer. You're living in the freedom of God."

There is no greater freedom than to be un-burdened by the consequences of your own sin. That's why people imprisoned, tortured and humiliated for their faith can smile and hold up those signs that say "You can burn our churches, but you can't take our faith." They get it!

----------

## How Free is Free?

If you don't remember the slogan "Free Love", you're too young to remember the 60's. It was the era where selfishness grew to monumental proportions, and godly values were dismissed and discarded because they put limits on self-expression and self-gratification.

Although that way of thinking was nothing new, it became pervasive and resulted in the problems our society experiences today. Instead of strong values based on absolute Truth, relative thinking has paved the way for all kinds of self-centered, harmful behavior. Those who don't believe in an absolute God are left scratching their heads and wondering, "What is happening?"

I was a teenager then – an adventurous person with no sense of mortality, no fear (that I let on to), and no morals. I hadn't found God yet, and many of my actions had devastating consequences. I believed the slogans espoused by my generation, and had no clue that "Free Love" would result in anything but freedom. Paul knew what it would lead to, back in ancient times.

In Romans 6, he asked the logical question: Since sin no longer tyrannizes us and we have freedom in God, does that give us the right to live any old way we want to? Here's his answer: "You know well enough from your own experience that there are some acts of so-called freedom that destroy freedom." He wasn't talking about incarceration, or physical freedom, but freedom of the spirit and freedom from the consequences of bad decisions.

Then Paul did something strange…he talked to me! "As long as you did what you felt like doing, ignoring God, you didn't have to bother with right thinking or right living, or right anything for that matter. But do you call that a free life? What did you get out of it? Nothing you're proud of now. Where did it get you? A dead end." Guess who I found at that dead end?

What a surprise! I discovered that God was with me all the time, and loved me anyway. I found "a whole, healed, put-together life right now, with more and more of life on the way!"

Living for self, indulging in sin, leads to death; not just ultimate death, but internal, spiritual death in this life. That's not freedom. "But God's gift is real life, eternal life, delivered by Jesus, our Master."

Special delivery. I accept. Thank you, Lord!

----------

## *Lawbreakers*

"Laws are made to be broken." Have you ever heard someone say that? It might have originated with the Apostle Paul. Wait, wasn't he a saint? According to him, he was as human as the next guy, and, he had some interesting things to say about God's law and how we, as humans, react to laws.

In Romans 7, Paul was speaking to the Jews, who knew the law inside and out. "When Christ died, he took that entire rule-dominated way of life down with him and left it in the tomb." We're no longer bound by what he called "the oppressive regulations and fine print."

So, does that mean the Ten Commandments no longer apply at all? Of what use are they, if we're not bound by them any longer?

Paul said, "The law code started out as an excellent piece of work." Yay, God! "What happened, though, was that sin found a way to pervert the command into a temptation making a piece of 'forbidden fruit' out of it." Human nature happened.

When I was growing up in Europe, there was no legal drinking age. Kids drank wine or beer at the dinner table right along with the adults. Because it was commonplace, they weren't tempted to drink themselves into a stupor when they were away from home.

American kids, on the other hand, can get into very dangerous situations because there is something in their nature that tempts them to break the law that was designed to protect them.

Paul said that sin looks dull and lifeless without the boundaries of the law. "The very command that was supposed to guide me into life was cleverly used to trip me up." That doesn't make the law a bad one. He said the law itself is "God's good and common sense, each command sane and holy counsel."

Paul anticipated the reaction to what he'd been saying. "I can already hear your next question: 'Does that mean I can't even trust what is good [that is, the law]? Is good just as dangerous as evil?' No again! By hiding within God's good commandment, sin did far more mischief than it could ever have accomplished on its own."

In this passage, I picture "sin" as a gremlin, waiting to pounce at every opportunity to cause trouble. So, simplistically, God's law is good, but we have this mischief-maker constantly tempting us to break it. Since Jesus buried the law and set us free, the gremlin has nothing to break. So where do we go from here?

----------

## Sabotaging Ourselves

Has anyone besides me tried dieting? After years of being overweight, you'd think I'd have come to grips with it by now and simply accepted how I am. But, no; I keep trying to lose the weight, and continue to sabotage my own efforts.

What about other challenges we have, such as character flaws we'd like to change, or the way we handle our finances? Paul nailed it on the head in this next section in Romans 7. I love his transparency here. He was as human as any of us, and freely admitted it. That endeared him to me much more than any imagined picture of what a 'saint' should be

He started out by admitting that God's commands are spiritual, but he wasn't. Really?

"What I don't understand about myself is that I decide one way, but then I act another, doing things I absolutely despise. [Like eating that piece of cake, and adding ice cream] So if I can't be trusted to figure out what is best for myself and then do it, it becomes obvious that God's command is necessary."

Some laws are oppressive; other laws protect. Paul was talking about God's laws meant to protect us from our impulses.

This passage needs no embellishment or interpretation. Paul described the human condition when he shared his struggle here: "But I need something more! For if I know the law and still can't keep it and if the power of sin within me keeps sabotaging my best intentions, I obviously need help! I realize that I don't have what it takes. I can will it, but I can't do it. I decide to do good, but I don't really do it; I decide not to do bad, but then I do it anyway. It happens so regularly that it's predictable." Can anyone besides me relate?

He'd tried everything, he said, and nothing helped. So what happens when we're at the end of our rope, dangling and helpless to change?

He told us, "The answer, thank God, is that Jesus Christ can and does." Jesus is the one who acted to set things right. So how does that help us?

----------

## *Judge and Jury*

There have been a few times in my growth as a Christian when I felt I'd finally arrived. I was saved, cleaned up, perfected, and now I could tell others how I did it. I shined up my Judge and Jury badge and wore it like I owned it.

It wasn't long before God took me down a notch or two and reminded me that I don't have the capacity to be better than anyone else. I can't even be better than my old self.

Now, many years later, I'm still learning that I'm not capable of doing anything right on my own. When I act in my own strength, I quickly find I don't have any. Anything I do on my own fails. So how do we rise above "my own"?

Paul addressed this in Romans 8. Because of Jesus, there is a new power at work in us. "The Spirit of life in Christ, like a strong wind, has magnificently cleared the air, freeing you from a fated lifetime of brutal tyranny at the hand of sin and death."

I love how he said "God went for the jugular when he sent his own Son." In order to take the focus off "my own," God sent "his own". Wow.

He did something the law would never have been able to do: "In his Son, Jesus, he personally took on the human condition, entered the disordered mess of struggling humanity in order to set it right, once and for all."

The law was a Band-Aid on sin, but God knew we needed real healing. So what do we do now?

Instead of trying to do it on our own, we simply embrace what the Spirit is doing in us. That's easier said than done.

----------

## What's Next, Papa?

When God led my sister to move from Germany to Florida, he paved the way in many miraculous ways. I couldn't wait to hear her daily reports because she was so excited, like a child opening Christmas presents.

Paul described exactly that in Romans 8:6-17. He began with a comparison of living a self-focused life and a God-focused life.

Do you remember the commercial that ends, "It's not nice to fool Mother Nature"? Paul said much the same thing, "God isn't pleased at being ignored." If Mother Nature can pack a wallop, imagine what a mess we can get into by ignoring God!

Paul acknowledged that we still struggle with sin, but that if we welcome God, we can experience life on God's terms. There's nothing in the old life for us. Paul said we should give it a decent burial and move on with our new life. "God's Spirit beckons. There are things to do and places to go!" I'll say!

"This resurrection life you received from God is not a timid, grave-tending life. It's adventurously expectant, greeting God with a childlike 'What's next, Papa?' God's Spirit touches our spirits and confirms who we really are … Father and children."

During Margie's and later our mother's move, God sent miracle after miracle. I often heard her say those very words, "What's next, Papa?"

Living in adventurous expectancy, on God's terms, should become second nature to us as we give more and more of our selfish nature to the Lord. Sin tries to trip us up and wrap us in self-this and self-that, but we don't have time for that, do we? There are things to do and places to go!

----------

## *Our Common Pregnancy*

I seriously doubt that Paul knew what it's like to be pregnant. We women know that God designed pregnancy to progress to the point where we cannot wait to deliver our babies. We get fatter, more ungainly, more uncomfortable, unable to sleep, unable to be more than a few inches from a bathroom; and the baby's kicks and squirms become stronger as baby gets bigger.

When labor begins, everything in us works like the dickens to deliver our baby. You'd think a man wouldn't be able to relate, but Paul did. In fact, in Romans 9, he described our current waiting for God as a pregnancy that he, himself, experienced along with all the rest of us.

He said everything in creation is being prepared for the final delivery. Waiting is not a passive act. We yearn for full deliverance. We're joyfully expectant. We prepare as best we can. We stock up on diapers, tiny clothes and supplies and make space in our home and our lives for the coming miracle. So it is with the world, waiting for the Lord to make his final appearance.

We get tired, but God's Spirit is right there with us, helping us along. "If we don't know how or what to pray, it doesn't matter. He does our praying in and for us, making prayer out of our wordless sighs, our aching groans. He knows us far better than we know ourselves, knows our pregnant condition and keeps us present before God."

Romans 8:28 is one of my favorite verses in the Bible. It has sustained me through some hard times. Its purpose is to get us through when things seem too hard to cope with.

In The Message it goes like this: "That's why we can be so sure that every detail in our lives of love for God is worked into something good." I also love it in the NIV, "And we know that in all things God works for the good of those who love him, who have been called according to his purpose." and in the King James version: "And we know that all things work together for good to them that love God, to them who are the called according to his purpose."

No matter how you read it, the fact is that God uses every trial, every challenge, every hurt, every disappointment, and everything that causes us to cry out to him for our good. One day, we'll be delivered of this baby we carry – the promise of forever, abundant, exuberant life with God.

For some of us, deliverance will come sooner than for others, as we pass from this life to the next. Meanwhile, all of creation is waiting expectantly for the promise to be fulfilled. Any day, Lord!

----------

## *Big Brother Is Watching*

I spent my fifth grade in a German school. My family moved from Texas to Germany, and Dad was no longer affiliated with the military. He and Mom couldn't afford the tuition that civilians were charged for the American schools, so we went to a local German school.

In retrospect, it was a wonderful educational experience, but it sure was tough at the time. No one spoke English to us, and we didn't know a word of German. By the end of the year, we were pretty fluent in the language and things were looking up.

Then we moved to Italy, and repeated the process in an Italian school. I had to learn Latin and Algebra right along with Italian. That's three foreign languages at once, since math was always a bit foreign to me.

The kids in those schools were like kids everywhere. At first, we felt as if they were always staring and talking about us. It hurt when they'd laugh and turn away. Some were friendly, others not so much. I longed for a big brother to shield me from the pain of perceived rejection. I felt vulnerable and a little lost. I wish I had known then, that I do have a big Brother who was watching out for me, every minute of every day, according to Paul in Romans 8.

How can we lose with God on our side? He sent his Son for us. What wouldn't he do for us? Jesus is in the presence of God the Father right now, sticking up for us. Who wouldn't want such a big brother standing against the bullies of the world?

"Who would dare tangle with God by messing with one of God's chosen?" God knows us by name. He called us. He chose us.

"Do you think anyone is going to be able to drive a wedge between us and Christ's love for us? There is no way! Not trouble, not hard times, not hatred, not hunger, not homelessness, not bullying threats, not backstabbing, not even the worst sins listed in Scripture."

Paul should know! He experienced it all! "None of this fazes us because Jesus loves us. I'm absolutely convinced that nothing – nothing living or dead, angelic or demonic, today or tomorrow, high or low, thinkable or unthinkable – absolutely nothing can get between us and God's love because of the way that Jesus our Master has embraced us."

Over time, I learned the languages of the countries we lived in and discovered that people are the same everywhere. We all need the assurance that we have someone watching out for us. I'm so grateful that Paul shared this assurance with us.

----------

## *It's Not Fair!*

"That's not fair!" I said it often enough to my parents. My kids proclaimed it to me, and now their kids are saying the same thing. What's not fair, I ask?

Usually, it's unfair that they don't get their own way when they want it. It isn't fair that one gets to do something first, or that one is using more Lego blocks than the other.

That particular outcry is as old as humanity. Cain killed Abel because it wasn't "fair" that God preferred Abel's sacrifice to his. According to Paul, in Romans 9, people were saying it in his time, too.

Paul was in deep mourning for the Israelites who rejected God's Son. They were his family. He grew up with them. He was one of them. They had everything going for them – "family, glory, covenants, revelation, worship, promises, to say nothing of being the race that produced the Messiah, the Christ, who is God over everything, always."

It wasn't God's Word that malfunctioned, it was humanity, and it goes back to Abraham and Sarah. "From the outset, not all Israelites of the flesh were Israelites of the spirit."

The Israelite identity was God-determined by promise, not racially determined by genetics. Paul explained how Isaac was the son of promise. God determined that his firstborn twin son would take second place, and so Jacob inherited the promise, instead of Esau. We can say "It's not fair!" all we want to, but the fact is, we don't measure God's decisions according to our standards. He sets the standards!

Paul asked, "Are you going to object, 'So how can God blame us for anything since he's in charge of everything? If the big decisions are already made, what say do we have in it?'" What was Paul's answer?

----------

## *Not Just Numbers*

During some of the hardest times in my life, I wondered where God was. Does he love me? Does he even know me? Why is this happening? I look at the crisis-filled lives of some of my Christian friends, or think about those precious people in the Middle East being tortured and killed for their faith, and again question God. Don't you love them? Do you know what's happening to them?

Of course he does, as Paul pointed out in Romans 9. Here was Paul's answer to the question of blame: "Who in the world do you think you are to second-guess God?" Paul put us in our place, didn't he? Yet there's so much promise in this.

He used an illustration to explain what he meant. Clay does not talk back to the potter. He has the perfect right to mold clay into anything he wants, from tall, slender vases to pots used for more mundane things. During our lifetime, we can be one or the other, or both at different times of life. Does the potter care about his clay?

Paul quoted the prophet Hosea, "I'll call nobodies and make them somebodies; I'll call the unloved, and make them beloved. In the place where they yelled out, 'You're nobody!' they're calling you 'God's living children.'"

He reminded us that Isaiah said something along these same lines. "If each grain of sand on the seashore were numbered and the sum labeled 'chosen of God' they'd be numbers still, not names; salvation comes by personal selection. God doesn't count us; he calls us by name. Arithmetic is not his focus." King David sinned by counting his people in a census. God punished him severely for that. We are not just numbers.

Paul summed up this chapter by saying that the people who did not seem interested in God actually embraced what he was doing as he straightened out their lives. "And Israel, who seemed so interested in reading and talking about what God was doing, missed it. How could they miss it? Because, instead of trusting God, they took over. They were so absorbed in their 'God projects' that they didn't notice God right in front of them, like a huge rock in the middle of the road."

Lord, help us to not become so busy with our 'God projects' that we lose sight of you!

----------

## Control Issues

I'm the oldest of five kids who were raised together. We have an older sister Mary who didn't grow up with us, but who is as loved and as much a part of us as if she'd been there all along. I longed to have my older sister around. She could have shouldered the responsibility of being the firstborn of our unruly tribe. As it was, that dubious distinction landed on me, and I was the most unruly of all.

In order to maintain a measure of control, I learned to be in everybody's business. I still struggle with control issues, so when Paul rebuked Israel in Romans 10, he was speaking to me, too.

Paul wanted nothing more than to see Israel saved. The problem was that they'd been so busy trying to do it on their own, they forgot whose business it is. Salvation is God's business, not ours.

Paul told us that the law "was intended simply to get us ready for the Messiah, who then puts everything right for those who trust him to do it." It isn't easy to live a life where every detail is regulated by law, and I'm grateful we no longer have to – because now, "It's the word of faith that welcomes God to go to work and set things right for us."

This is the core of Paul's preaching: "Say the welcoming word to God – 'Jesus is my Master [or Lord]' – embracing, body and soul, God's work of doing in us what he did in raising Jesus from the dead. That's it. You're not 'doing' anything; you're simply calling out to God, trusting him to do it for you. That's salvation."

That's it? I don't have to work hard, be good, eat right, exercise, or stay in control? Not for salvation. God does that all by himself. That's why anybody can be saved -- in any situation, in any lifestyle, speaking any language, with any religious or non-religious background, of any race or nationality!

It is not about us and our rules. It is all about God's grace and his work. It's good not to be in control of everything!

----------

## *Someone Has to Tell Them*

Here's something my brother Mark wrote in his blog *Just Drive The Bus*. It could have come from my own heart. "So, no, I am not pious nor religious. I don't follow much pomp and ceremony, and I don't like pasted-on smiles and insincere syrupy platitudes. I really don't like legalism or religious bondage of any sort.

"That being said, I consider Jesus Christ to be my closest friend and most valued companion, throughout this life and the next. I love him fully. He's my role model, teacher and guide. Wanting to please him motivates me. Trusting him gives me courage. Knowing he is forgiving gives me hope – and time for my character to improve. Studying him increases my wisdom. I have never felt abandoned by him. We don't have anything to prove to each other. I don't require signs and wonders to know he is here. He promised the companionship of the Holy Spirit to all who believe. I believe. He has not disappointed me."

In Romans 10, Paul said this about faith like my brother's: "Scripture reassures us; 'No one who trusts God like this – heart and soul – will ever regret it!' It's exactly the same, no matter what a person's religious background may be: the same God for all of us, acting the same incredibly generous way to everyone who calls out for help. 'Everyone who calls, 'Help, God!' gets help.'"

So why doesn't everyone believe? Why not grab onto this incredible gift of life? Paul reminded us that people can't trust the One who can be trusted if they've never heard of him! Someone has to tell them!

That's one side of the equation. The other side is this…they have to listen before they can trust. Here's the problem: too many don't listen, don't want to hear about it, or choose not to believe what they hear. Paul addressed this in the next verses.

----------

## Is God Fed Up With Israel?

It's hard to believe how many years it's been since the United States was attacked and the World Trade Center fell. The nation united in grief and outrage in a way it has not done since. People turned to God in droves. Patriotism was at an all-time high in modern times, and too many families grieved, and still grieve, their lost loved ones. As horrible as it was, it drew Americans together.

Israel has always been like that. They have suffered incredible injustices and endured unimaginable pain and suffering throughout the ages. They have also seen miracle after miracle as God intervened on their behalf. Their very existence as a modern country is a miracle, and was foretold by their prophets. Perhaps that's why Paul was so hard on them in Romans 10.

Paul questioned why Israel didn't understand that they, as the chosen ones, don't have ownership of God and his ways. They've had plenty of opportunities to listen and know what God said about it.

He goes all the way back to Moses, who predicted "When you see God reach out to those you consider your inferiors – outsiders! – you'll become insanely jealous. When you see God reach out to people you think are religiously stupid, you'll throw a temper tantrum."

I have never known any of my Jewish friends to throw a temper tantrum! It must have been different when Gentiles first started turning to God because of Jesus.

Paul also quoted the prophet Isaiah, "People found and welcomed me who never so much as looked for me. And I found and welcomed people who had never even asked for me. Day after day, I beckoned Israel with open arms, and got nothing for my trouble but cold shoulders and icy stares." Again, remember that all the first Christians were Jewish!

Paul started the next chapter with a question: "Does this mean, then, that God is so fed up with Israel that he'll have nothing more to do with them?" What was the answer?

----------

## Utter Frustration

One of my favorite lines in my all-time favorite movie, James Cameron's *Avatar*, sounds something like this: "AAAAAGGGGHHHHH." It's Neytiri's expression of utter frustration when her priestess mom says she has to do something she's very much opposed to.

Now I own it, too, often using it to express my frustration with rude drivers. It beats the more colorful words I try not to say. I imagine Paul used it once or twice, too. He seemed to be at that level of frustration as he talked about his fellow Jews in Romans 11.

He asked if God is so fed up with Israel that he's given up on them. His answer was "Hardly."

He reminded us that he was also an Israelite, from the tribe of Benjamin. "God has been too long involved with Israel, has too much invested, to simply wash his hands of them." So what is God's plan?

Paul went back to the prophet Elijah, who felt like he was the last loyal God-follower. God told him, "I still have seven thousand who haven't quit; seven thousand who are loyal to the finish." There has always been a fiercely loyal minority who hold on to God because they're "convinced of God's grace and purpose in choosing them." That can be said of anyone who loves God.

The Israelites tried to get right with God on their own, and failed. They became hardened toward God. Moses, Isaiah and David all commented on the self-centeredness and self-serving ways of the people. When we focus on doing it ourselves, we forget to trust God. They were no different.

So, were the Jewish people on the outs forever? Paul said the answer is clearly NO. "Ironically when they walked out, they left the door open and the outsiders walked in. But the next thing you know, the Jews were starting to wonder if perhaps they had walked out on a good thing."

So, if their leaving triggered such an influx of non-Jewish outsiders to God's kingdom, just imagine the effect they'll have when they return to God.

In the next section, Paul turned his attention to the outsiders.

----------

## *Mine! Mine!*

On a typical summer day in Florida, with plenty of thunderstorms and soaking rain, we had the grandkids over. Grampa was grounded because the tennis courts were too wet to play, so he and the kids formed a drum line. I had saved two enormous popcorn tins from a long-past Christmas, and they took turns drumming on the cans. Then Anthony decided our children's workbench and plastic tools made a great drum set. As soon as he started playing with it, Ashley decided she wanted those "drums."

According to Paul in Romans 11, it seems we never outgrow wanting what someone else has. Here's where Paul turned his attention to the outsiders. He figured that the Israelites would want what they discarded because now the outsiders have it. He said that when they figure it out, there will be a mass homecoming – back to God.

He used an analogy that gardeners will have no trouble understanding. In fact, he talked about God's use of natural genetic modification – grafting. First God planted and tended an olive tree with holy roots, namely Israel. "If the primary root of the tree is holy, there's bound to be some holy fruit." What did God do to the branches that didn't produce fruit? He pruned them. Then, he took some wild olive branches, Gentiles who love God, and grafted them in.

Paul warned us about feeling superior to the pruned branches. We are, after all, being fed by the same holy root that grew the tree. God didn't prune the branches to make room for us. He pruned them because they were "no longer connected by belief and commitment to the root." The only reason we're on the tree is because our graft "took" when we believed.

"So don't get cocky and strut your branch. Be humbly mindful of the root that keeps you lithe and green." God can just as easily prune us!

Paul said, "Make sure you stay alert to these qualities of gentle kindness and ruthless severity that exist side by side in God – ruthless with the deadwood, gentle with the grafted shoot. But don't presume on this gentleness. The moment you're deadwood, you're out of there."

Does that mean that if we mess up and go through a time of rebellion and doubt, we've lost our chance with God? Not necessarily. Paul told us that God can graft the deadwood back in.

Our job is not to judge the pruned branches. Our job is to be glad we're in the tree and to hope for the best for the others. The day is coming when it all comes together for Israel.

----------

## *Bullying*

It's been so long since I was a little girl that most of my memories are pretty vague, but here's one that I'd like to forget because it hurt. I was a skinny kid, about 9 years old, with crooked teeth and stringy hair -- the antithesis of pretty and popular -- and I had a crush on the cute boy across the street. We lived in Texas, and all the neighborhood kids went to a local muddy, tadpole breeding swimming hole to cool off. The first time we went that summer, I didn't have a bathing suit that fit me, so I wore an old leotard.

The other girls had cute new outfits. Kids can be really mean to each other, but the worst was when the boy across the street joined in the verbal bullying. Words can crush the spirit. What I've understood since then is that all of us are susceptible to thinking we're better than someone else, for one reason or another. Paul addressed this in Romans 11.

He admitted that it would be easy for us to arrogantly believe we're royalty and the pruned branches are just "rabble, out on their ears for good," but he reminded us that Israel's hardness toward God is just temporary, so that the doors could open to us outsiders. "Before it's all over, there will be a complete Israel."

We can assume that the prophecy Paul quoted here refers to the second coming of Jesus because it hasn't happened yet: "A champion will stride down from the mountain of Zion; he'll clean house in Jacob. And this is my commitment to my people: removal of their sins." Far from being God's enemies, the Jews were his oldest friends. "God's gifts and God's call are under full warranty – never canceled, never rescinded."

Paul said, "In one way or another, God makes sure that we all experience what it means to be outsiders so that he can personally open the door and welcome us back in." Wow.

If I could talk to the little girl I was that day, I'd comfort her with the knowledge that God loves her and doesn't mind that she's wearing an old, ratty leotard, and that the ones taunting her are also outsiders who need his love. Paul said, "Have you ever come on anything quite like this extravagant generosity of God, this deep, deep wisdom? It's way over our heads. We'll never figure it out." If the Apostle Paul couldn't figure it out, who can?

All I know is what Paul says next, "Everything comes from him; everything happens through him; everything ends up in him." Along with Paul, I give glory to God and praise him always!

----------

## *Be Yourself*

We've all heard of the fear of failure, but did you know there's also a fear of success? When Bill and I were on the verge of reaching a level in our business that included some new responsibilities, I began to panic. I had no doubt that Bill would fit right in -- but would I?

Would I have to be more self-confident? Would I be able to live up to the added responsibility? Would I let everyone down? Self-doubt set in like cement in my belly. Then we got the phone call from the Vice President of Sales, and he gave me some of the best advice I've ever gotten. "Just be yourself." Those simple words broke up the cement, eased my fear, and opened the way to much joy and fulfillment. I am a different person because I didn't have to do anything except be myself. The experience has grown me and given me confidence. Guess what?

It's the same advice Paul gave us in Romans 12, "So here's what I want you to do, God helping you: Take your everyday, ordinary life – your sleeping, eating, going-to-work and walking-around life – and place it before God as an offering. Embracing what God does for you is the best thing you can do for him." When we simply offer ourselves to God, as we are, he does all the work. He changes us from the inside out. He develops maturity in us.

"The only accurate way to understand ourselves is by what God is and by what he does for us, not by what we are and what we do for him." God sets the standard and helps us grow up to it.

Paul gave us a little anatomy lesson. "We are like various parts of a human body. Each part gets its meaning from the body as a whole, not the other way around." As believers in Christ, we're now members of his body.

"So since we find ourselves fashioned into all these excellently formed and marvelously functioning parts in Christ's body, let's just go ahead and be what we were made to be, without enviously or pridefully comparing ourselves with each other, or trying to be something we aren't." There it is!! Just be yourself!

Paul listed some examples, with the admonition to not go overboard. Here are a few that speak to me. "If you help, just help, don't take over. If you give encouraging guidance, be careful that you don't get bossy. If you work with the disadvantaged, don't let yourself get irritated with them or depressed by them. Keep a smile on your face." I'm a work in progress. That's why the self I am now might need some of God's tweaking.

----------

## How To Be Yourself

There's something to be said for birth order and how your position in the family affects your personality as you grow up. I was number one in our immediate family. I have a tendency to take control and be bossy whether I know what I'm doing or not. I have strong opinions and I'm vocal about them. I tend to be insensitive to others' feelings when I speak what I'm convinced is the truth.

So, how can I call myself a Christian and still be myself? Paul must have given that some thought, too, because in the next verses and some upcoming chapters, he sounded like he was reading right from Proverbs.

First he said to "be yourself," and then he had the audacity to give us a list of what we should be like in Romans 12.

He said, "Love from the center of who you are; don't fake it." So far, so good. Is the rest of his advice as applicable? I definitely need some of God's tweaking.

Here are a few more: run from evil, be a good, loving friend, don't grab the limelight. Stay fueled and fired up. Be alert and cheerfully expectant. Don't quit when things get tough -- pray harder. Help needy believers. Be hospitable.

This is hard for me: "Bless your enemies, no cursing under your breath."

It's easy to laugh with your happy friends, and not so easy to cry with them when they're sad. Get along with each other. Don't be stuck-up. Don't think you're better than anyone else. Don't retaliate. See the beauty in everyone. Don't take vengeance into your own hands – that's God's prerogative.

Paul reminded us, "Our scriptures tell us that if you see your enemy go hungry, go buy that person lunch, or if he's thirsty, get him a drink. Your generosity will surprise him with goodness. Don't let evil get the best of you; get the best of evil by doing good." How often has God surprised you and me with goodness? Good trumps evil.

If we're being ourselves, what if we don't measure up to everything Paul has told us to do? We go back to the beginning of this chapter, where Paul said, "Take your everyday, ordinary life – your sleeping, eating, going-to-work and walking-around life – and place it before God as an offering." Here I am, Lord. Do your work in me.

----------

## Good Citizenship

What does it mean to be a good citizen? In our country, I believe it means to be engaged, to obey the laws, and to do what we can to ensure that the values of the United States Constitution are kept. Our Constitution gives us rights we're obligated to defend, and it takes precedence over oppressive regimes that are bent on destroying those rights.

Here's where it gets sticky. You may think the government leaders are doing the best for the country, and I may believe they're trying to tear it down. Regardless of which of us is right, Paul said some things in Romans 13 about being good citizens. I have to admit, it raises some tough questions.

When Paul said that all governments, even horrible ones, are under God, did he mean that our getting involved in politics is interfering with God's plans? In the NIV, it says that we're to submit to the governing authorities because they have been established by God. What does that mean for believers in our country? According to Paul, if we're not responsible citizens where we live, then we're being irresponsible to God. He assured us that we should have nothing to fear from authority if we live as decent citizens.

That may be true, or nearly so, in the United States, but in light of what's happening to the churches in the Middle East, it sticks in my craw. How could he give us that assurance when he, a law-abiding citizen himself, was persecuted?

Paul told us to obey the laws, not just to avoid punishment, but because it's the right thing to do. Does that include obeying laws that God clearly does not approve of?

He went on, "That's also why you pay taxes – so that an orderly way of life can be maintained. Fulfill your obligations as a citizen. Pay your taxes, pay your bills, respect your leaders."

I find that to be the hardest of all. God says we're to respect our leaders, but what if they are not respectable?

----------

## *Obligations of a Good Citizen*

What are my obligations as a citizen of the United States? As long as we have elections, we have the responsibility to participate in those elections – to vote, to speak out for our candidates of choice, to uphold the values we believe are right.

We also have a duty to stand against laws that are wrong. The Civil Rights Act would never have been written had people like Martin Luther King, Jr. not stood up to unjust laws.

Paul, the Jew, was oppressed by the Roman government. Paul, the Christian, was persecuted by the Jewish leaders. We may not be happy with our government, and Paul couldn't have been happy with his, yet he asserted in Romans 12 that all governments are under God.

Jesus was rejected as the Messiah because he didn't do what the Jews believed the Messiah would do – deliver them from their oppressors. Yet, in fact, that's exactly what Jesus did, and the fulfillment of it will happen when he returns.

Government is not our oppressor. Sin is our oppressor, as Paul has made clear in previous chapters.

God has an agenda, and the governments he's put into place all play a role in it. The government we now belong to as believers in Christ is ruled by the King of kings and Lord of lords. I hope to be considered a good citizen of God's kingdom.

----------

## *The Good Debt*

$16,738,533,025,135.63 was the United States' national debt as of September 13, 2013. That's 16.739 Trillion Dollars. The average credit card debt per U.S. adult with cards that carry a balance was $8,220. We are a nation that has made buying on credit a national pastime.

It's as if being in debt is part of the American Dream of owning anything and everything we can get our hands on. We know we're in trouble, but how do we stop it? Did you know there is one debt that God wholeheartedly approves of? Paul mentioned it in Romans 13.

"Don't run up debts, except for the huge debt of love you owe each other. When you love others, you complete what the law has been after all along." That's it. Love is the debt that God wants us to have.

All the 'don'ts' of the law are summed up in this, "Love other people as well as you do yourself. You can't go wrong when you love others." Love is the sum total of the law.

Paul also gave us advice on how to stop over-spending. It's simply a matter of taking our focus off of ourselves. We tend to put God on the back burner as we go about our daily lives, and that's when we get into all kinds of trouble, including racking up debt.

He said, "The night is about over, dawn is about to break. Be up and awake to what God is doing! God is putting the finishing touches on the salvation work he began when we first believed." Stay focused on God. Time is shorter than you think.

----------

## *Who's Right?*

Through our business, our church, and in our neighborhood, we've met the most interesting and wonderful people you can find anywhere. They come in all ages, ethnic backgrounds and nationalities -- and they come with all kinds of beliefs.

The Christian believers attend churches in different denominations, and have widely varying belief systems that are all centered around Christ, but with a lot of different interpretations of Scripture. So what do we do with all these differences? What if I'm right and you're wrong, or you're right and I'm wrong? Paul addressed this issue in Romans 14.

He was speaking directly to me. "Welcome with open arms fellow believers who don't see things the way you do. And don't jump all over them every time they do or say something you don't agree with – even when it seems they are strong on opinions but weak in the faith department. Remember, they have their own history to deal with. Treat them gently."

I believe we can eat anything. You might believe we should all be vegetarians. Paul said it's rude to criticize what one eats or how one eats it. "God, after all, invited them both to the table. Do you have any business crossing them off the guest list or interfering with God's welcome? If there are corrections to be made or manners to be learned, God can handle that without your help."

You may worship on Saturday, and I may go to church on Sunday. Paul said, "Or say, one person thinks that some days should be set aside as holy and another thinks that each day is pretty much like any other. There are good reasons either way. So, each person is free to follow the convictions of conscience."

It's important that we do everything for God's sake. He's the one we answer to – not each other. "That's why Jesus lived and died and then lived again: so that he could be our Master across the entire range of life and death, and free us from the petty tyrannies of each other."

Those "petty tyrannies" start in early childhood and plague us the rest of our lives, don't they? If you've ever had a child or been one, you'll know what I mean.

The bottom line is that we're each going to be facing God in the place of judgment. Our critical and condescending ways won't give us any advantage there. Paul said, "You've got your hands full just taking care of your own life before God."

Why waste time and energy criticizing others? Paul had more to say about this.

----------

## *What You Eat Doesn't Matter*

Bill and I met in a little storefront church in Pennsylvania. The pastor often joked that the motto of the church was, "Until we eat again," because the explosive growth of that church was partially attributed to food. We had a catered dinner before Bible study on Wednesday nights. Each person paid a set amount to eat. We loved it because there was a ridiculously low family rate – at least low for our gang of kids.

Bill and I had our very first conversation at that dinner, where we quickly established that we had nothing in common except for kids and our love for the Lord. That was enough for a friendship, and here we are today, happily married more than 20 years later.

Most gatherings of believers of any faith include food, so it's no surprise that, in Romans 14, Paul used food as an example of how we should behave.

He said, "Forget about deciding what's right for each other." You mean everyone doesn't have to do what I say is right? Paul said we're not to make someone's life more difficult than it already is. He was convinced that everything is holy. We're the ones who contaminate it by the way we treat it or talk about it.

He told us to stop making a big issue over what people eat. You risk turning people for whom Christ died away from him (he put it more strongly). We can extrapolate from this that food isn't the only issue here. Our way or the highway is not the way to win people to Jesus!

God's kingdom is not about what goes into your stomach. "It's what God does with your life as he sets it right, puts it together and completes it with joy."

Paul said, "Cultivate your own relationship with God, but don't impose it on others. If the way you live isn't consistent with what you believe, then it's wrong."

Our job is simply to serve God wholeheartedly, using all our energy to get along with each other. "Help others with encouraging words; don't drag them down by finding fault."

In other words, do nothing that might interfere with love.

----------

## What Would Jesus Do?

Did you ever wear one of those bracelets with the letters WWJD? It stands for "What Would Jesus Do?" We like to think that if everyone lived their lives asking themselves that question, and then acting on it, what a loving, peaceful world we'd have.

So what did Jesus do? He overturned the money tables at the temple. He called the religious leaders of his day "dead bones" and "vipers". He told those who religiously kept the law but considered themselves more important than the common people that they were the blind leading the blind. He wasn't politically correct. He pointed out that we might be doing it all wrong.

So how do we get it right? Paul gave us a hint in Romans 15. He reminded us that Jesus jumped right into the middle of people's troubles in order to help them. He didn't make it easy for himself.

That's probably what WWJD is referring to. God wants us to be alert for whatever he wants to do next. "May our dependably steady and warmly personal God develop maturity in you so that you get along with each other as well as Jesus gets along with us all. Then we'll be a choir – not our voices only, but our very lives singing in harmony in a stunning anthem to the God and Father of our Master Jesus!"

Paul said, "So reach out and welcome each other to God's glory. Jesus did it; now you do it!" Jesus reached out especially to the Jewish insiders "so that the old ancestral promises would come true for them." The result is that non-Jewish outsiders also get to experience the mercy of God.

Verse 13 is a benediction. "May the God of hope fill you with all joy and peace as you trust in him, so that you may overflow with hope by the power of the Holy Spirit." (NIV)

WWJD? He would offer you a life of hope. This is my prayer for you as well.

----------

## *Praying For Each Other*

The more I get to know my social media friends, the happier I am to be a member of this community. We get into some lively political discussions, share business information and testimonials, and enjoy photos and stories of each other's lives and loved ones.

Mostly, I've found that we're a supportive and loving group of people. When we ask for prayer, we're prayed for! Then our requests are shared on our friends' pages, and even more people are praying and sharing.

God, of course, knows each of our hearts and doesn't need social media to hear our prayers, but I imagine that he's pleased with the way we're using this amazing tool! Paul asked for prayer, too, in Romans 15.

In this section, Paul assured the Roman believers that he did not mean to be critical of them. He was simply instructing them so that they could participate in his work of getting the message out to people who haven't heard about Christ.

He didn't take personal pride in his work because, he said, it was "only the wondrously powerful and transformingly present words and deeds of Christ in me that triggered a believing response among the outsiders." They weren't responding to Paul's articulate and impassioned preaching. They were responding to the call of Christ in him.

The remainder of this chapter was Paul's coming itinerary. He was letting his friends know where he was headed and what his plans were. Then he ended the chapter with this:

"I have one request, dear friend: Pray for me. Pray strenuously with and for me – to God the Father, through the power of our Master Jesus, through the love of the Spirit."

Imagine if he had put that on social media! He would have had much of the world praying for him. As I pray for you, my friends, I add, with Paul, "God's peace be with all of you."

----------

## *If I Forget Your Name...*

I have the unfortunate tendency to forget people's names. Most people I know have to scroll through their children's names to get to the right one – like I do. I can honestly say I've taken it a step farther.

At one event, I intended to introduce my daughter to someone and forgot her name – the very name I gave her at her birth. I've been calling her by that name for more than twenty years! How could I forget?

It's one reason I love this last chapter in Paul's letter to the Romans - chapter 16. He didn't want his friends' names forgotten, so he wrote them down.

Not only that, he wrote something nice and memorable about many of them. He even had his scribe, Tertius, mention his own name as he dictated the letter.

He added one final word of counsel, "Keep a sharp eye out for those who take bits and pieces of the teaching that you learned and then use them to make trouble. Give these people a wide berth. They have no intention of living for our Master Christ. They're only in this for what they can get out of it, and aren't above using pious sweet talk to dupe unsuspecting innocents."

It seems that scam artists have been around for millennia. So has our innate ability to fall for a "good" thing. He said, "Don't be gullible in regard to smooth-talking evil. Stay alert like this, and before you know it the God of peace will come down on Satan with both feet, stomping him into the dirt. Enjoy the best of Jesus!"

In Paul's summary he said, "All the nations of the world can now know the truth and be brought into obedient belief, carrying out the orders of God, who got all this started, down to the very last letter."

Praise God! I find great comfort in knowing that God, who started it all, has it all planned out, down to the last letter. We can relax and enjoy the journey.

----------

## *Giving Thanks*

I started my gratitude project on November 8, 2012 in response to a social media friend who started thanking God daily for her blessings. I liked the idea and did the same. I meant it to be short-lived, but it never ended.

Gratitude to our loving God, who won't stay in any box we humans want to keep him in, is food for growth. It's the secret that changed me from a negative, depressed person into one filled with joy and zest for life.

King David described what I feel so much better than I can. Here are a few nuggets from Psalm 145:

"God is magnificent; he can never be praised enough. There are no boundaries to his greatness."

"God is all mercy and grace – not quick to anger, is rich in love. God is good to one and all; everything he does is suffused with grace."

"God gives a hand to those down on their luck, gives a fresh start to those ready to quit."

"God's there, listening for all who pray, for all who pray and mean it. He does what's best for those who fear him – hears them call out, and saves them."

"My mouth is filled with God's praise. Let everything living bless him, bless his holy name from now to eternity!"

Gratitude gets God's attention. It opens a life-changing cycle of blessing. My prayer for you is that God will set you on your own adventure in gratitude. I had no idea he would lead me into writing this book. Only God knows where your journey will lead you. I can say with complete assurance, it will be good!

Like David, my mouth is filled with God's praise, and I bless his holy name from now to eternity.

The End, For Now

Made in the USA
Middletown, DE
03 December 2014